THE SUBTLE
THIEF OF YOUTH

DJ WISEMAN

First published 2012

Askance Publishing
Cambridge

askance-publishing.com

ISBN 978 1909009 066

British Library Cataloguing in Publication Data.
A catalogue record for this book is available from the British Library.

Typeset in 11pt Aldine401BT by Askance Publishing

Cover photo by Daisy Botha

Printed in the United Kingdom by PrintOnDemand-Worldwide.com

THE SUBTLE
THIEF OF YOUTH

For Sheila
with my best wishes
David Wilson
January 2013

"How soon hath time, the subtle thief of youth,
Stol'n on his wing my three-and-twentieth year!"
John Milton - Sonnet VII

1

It rained. It started in a small way, just a few dollops of water plopping into the dust at the side of the road, few enough for the pattern of their falling to remain imprinted in the dirt. It tapped on the car roofs of the mothers delivering their children to school and streaked brown lines across their windscreens. Up Whyn Hill on the heath it splattered onto the hard rutted farm tracks that hadn't seen rain for more than two months and it battered the drooping leaves of the trees in Whyncombe Wood. It came out of a heavy sky on a still and humid day in the middle of July, hinting at a summer downpour that would soon pass, as summer downpours tend to do.

For a few minutes around nine-thirty it seemed the threatening clouds would be no more than that, would carry their millions of tons of water further across the land, towards Birmingham or Warwick perhaps, and leave this parched corner of the Cotswolds as dry as it had been since Easter. Through the dense atmosphere a ghostly sun cast a sickly light and the villagers turned their attention from the sky to the business of their days: the mobile library set up shop, the postman continued on his round while the district nurse set out on hers, and it being Wednesday, the refuse collectors blocked the narrow roads as they emptied bins.

Unseen and unremarked, the dark mass above them gained heat and energy, drawing the column of vapour ever higher. In a critical meteorological anomaly, the leading edge of the front turned back on itself and collided with an even denser mass right behind it to the west. As it did so the real rain began, heavy and steady, huge drops of water bouncing from every surface, hard or soft. And still it seemed to all those in the twin villages of Germans and Whyncombe St. Giles that it was a summer squall, heavy enough, but a squall none the less, and wouldn't John Westerleigh up at High Whyn Farm be pleased with the respite from endless sun, hadn't he been desperate enough lately for something to wet his crops and his livestock?

But it was not a squall to slake the thirst of the farmers and their animals, not a passing shower to deliver a drenching before moving on to spread its favours on another desperate district.

There would be no pretty rainbow shimmering across the vale to the east, no refreshment of the earth in which to rejoice. Instead, it rained harder and heavier until the whole air seemed full of water, each drop massive and merging with its neighbour to grow even larger. The gutters filled and flowed in torrents down the drains and down into the combe, to the dry stream bed and the newly-made Centenary Wood. It rained so hard that people stopped their business to look out of their windows to wonder at the sight of it. As there was no wind to blow the storm inside, some opened their doors and stood in their porches to be closer to the spectacle.

One or two ventured so far as to extend an arm to catch the flow and feel the pulsing liquid in their hand. Such a downpour would be something to remember, something to tell distant friends about, something to report to mother in the weekly phone call. A few remembered a similar cloudburst a few years back, also sometime in July, and it had lasted for more than an hour.

It rained as hard as anywhere a mile away in Maiden Quarry where Peter Staples could hardly hear himself think for the thunderous din from the corrugated iron roof of his workshop. He put down his tools and stood by the open doorway to marvel at the volume of water and the blackness of the sky. The quarry was a hard and dusty place at the best of times, nowhere more so than in his workshop where he cut and shaped the stone. But the endless heat of this endless summer was far from the best of times, each day the rock had become a little more dazzling, the tin workshop a little more unbearable, his shirt more quickly caked in a paste of sweat and dust. Now as he watched, the very ground itself appeared to melt and flow. He was a steady, quiet man, all the quieter in recent years for having suffered the loss, one way and another, of his son, his daughter and his wife. Despite his misfortune, he wasn't given to forebodings or premonitions, but a deep unease welled inside him, a primeval, instinctive reaction to the awesome power now displayed.

In the parish church of St. Giles, The Reverend Philip Fox-Lomax cast a wary eye at the vestry ceiling. He knew all that lay between him and the deluge was some already water-stained medieval plaster, a few ancient timbers and a green tarpaulin, placed there only yesterday by the builders repairing the holes in the roof. They had worked painstakingly and skilfully for more

2

than a month and had all but completed their task. Fox-Lomax was tired of their presence, tired of the scaffolding defacing his church, tired of having to step round the caged enclosure where they kept their tools and machines. More than all those things, he was tired of not having the place to himself and his coterie of loyal parishioners. Now they would be delayed another day, perhaps longer.

Even as he watched, a drip formed and fell to the vestry floor, then another became a trickle, a stream. As the rector reached into the cupboard for a bucket, a wrenching metallic crash announced the collapse of a section of guttering, rusted after a hundred and forty years of faithful service and now forced from its mounts by the weight of water cascading from the roof. To his horror, the Reverend Fox-Lomax saw water seeping beneath the heavy oak of the long-disused door from the vestry to the churchyard. From the window he could see the remains of the fallen gutter now channelled a huge flow of water directly to the doorstep. He could also see the truly biblical proportions of the deluge.

Above Lisle House, on the heath, it rained on the sodden fields and pastures until they could take no more, hard and resistant as they were. It rained with no hint of a wind to carry the storm away, the water gathering in huge puddles even on the tops of the hills. On the edge of the estate, where St. Germaine's stone effigy had looked across that most pleasant fold in the land for more than a century, the water from the plateau above gathered at the brow of the hill. It ran down in a trickle by the monument, slowly at first, finding its way through the ruts and crevices. As the volume grew the course became deeper and wider until the trickle was a stream and the stream became a torrent. This sudden unnatural flow carried down the footpath, through the narrow gap in the bank, across the lane and through the gate opposite, bearing its load of mud and rubble down towards the manicured lawns and immaculate borders of Sir Bernard Stoner, the greatest of all among the great and the good of both Germans and Whyncombe St. Giles.

As the flow increased, so the pressure behind the bank increased. Where the water sprang through the gap that had once been a path, it quickly ate away the earth and carried more stones down into the valley. The breaking point for this dam was the sudden arrival of the old monument from eighty feet above. As the masonry struck, the statue itself somehow cartwheeled across the edge of the breaking dam and smashed into the little Rover whose driver had stopped, unable to see the road. A few seconds later the whole bank gave way and carried both car and driver away.

'Oh my dear God,' were Mary Radcliffe's last words but her god was very busy that morning with a leaking roof and he didn't hear her.

By fate, or the extraordinary nature of coincidence which defies all logic or probability, the tribute to the saint had been erected in 1868 by one William James Radcliffe, the great-great-grandfather of the man who owned the car. His wife became the first to die on that water-filled day. She was not drowned as might have been expected, but had her head split open by St. Germaine's right hand. The chronology of death is rarely precise, but it is most likely that the second, a drowning, followed soon after, but Mary neither knew nor cared by then.

At the back door of The Chequers, Alan Miller looked out at the half dozen tables and chairs in the pub garden and beyond them to the dry-stone wall separating the car park from the garden. He was puzzled to see water was spouting through the wall in several places, and for a few seconds he could not imagine how this could be happening. Looking beyond the wall up to the fields above the pub, he had a sudden appreciation of the volume of water cascading down into the car park. So dense was the rain he could see no more than thirty yards or so but once he understood the situation he acted quickly. Unless he released the growing lake of water in the car park, pent up as it was by the wall, the whole thing might easily be swept down onto the pub itself. Luckily, Alan was a big man, still with much of the strength and fitness of the marine he used to be. Within two strides he was drenched through, but he reached and vaulted the wall in seven more. If he could just make a break in the wall a little further along from the garden, the resulting flow might miss his pub completely and run harmlessly to the road and down the valley to the little lake by the Centenary Wood.

Although no mortar held the stones in place, they were capped with concrete. Standing knee deep in water the landlord chose a spot he thought weakest, and launched a heavy stamping kick at the top of the wall. It gave way far more easily than he'd imagined it might and he landed on his back half way through the wall, his standing leg bent awkwardly underneath his body. He not so much cried out as grunted through gritted teeth. Something was broken, or dislocated at the very least. His efforts had partially breached the dam and water flowed round and under him. The greatest obstacle to the flow at that point was now Alan himself. With a great effort and the resolve of a soldier, he twisted his body to relieve the unnatural angle of his left leg and dragged himself a few feet from the gap. Lying on the ground, water streaming over him, blood streaming from lacerated elbows, fighting back the pain in his leg, Alan pushed aside a dozen more stones, satisfied that he had accomplished his mission.

In the new houses, a hundred or so homes built on the old Lisle orchards in the 1980's but still 'new' in Whyncombe St. Giles terms, the downpour was no more than a curiosity for many, something unlikely to have any bearing on the daily lives of those in Lisle Gate, Orchard Way or Cherry Close. But after two hours of incessant rain even these homes with their new drains and their new patios and their new water features succumbed to the relentless flow from the higher ground behind them. Those backing onto the fields ironically suffered the least, being attacked on a broad front with the cleanest water. Worst effected were those at the bottom of the development, the fifth row down the hill. Not only did they suffer the greater volume of water, but by the time it reached them it had been channelled by the roads and gardens and driveways of the houses above and had gathered to itself mud and sewage and stones and debris of every kind. The torrent broke windows, smashed doors, burrowed into every house in Combe Road, and burrowed under a good many too.

At the end of the top road, spared the worst of the damage, were a group of larger houses, the 'executive' enclave of Upper Orchard. These were the five-bedroomed houses, with double garages, cobbled driveways and matching his 'n hers Range Rovers. Some had lately acquired higher walls and substantial electric gates. Whether these defences were to repel an imagined tide of rural crime or to conceal the crimes within had been the subject of some malicious talk amongst the contractors who installed them.

From his window at the front of number eight, Thomas Samarasinghe looked out in wonder, his mother Upeksha at his side. Both wore a slightly quizzical look, amazed not so much by the tropical deluge as that it should be happening here in their

5

adopted Cotswold home rather than Kollupitiya in their native Colombo. Theirs was the highest of all the new houses, safest of all from the flood. At his mother's insistence, Thomas had twice been round the house and checked as best he could for any incursion: the house was secure for the time being at least. Not so their immediate neighbour, for through the hammering downpour they could see the river flowing down their drive went straight under the wrought iron gate of number seven, where the open garage was already a foot or more deep in a growing muddy pool. Thomas idly speculated on how the gates could be opened without electricity.

'This is very bad,' Upeksha Samarasinghe said flatly.

'It's amazing, it's like being at opa Wikram's,' Thomas replied, referring to his grandfather's house in Kollupitiya.

'It will be worse than that, much worse. We don't have this here.'

'I've never seen it like this.'

'Once, once before, I think. You were still at . . .' her voice trailed away as a cloud passed across her face.

'Yes, Amma, once. I remember,' and the same cloud cast its shadow on her son's face.

Later, much later, when the world would be told of The Great Whyncombe St. Giles Deluge, it would be said that the village was the very centre of the downpour, that nowhere did it rain harder, nowhere did more rain fall, nowhere since records began and probably long before. Strictly speaking, none of that would be true, for the heaviest rain and the greatest volume of water actually fell on Six Lanes, the little hamlet a mile and a half to the north-west. But the two inhabitants of Six Lanes were both elderly and both poor, and besides, nobody heard from them until late the following day, so their voices never had a chance to stake a claim to the deepest or the wettest or the most destructive. However, despite age and poverty, they were both resourceful. As the water rose and the electricity failed, they looked at each other, and joined forces in the larger of the two houses, Sweet Pea Cottage, the one with two bedrooms. They quickly gathered fresh water, a bucket, biscuits, bread, some cheese and their mobile phones and ascended the stairs to wait out the flood.

Colin Deeley gave his friend and neighbour Margery Webster the spare bedroom to use if she should need it. In his own room he arranged a couple of chairs and a table for them to share while they peered out at the widening lake surrounding their homes. They had neither boat nor honey, but he had large spectacles and she had a few grey whiskers, which when combined with the name of the house and a pint or two, caused them to become known locally as The Owl and The Pussycat, a touch of humour much needed in the grim days that followed.

As two o'clock arrived, there was the slightest easing in the intensity of the rain. After nearly four hours of the monsoon, any suggestion of an end was seized on anxiously by the villagers. The curiosity and wonder had long been overtaken by fear and tears. Nowhere more so than in the brand-new study centre by the pond in the Centenary Wood, where nineteen children were in the care of their teacher, the tiny Miss Glazer, the classroom assistant Mrs Hoblin and Michael Radcliffe, school governor. To be precise, the governor did not legally share the care of the children, he was subject to Miss Glazer's overall command, and he was very careful to maintain that position throughout the day. He had called in for a couple of hours, to see how things were going, a regular habit of his with school expeditions. His was a familiar and generally welcome face in the school, even if he did appear strained and distracted on that Wednesday morning. But two hours had turned to four and five as the impact of the rising water became apparent. Fortunately, the centre was built on a raised platform and so was still clear of the water, although rather than being beside the pond it was in the middle of a growing lake. There was no question of leaving, with or without the children, some of whom wept miserably at regular intervals.

Miss Glazer had been discreetly monitoring the depth of water and was reassured by the fact that it had not risen beyond the fifth step since midday, despite the unabated downpour. She was entirely confident that when the situation became known, a rescue party would arrive and ferry the children to dry land, although beyond the lake and trees surrounding them, the prospect of any dry land seemed unlikely. There was no signal for her phone, nor anybody else's. She made a mental note to include the strength of mobile signal as part of the risk assessment for future trips.

From time to time the teacher fretted about Eysha Duncan, who was supposed to have joined the group directly after a visit to her dentist. But she wasn't there, and in truth Miss Glazer was not entirely sorry, for the girl could be wilful and difficult at the best of times and these were far from the best of times. Like many children in their last term or two at primary school, Eysha had suddenly outgrown her surroundings, awkward and out of place as childish things fell away and puberty beckoned. What nagged at her teacher was Eysha's friend Molly insisting she had seen the girl at the start of the day walking down the track to the wood. Miss Glazer was not exactly sure when and where her responsibility for the girl would have begun.

At two-thirty, just as it seemed the worst might be over, the electricity supply to all of Germans and Whyncombe St. Giles failed.

In Whyncombe Wood, where two millennia of use had already made the old sheep track a deep groove in the hillside, the run-off from a hundred acres of grazing gouged new scars in the earth. As the volume grew, so more soil and stone were added to the abrasive flow being channelled down the track. At the very centre of the wood where the path had been cut the deepest, the trees clung precariously to unstable ground, every year of growth a struggle and none more so than this dry season. Now the water they needed for life threatened to destroy them utterly. As it gathered speed and force, the ground beneath their roots was cut away. One by one, the trees nearest the torrent were undermined and slid at crazy angles into the stream. Some blocked its path and formed dams over which the mud and stones and splintered branches formed deadly waterfalls.

Of all the trees in the wood, none hung on to its place more fiercely than the sycamore which stood guard over the remains of Melanie Ann Staples. It had grown a few steps back from the edge, in deeper soil and with the slight benefit of the additional light afforded by the track. The injury caused by the symbol carefully inscribed into its bark years previously had been more than compensated by the additional nutrients provided by Melanie's body. As if to commemorate that season, the eleventh ring in its record of growth was a subtly different colour to those on either side. As the roots had reached out and touched her neglected remains, they had embraced her in their tender grasp and even now held her tightly as they clung to the slope.

They might have remained so had it not been for the weakened banks of the slurry pit at High Whyn Farm. John Westerleigh had seen the danger a little after mid-day and had worked all that time to avert it. The day would be a disaster by any measure, but it would be infinitely worse if two thousand cubic metres of excrement burst through the lagoon walls and cascaded down towards The Chequers, the school and the houses of Germans. As fast as he repaired the banks they were undermined by the flow of water through the farmyard. In desperation he tried blocking the yard completely but as soon as he dug channels or dumped earth it was washed away. The lagoon was full and overflowing, eroding the banks from the top, while beneath the walls the whole hillside was inching downwards. Almost too late the farmer sensed the final moment, scrambling backwards and crying out in despair as the dam disintegrated.

The tidal wave of faeces, mud and concrete reached the wood in a matter of seconds, carrying all before it. Trees that had fallen barely half an hour previously were now swept down the slope, those that had resisted the calamity thus far were carried away with them. The guardian sycamore was amongst the last to fall, and even in its falling still clutched Melanie to itself.

As if determined that she should not be buried again, the tree twisted on its journey, the exposed roots enfolding the girl and the red plastic mac which had been her shroud, were held high above the stream. Down, down they tumbled, surfing the river of sludge and debris, surging over the splintered gateway at the bottom of the wood, through the wreckage of The Chequers garden, rushing to meet the children finishing school. The brown tide that carried them was first deflected by the playground wall, then filtered of the larger items by the railings. Finally the splintered remains of the faithful sycamore and its precious cargo came to rest beside a drowned sheep atop a vast pile of branches and rubble, right by the school gate.

The poor girl would have to wait a little longer before her bones were recognised for what they were, and longer still to be given back her name, but for those who were alert to such things, her re-appearance at precisely that spot at precisely that moment was said to be a miracle. It was a moment to prove the very existence of their god: retribution and justice all rolled into a single event. Whether by divine intervention or simple chance, it certainly made perfect symmetry, for it was exactly at that place at exactly that time of the same day of July that Melanie had last been seen alive eleven years previously.

2

Having so narrowly escaped with his life, John Westerleigh was left gaping at the trail of devastation leading down from the remains of his waste lagoon. He had struggled so hard to avert this catastrophe, pouring every ounce of energy and imagination into the task. Now the worst had happened and he could do no more than stare, half kneeling, half crawling in mud and excrement. In his shocked state, he wondered if this was the end of his life at High Whyn Farm, all he had built wiped out in seconds, and all his own fault for ignoring the advice he'd been given. He and his wife Margaret, where would they be in a year's time, which of their friends and neighbours would still be counted as such? The good farmer saw these things, wondered these questions, as though from a distance, floating high above the waterworld around him.

The trauma of the moment, the awesome scale of the events, numbed his brain to any action until, through the unabated rain, he heard his wife screaming his name. She struggled to him and fell on his neck so that they both lay grasping each other in the swirling muck. She could say nothing but his name, over and over again, as the water poured over and round them. He, finding his senses returning, began to comfort her, tell her everything was all right, and not to be worried, he was safe and well, and nothing more than a little dirty and wet. With this wakening from his reverie John found fresh resolve. He eased himself free of his wife's embrace and took her by the shoulders, 'I'm alright,' he shouted.

Her hair was plastered to her scalp and straggled down her face. The mud and slurry was fast being washed off by the deluge enveloping them but dark solids remained lodged in her nose and ears and trickled from her mouth. Her glasses hung uselessly bent, caught in her collar. In a moment of rare tenderness he wiped her face with a huge hand. In a blink it had passed as practicality re-asserted itself.

'I must get to the village. Call down to The Chequers, tell Alan I'm on my way.'

'There's no phones.'

'Mobile?'

'No.'

Back in the house Margaret pulled the wet and clinging clothes from her still shaking husband and found him fresh ones. 'When I'm gone get on the radio, channel nine, and get hold of some help,' he instructed, then added, 'God knows what's happened down there.'

Standing by the yard door she watched him dash to the tractor, calling after him in a voice too small to be heard, 'Be careful, John.'

As she did so, the hammering on the corrugated roofs of the barns eased slightly, rose once more to a deafening thunder, then ceased. The tractor was almost out of the gate, red tail lights twinkling through no more than a light shower.

★

Upeksha Samarasinghe was not pleased that her son wanted to leave the house, even though the deluge had ended as abruptly as it had started. Despite the lightening sky she remained deeply uneasy, distrusting the promise of relief that it offered.

'Go if you must, but look at the house first. And come back immediately if it starts again,' she insisted. This was a strange day in a strange land, for all she had lived in it for thirteen years and been one of its citizens for twelve.

Thomas did as he was asked, accustomed to compliance with his mother's wishes, even though he knew of many ways of persuading her differently. The house was as dry as the day before, although a little sticky with the doors and windows all closed up. But the air inside was as nothing compared to the humidity he found when he ventured into the garden. Already the heat of the sun was recycling water from the sodden earth back into the atmosphere. Steam rose in clouds from the hard surfaces of the paths and driveways all along Upper Orchard and a light mist was already hung out across the valley.

At the end of the road where it joined Orchard Way, Ben, the ancient black Labrador who lived at number one, stood and stared warily at him. Thomas' instinctive move towards the dog, hand outstretched to meet the familiar wagging welcome with a pat and a stroke, was rebuffed with a distressed growl and a lowered head. The dog turned and slinked back up the driveway to its house, casting a furtive glance back at Thomas, who stood watching in dismay.

As he walked towards the centre of Whyncombe St. Giles, down through Lisle Gate and Orchard Way, the damage increased - gutters torn from roofs, whole gardens washed away, corners of houses undermined and one already cracked from top to bottom. At the turn to Cherry Close a great chasm had appeared in the road, almost swallowing a little black Peugeot and the street light it had been parked beside. This lamp-post now protruded from the hole like a periscope. Further along the road the drain covers had been lifted by the force of water which still gushed out of the pipes beneath. Some were broken and scattered amongst the litter of stones and rubble, making the road more like the bed of a stream, while the stink of sewage pervaded the whole steaming scene.

And these were all the new roads and houses, with careful planning and modern drains, what might he find lower down, where the houses of several centuries clung to the steep sides of the combe and the narrow road was as old as the hills themselves? And what of the school, the first place to have welcomed him all those years ago, what might have happened there, perched on the edge of the drop below Whyncombe Wood?

Instead of wandering like a ghoulish tourist, Thomas set his course to the school. He'd fallen into the habit of visiting at the end of the summer term to say hello to those he still knew. And today, after such a day, he might even be able to help in some way. His ties to the place loosened a little as each year passed, staff changed and once familiar families moved away from the village, but it was where he had first tasted English life. On each return he'd had the same friendly welcome from Frank Wheeler, the head teacher, as he'd had on that first day when he was just ten. Frank had retired a year ago now, so another link was gone, but he was still bound to Germans Primary by memory and affection. Not that the little village school was called by that name any longer, for it had lately adopted a new uniform upon which a new badge spelled out the full St. Germaine and St. Giles Church of England Primary School around a red cross on a deep blue background. To most in the village the change meant nothing, but to a small group it represented the reassertion of faith and tradition, a small triumph of decent values over indifference.

These subtleties were of no concern to Thomas as he made his way past the village store, through the front of which a sticky flow of muddy water was being helped by Chris Rogers, the beleaguered owner. As he was about to offer a greeting or a word of sympathy, Thomas caught something in the face of the shopkeeper that in thirteen years he had glimpsed only once before. It was pure anger, anger seeking someone to blame for all the misfortune of his life. Who could be better suited to take that blame than a brown face in a white-faced corner of the land? And which brown face could be more blameworthy than that of the golden Samarasinghe boy with all his privilege and opportunity? A deep chill passed through Thomas and he hurried on, averting his gaze from the wrecked shop and its impotently raging owner.

He was still coming to terms with this unwelcome insight into human nature as he passed the parish church of St. Giles, where the rector was standing by the lychgate with some workmen, looking up at the ancient building. He couldn't hear the words of their conversation, but their tone seemed clear enough. An argument was in progress and the subject was obvious. Instead of being stretched across the roof, a green tarpaulin hung limply by a single rope, revealing an area without any roofing stones at all. It took little imagination to guess the damage caused by six hours of torrential rain pouring through the gap. As Thomas paused to look at the church and the three men clustered by the gate, they turned and looked at him. Perhaps it was the close encounter with Chris Rogers that made him super-sensitive, perhaps it was a day for anger and hostility, but Thomas felt no warmth in the steely stares. As if suddenly remembering his calling, The Reverend Philip Fox-Lomax adopted a lopsided smile, so insincere that it simply underlined his animosity.

Again Thomas moved along quickly, unsettled by everything and everyone he had found. This was the place he called home, this was where he had been welcomed, been brought up and grown up, even if he had been away to boarding school and university for these last few years. Quite suddenly he was the alien, the distrusted outsider.

A little further along the lane, just before the post office on his right, a steep track ran down and afforded a view across the valley. Through the rising mist he could make out the school and behind it Whyncombe Wood. A dark brown scar ran through the wood, behind the pub, then down into the combe beside the school, or perhaps through the school. In the mist he could not be sure, but it filled him with foreboding. Further round he could see the whole of the new Centenary Wood was flooded, and he guessed that the study centre would be under water too, as would the bird-hide a little further down the valley.

For all the damage and destruction he had so far seen, for all that he could imagine far worse down the valley or across by the school, he was suddenly struck by the absence of people on the streets, of traffic, of police or fire engines, of any noise or disturbance in the steaming heat. Fearing what he might find, he quickened his step towards the school, but got no further than the turn which ran up to the main road. A grey-brown river gushed down from the heath, channelled by the lane, and cut across the route to Germans and the school. All manner of debris and rubble had already been strewn across the road, where clearly the volume had been even greater a short time previously. Beyond the flow Thomas could see other streams pouring from the higher ground, each sending more mud and stone across the road. Little wonder there was no traffic.

★

John Westerleigh was used to manoeuvring the tractor round the lanes, but not with the big front bucket on it. He'd been using it in his vain attempts to shore up the slurry pit, now he was glad he'd chosen to keep it attached. Past Six Lanes, as he rounded the head of the hill above Lisle House, the road was blocked by a landslip. Where the path up to the monument came down to the road, right by the old gate to the Lisle estate, it seemed as if half the hillside had slid across the road. A river of mud and stones still gushed down it. Down to his left the pristine gardens of Lisle House, so recently the setting for Pimms and croquet, were unrecognisable under their new coating of soil and rubble. From the middle of a huge brown lake where once there had been an immaculate lily pond, the rear end of a car protruded, doors and boot lid sprung open.

In his shock and confusion he thought at first that all this was his fault, the result of the catastrophic collapse of the slurry pit. He stopped the tractor and stared around wildly, unable to comprehend how the devastation could have spread so far from where he feared, by The Chequers, round the school and the houses below Whyncombe Wood. Slowly the extent of the destruction, the sheer scale of the event of which he had been only a part, began to dawn on him. Who knew how far and wide this flood had spread, who knew what terrible consequences would unfold? He looked again at Lisle House and the little blue car nose down in the moat of mud, the whole unearthly scene beginning to steam, apparently simmering gently in the afternoon sun.

And once that greater understanding of the day and its events had taken hold, John Westerleigh had a second revelation. If none of this was his responsibility then perhaps, just perhaps, the small part of it which might be laid at his door, well, that might somehow be lost in the bigger picture. And from that glimmer of light on a very dark day, John Westerleigh was able to think again of the future and of rebuilding his business and his livelihood. From the edge of the abyss he could see the way back, see the way to retaking his place in the world, in the twin villages of Germans and Whyncombe St. Giles. The claims he would be making on his various insurances also began to take shape in his mind.

This greater confidence was tested to the full as he rounded the last bend into Germans to find the road ahead blocked to shoulder height with the stones and trees brought down the path from the wood. From the vantage point of the tractor's cab he could see across the debris to where a small group of villagers were bringing children out of the school. To his enormous relief the building appeared to be largely undamaged, but appearances can be deceptive. The filthy water of any flood can render a building unusable in minutes, and this particular flood was filthier than most. A brown stream still cascaded down the track by the pub, but its course was diverted by the bank of earth and broken branches, so it continued less harmfully down the slope through the school playground to the valley below.

The Chequers too looked undamaged, although much of the track was washed away and it would be a while before anybody used the car park or the beer garden. The wall between the two had been spread in a thousand pieces across the grass. Of his friend Alan, the landlord, John Westerleigh could see no sign.

To his amazement when he looked again at the bank of rubble and twisted branches his eye fell on the legs of a sheep poking out from under the shredded red plastic of an old fertilizer bag. How had he not seen it before? It would certainly be one of his, for there was not a sheep for two miles that belonged to anyone else. It would have to wait where it was for the time being, then he would need to go through the bureaucratic processes of recording and reporting that were the bane of a farmer's life in that closely regulated world. But it would be one more item to add to the tally of losses.

On the school side of the bank Lorraine Gregson, head teacher of one year's standing, had spotted John Westerleigh and was waving frantically at him. She'd found him a helpful and welcoming governor since her appointment, and now she had urgent need of both his help and his tractor. He leapt down from the cab and climbed round the stinking mound to where she was supervising the dispersal of her pupils into the care of suitable adults. Quite what were the exact criteria for 'suitable' in such an emergency, she was not sure. While the school appeared to have suffered little lasting damage, the day had been alarming for staff and pupils alike. Excitement and wonder had very quickly turned to fear and anxiety.

'Need some help?'

'Oh yes please, especially as it's you. Advice and help. I've heard nothing from Ann Glazer all day and she has her class down in the study centre in the wood,' she swung round to point down into the combe, as if he might not know the place she was speaking of. 'No phones and I can't get her mobile. I'm not sure what to do for the best. Some parents have already gone down.' There was the slightest tremor in her voice, an awkward shape to her mouth, suggesting how close she was to tears.

'I'll get down there and see what's happening,' he said with a measured calmness he did not feel. 'How many?'

'Twenty, plus Ann and Joan Hoblin.'

'Get me the names.'

She had the list ready.

The simplest and quickest way to bypass the road block was to break through the low wall at the front of The Chequers and drive across the sodden grass to the back edge of the rubble pile, then back out onto the road beyond the obstruction. Tangled in the mess he was surprised to see another fertilizer bag. It was hardly important on such a day, but he was usually so careful not to leave these things lying about.

Once past the school the going was easier, where earth and rocks were strewn across the road they offered no challenge to the power and size of the big John Deere. The bottom of the combe was barely visible through the trees and the mist, so there was no guessing what might have happened down there. A deep foreboding welled inside the school governor as he negotiated the road round to the parish church. He was almost there when his wife's voice crackled on the cab radio to tell him that she had contacted the fire brigade who were overwhelmed by calls and would get there when they could. Before she had finished speaking the clatter of the first helicopter could be heard above the engine of the tractor.

Just by the church, another familiar figure, the black-frocked priest, flagged down the tractor.

'John, glad to see you, could you clear the road up to the heath, no one can get in or out at the moment?'

'In good time, rector, but there are some children down in the wood who need some help.' Again, the steadiness of his tone belied the anxiety he felt. 'And the school will need some attention too, Lorraine looked a bit wobbly when I saw her just now.'

Neither the school nor its pupils were high on The Reverend Fox-Lomax's list of priorities that afternoon. He would attend to the school tomorrow, the last day of the summer term when by tradition he would chair the final governors' meeting of the academic year. Despite recent changes to the role of governors, he maintained a largely hands-off approach, delegating anything practical to lesser mortals while retaining the final word on anything he chose to take an interest in. Which is how it had come to pass that with Frank Wheeler's retirement the school had formalised its name and adopted the new badge.

Past the church, out towards the quarry near the edge of the village, a knot of people stood at the top of the track down to the study centre in the Centenary Wood. Blocking the way down the slope was a car, two wheels off the hard surface and tilted over where the ground had been washed away. The driver had long given up trying to get up the last few yards of the hill and stood uselessly beside his vehicle. More delay to John Westerleigh's rescue mission. One shove from the tractor would shift it easily enough, but even in such times as these people have a strong attachment to their cars. And besides, there was as yet no indication of any real emergency. A little patience and persuasion would be required.

★

With the end of the rain a new spectacle came to Maiden Quarry - rising curls of steam amidst the still dripping stone. The tin roof of Peter Staples' workshop was the first to absorb the sun's heat, creaking and groaning as it did so, then the first to steam. Ten minutes more and the cut stones, stacked in the enclosure, raised their own curtain of mist. Finally, clouds began to form and rise from the floor of the quarry itself, turning the whole into a fantastic stage set, wreathed in the smoke from dry ice.

Just as he had done in the morning as the deluge commenced, and later when the electricity failed, the stonemason stood at the door and watched in wonder at this new atmospheric party trick. A day of wonders, he thought, and a day not yet done. As he considered the idea that it was, and still would be, a remarkable day, he remembered that it was the anniversary of the loss of his daughter. He had never forgotten the date, never would, but he was not one for keeping vigils, laying flowers or saying prayers. He thought about her often, sometimes with great anguish, sometimes with pleasure, but he'd never thought about her any more on this day of the year than on any other. It was just another day, like birthdays and weddings. Another day like the one on which his son Anthony had died, another day like the one his wife had disappeared leaving him only a note and an empty wardrobe.

With no power for his machines he'd used the old generator to provide some light to hand-finish the piece he'd been working on, a faithful reproduction of a tricky corner piece from the tower of the parish church. Helping maintain the fabric of the ancient pile was a never-ending task, and one he had mixed feelings about. Even though in recent times he was hardly ever short of work, the church was a sure thing to fall back on, and being paid was never a problem. In fact he was frequently paid in advance, which was part of the ambivalence he felt. Being pre-paid put him in debt to the church, or more especially to the rector, and it was not a position he was comfortable to be in.

The generator had spluttered to a halt just as the rain had stopped. Now he could refill the tank and attend to a few other jobs, or he could lock up for the day and get home. Home was just a few minutes' cycle ride away, the end cottage in a terrace of four built for the workers when the quarry was in its heyday at the end of the nineteenth century. The day had already taken such unnatural turns that the mason saw no point in any attempt at normality: he would lock up and cycle back to Whyncombe St. Giles. He'd been so pre-occupied by the extraordinary happenings in his quarry, he hadn't given a single thought to the wider world and what, if any, effect there might have been. Now, as he cycled

19

back along the familiar lane and found it littered with soil and rock brought down from the hillside, as he saw the valley below shrouded in the same unearthly mist as his workplace, so he sensed the wider scope of the events around him.

★

When he'd heard of the class marooned at the study centre in Centenary Wood, Thomas had run to his friend Jack's house to borrow his canoe. For whatever reason, he'd always been popular with all his friends' parents, and Jack's mother was only too happy to agree to his request, distracted as she was by her rapidly defrosting fridge. He'd only ever used the canoe once before, and then under Jack's close supervision, but he didn't rush foolishly into the water. The fibreglass vessel had been easy to drag down the slope to the edge of the muddy lake, where he'd donned helmet and life vest, just as Jack had shown him. There was no current to deal with and with great care he'd paddled through the trees, following what in normal times would have been the path.

As the first to reach the castaways, he was the first to see the drawn faces of the adults in the doorway, the pale, wide-eyed anxiety of the children looking down at him through the open windows.

'I can't rescue anybody,' Thomas called up to Ann Glazer, 'but I can take a message back. Some parents are getting worried. They're trying to find a bigger boat.'

Had he been standing next to her she might have hugged him, so relieved was the teacher to see him paddle up to the steps. She'd only met him a few times but recognised him, even under the helmet. 'It's Thomas, isn't it? Thank you for coming over, tell everyone that we are all quite safe and dry.'

To involve the children in the process and let them share her joy, she invited them to give Thomas a cheer, to which every one responded enthusiastically. Then, as an afterthought, the teacher added, 'And don't forget Mr Radcliffe, he's here too.'

Thomas looked beyond the teacher to the less than ecstatic face of Michael Radcliffe and for the second time in the day received the doubtful blessing of a twisted smile.

With little expertise but great concentration he paddled a slightly erratic course back through the trees to the foot of the slope and the little parking area where the group of parents, mainly the mothers, were waiting. Before he touched ground he was shouting out to them, 'They are all safe! They're all dry!' As the bearer of such happy news he was quickly surrounded and eagerly helped from the blue boat. One parent thanked him profusely, another slapped his back, while a third enquired if he had seen some child whose name he did not recognise. Thomas offered his reassurance, 'They are all fine, you must not worry. Is there a boat coming?'

Before an answer or a boat could be found, John Westerleigh's tractor purred into view. After a short discussion and a calculation of the likely depth of water along the submerged path, it was agreed that the farmer should make a trial run to see if the castaways could be rescued with a few at a time riding in the big bucket hoisted high above the water.

The first journey went smoothly enough, with one mother making the trip out, then returning with her son to a round of applause. A limit of two adults and two children was imposed for each subsequent journey and in less than forty minutes the centre had been evacuated. Last back were Ann Glazer and a nervous Michael Radcliffe, clinging white-knuckled to the rim of the bucket.

'Michael, are you OK? You don't look very well,' John Westerleigh asked with genuine concern, for his fellow governor looked distinctly grey.

'I'll be all right, it's been a long day.'

'Come up in the jump seat, I'll take you home.'

The older man held up a hand to decline, then waved towards the hedge bordering the gravelled parking spaces, 'No, but thank you, my car's just here.'

But it wasn't.

It was not as if the area in question was very large, far from it. Michael Radcliffe could not believe that his car was missing. He was extremely agitated, and cast about wildly for some sign or explanation of the loss, even walking around as if a different view would reveal the missing vehicle behind a bush or tree.

'Could your wife have taken it?' asked John Westerleigh gently, finding himself in the position of calming authority once again.

'My wife?' Michael Radcliffe looked totally perplexed, as if he had no recollection of ever being married. 'My wife?' he repeated. 'Why on earth would my wife take my car?'

'Well, I don't know, but maybe she needed it for some errand or . . .' The sentence went unfinished, for Michael Radcliffe had wandered off, both mentally and physically. He stood apart from

21

those who remained at the scene, staring blankly up the sloping track to the village. His wife, yes, she'd been at the centre when he arrived, she'd opened it up that morning for the school visit, she'd made sure they had everything, she'd said something to him as she left, but what? He'd been so pre-occupied, she'd called him hot and bothered, taken his jacket and hung it up. He slid his hand into the pocket, a familiar pocket in his favourite jacket, worn every day, even in this sweltering summer. His keys were gone. His car was gone and his keys were gone. His wife had taken his car. And if she had taken his car where was she? Why had she not returned it, where had she taken it? Wait, something she said, some reference to having to go over to somewhere. To where? And why had she not taken her own car? These and other questions piled into his head, one after the other, each unanswered, most unanswerable.

John Westerleigh took him by the arm. 'Michael, come over here and sit down for a while, you look absolutely awful.' He guided him to a bench by the visitors' map to the paths through the wood. 'You sit a bit and get some colour back. Here, I brought this from the cab.' He passed across a cereal bar.

'I'll be all right in a minute. Thank you. I must get home, I'm sure Mary has the car, she said as much this morning, I'd just forgotten, I thought she would have returned it, maybe she changed her plans.' His voice trailed off, his mind on something completely different.

His friend was about to offer a consoling platitude about Mary Radcliffe turning up soon, but a sudden vision of a blue car half buried in the mud at Lisle House changed his mind. He had no desire to become involved in another of the day's dramas, nor to precipitate one.

'There'll be a lot of people who've changed their plans today. I dare say you changed yours too.'

'Yes, yes you're right of course,' and with these words he seemed to snap back to the present.

Thomas idly watched the two men on the bench, for lack of anything else to do as much as for any great interest he had in them. He knew them well enough to exchange a greeting, perhaps even have a brief conversation, but he was wary of them both for quite different reasons. His first impressions of them had been as school governors. At ten he was the cautious new boy in both school and village, without any idea of the importance of such people. He adopted his natural default position of respect and deference, and called them both 'sir', as he did with every man he met until he learnt English ways. Later he came to know a little more about each man, in the casual way that knowledge is accumulated, but also because he observed closely, listened acutely and remembered well. These gifts were complemented with an ability to look as if he'd heard nothing, seen nothing and understood even less, a powerful combination which had fooled many people over the years.

After a while Michael Radcliffe rose a little unsteadily, then seeming to gain strength and confidence, he strode off up the slope. Thomas was about to follow, dragging the canoe behind him when a woman, the last of those who had received the rescued children, approached John Westerleigh. She had three young girls in tow, the oldest of whom Thomas recognised as Molly Gardner, presumably her daughter. She was enquiring about another child, the name Duncan floated across to Thomas, but the farmer shook his head. Molly looked distressed but her mother thanked him and turned away.

Then to Thomas' surprise he called across to him, 'Good work there with the canoe, well done.'

'Thank you, Mr Westerleigh,' he replied, 'but I carried only a message, not the children as you did.'

And with that simple comment, John Westerleigh was reminded of how direct and concise the boy had always been, how naïve his manner appeared, and yet how deceptive that appearance almost certainly was. Hadn't the boy, a man now despite his boyish figure and feline looks, hadn't it been said he'd got a good degree at Cambridge? You don't do that with just being polite and naïve.

'Put that in the bucket,' he said, pointing to the borrowed canoe, 'and hop up. I'll give you a lift up the hill. I must get back to the school.'

Back on the road, at the top of the slope, there were a few more people about. From further along by the church the cold reflections of flashing blue lights were visible. A distraught young woman, not much older than Thomas, ran over to the pair as soon as they dropped down from the tractor. Trailing a little way behind her was Molly Gardner's mother with Molly and her two sisters.

'Did you fetch them back?' the woman asked urgently, accusingly, of John Westerleigh, pressing herself forward almost into his face.

'The children? Yes, is everything all right?' The idea that one of the rescued pupils might have somehow injured themselves in the bucket came to his mind. He'd been very careful to check every child had an adult with them, and had left the tractor completely unharmed. Even in today's special circumstances, or perhaps because of them, he'd been especially conscious of their safety. And his potential liabilities.

'No, it's not all right,' she yelled, 'you never got my Eysha!'

He was a little taken aback by the ferocity of her response and sought to calm her. 'It's Laura, Laura Duncan, isn't it?'

She nodded. He recognised her as a girl who'd been born in Germans, been a pupil at the school, and who now had her own daughter there. He was not sure of the daughter's name or that of the father.

'Laura, you must check with Miss Glazer, I know it's late but she's probably still back at the school. I'm certain nobody was left behind.' He was as certain as a reasonable man could be, but he had only now remembered the list of staff and pupils that the head teacher had given him. He could feel it folded in his inside pocket as he spoke, but resisted the temptation to check it for Eysha Duncan's name.

'She says she were never there, but I saw her go down, I know she were.'

Thomas was watching this exchange when he became aware of movement beyond the tractor, by the houses that were the last few cottages on the road out towards Maiden Quarry. Peter Staples was lifting his bicycle over the mud and rocks brought down his garden path from the hill behind. Here was another man in the twin villages of Whyncombe St. Giles and Germans with whom the boy from half a world away had a particular relationship, but quite different from his wariness of Messrs Radcliffe and Westerleigh.

Thomas smiled at the stonemason, a smile from such brown skin over such white teeth could not be mistaken for anything else, and Peter Staples returned it with a nod and a lesser smile of his own. He liked the boy well enough, always had in his way, but he'd never quite understood why his daughter had taken up with him right from the start. She'd said it was the maths and because he was not like all the rest, but her father was less sure. And when she'd gone, hadn't Thomas been one of the last to see her, maybe *the* last. And when he'd looked for her not more than an hour later,

24

wasn't Thomas the first person he found, wandering down the track by The Chequers, smiling that winning smile. Here he was again, on this day of all days, still smiling and now a grown man, but there was no sign of his Melanie.

Something of this shadow of time may have passed across Peter Staples' face, for even at a distance Thomas sensed the moment of change, shared the deeper reflection. He hardly ever thought about Melanie, could hardly remember her at all, and when he did, he was not at all sure that the mcmories were real. Many things had been said, many ideas explored, many theories advanced and they all involved Thomas to a greater or lesser extent. Now what he'd heard or read was almost indistinguishable from the memory of real events. As this thought came to him his attention was again drawn to the farmer and the now-weeping mother of the missing child. The haziness of one memory reminded him to be alert to the present.

'There must be plenty of places she can be,' John Westerleigh was saying, attempting to soothe her. 'On a day like today, when who knows what has happened, she could be safe with any of her friends.'

Laura Duncan had become too distraught for sensible conversation; her attempts to speak were trapped and distorted by gasping sobs. Tears and mucus streamed down her face as fast as she wiped the backs of her hands across it. As she fell onto her friend's shoulder so Molly caught the miserable anguish of the moment and burst into her own flood of tears.

'Let's try and be practical about this,' John Westerleigh urged, but with little chance of being heeded. The events of the day appeared to be unfolding in a relentless procession, each one more awful than the last. No sooner did he get to grips with one thing than the next threatened to spiral out of his control as he stumbled from one terrible scene to the next, unable to wake from the nightmare. Now he was being dragged into another and he cast around desperately for some assistance or an exit.

For a moment Laura rallied enough to lift her head and cry out in anger, 'If she's bunked off somewhere I'll kill the little sod!' Then, catching sight of Thomas as if for the first time, screamed into his face, 'Who the fuck are you looking at?'

3

Nobody in the twin villages would normally think of The Reverend Fox-Lomax as a cheery man, least of all his wife, Acantha. She did not see as much of her husband as many of his parishioners did, a fact for which she was grateful since what she did see was almost completely unsatisfactory. The awful day had brought her one small blessing, not that she would have used the word, which was that she hadn't seen him since he'd left the house at twenty past eight in the morning. Even that had been an accidental sighting, since they habitually shared neither bed nor breakfast.

Now, from the drawing room windows she watched as he strode along the flagstone path from the private door in the wall between churchyard and rectory garden. The smoothed stones bore the imprint of five centuries of parsons, some no doubt jollier than others, but few can have been in such a foul mood as the present incumbent. Acantha Fox-Lomax allowed herself a private smile before her husband entered the house. She had a pretty good idea that the church was likely to have suffered some water damage, although she was unaware of the full effects of the drooping tarpaulin. But what she did know, and which he did not, was that all day water had been seeping through a particular weak spot in one of the roof valleys of the rectory. She'd seen the results on the landing outside his bedroom and when she'd checked downstairs a damp patch was showing on the ceiling of his study. Later, she'd seen little rivulets of water on the panelling behind the study door. That had been more than two hours ago. She anticipated his discovery of the current state with great pleasure.

'Home from work early, vicar?' she asked without a trace of irony and without lifting her eyes from *Good Housekeeping*. The words were, as ever, carefully chosen to offer the maximum irritation to her husband. Some days she played the game more seriously than others, scoring herself marks out of ten for the brevity of the comment and its ratio of irritant words. Had it been such a day she would have given herself a nine-point-five.

'And good afternoon to you too,' Philip Fox-Lomax did not look at his wife as he spoke, he was intent on getting to his study to see if the telephone worked. He urgently needed to call the diocesan office, a call that would almost certainly be the first of many needed to deal with the aftermath of the deluge.

Acantha Fox-Lomax listened intently as the study door closed behind him, she heard his muffled step across to his desk, the faintest beep as he dialled a number. Then silence. The silence continued for perhaps a minute, perhaps five, she could not be sure how long she enjoyed it. And there were still the pleasures of the upstairs discoveries to come.

'Have you seen what has happened in here?' He stood at the study door, speaking with that icy calm that sometimes accompanies the extremes of anger.

'In there? In your office? Your office is not somewhere I go, Philip. *Persona non grata*, remember?'

'Upstairs. Have you checked upstairs?'

'Only our bedroom, which was fine. And our bathroom was fine, in fact I had a nice long shower at about two.' As she spoke, Acantha's left hand traced an imagined flow of water down her hair, across her shoulder and down her body. Score only seven for brevity but another nine-point-five for irritation: perhaps it was a day for serious play after all.

He turned and left her, ascended the stairs in a few steps, reached his part of the old house in a few more, then stared in horror at the soaking carpet covered in plaster, the still dripping beams. Nowhere near as bad as in the church, but bad enough. Cautiously he opened the door into his bedroom. There was less visible damage but the line of drips extended across the ceiling well into the room.

The rector sank on to the edge of his bed, the still centre in a perfect storm of anger with all the day had brought him. He was beset on all sides by disorder and chaos while for his whole life he had sought to impose unchallenged order and obedience. Chief culprit for this purgatory was his wife, and it was on her that his rage found focus. One by one he rehearsed the familiar litany of her faults: headstrong, independent and assertive; too clever; too sensual by far; disloyal and disobedient. To these long-standing failings in more recent times he'd added malice, hostility, infidelity, provocation, mockery and betrayal: a fine set of sins to challenge the calling of any priest. Not that Philip Fox-Lomax had ever felt his calling to be in doubt. He was the rock around which a sea of doubt, heresy and non-belief might thrash, but his convictions never wavered, least of all in his own righteousness.

He led his admittedly small flock, some might even say a diminishing flock, according to his unswerving beliefs in the proper interpretation of the teachings of the true church. He had no truck with fads or fashion, but he did see the virtues of adopting a softer stance on contentious issues if it might gain some advantage in the longer term. As a result of this strong conviction combined with perceived flexibility, he was generally well regarded in ecclesiastical circles. But for a long-past, but not forgotten, misdemeanour he might have gained high rank. In earlier years there had been talk amongst some of a place in the bishop's palace for the devout and talented Fox-Lomax, but lately the bitterness of unfulfilled promise had hung round him like a cloak.

*

John Westerleigh carefully positioned his tractor by the mound of debris in front of the school so as to obscure the sheep's carcass from all but the most inquisitive observer. To be extra sure he raised the big bucket close to the remains in readiness for the animal to be lifted into it without attracting too much attention. Satisfied with his forethought, he found Lorraine Gregson still fretting by the school gate. A good looking woman, he had always thought, despite being taller and stronger than most of her sex. This, combined with intelligence and ability, put him a little in awe of her, as it did for most of his fellow governors. Many of the children of St. Germaine's, and certainly their parents, would have said the same. Now he found her slightly dishevelled and wild-eyed, casting around distractedly, just as Michael Radcliffe had done previously.

'You look as though you've lost something,' he ventured with a calculated lighter air.

'I hope not, that is I hope we haven't lost anybody,' the head teacher replied, with emphasis on the collective 'we'. 'One of the parents has told me that a girl was left at the centre and now she's gone missing.'

'What? You mean Laura Duncan's girl? There was no one left down there! I brought them all back across, I'm absolutely sure of it.' He was dumbfounded by the suggestion that he'd left anyone behind. The girl's mother must have repeated the accusation and now the nonsense was spreading like a virus. 'Where's Ann Glazer?

She knows I brought everyone back, she knows . . .' he was about to say the teacher knew who was there, but the thought of the folded paper in his breast pocket, untouched since the moment Lorraine Gregson had given it to him, made him hesitate. He couldn't exactly see how his failure to consult the list of pupils and staff made him responsible for the lost girl, but he had deep foreboding that unless the story was put right quickly, he would somehow become accountable. He had a great urge to look and see if the Duncan girl's name was on the paper. If it was, then however unjustly, he would have a question to answer, but if it was not, he would be instantly exonerated. John Westerleigh chose to defer the moment of discovery until a more private opportunity presented itself.

'Ann's gone back there to see if she can find the girl's mother.'

'I left her by the church, talking to the police.'

'Oh. The police,' she said flatly. What resolve remained now seemed to evaporate and the head teacher sagged visibly. A term that had started full of summer promise was ending with the same sour taste as each of the previous two.

At the end of her first, a trouble-free and happy introduction to headship, it had been a simple visit to a museum in Oxford, a treat, an enjoyable day before the Christmas break. It hadn't been her fault, she was not even on the expedition. It hadn't been Ann Glazer's fault either. It hadn't been anybody's fault other than the boy's. He was wilfully disruptive, would not do what he was instructed to do, and would frequently do what he was instructed not to do. So when he tripped and fell awkwardly on the marble floor while scuffling with another boy, when he cried out in agony as his wrist went back and splintered in the way that young bones tend to when bent too far, when he wailed and wept, he was not at first believed and was treated with less kindness than a better behaved pupil might've been. Which did not alter the injury in the slightest, but it did set the tone of the confrontation between the school and the boy's father, who threatened to sue. Despite a long protest and support from the governors, Lorraine Gregson had been dismayed when the County Council chose to pay uncontested and undisclosed damages into the father's bank account. The amount was later rumoured to be roughly twice the annual salary of the classroom assistant the school urgently needed but, thanks to financial restrictions, was unable to recruit.

Then, two days before the welcome prospect of the Easter break, eight year-old Aaron Price had dashed out of the playground straight into the path of a supermarket delivery van. The boy was knocked unconscious and later found to have cracked his skull. It was his good luck that the driver was new to the route and was progressing slowly, looking for an address unknown to his sat-nav. Some said that the driver was not paying proper attention to the road, others that it was Aaron's mother Tracey who was not paying proper attention to her son, encumbered as she was by his three younger sisters. He made a full recovery, was back at school within a few weeks and no prosecution for neglect was made of driver or mother. But for a while afterwards and purely for the sake of goodwill and without the slightest suggestion of liability, the Prices had enjoyed a one-hundred-percent discount on their weekly grocery shop. The effect on the school had been sombre but one practical result had been the erection of a barrier on the footpath outside the school gate to prevent such reckless dashes in future.

Those same railings would need replacing now they'd been buckled by the weight of rubble and boulders borne by the torrent, but nobody could have foreseen the vital role they'd play in deflecting the destructive flow from more serious, perhaps deadly, results. Neither could anyone have predicted that one consequence of Aaron Price's near-fatal rush would be to bring Melanie Staples, or at least most of her bones, right back to where they had last been seen walking upright. Yet still those aching bones went unrecognised, still they waited for discovery and final indignities.

★

The very first thing Michael Radcliffe did when he got home was dive into the top drawer of his desk and seize a new packet of cigarettes. It was the second new packet of the day, the first having gone missing much earlier. He'd been without a smoke for nearly six hours, most of them spent cooped up with Miss Glazer and her class. An hour or so he could just about manage, he'd planned on that, knowing full well that he couldn't smoke with the children. But an hour turned to two and two turned to an age. When finally he'd been liberated there were no cigarettes in his pocket. They would surely be in the car but there was no car either.

After a few minutes searching, during which he'd found no trace of his wife in the house nor the waterlogged gardens, he stood by the kitchen window drawing smoke deeply into his lungs. It was the first cigarette he'd smoked in the house for twenty-five years. Beyond the glass the garden dripped and steamed as if it were a mere clearing in a rain forest. Somewhere in the middle distance a siren wailed, then stopped mid-note as it drew nearer. Reason seemed to have left him completely for he could make no sense of the day's events, try as he might to calm his racing thoughts. In the flooded garage he'd found Mary's car, which puzzled him further. Although it now stood in a couple of inches of water that was no reason for Mary not to have used it earlier. She'd driven to Oxford and back the previous day and made no mention of a problem. When she'd chosen to walk to the study centre that morning it was not unusual, she nearly always walked on local errands, sometimes more distant ones too.

His reverie was broken by the sudden clatter of a helicopter, overhead but hidden from view. The noise receded abruptly, but it galvanised him to manic activity. He set about searching the house again, ever more feverishly, ridiculously looking in cupboards and under beds. In desperation he eventually unlocked the cellar and went down into the gloom, feeling his way on the stairs until he found the torch hanging near the bottom. Even before he clicked it on, the smell of mud and water told him what to expect. The whole area was flooded. Floating here and there were various possessions; an old cricket bat, a table tennis ball bobbing beside it; a few paperbacks, long waiting to go to jumble; a plastic crate lay capsized, its cargo of old clothes trailing just beneath the surface. Some movement of water or expansion of sodden timber seemed to speak softly to him.

'Mary?' he whispered, then louder, 'Mary! Where are you? Are you here?' and there was as much anger as desperation in the shout.

A temporary insanity possessed him, all reason and logic absent as he raged round the house, his focus switching from his missing wife to his missing car and back again. He feared the loss of the latter at least as much as the former, and could not even be sure the two were connected. A dozen improbably wild scenarios paraded themselves through his distracted mind but none came close to the even more improbable facts. And not a single one of those wild scenarios featured concern for his wife's health or fear for her life.

At length the fever passed and a calmer mood prevailed, though he was still distracted by strange thoughts and imaginings. For a while he patrolled his garden paths, wreathed in smoke. Briefly it swirled in his wake before hanging in the atmosphere, a pungent mix of tobacco and water vapour. Some action on his part was required, but in the circumstances it was difficult to decide what. The idea of paying a visit to his priest, The Reverend Philip Fox-Lomax, kept recurring but he pushed it away. That man's mood would be foul, no doubt made worse by the church repairs being held up for another day. Yet on a day like today, with who-knew-what still to be revealed, Michael Radcliffe felt in need of the solace his church might offer nearly as much as he felt the need for another cigarette. He must also decide soon what to do about his car, his flooded cellar and his wife.

★

On the road above Lisle House, close to where the footpath had branched off up the hill and where St. Germaine had dealt his mortal blow, a solitary onlooker watched intently as the Sea King made first one pass and then another across the house. With the fire and police overwhelmed by calls on their services, the RAF had been summoned from their base in Suffolk. On the third approach the helicopter slowed and hovered to more closely inspect some point of interest below. The heavy thump-thump-thump in the thick air, the undeniably military nature of the machine despite its yellow coat, brought to mind images of conflict in distant lands. The downdraught raised a brown spray through the swirling mist; it could as easily have been the desert sand as muddy water below the churning blades.

It was impossible not to watch, even though Thomas Samarasinghe felt a certain guilt at doing so. He'd been attracted by the sight of the machine clattering across the villages. His first thought had been of the school but it had flown on further, then banked round and lower into the combe, briefly disappearing from sight below the tree-line. He could only think that it would be searching for Eysha Duncan, then when it swooped lower he imagined it landing at Lisle House. Only as he came to the gap in the hedge where the gate had once been and a steady stream now flowed off the hill and across the road, only then did he see the true extent of the devastation at this end of the villages. The great house was surrounded on three sides by a huge expanse of brown water where once there had been lilies and lawns. The ornamental stone bridge remained just visible above a milk-chocolate sea, while a couple of trees marked the former edge of the lake, otherwise nothing recognisable remained. For a few moments he struggled to see what could be the focus of such attention. Then, amongst all the mud and rubble he recognised the rear half of a car. Thomas thought it was probably a blue car, although he could not be certain.

Having been drawn to the sight, he couldn't stop, couldn't turn his back and walk away, feigning disinterest. He was transfixed by the scene unfolding before him, imagining that he might soon witness a dramatic rescue. From his vantage point on the slope he was roughly level with the hovering machine. Below it, hanging by a thread, an orange suited figure was lowered close to the car. The crewman manoeuvred deftly to inspect the open boot then reached out to pull it half closed and inspect the number plate. A moment later he was lowered a little further. Up to his waist in the brown water, he reached down below the surface into the side of the car. After a few moments Thomas saw him signal to the winchman and the helicopter shifted its position fractionally before drawing the dangling crewman up to the open hatch. For an instant Thomas felt a twinge of disappointment that there would be no rescue, simply an empty car caught in the flood. Then, quite shockingly, some sixth sense, some silent logic that had been ticking away in the back of his head gave him a different answer, an answer that included Michael Radcliffe, his absent wife and his missing car.

Slowly the big machine swung round to point back towards the school, The Chequers and the debris that surrounded them both. It gained a little height before heading up the valley. As it disappeared round the shoulder of the hill, it slowed and hovered again, then began to descend to some new investigation beyond Thomas' view. He followed it again, not this time to watch, but because it was the way home and he was suddenly tired of being the onlooker at these scenes of anguish.

★

Midway between Chris Rogers' shop and the churchyard was a little pull-in area, enough for the few cars that brought the Sunday worshippers or the overflow from the two spaces outside the village shop. A small but growing crowd had begun to gather there, at the centre of which were police Constable Simon Lessing and his companion in uniform Sharon Whitlock, a probationary support officer. PC Lessing was already out of his depth with the tide still rising. He had twice called for assistance but as yet had no word of when it might arrive.

'What're you *doin*?' Laura Duncan insisted. A little crowd had gathered in support of her initial distress and was indignant on her behalf. Word of Eysha's disappearance had spread quickly and in addition to well-meaning friends, the numbers were being swelled by those who felt the need to be part of the slightest drama.

'Mrs Duncan, I have reported what you have said, and assistance will be on its way,' PC Lessing reassured her. A murmur of discontent rippled round the policeman and his colleague, enough for him to use his radio for another call to the control centre, this time making sure that Laura Duncan and her supporters were aware of all that he said. Again the response was a simple crackling acknowledgement.

'I'm not Mrs Duncan, not *Mrs* bleedin' anyone.' The crowd's sense of dissatisfaction grew at this new slight to the distressed mother.

'The very best thing you can do,' he paused, unsure how to address her without giving some fresh offence, 'is to go home in case your daughter is there or someone is trying to get in touch to tell you she is safe.'

From the back of the crowd came a comment about the policeman's parentage. This was something altogether more familiar for PC Lessing to deal with, a daily insult to be ignored or used as an excuse to escalate a confrontation. For now he let it pass, not only was he outnumbered by an unsympathetic crowd, but he had a fair idea whose voice it was. There would doubtless be another opportunity to exact some small retribution.

'Mum's at home, she's waiting for her.' Laura said sullenly. Her shoulders sagged and her face twisted into fresh despair as she started another decline towards the awful parental mix of tears and anger with her missing child.

Finally the constable grasped the need to be seen to be doing something, even if that something was unlikely to yield any results. In a moment he had the answer. 'OK, let's have a little tour round, you hop in the back and we'll see what we can see.' He motioned Laura towards the door of the Land Rover. Now the crowd's mood lifted and the mutterings carried a note of grudging approval. A lone voice suggested what several were thinking: that it would not be the first time Laura Duncan had been in the back of a police vehicle.

So it was that they drove slowly along the road towards the school, blue lights flashing, Sharon Whitlock's voice, harsh and metallic through the loud-hailer, asking for any knowledge of the whereabouts of Eysha Duncan. Near the school they encountered Thomas, who was trudging heavy-hearted back through Germans to Whyncombe St. Giles, to his safe dry house high above the village's distress. Neither the constable nor the probationer knew Thomas or any other member of the Samarasinghe family. Now, at Laura Duncan's behest they asked him directly if he had seen the missing Eysha.

'No, I don't think so,' Thomas replied.

'You don't think so?' queried the constable.

'I am not sure that I know her, know what she looks like,' expanded Thomas.

The precision of the answer confused the officers, more used to evasion or false confidence than an exactly correct answer. From the back seat Laura Duncan leaned forward, shouting accusingly, 'You was there, you went and saw them all, you came and said they was all safe and dry!'

This was true, he had said that, but only by way of relaying a message from the teacher, Ann Glazer. Now he regretted ever having become involved, ever having thought he might help his fellow villagers.

PC Lessing now took up the challenge. 'So you were down at the centre. What were you doing there? It was a school trip as far as I know, what business had you at that?'

How quickly a series of events slips and slides in the memory, how easily the story is told and retold with subtle changes that bring new light, new slants to bear, how softly do fancies take on the appearance of fact. Now was the time to correct the path the story was taking, but Thomas hesitated. Restating it all would take too long and his inquisitors were not in listening mode. Instead he simply said 'I had no business there beyond trying to bring help to stranded children and news to worried parents. That's all. I'm sorry your daughter is missing, but I cannot help.'

'I'll have your name anyway, and your address, just for the record,' the constable persisted.

Thomas gave both without hesitation, spelling his name without prompting, knowing very well that for all the changes in his adopted country, English ears were still unaccustomed to multi-syllable Sri Lankan names.

35

As he wrote the address, some spark of recognition flickered in PC Lessing's head. He knew enough of the villages to remember that Upper Orchard was home to some of the wealthier and more influential names in the community. His thanks for Thomas' assistance had an almost imperceptible change of tone, and a 'sir' added to the end, just in case.

★

John Westerleigh had been keen to get back to the farm, to restore some semblance of order to the mess he'd left in his dash to discover the extent of the damage he'd caused. With that burden lifted and with all that had happened since, the disaster of the slurry lagoon collapse had been pushed from his mind. Just as he'd begun to focus on his own affairs once more, the sight of the big yellow rescue helicopter in The Chequers' car-park distracted him again. Leaving the tractor still parked by the rubble pile at the school gate, he'd clambered over the debris in time to find Alan Miller being strapped into a stretcher and lifted into the aircraft. It seemed the landlord would survive his ordeal of broken bones and near drowning. He'd lain twisted where he'd fallen all that time, washed over by the mix of soil and stones carried by the water flowing down through the wood, until being spotted by the crew.

'You'll let us know if you need anything,' John Westerleigh shouted in his ear.

Whether he didn't hear above the noise of the rotors, or whether the morphine had begun to take its drowsy hold, Alan Miller did not answer or open his eyes.

The rescue team were ready to lift off and deliver their wounded soldier to the hospital helipad in Headington and signalled that visiting time was up. The farmer leaned down close again and wished his friend well, promising to call and check his progress.

'Tell the rector I'm sorry,' was the unexpected and slurred response. Any chance to clarify the comment was denied him as the pitch of the engines changed and he was waved away. For a few moments he watched as the machine rose slowly, spattering him with a muddy spray until it turned and headed for Oxford.

He puzzled over the comment as he walked back down the track and forgot for an instant why he'd left the tractor and bucket in such an odd position. The red fertilizer bag on top of the still-steaming pile reminded him that he had farm business right here before he headed back home. Recovering dead animals was all part of the job, not an everyday thing, not a pleasant thing, just something that came with having livestock. There'd be some compensation for the dead sheep from the ministry or the insurance, or, if he was astute with the timing and the form filling, perhaps from both.

He adjusted the bucket a little and turned it ready to accept the carcass, then scrambled up the pile. The old ewe was heavy enough alive, but its dead weight was made all the more unwieldy by the sodden fleece. After a little struggle he managed to flop the beast over the edge of the bucket where it slid on its back to the bottom. Then he turned to pull the red plastic clear of the roots and stones holding it. Even as his hand closed on the corner of the bag it felt wrong, something other than the heavy-duty smoothness of industrial plastic. But his hand was already in motion, the jerk on the material already delivered, there was no undoing what was done. Melanie Ann Staples was once again revealed to human gaze. As the remains of her red plastic raincoat were wrenched from under her bones, the movement twisted her skull to face the farmer. For a frozen moment that would last him the rest of his life, John Westerleigh stared into the girl's empty eye-sockets, seeing deeper into her than any man should ever have seen. A stray wisp of vapour, released by the movement, escaped from the damp pillow of sticks and stones on which the girl's head lay. In the ugly madness of the moment it seemed she might have whispered a final word to her stupefied discoverer.

*

Michael Radcliffe was still alternately pacing his garden and wandering around his house like a man who's entered a room and forgotten why he opened the door in the first place. He had no idea what to do, or even if he should do anything at all. From time to time he walked down the little drive and peered about, but was barely aware of the activity in the village. On each occasion when he returned to his house he went from room to room, not exactly looking for anything, more to check that he had not missed some clue, some sign, on his previous search. The flooded cellar too, attracted him more than once, the unfamiliar sounds and smells posing their own questions.

At length he sagged into a chair, clutching a large glass of scotch. After a couple of gulps he quite deliberately drew out a cigarette

37

and lit it. He inhaled slowly and deeply, then breathed the smoke steadily out into the sitting room in a second, more deliberate polluting of the pristine air. He stared at the blue cloud as it settled in layers across the room, lit by the evening sunlight. The fresh smoke straight from the burning cigarette made its own twisting way to one level, while the exhaled cloud found another.

He sat in this way for some time, mesmerised by the drifting blue patterns, with little of consequence passing through his mind. His wife, the church, his car, the rector, the school and other trivial subjects flitted through his head. Some notions lingered longer than others, but he saw them all as if from a distance, mere dots in a receding landscape, growing less and less significant. He was considering a second glass and a fifth cigarette when the doorbell disturbed his reverie. For a moment he thought his wife must have forgotten her key.

When he opened the inner door two figures stood beyond the outer glass, both police officers, one male, one female, both young, both nervous, both wishing that they might be somewhere else. He saw them before they saw him. Many things can enter and leave a person's thoughts in the tiniest fragment of time. In the blink between seeing the police and them seeing him, many things passed through Michael Radcliffe's mind, his car and his wife among them.

The female officer spoke first. 'Mr Radcliffe?'

Michael Radcliffe nodded and only then noticed that he was carrying an empty glass.

'Can we come inside?'

Dumbly he waved them in and for no apparent reason that they could understand, he put on his jacket as if he was about to leave them to themselves in the smoke filled room.

Now it was the other constable's turn. 'Do you own a blue Rover, Mr Radcliffe?'

The car. They had found his car. Michael Radcliffe struggled to concentrate on the events unfolding around him. Since the morning he had been swept along on a tide, almost literally, with no apparent control. Now they threatened to carry him along again.

'Yes,' he said, with more assertion than he intended or felt. And then as if to justify his tone, added, 'It's missing.'

'Missing?' queried the female officer, 'Since when?'

'Well, no, it's not exactly missing. What I mean is I don't know where it is, I think my wife took it.' Nothing of Michael Radcliffe's usual confident authority was apparent in his strangely contorted voice. Both constables assumed he'd drunk far more scotch than in fact he had.

'Ah, yes,' she replied, looking to her colleague.

'You've, found the car then?'

'Yes, Mr Radcliffe, we've found a car we believe is yours,' confirmed the boy-constable. Neither officer was yet willing to tackle the main point of their visit.

The registered keeper of the blue Rover could scarcely breathe, waiting for them to say what else they had found. 'Where, erm, where . . .?' his voice trailed off.

The female of the two, not much more than a girl in Michael Radcliffe's eyes, looked again at her fumbling partner, who made a despairing face. Neither had previously been delegated to perform this particular duty and they had agreed that however the conversation progressed, he would be the one to break the news, he would be the one who actually said they had reason to believe that Mrs Mary Sylvia Radcliffe had been killed when Mr Michael Joseph Radcliffe's car had been swept off the road. She would be the one who made a cup of tea, asked about getting a friend or neighbour in, asked about family. She would be the one who might even hold an old man's hand if she had to. Now it looked as if she would need to do the telling and the hand-holding.

'Mr Radcliffe, yes, we have found a car, your car we believe. There was a lady driver who we think may be your wife. The lady is deceased.' Even as she grasped the nettle she could not quite bring herself to say 'dead'. She aimed an accusing sideways look at her partner.

Michael Radcliffe feared he might burst, so long had he been holding his breath. The air rushed from his lungs making an involuntary noise in his throat which the anxious officers took for anguish.

*

At the same time as one female police officer was engaged with Michael Radcliffe, another was sitting in the equally comfortable, but smoke-free, lounge of the Samarasinghe house in Upper Orchard. She too was young, but she wore no uniform. She was attached to the CID, hand picked from last year's recruits and

39

already marked out by senior officers as a potential high-flyer. This was entirely justified since she was bright, enthusiastic and diligent, but Lavi Pitesteanu was also blessed by belonging to an ethnic minority and by living in an olive brown skin. Which of these particular attributes had brought her to interview Thomas was open to question.

Thomas was as keen to have the correct version of events recorded as the detective, who had been summoned to help with the disappearance of Eysha Duncan. She had few names on her list of interviewees: Molly Gardner and her mother, plus Eysha's mother Laura, Thomas and John Westerleigh, the last on her list. There were plenty of others with opinions and ideas, yet more who repeated rumour and wild guesses, but only these names had been noted by PC Lessing.

Upeksha Samarasinghe kept a watching brief, sitting quietly listening to the questions and her son's fluent answers. She was immensely proud of both her children and was always most proud of the one she was with. Today it was Thomas' turn, at least until his sister Diana returned, probably late in the evening, from the BBC news office in Oxford where she too had been earmarked for rapid progression. Diana Samarasinghe shared all Lavi Pitesteanu's positive attributes, plus she looked very good on camera. But for now it was Thomas who was the centre of his mother's attention: how easy and confident he was, how clear and precise was his description of the afternoon's events, what great prospects he had as a brilliant lawyer – even if a brilliant doctor would have been slightly better, what a handsome young man he was, what a fine pair he and the detective would make if only she were something more than a junior police officer.

'That is all I can tell you,' Thomas was saying.

For all her diligence and dedication, Lavi Pitesteanu was also flesh and blood. She was unwilling to leave such a lean and attractive young man after so short and precise an interview. A more general discussion might not only shed much needed light, but it would extend her time in his company.

'All you can tell me about the canoe and the rescue, perhaps, but what about the rest of the time you were out, who you saw, what was happening. You have an eye for detail, and there won't be many CCTV cameras in the village,' she hesitated a moment before adding, a little awkwardly Thomas thought, 'if we were to need one, of course.'

Thomas closed his eyes and collected his thoughts. 'I'll see what I can remember,' he said, then began a steady recounting of his travels that afternoon. He stuck to who and what he'd seen, where he'd been, leaving out what had been said and his own discomfort as he'd encountered various people, just as he'd omitted Laura Duncan's hostile blast from his account of the rescue.

He'd reached the point at which the helicopter hovered over the sea of mud at Lisle House, when the buzzing of Lavi Pitesteanu's mobile interrupted him. Excusing herself, she stood and turned away from Thomas and his mother, walking to the window and speaking curtly.

'Some news?' asked Thomas, hardly expecting an answer.

'Perhaps. Something's been found. It may be . . . it may be better that I say no more. But it seems the search has been called off, for now at least.'

'For such bad things to happen in such a place,' Upeksha said sorrowfully, as much to herself as to her son or the constable.

Thomas looked at her quickly. He knew exactly to what she was referring, but it was something of which they did not speak, and as far as Thomas was aware, nobody in the village had spoken of for years.

The constable caught none of this, heard nothing surprising in Mrs Samarasinghe's comment, but then again the constable had never heard of Melanie Ann Staples. Her mind had already moved on to the processes and procedures to be followed and what role, if any, she might play. On a day such as this the poor child had probably drowned, she thought, been trapped somewhere she shouldn't have been and drowned in the rising water. It was not an unreasonable idea, given all that had happened, and closer to the truth than she could possibly realise.

4

Under the blazing sun of another stifling day in a stifling season, white-clad figures picked their way over the slowly diminishing mound of rubble outside the school. White caps and white masks, white slippers scuffed brown by the soil, white latex gloves tucked in to white sleeves: as hooded apostles of an ancient cult performing the sacred ritual. The process had begun at six that morning after a night of floodlit activity. Rocks lifted one by one, each checked carefully before being thrown into a skip, smaller pieces all sieved and graded according to size before they're washed and examined in their turn. Once it had been agreed that the bones were both human and modern, a full investigation had swung into action, painstaking in its attention to detail where yesterday's sloppiness could only partly be excused by circumstance. The grubby, muddy pile might have been the sepulchre for an ancient princess, such was the care lavished on the excavation. Instead, it was the latest resting place of humble Melanie; not that she had been formally identified, that would take another day or two. But there was nobody in Germans or Whyncombe St. Giles who had any doubts as to whose bones had come back to the school gate, even if they had been equally convinced of a different name only a few hours previously.

When John Westerleigh's trembling hand had pulled back the red fabric for a second time, revealing his grizzly discovery to a white faced constable, his eye had fallen briefly on the purple-smudged but still legible letters 'MAS' written in the lining. Put there most likely by Melanie's mother he'd thought, in that millisecond of recognition, its survival a tribute to the indelibility of modern inks. He didn't point out the inscription, nor did he mention it to anyone apart from his wife. As it turned out, this silence was a great mistake, for word spread rapidly of a discovery, but it was the wrong word. Without reference to fact, the whisper was of the missing girl being discovered at the school. Conclusions were jumped to and assumptions made, not least by those who should have known better, and the tentative search for Eysha Duncan was aborted before it had properly got under way. Her distraught mother and her family were spoken to and prepared for the worst of all possible findings, although they were mystified as to how she could have been found at the school. The last strands of daylight still lingered in the summer sky before the cruel error was understood, but by then precious hours had been frittered away. Eysha's whereabouts went unquestioned until a suffocating darkness had settled over the little fold in the hills that held Germans and Whyncombe St. Giles. Only then was the awful reality realised, only then were the old files dusted down ready for the glare of fresh scrutiny, only then was the new file, Eysha's file, quickly made up to what it should have been from the moment her absence was reported. And only then, when those not still sweeping mud and raw sewage from their homes were thankful to be in their beds, only then were two more officers despatched to two addresses, one in Germans the other in Whyncombe St. Giles. The first, and more senior, had taken deep apologies and fresh hope to Laura Duncan, the second took the prospect of hope extinguished to Peter Staples.

All these aspects and more touched upon The Reverend Philip Fox-Lomax who stood sour-faced at the staffroom window, surveying the shrinking pile of debris beyond the playground railings. Behind him Lorraine Gregson, head teacher and only other governor present for the end of year meeting, sat in silence, slumped in her chair. The school had been closed for the day, the last day of the school year. The governors' meeting was the very last business of the year, a tradition preserved by the chairman despite the awkwardness of the hour for the majority of members. The events of the previous day, perhaps even the events of many years past, had kept all but the rector and the teacher from their governing duties. The priest grudgingly conceded that Michael Radcliffe, Alan Miller, Colin Deeley and Peter Staples had good enough reason, but Ann Glazer had little excuse and John Westerleigh might surely have taken an hour away from his farming labours. The rest of the governing body, parents and appointees from the county, rarely attended these inconvenient gatherings. Which was another reason the rector maintained the tradition.

The absences only partly accounted for his ill-humour. Many and varied had been the calls upon him that day. Not only did his house and the church need his urgent attention, but he'd been required to minister to a steady stream of parishioners, some he scarcely knew. As whispers had spread, he'd also felt the need to visit Peter Staples, but had found the house empty. A neighbour suggested the stonemason had gone as usual to his work in the quarry. With some hesitation he'd also called next-door at The Glebe House, home to the Radcliffes, but to his relief received no answer there either. In all the comings and goings, the closing of the school, the visits and the phone calls, he had found but one small consolation, and almost immediately regretted the little pleasure which the news of Alan Miller's hospitalisation gave him. In its way, this relatively minor incident amongst all the major events of the day, reinforced his unassailable faith that there was indeed a God: in a recent exchange with his wife she had casually mentioned the publican as being an attentive and energetic lover. It hardly mattered whether it was true or not, but retribution had been swifter than is often the case.

Disordered and pressured as his day had been, he saw worse in those to come. If it was indeed little Melanie Staples' remains that had been found, then all the old stories would fly round again, all the questions would be asked again, the same suspicions would resurface and probably some new ones too, as ill-founded as the old. And then there was the business with the Duncan girl. Not good, thought the rector, not good at all. More questions to be answered, more movements and responsibilities to be accounted for. Nothing to do with the school of course, nothing at all, yet it was a school day and a school expedition from which she had in theory gone missing, even if she hadn't arrived in the first place. The Reverend Philip Fox-Lomax sighed deep and long as another white-masked apostle stepped gingerly down the rubble pile carrying a shallow plastic box.

Lorraine Gregson was also occupied with the past, but the more recent past. Whyncombe St. Giles would be forever on her record as a place of accidents and mishaps, perhaps worse if Eysha Duncan were not soon found alive and well. It could all have been so different, this first headship was to have been the first step to better things. She still enjoyed teaching, which was just as well in such a small school, but she had her eyes on a post that took her beyond little Jack's SATS results and evening meetings with Jill's disinterested parent. It might have taken her another step, a bigger school in Oxford or Cheltenham perhaps, but even that idea seemed distant now. Whatever she might be good at, the 'notable incidents' column would forever contain a broken arm with compensation paid, a fractured skull and a missing pupil. Even if the child were found safe and sound she would still be on the record, still be noted as the lost Eysha Duncan. As much as she was distracted by her career prospects being irreparably damaged, she silently railed against the injustice of it all. Not a shred of blame could be laid at her door, nor the school's. If anyone could be held responsible it should surely be the parents, yet there would be no mark against them, no sanction to hang as a shadow over their lives.

★

Michael Radcliffe walked as in a dream down the soft lit, soft floored, soft sound corridor. Another man might have had a son or daughter to support him, a close friend at least, but he had none he'd thought to ask. He had no idea what to expect, no idea what state his wife might be in, no idea if he would recognize her laid out on a slab. And what if he didn't recognise her, what if it wasn't Mary at all, this body prepared for his inspection, this corpse waiting for his identifying word? What if it wasn't even his car they'd found her in? Even in his half-dream world, he could see such a mistake was unlikely. But they'd got the wrong girl yesterday hadn't they, so why not the wrong car or the wrong body? What if they rolled out the wrong body from the wrong drawer and showed him some stranger? Under his jacket he could feel his shirt sticking to his skin. This day, this appointment with death, was an ordeal to be dealt with, no more than that. He would play the game, match move for move, take his cue from those around him, until he understood what he was supposed to say, supposed to feel in this alien world.

With each step his legs weighed heavier. The spongy floor stuck to his shoes, simply lifting his feet became an effort. He reached out to steady himself against the wall but it was marshmallow, sucking in his hand, his arm, right up to the elbow. With all his strength he pulled himself free, gulping great breaths of air and tasting his sweat as it touched his lips. At the far end of the passage a green light twinkled above a doorway, yet it was further away than when he set out. Every glutinous step seemed to be taking him further from it.

'Mr Radcliffe, are you alright?'

The policewoman, the one who'd called to see him, caught him unawares. He turned his sickly, sweaty face towards her and,

45

unsure who she was, muttered, 'Difficult day, difficult day,' with as much composure as he could muster.

Yes, she thought, a difficult day for anyone, and with the day nudging another record high not made any easier by wearing a jacket. And a job today that she could have done without, a job for a liaison officer, a specialist, but lack of numbers and her 'previous knowledge' had pushed her into the firing line.

'In here,' she said, guiding Michael Radcliffe through the swing doors to the mortuary.

After a few minutes in the little waiting room, he was called through to where a body lay under a plain white sheet. He could tell it was a body because it was body shaped, despite being obscured by the pale folds. The constable hovered awkwardly beside him, telling him to take his time, to say when he was ready and they would show him her face. She was telling him that she looked very pretty, that they had made her look nice for him and that he was not to worry. Michael Radcliffe kept thinking that the room had no echo and that it was very small and cool and windowless. In his jacket pocket he felt the familiar round-edged smoothness of his lighter, a present a lifetime ago from someone who'd had his initials engraved on it, someone he couldn't quite remember.

At length, receiving no sign or word from the potential widower, the constable nodded almost imperceptibly to the technician who was waiting patiently to lift the sheet. For a moment Michael Radcliffe's worst fears seemed to be confirmed, for the woman he saw seemed to be far too young to be his wife. Added to this, her hair was covered by a white cowl, as a nun might have, which gave the impression of a sleeping Madonna. It needed only a crucifix to have been laid across her breast to have completed the picture of sainthood. Despite these distractions it was definitely Mary Radcliffe, of that he was sure. Not perhaps how he had last seen her, not even how he had ever seen her, but the more he looked, the more he thought it fitting that she should have been laid out like that.

'Mr Radcliffe?' the officer enquired gently.

'Yes?' he responded, uncertain of what was wanted of him, then remembering the purpose of the appointment, added, 'Oh, yes, that's my wife, that's Mary.'

In his pocket his fingers closed round the comforting shape of the lighter and he remembered who'd given it to him.

★

It wasn't any particular stoicism that drove Peter Staples to work in the quarry, nor was it dedication to his craft, it was more a matter of giving himself something to do after his visit the previous night. Each year since his Melanie's disappearance, around about the anniversary but never on the day itself, he would get a call or a visit from the police telling him that there was no news, no new leads, but that Melanie had not been forgotten, the file was not closed, they still felt confident of finding her. They called twice the year they found two other girls and the men who'd stolen them, called to say they were sure there would be some developments soon. But there never were any developments. Now this year was different. On the very date she'd gone away, here they were knocking on his door late in the night, telling him in gentle tones he should know something had been found near the school. There were indications of this, the possibility of that, and he should prepare himself for some hard days ahead. As if he didn't know hard days already. And Melanie's mother, would he contact her or should they? He'd never given them an address, never told them where she went. Most likely they knew, but not from him. Now he'd see her again, now the old bitterness would be back, rising like bile in the throat.

Maiden Quarry was also a good place to keep out of people's way. Nobody just happened to be in the quarry, it wasn't a place where anybody ever bumped into anyone else. So despite the whispering and the knowing looks that abounded in the twin villages, Peter was untroubled by any of it until mid-afternoon. He had a second piece of work to do for the church, more complicated than the straightforward corner block of yesterday. This was something he'd fiddled at on and off for a few weeks, but never had his heart in. He'd been paid for it a month ago, another of the little debts he owed the rector. For no good reason other than a sudden desire to be done with the job, he'd set about it as soon as he arrived. He'd already fashioned the stone into the rough shape that he needed to form the gargoyle, and he'd worked on the base where it would sit snugly into the space waiting for it. Power tools had their place and he'd use them wherever they were called for, but now a few hours of careful work with his chisels would see the job done. He had a pattern to work to as well as the crumbling piece being replaced, so eroded and disfigured it was barely recognisable as a goat's head.

The work went well, until around three-thirty when the mason was interrupted by another visit from the police, a couple of uniformed officers wandering in from a patrol car left at the gate. He put down his tools and waited for them to approach him.

'I didn't expect to see you today,' he said by way of greeting.

'Oh, when did you expect to see us then?' was the less than amiable response. Both officers were clearly suffering from the heat, festooned with belts and devices, their white shirts already stuck to their backs. A little dust devil danced across the quarry floor and blew grit in their faces.

'I didn't think there would be any news today, that's all.'

'News of what?'

Peter Staples looked at the pair and guessed that they were maybe a couple of years older than his Melanie would be, no more. They'd never heard of her.

'Never mind,' he said, with such a deep sadness in his heart and his voice that even the youthful officers caught some hint of it.

'You work here?'

The question hardly needed an answer but Peter nodded.

'There's a girl gone missing, we're calling on everyone in the area, asking them to check buildings, skips, dumps, anything where she might be. You seen anything?'

Peter Staples' arms hung limp at his sides, his chisel slipped from his fingers. For an instant it seemed he might crumple completely, be blown away with the dust, leaving an empty green overall on the scorched stone. A girl, another girl missing. He made as if to ask her name, to ask if it were the Duncan girl he'd seen the fuss about yesterday, but no words came. It was not enough that he must re-live all the dark days, recall all the incidents, remember all the pain. Now he must see it all played out again, new players on the stage, retelling his story, his Melanie's story, even right here in the quarry. They'd swarm over the place in a day or two if she wasn't found, just like they had for his girl. Maybe it was because it was such a foreign place to all but him, maybe that was why it seemed a place that a lost child might hide. Or be hidden. Maybe they'd think it was him who'd hidden her, like they'd thought he could have hidden his girl all those years ago.

'Have you seen anything?' one of the officers took a step nearer as he spoke.

'No. Seen nothing now and saw nothing then.' He held out his hands, palms uppermost towards the blue, blue heavens as if to show that they were unstained by any blood. Swinging round he encompassed the three acres of Maiden Quarry in a great sweep of his arms, 'Look here, look at it, there's no lost girl here, what would a little girl be doing in this hard place?' and as he spoke tears fell down his face and mingled with the sweat from his brow and no one but he knew that he wept for his daughter. No one but Peter Staples had ever known that he wept for his daughter.

'We'll have a look round anyway,' said the second officer, unsettled by what he saw as a strange, even manic, response.

Suddenly all the anger, all the misery of Melanie never having been found, all the time wasted looking in the wrong places, looking at the wrong people, it all welled up inside him. 'Yes, look round everywhere, look at everything, look under everything and behind everything, I'd help you if it would do any good.' Then the promise that had echoed so hollow down the years came back to him, one of many promises made, and the irony of the words made him spit them back at those same uniforms that had uttered them. 'Go on,' he cried, 'leave no stone unturned. For all the good it'll do her.'

In the heat of the day, and of the moment, a useless confrontation could easily have followed this angry outburst, but for once a kind of sanity prevailed. 'We'll just look round ourselves for now, perhaps you'd just show us what's kept where, that'll be best. But a place like this, with all these places to get lost, they'll more than likely want a proper search done later.'

'Later? A proper search later? No. You take a proper look now, later's not good enough. Someone's waiting for this girl. Come on,' he commanded, 'we'll look together.'

So, after a brief radio exchange, the three men searched the quarry for the next hour, Peter Staples with a labouring, sweating constable in his wake, while the other struggled queasily along the quarry edge surveying the place from above. Also at the stone-cutter's insistence they opened up the old tunnel, wrestling with the heavy wooden doors and pulling back the iron grating just far enough to slip into the dark and dust of decades. After the brilliant glare of the limestone it took them a few moments to become accustomed to the gloom of the long abandoned tunnel. The cool air surprised them, a small and welcome relief from the sun. They ducked down beside the disused trucks and groped their way along the old track, stumbling on sharp stone, until in near darkness they reached the old rock-fall blocking further progress. Their search could hardly be called thorough, but the quarryman knew well enough they would find nothing and the constable was keen to be out of the place. When he stumbled and half fell to his knees and felt the softness of old hessian sacks beneath his hands he recoiled in anticipation of far worse. By the time they emerged blinking into the blinding light of day, the cool dry air of the tunnel had caked the sweat and dust onto their skin so that each had acquired a ghostly pallor.

Throughout the whole hour the men barely exchanged a word apart from essential warnings and instructions. More than once the two policemen regretted ever stopping on their comfortable air-conditioned ride round the countryside to have a quick look in Maiden Quarry, a place they imagined might be disused and prettily overgrown. A hard hour's toil over hot sharp rocks for one and a battle with snagging brambles and sickening vertigo for the other had not been what they'd expected. But with Peter Staples demanding it and their base endorsing it, they'd had no choice. If the girl were to be found there after they had declined to look, after they had been invited to do so, and offered assistance, well, there would be hell to pay one way or another. But by the time they'd finished looking as much as they could possibly look, they were both feeling quite pleased with themselves. They'd done a thorough job and had the scars to prove it. And found no sign of Eysha Duncan.

*

Upeksha Samarasinghe was not happy with her husband. She was not very happy with her two children either, but her husband had particularly displeased her. She had phoned him in his office in Berkeley, California, something which she was never supposed to do apart from the direst emergency or the most exceptional circumstances. She had deemed the events in Whyncombe St. Giles to be exceptional but her husband Clarence had not. And since it was not an emergency either, he was unhappy to have had his day disturbed. He was very abrupt with her, making his displeasure quite clear and suggesting that none of it had anything to do with him and little to do with her since she, their house and their children were all unscathed.

B W C Samarasinghe had chosen to be called by his third name, his very Anglo-Saxon name, Clarence, since his university days. He'd always considered the name lent him a certain gravitas which his brown skin might otherwise deny him. Besides, his other names were too difficult for English ears and did not lend themselves to abbreviation. So it was as a young Clarence that he'd first been noted by talent-spotters in Cambridge, although he claimed to have spotted them first. It was a lesson he'd thought of passing on to his son, but never found the moment. The British had kept tabs on his progress for several years, quietly smoothing a path here, ensuring an invitation there, until the day came when the highly qualified and well-travelled Clarence was discreetly encouraged to take up an obscure but significant post in the civil service. Later, it was Clarence the Anglophile who'd been invited, along with his young family, to lay their hands on the flag and take citizenship. Now it was as Dr Clarence Samarasinghe, renowned expert in digital encryption that he was currently enjoying a year seconded to the Golden State. It was even whispered by those with an interest in such things that he might one day acquire a title. Within his own sphere he was well regarded by many people around the world, although on that particular day his wife could not be numbered among them.

Upeksha's children were out of favour because although they agreed with their mother that the events were exceptional, they also agreed with their father that a special phone call during his sacred working hours was not justified.

'He could have listened to me,' Upeksha complained, 'instead of interrupting and asking all the time what he was meant to do.'

Her children nodded their sympathetic agreement.

Diana Samarasinghe was delighted to find her dull little village to be at the centre of events for once, instead of the usual sleepy backwater. She'd been out making notes and taking pictures since early morning, phoned in a short report for radio and met up with the TV crew from Oxford. She'd prepared a little piece to record in case it was called for, but the niceties of seniority had to be observed. The veteran reporter assigned to the job was hardly going to volunteer any of her own camera time to the dusky talents of the Samarasinghe girl. Diana blessed the ageing journalist and the mesmerised young cameraman with one of her sublime smiles. She could wait, other chances would come soon enough.

Thomas had planned a trip to an exhibition at the Bodleian, but postponed it for no particular reason and then spent the rest of the day regretting it. He'd felt the need to stay near home, to be on hand if he were needed, although for what he could not say. His mother's ill-humour made him all the more restless, a feeling only heightened by his sister's return with the news that Eysha Duncan remained unaccounted for but the village was buzzing with rumour that the body of another girl had been discovered.

'Melanie someone,' Diana told him, 'Didn't you know a girl who went missing, years ago, while I was with opa Wikram one time?'

Her mother looked up sharply and scowled at her daughter over her glasses. She and Thomas had shared a thought about the girl while watching yesterday's flood, but neither of them had spoken of her. Now, thanks to Diana, the spell had been broken.

'Staples. She was Melanie Staples,' Thomas said flatly. The words had not crossed his lips in more than a decade. On those rare occasions that reference had been made, it was always obliquely, never direct, never with her name being spoken. It felt odd to hear himself speak the words again now. His mother looked disapprovingly at him and moved her mouth to speak but made no sound.

'Yes, Staples. Well, people say she's been found. It'll be a big story.' And with the prospect of that excitement ahead of her, Diana Samarasinghe escaped her mother's censure and headed to Oxford and the Banbury Road.

A big story. Yes, and much else besides, thought Thomas. A new investigation, another round of interviews, another set of questions. And once again he'd be involved, he'd be asked to remember the day and the days before it, asked who he saw and when he saw them, which cars passed, which stopped. How much had he forgotten, how much had he ever remembered? He was only just eleven, he and his mother sitting in the police station, still an adventure then, still just Melanie missing, probably just being Melanie, you couldn't tell with her, that's what made her so exciting. Always slightly on the edge, always daring him to do things, always hinting at plans and schemes and adventures of her own. A big story even without the new complication of Eysha Duncan. It occurred to Thomas that he'd seen most of the same faces round the villages yesterday as he saw whenever he was at home, faces that were part of the very fabric of the twin villages. How different he wondered, was the cast of players all those years back when he was eleven? There were certainly some constants: the stone-cutter, the rector, the farmer, the shopkeeper, the governor, and probably many more behind their walls and hedges. In a moment of insight he saw himself and realised that he must be added to the list of constants, along with his mother, although neither would be classed as part of the fabric, not if they were to live there the rest of their lives.

★

For many residents of the twin villages, the day after the deluge was even worse than the deluge itself. Those with the slightest connection to the Staples or Duncan families had their own additional fears and concerns, but for the majority it was the sickening matter of clearing up as best they could from the invasion of their homes. For some the water had burrowed into their houses and, slowed in its progress, dropped some of its load of mud and sludge before leaking out under doors and through windows. The rain had stopped long ago, but the heat was unrelenting and water still ran in the new courses cut in the hillsides. For those worst affected, clearing up was impossible, instead it was a job for contractors, a long drawn out engagement with insurance companies. Weeks, perhaps even months, in temporary accommodation stretched ahead of them, willing friends and family now would become resentful hosts by the time autumn was in the air.

Not every house was damaged, made uninhabitable by the flooding. Many survived completely untouched, amongst which were a handful of empty houses that had waited for a suitable tenant for months, even years. Suitable tenants were defined as anyone who could afford the rent in such a highly desirable district. Some owners of these houses and their agents were not slow to spot the opportunity. Presented with an increase in demand coinciding with a reduction in supply, asking prices would rise accordingly.

Although only twenty-four hours had passed since the rain had stopped, the streets and lanes were lined with soaked and stinking piles of furniture and all manner of possessions made useless by the water. Some poor families found that even perfectly dry and salvaged goods, especially those electrical items which were

53

outdated in their style or capabilities, were found on closer inspection to have been rendered useless simply by having been in the same building as a few millimetres of water. What to do with such items other than throw them onto the heap of furniture in the front garden? The astute answered this question by listing them, or at least, listing something like them, ready to claim the latest models from the insurance company.

The claims being considered by John Westerleigh featured no such goodies as games consoles or laptops. Apart from some rather more catastrophic losses, his house was largely unaffected, a testament to Victorian builders and timely maintenance. A gutter had broken and caused some water to get under the roof of the old dairy which he'd converted into the farm office, but the damage was slight. As he sat at the desk trying but failing to make notes ready for the assessor's visit, he did eye the old printer which had some wet plaster splattered across it. The thought of a new one was momentarily attractive but he quickly rejected the idea of such trivial fakery. It would endanger his major claim which would be detailed and comprehensive in all aspects bar one: the contrary advice he'd received about the site of the lagoon and the cost-cutting construction methods. Weighed against that engineer's unofficial opinion had been the bank's, which had loaned the money for the project, and a land agent's report which endorsed the need. It was going to be a tricky business assessing both the immediate and consequential losses, something not to be rushed, something to take expert advice over, something a friendly agent could be relied upon to help out with, especially the one relied on so heavily by the bank. And he must remember the dead sheep.

Recalling that carcass brought his thoughts full circle. The girl clawed at his mind, demanding he see her again. He kept her at bay by thinking of the sheep, how heavy it was, how it slid down the bucket side and flumped into the bottom, legs uppermost. 'MAS' he was sure of, there would be no other name than Melanie Staples attached to those sad remains. He watched the sheep slide down again, smearing the bucket side with its sodden fleece. Again it quivered as it hit the bottom. Melanie's skull had a tooth missing, front top left as he looked at it. Did they find it as they sieved the mud, did they spot a child's tooth, brown from the soil amongst all the little brown limestone pebbles? The sheep and the fertilizer bag, the other red bag that he never did go back for. The red bag he clutched at, tugged at, would have pulled free but for the tree roots gripping it, the red bag that felt wrong the moment his fingers closed on it, only the colour was right, all else was wrong. The colour had faded, dulled by the years of burial, dulled to become a fertilizer bag when once it had been vibrant, shiny pillar-box red. 'MAS' still written, still purple, smudged and streaked but still there. Her jaw hanging open but no tongue to speak, no eyes to see him with. Again the sheep slid down, dead and heavy, legs up, head back, mouth wide.

Margaret Westerleigh had stood a few moments in the open doorway, watching her husband rocking slightly to and fro, eyes closed, a twist to his mouth that she didn't recognise. She'd called him for tea but had no reply. Now she guessed at what was in his mind, guessed it was finding the girl, guessed how he felt about it. She guessed as she always did, because he hadn't told her, he never told her, never showed her. He took animals to slaughter often enough, he'd think little of shooting rabbits, he'd castrate a lamb in a moment, but this was the practical farmer, brought up as such and lived as such. Somewhere hidden she was sure, was tenderness, caring, perhaps even love, but for years he'd been detached from her, sometimes to the point of coldness. For Margaret it was a wonder he was able to function anywhere near normal after the collapse of the lagoon and the traumas that followed.

She'd called and called him on the radio without any answer and had been on the verge of chasing him down in the pickup when he'd swung the tractor back into the yard. He'd looked strained and white and muttered about getting a dead sheep sorted out, brushing past her without really seeing her. When she'd asked what'd happened down the hill, he'd stared at her blankly for a second or two, motioned with his hand, said it was all right, the village was inundated, but it was all right, it wasn't anything to do with them. He'd said it almost casually, as if the whole disaster had been no more than a minor incident. Only later, eating his supper, had he stopped, fork midway between plate and mouth, to tell her that he could still read the initials, still see 'MAS'.

'John,' she said softly so as not to surprise him.

He opened his eyes and stared at her as vacantly as he'd done the day before.

'John, here's your tea.' She laid the cup on the desk in font of him.

'Thanks.'

'I meant to tell you, the rector phoned. He asked how you were.'
'How was I?'
His wife shuddered a little. Feelings buried deeper than ever, beyond even his own reach.
'I said you were fine, but very busy and tired.'
'I was.'
'Yes, but he said something about a governors' meeting too.'
'Oh?' he said, puzzled, then 'Oh yes, the last day of the year. How could I have forgotten?'

★

Late into the afternoon, extra police were bussed in. New recruits, special constables, support officers, anyone who could walk and wear a uniform was pressed into service in the search for Eysha Duncan. The authorities were acutely aware of how seriously the mistakes of yesterday would be viewed once the facts were known. The appalling conditions, the stretched services, the broken communications would all be forgotten long before they were allowed to forget the mistake of calling off the search. So they made sure they were seen to be doing everything that could be done.

They walked in lines on the heath, they knocked on every door, looked in every garden shed and outhouse. Overhead the blue and white helicopter fluttered and buzzed, now moving to get a new line of sight here, now directing a dog handler there. Frogmen paddled and dived around the study centre in the Centenary Wood which remained an island in an ever muddier lake, widening still as water flowed from the saturated ground. They took over the village hall and parked a mobile incident centre across the car park. Half a mile away on the main road they set up road-blocks and spoke to every driver. On TV and radio they spoke to the county and by half past nine they'd spoken to the nation. Eysha Duncan was reported to be in Edinburgh, Wallasey and Truro in quick succession. Each false report was followed up immediately and publicly.

They had one other line of enquiry, not fully grasped when she'd been reported missing, and known only to a handful of people. But that evening it was being pursued with surprising delicacy in a shabby little house in Germans. Two female officers were at the Duncan home gently trying to persuade Laura Duncan to reveal the name of Eysha's father.

5

The first official day of the school summer holidays dawned as hot as the short night before it and promised to break yesterday's record. The clinging, sapping humidity made the heat all the more unbearable and frayed tempers before the day had even begun. For those waking in unfamiliar beds or on uncomfortable sofas, the misery was compounded by the need to maintain a level of politeness with their hosts. For those wage earners who had the good fortune to live in unaffected property there remained the unwelcome daily commute, relieved only slightly by the lighter traffic brought by the holidays.

There were signs that the flow of water from the hills above the twin villages was abating and the vast lake at the bottom of the combe had stopped growing. Down beyond Six Lanes, at the far end of the Lisle estate, diggers and pumps were at work carefully relieving the choked watercourse damming up the millions of tons of water. At several points around the villages the fire brigade were still in attendance, pumping water from blighted homes. They and their fellows had worked in shifts tirelessly through two days and nights. Neighbouring brigades had sent extra vehicles and men and, along with a belated response from cash-conscious government, most of the immediate needs of the stricken villages were being met. Added to the distressed scene were more than eighty police, with all their usual vehicles and now a mobile canteen to increase the congestion. Since first light their helicopter had again been in the sky, quartering the ground in the fruitless search for Eysha Duncan.

Another, smaller, group was walking slowly along the old track beside The Chequers, up past the car park toward the woods, tracing in reverse the route that Melanie and her sycamore took on the tidal wave of mud and slurry. It was hard going, a steady stream of water still flowed down the hillside and the track surface formed over centuries had been gouged out in many places, leaving great pot-holes half full of fetid brown liquid. Rocks and splintered branches, a few whole trees, littered the way. The little party consisted of four police, two in uniform, two not, plus John Westerleigh, chosen as a solid reliable citizen of long standing and for his knowledge of the land. The more senior of the two detectives, Donald Smallborne, had thought it was also a good excuse to talk a little more with the man who had discovered the girl's remains. He'd been put in charge of the new investigation but had little enthusiasm for it. These old cases had a reputation for being tedious affairs, covering ground that had been covered many times before, and they rarely brought any kudos to those involved, regardless of the outcome. Resolve it or not, you either looked bad or made someone else look bad. And besides, it threatened to disrupt his annual leave in a few days when he and his family should be heading to cooler climes in South Africa.

He'd brought a couple of uniforms along as extra pairs of eyes, and the pushy little eastern European, Pitesteanu, as an extra pair of ears. And also because he thought her backside looked particularly fine, particularly round, in the thin summer trousers she was wearing. Lavi Pitesteanu had been rapidly switched from the Eysha Duncan team after the little misunderstanding about a body being found. She was not alone, every officer involved had been found new tasks and a whole new team assembled. With numbers so stretched, this meant some of those not considered competent to find Eysha twenty-four hours previously were now expected to solve a far older disappearance.

'So, your place is up on the hill?'

John Westerleigh nodded. He'd had little rest and less sleep. His normally wiry frame was even thinner, his face haggard and drawn. The last thing he'd wanted that morning was an early call from the police with their request for assistance. Refusal was not an option, despite Margaret's objections. Better he went and walked with them than someone else who might see the wrong things, draw the wrong conclusions. So far as he was aware, nobody but he and his wife yet knew the extent of the lagoon collapse, knew of the part it played in Allan Miller's misery, the school's near miss nor his shocking discovery. The girl still called to him, still wanted to catch his eye, still had a tooth missing. The dead ewe still flopped into the bucket, still quivered as it hit the bottom, its belly bloated after a few hours simmering on top of the mound. He shook his head as if it might dislodge the images.

'Yes, that's my place,' he said, pointing above the trees to the brow of the hill a little to their right. Just visible was the red roof of a barn and beside it the chimneys of High Whyn.

58

They struggled on until they came to the bottom of the wood where it seemed the most damage had been done. The awful torrent and its destructive cargo of rock and concrete would have been at its worst here at the foot of the steepest slope. The little track, just a few meters wide before the deluge, had been washed away, its place taken by an ugly gash perhaps twenty metres across. Looking up the slope there was nothing recognisable, the scar ran right up the hillside, right through the wood to the skyline above. The going looked even tougher, more like rock climbing than a good walk up an ancient Cotswold path.

'Is there another way up through the wood?' The detective was disappointed there was little to see and that his exploration would be so soon completed.

'Not really, you could scramble up, but there's no path as such.'

'You wouldn't think just water could do all this. Just goes to show.'

'What do you think, Mr Westerleigh, just water?' his junior enquired, poking a broken branch into the nearest brown puddle.

'Well no, not a hundred percent,' the farmer responded. He had been ready for exactly such a question, and rehearsed his answer. 'There was a problem with the slurry in such a downpour as we had. They're calling it a thousand year event, did you know that? It overflowed for a while then that side of the hill just slid away. I was up there, tried to stop it. That's why there so much concrete in the mix.' To demonstrate the point he bent and picked a lump from near his feet. Beneath it were two little smooth limestone pebbles, which could easily have been mistaken for teeth. He stepped back shaken, almost losing his balance.

The two detectives examined the concrete fragment as if it might have some significance. Its crumbling breadcrumb texture did indeed hold significance, but not for them.

'Is all this part of the farm, right down to the school?' Lavi Pitesteanu asked, keen to keep the conversation going, keen to remind her superior that she also had a brain.

'No, the wood's not part of the farm. Up there, pretty much to where you can see, that's the farm there, grazing mainly, beyond the wood.' Again he gestured up the hill.

'Who owns all this then?' said Donald Smallborne quickly.

'Ah, well, thereby hangs a tale. Strictly speaking it's the subject of a dispute, but for what you're asking, the village owns it, the parish council if you like.'

'You'll have to tell me more.'

'A while ago, a few years back, the estate,' he pointed back towards the combe in the direction of Lisle House, 'the Lisle estate, they owned half the county once, well they were going to sell it, but the lawyers came up with a snag, it seemed the property title had a fault and it looked like a section had been sold once already, to the church. Then once the argument got going, the brewery joined in and said the church had sold part of it to them. It was all a matter of maps and fence posts and there was no agreement to be had. Each thought some of it was theirs and they had the plans and sketches to prove it. I checked my title, and a few others did to, in case they had a claim as well.'

'How long ago was this?'

'Maybe ten years or so.'

'So what happened?'

'Well the estate couldn't sell, none of them could, so they all agreed to disagree and let the parish council have it for the village. The path we've been on and all the wood along the side of Whyn Hill was given over for the villages to use.'

'Who used it before that?'

John Westerleigh smiled a thin smile, perhaps the first of his day. 'The same people as used it after. There was no right of way, never was, still isn't, but people have been using the path and the wood for centuries.'

'Over the farm too?' Lavi Pitesteanu chipped in.

'No, there's a fence round the field,' then as an afterthought, 'or there was a fence.' Which reminded him that the assessor would be knocking at his door very soon. He checked his watch in the universal way of suggesting another appointment.

'Thanks for coming out this morning, we might need to talk again. You've been a great help, can't have been easy, finding the girl like that.' The policeman looked straight at John Westerleigh as he spoke, a calculated comment, delivered casually, but precisely at the moment that the man thought he could turn and leave. It was also the first suggestion that Melanie's remains had been identified.

'No. Not easy at all. It was her then, it was . . . ' he was going to say her name but couldn't bear to utter the words, 'it was the girl then.'

'Nothing certain yet, but it looks like it. You'll keep that to yourself for now, please, still some checks to be done, the usual things. But you have an idea who it might be?'

John Westerleigh turned and looked down the track to The Chequers, to what was left of the pile of debris, to the blue and white tape hanging limp from the school railings, and shook his head before turning back to face the detective. 'There's surely only one isn't there, only one it can be?'

★

Peter Staples had been awake as early as anyone in Whyncombe St. Giles. He'd stood at his bedroom window breathing in the only freshness there might be in the day, looking over the little valley and beyond as the light grew in the east. A new day, but one certain to bring old pain. More than likely they'd be knocking on his door today, telling him his girl was found, then after all the politeness they'd want another statement, they'd want to go over every moment again, every second of every minute of that day and where he'd been and who he'd seen and what he'd done. And he'd remember all those things like they were yesterday, because he'd never forgotten the day his Melanie didn't come home. He never forgot his son, either, never forgot his wife, though he'd tried hard enough.

He'd sat a long time trying to order his thoughts and gather strength for the day, then at the first sound of the helicopter, he dressed and breakfasted. One thing he never missed, whatever the day, whatever the occasion, was his breakfast. As a child the importance of breakfast had been repeated daily. The anchor to the day, his father called it. He'd need an anchor this day. He was glad his father hadn't lived to see it, losing his granddaughter had been the death of him, or so people had said. He'd doted on her, all the more so after her brother died. Then the day she went there was no consoling him, all the worse that they'd had a little falling out the day before. Two weeks later Peter Staples senior had the test results back from the hospital and his son buried him on a freezing day in December. Happy Christmas. Susie, his wife, left in the January. Happy New Year.

A siren, sudden and urgent, loud and nearby, brought him sharply back to the present. The noise died as abruptly as it had begun, as if it had been a mistake, a slip of the fingers on the switch. But it brought the grieving father back from past miseries to current ones. For one of the few times since he started working on his own account, he decided to take a day away from shaping stone. The goat's head gargoyle had waited long enough, it would

61

wait a few more days. Instead he would get some overdue domestic jobs done, and clear the soil and pebbles still littering his little garden and the path by the house. He gave himself these good reasons, but there was another. When they came to see him, came with the news, he wanted it to be here in the house, close to her memories, not in the dust and glare of the quarry.

Upstairs he went to the cupboard where he kept what was left of Melanie's things in a couple of boxes. He usually kept one or two items out, just to be reminders. There'd been nothing in the last few weeks but today he reckoned he might find a couple of her favourites, put them downstairs so they'd be around when the words were said. They might let some part of her, some hint of her, live on a little longer in the only house she ever called home. There wasn't much to choose from and it was a seemingly random collection after her mother had taken everything else away in a suitcase. He looked through the boxes, turning each item in his hands- the hair brush she'd had as a baby, some favourite first books, a piece of sewing she'd done, heart-shaped pink sunglasses, a dyed tee shirt. After a few minutes he chose a little bear named Princess, a precious birthday present from her grandpa Staples, and her duvet cover from when she was a toddler and which had forever been her comforter. He made no great show of these things, the cover was folded and put on top of the cabinet with the bear sitting on it. They were not displayed, they were simply there, as if she had left them lying about and her mother had tidied them ready to go back upstairs. It was how he liked to see her things when they were not in the cardboard box.

★

Margery Webster and Colin Deeley had not exactly relished their time cooped up in the little house at Six Lanes, but they had made the most of it. Neighbours and friends, both with partners deceased a respectable length of time, they had found a new level of friendship during their voluntary confinement in Sweet Pea Cottage. For much of the time they'd peered out in wonder and been grateful that their two cottages were built on a little outlying hump of Whyn Hill. Behind the houses the great lake spread across the valley, while in front the torrent from the hills above was unrelenting. At the height of the flow, water had lapped at the front steps but it had risen no higher, a blessing which Margery felt owed something to the sincerity of their prayers, a sentiment Colin willingly supported even if he lacked her conviction.

Cut off down their little lane from any passers by, and unthought of by those who had their own difficulties to deal with, the two waited out the flood until they could see the way clear enough to walk to the road. From there, one or both of them, could get to the village shop to fetch fresh supplies of essentials. They'd seen the helicopters buzzing but not waved or signalled as they'd become quite cosy together. Distant sirens and the flashes of blue lights during the night simply confirmed they were not alone in their watery distress, but of the missing girl and the found girl they knew nothing.

Accepting her neighbour's offer to collect her milk and newspaper, the widow Margery returned to her own house wondering if she would ever again spend a night in her neighbour's bed, and wondering too if the previous night had been as good an idea as it seemed at the time. She was very unsure of her feelings towards both past action and future possibility. But she did allow herself a very satisfied smile at the thought of what her children, or better, what her grandchildren would have said about it. Not that she was ever likely to tell any of them.

By contrast, Colin Deeley gave little thought to past or future that morning as he set off on his errands. He too allowed himself a satisfied smile, but for different reasons than Margery's. Had he been walking he would certainly have had a spring in his step, but he was cycling, albeit with more energy than usual, despite the sultry heat. The way from Six Lanes took him up round the hill to where the path from the monument met the road above Lisle House. Like most who had passed that way in the previous two days, he was astonished at the view now presented. He'd seen his little corner of the world inundated, but not dreamed what it might mean to the village and beyond.

Further along he was more surprised still by all the activity round the school. The building looked intact, and the sight of it reminded him he was a governor and he'd missed the end of year meeting. He missed most meetings but never with such a good excuse, he thought. It wouldn't be the first time that he'd been sat in The Chequers of an evening and seen the lights on across the road in the school before he'd remembered he should be there. He turned up the path and banged at the door of the pub but got no reply. The building looked alright, but all around was smashed and levelled. Then, wondering how he could have missed it, he saw the great gash through the wood on the hillside and began to understand the enormity of the event that had struck. The whole path had gone, it looked like half the wood had been swept down with it. He let his eye follow the line upwards to where a few people, police by the look of it, were struggling to climb up to John Westerleigh's place. He wondered if someone was in trouble up there, trapped or caught in the landslide. Or maybe some of the High Whyn sheep.

He cycled on through Germans towards Whyncombe St. Giles and the village shop, open mouthed at all he saw, hoping to meet someone who'd tell him more. But he saw nobody but police standing about and firemen pumping and hosing. He'd have stopped at Alex Duncan's house and talked to him, but there were police parked outside and one on the door. The house looked alright so he guessed there'd been some trouble, which would be nothing new for Alex's family.

Eventually he reached the shop where a little skip was parked outside with half Chris Rogers' stock tipped into it. The shopkeeper had just opened again after non-stop work getting the water and damaged goods out and the electricity re-connected. He should've been pleased to see a customer again but he wasn't.

'Bad do then, Chris,' Colin Deeley offered by way of a sympathetic greeting.

Chris Rogers was hesitant. 'Yes,' he said in a non-committal way. 'How's it been down your way?'

'Cut off. Been stuck indoors for two days,' then, lowering his voice in a confidential tone, 'Not all bad though.'

'Ah. Right, not seen or heard much then,' the shopkeeper nodded slightly, his puzzle solved.

'Seen a lot of water. Still got some dry smokes?'

'Yes.' Again the response was flat, unwilling to engage in conversation, which was unusual because the shopkeeper was well known to be miserable, and never missed an opportunity to let his customers know how miserable he was. And if ever there was a day for Chris Rogers to complain of the injustice the world heaped upon him, it was surely today.

'Any milk?'

'No.'

'What's going on with all the police? The Duncans been up to something again by the look of it.'

64

'Yeah, maybe. Twenty fags, only got the Lites, ok?'

He was very keen to get the transaction completed and Colin Deeley out of his shop. The man clearly had no idea what had happened, no idea the bones of his granddaughter had been washed up at the school gate. And Chris Rogers did not want to be the one to tell him.

★

They knocked so quietly on Peter Staples' front door he wouldn't have heard if he hadn't been listening for them, waiting to see who they'd sent, wondering how they'd say the words. They'd sent Donald Smallborne, or rather he'd chosen to go, and he'd brought his new favourite, the dark eyed constable with the east European name and the well-rounded figure. Outside at the garden gate they left a uniform to deter the gawpers, but a uniform attracts interest where there was none before. The two introduced themselves and he showed them in to the back room. He'd cleared the mess round the house, cleared the mess in the house, got everything tidy, all ready to receive visitors. They sat with their backs to the cabinet with Princess gazing glassily over their shoulders.

'Mr Staples, we have the news you were contacted about.' No small talk, no messing, the senior officer was calm, deliberate, business-like, but he found a softer edge to his voice.

'It's Melanie then? You know for sure?'

'Years ago we wouldn't question it, we'd be saying yes for sure. Today, we still have the DNA result to come, but yes, we think it is Melanie. There is very strong dental evidence, as near conclusive as it can be.' He was very careful to avoid any reference to the missing tooth, which records showed had not been missing on the day she was last seen alive.

'Dental evidence. There'd be plenty of that. Never looked after her teeth, always on at her, but she never . . .' the reminiscence trailed away to nothing.

The policeman paused, let the memory fade, then to be sure that the girl's father would know all that he needed to know, added, 'And there is another thing, remarkably in its way, her coat has been identified. It seems unlikely that anyone else would have Melanie's coat.' Again he chose his words with the utmost care.

'Her raincoat? You've found her raincoat?' He could not reconcile a dead Melanie, decayed beyond recognition had been yesterday's suggestion, with an identifiable raincoat.

'Yes, Mr Staples, we're sure it's hers.' Again he avoided graphic detail.

Peters Staples looked desperately from one officer to the other.

'It has her name written in the lining,' explained Lavi Pitesteanu with great gentleness. Even so it did not please her superior, who'd been anxious not to disclose any detailed information, however trivial or apparently obvious it might be.

As is so often the way with tragedy, it is not the big picture that breaks the heart, but the tiny fragment. An appalling air crash creates great sadness and sympathy, but it is the picture of the charred teddy-bear lying in the wreckage that springs a tear in the driest eye. So it was with Melanie's father, who'd prepared himself as well as any man could for such an interview, but was overwhelmed by the vision of that fragment, that totally personal thing, her name written in purple ink on the cream linen lining of her bright red mac. He knew the day they'd bought it for her, the day his wife had written it, the day she'd said how it would never wash out.

He stared at Princess sitting on the cover, stared until he couldn't see the toy through the tears in his eyes. He put his head in his hands, letting tears and dribble mix and run through his fingers. He'd wept for her before and probably would do so again, but these were fresh tears for the final chapter. His only movement was the juddering intake of breath. He didn't speak or cry out, his voice was reduced to an intermittent low moaning, like some injured animal waiting for death.

They let him weep for a while, they would have let him weep for as long as he wanted, but after a few minutes it subsided. The young officer rummaged in the kitchen until she found a glass and brought him water. He pulled a clean white handkerchief from the pocket where he'd carefully thought to place it an hour or so previously and wiped the tears from his cheeks and the dripping mucus from his nose and swollen lips.

Lavi Pitesteanu made as if to speak to him, her hands and body shaped by sympathy, but her boss looked at her through narrowed eyes with a tight little mouth and the words died in her throat. Donald Smallborne took no pleasure in watching a man grieve for his daughter, but seeing him do so might tell him more than a hundred questions. He'd once been told that some of the worst of criminals, the most sadistic of killers were also the most accomplished of actors. He had no reason to think Peter Staples was anything but genuine, anything but distraught, but he had no reason to think anything at all after such brief acquaintance. Genuine grief, genuine distress, might easily accompany genuine remorse, genuine guilt. Quite rightly in his opinion, the original investigation had never excluded Melanie's family from their enquiries.

At length he recovered himself enough to be able to look at her Princess again and quiet filled the cramped and airless room in the stone-cutter's cottage. Sweat ran down the policeman's neck and lingered on his shirt collar before joining the dark streaks leaking towards his waist. Lavi Pitesteanu sat in her own pool of discomfort, taking her cue from her boss and determined not to be the one who broke the spell of silence. They sat that way for a few minutes more, as if deferring to the father's right to speak first in his own house, but the truth was Donald Smallborne simply wanted to know what the man would say without a prompt.

'When can I have her back?' he said thickly through puffy lips.

This simple question seemed to satisfy the policeman, for he turned to his companion saying, 'Shall we see about some tea?' then to him, 'Would that be alright Mr Staples, if she went and got some tea?'

Still with his soft-edged voice, he spoke of tests still to be done, observations to be made, a coroner to satisfy. He didn't touch upon the question of recovering all of Melanie's bones. The guardian sycamore had performed its task well, but such had been the upheaval, some losses were inevitable and the area to search was wide. The policeman didn't expect to glean any critical knowledge from the girl's missing parts but it was possible. And there was the delicate matter of what should be done with a newly discovered tibia or fibula if the rest of the owner had been buried a while back: a wasteful new investigation might well be started at great expense and distress to everyone concerned. But he did touch on the need to re-examine all the old statements and take new ones, to look carefully at the implications of where Melanie might have been buried. And he did ask Peter Staples to go to the police station as soon as possible to provide a new DNA sample, his previous one having been 'compromised'.

Making the tea was not what she had been trained for, but Lavi Pitesteanu was savvy enough to do it without any hint of protest, but to watch and listen. She was annoyed with herself over the foolish slip of mentioning the name in the coat, for letting sympathy and feeling get the better of her. She hadn't even seen this Chief Inspector Smallborne before yesterday, but after being summarily dropped from the Eysha Duncan enquiry she'd jumped at the chance to work alongside him. And the hot weather had at least let her exploit her wardrobe to its best advantage.

★

There were tears too in the Duncan household, not of grieving, not yet, but tears all the same. Another interview with the same two officers who had spent half the night there ended with the same result, namely Laura refusing to give up a single name for Eysha's father. She insisted she didn't know, there were several who might have been the father and whoever it was she was certain none of them even knew of her daughter's existence. Gossip about who it might be had abounded in the first few weeks of the pregnancy, and included some predictable if unlikely names, but interest had quickly waned. It was exactly the story she had always told, and she couldn't see why it was being questioned again now. Quite reasonably, the police thought it possible that Eysha might have been taken by the anonymous father, that she might even have gone willingly. Just as reasonably, the Duncans thought the police should get on with finding her and worry about who her father might be another time.

The family also deeply resented hints of them being involved or Laura somehow being complicit in the child's disappearance. Her two brothers were quick to defend her, even to the point of being threatened with arrest for obstructing the enquiry. Both men were already known to the criminal justice system for a series of relatively minor offences and there was little love lost between them and the forces of law and order. As a result, the perception of a biased and ill-judged police operation was growing, not only within the family but also among their wider circle of friends and neighbours. They had taken their eye off the ball once and as far as the Duncans were concerned, were doing so again.

Laura continued to yo-yo between anger and despair at the unknown plight of her daughter. A surging rush of emotion accompanied each high and low, alleviated only slightly by

68

frequent nicotine intake. At three in the morning, when she'd emptied her last pack, she'd raided her mum's handbag, just as she used to do as a child. Later she'd pleaded with her brothers to fetch her some more from the petrol station up on the main road. That fresh supply was severely depleted by the time the morning inquisition about Eysha's father had finished. Laura was left sprawled abjectly across the sofa, her bloodshot eyes sunk in deep purple rings, all the more marked by her pale skin. She hadn't been to her bed for two days, instead she'd slept only fitfully on the ever-compliant sofa.

Her friend Vicki, Molly Gardner's mother, the one who was meant to have collected Eysha from school, called round as soon as she saw the police leave. She had taken the whole affair very badly, blaming herself for not getting to the school on time, even though it was crystal clear Eysha had never even got to school. But it did allow her to share Laura's distress, and to keep herself close to the centre of interest.

'Fuckin' cops.'

'Nothing yet then?' asked Vicki, her own face smeared with tears, refreshed the moment she'd set eyes on Laura and they'd fallen on each other's necks.

'Fuckin' cops.'

'What they reckon, then?'

'Seem to think either her dad's got her, or I've hidden her some place to make money from it all.'

'Her dad? You never said did you?'

Laura looked at Vicki as if she was too stupid for words, a look she'd given her a million times in the twenty or more years they'd been friends.

'What d'you think, Vics?'

'No.' Vicki cast her eyes down, her well-practised response to Laura's frequent reproaches.

The pair lit cigarettes, pushing the butt ends of the last couple of dozen round the ash-tray to make room for more, spilling a shower of ash onto the table in the process.

'Where's Molly, then?'

'Left her with Mum.'

'You could've brought her. They talked to her yet?'

'They talked to her, but only for five minutes. She told 'em what she saw, they said thanks, then that was it.'

'If she's run off somewhere, I'll bloody well . . .' The conflict between anger and distress had no outlet other than tears and more came quickly and easily, rolling down her white cheeks.

'She'll come back, Lor, she'll be alright.' Vicki Gardner hugged her friend again, shedding a few more tears of her own in the process.

'Did you speak to Molly, ask her yourself, like we said?'

'She swears she knows nothing, swears she ain't telling lies, swears she saw what she saw. She says she knows it was your Eysha for sure. Right up there at the top of the track.'

'Then where the fuck is she?' Laura shouted, her voice rising with each word as anger and frustration briefly gained the upper hand. 'Why don't they find her? Wasting their bloody time asking stupid questions or standing around, like that knob-head outside.' She directed her fury at the unseen policeman posted by the front door, well aware that with every window in the house wide open, he, and half the village, were certain to hear.

Despite the continuing presence of many uniformed officers, dog handlers, volunteers and a circling helicopter, it had been whispered maliciously that these resources were a direct result of Melanie Staples' body being found rather than the urgent need to find Eysha. The age-old antagonism between Germans, the poor twin with the unfortunate name and Whyncombe St. Giles, home to the wealthy and powerful, was already colouring opinion and debate on both sides of the divide. As usual at such times, fact and reason were among the first casualties. No one wished to be reminded that Lisle House, the grand home of Sir Bernard Stoner, was the last house in Germans on the road to Six Lanes. Neither did anyone recall Peter Staples' humble cottage being the last one on Maiden Lane for anyone taking that route out of Whyncombe St. Giles.

★

'I'm going to Oxford, taking the car.' Acantha Fox-Lomax called through the study door. Her husband rarely drove, and it would have been quite usual for her to have said nothing and simply driven away. But she was fairly sure he would want to use it during the afternoon and it was a lot more fun to see his displeasure than to imagine it after she'd left. As she'd anticipated, he opened the door to argue the point.

'Must you? I may need it later.'

'Yes, Philip, I must. I really must. I have an appointment.'

'An appointment?' He couldn't keep the sneer from this voice or his expression. 'Well, that does sound important.'

'Not to you perhaps, but certainly to me.'

'An appointment you say? Sure you don't mean a visit?'

For a moment the rector's wife was thrown by this, not quite recognising the reference. Then the penny dropped and she allowed herself a little smile. A visit, yes, a visit to a friend in hospital with a broken leg, perhaps. She'd been intending to leave quickly, this encounter was to be no more than a minor amusement, a tweak of the parson's nose as she liked to call it, but now he wanted to play. He so rarely offered her any competition that she sometimes became bored with her own games and the ease with which she scored. Setting herself higher and higher targets gave some satisfaction, but there was nothing quite like having a competitor, even if he was rarely a match for her, as this clumsy taunt confirmed.

'Oh vicar,' she gushed, as if about to throw herself upon him in a fit of passion, 'Have you been playing with a little green-eyed monster in that private room of yours?' Then coyly, licking her lips and in her most suggestive of voices, 'Will you show him to me?'

'Acantha, you are . . .' he struggled for a word he could trust, then found, 'insufferable!' As he spoke, little flecks of saliva leaked from the corner of his mouth, a familiar sign of greater stresses beneath the surface.

'Oh but Philip, that's what you do isn't it, suffer.' It was all too easy for her, and pleased with a small success tried something more ambitious. 'Have you forgotten your commandments, vicar?'

'No, Acantha, I haven't,' he replied with disdain, then unable to stop himself, asked, 'What do you mean?' and immediately regretted it.

'Surely I don't have to spell it out? Perhaps as a penance --'

The arrow was stopped mid-flight by the doorbell, two long insistent rings. The rector's wife chose to bide her time, it might even nag away at him, her undelivered barb. Instead she changed tack. 'Oooh,' she purred, 'sounds like another customer. Sounds like a regular, makes you shiver with anticipation, doesn't it?'

The visitor was indeed a regular customer, it was Michael Radcliffe. Acantha Fox-Lomax offered him the very sweetest of consoling smiles and a touch on the arm by way of sympathy, as

71

she left for her Oxford appointment. Her husband showed him into the drawing room, and opened the French windows ready for the inevitable cigarette smoke. Of the many trials in the rector's life, smoking remained one of the hardest to bear. He had given up the habit with great difficulty many years ago, yet felt unable to demand any of his visitors should abstain or confine their smoking to the garden. Those who sought his spiritual help were frequently distressed, to refuse them the balm of nicotine would only add to their woes. From time to time, particularly if his wife had vexed him more sorely than usual, or if certain members of the congregation called round in trying circumstances, he had been known to succumb to a sudden resurgence of the craving.

Michael Radcliffe was one such member of his flock and the rector's wife had hugely irritated him, although little more than usual. No sooner did he see the silver lighter flip and flame in his visitor's hand than the desire to draw deeply on a cigarette surged through him. For a confusing moment he thought it might be this sin that his wife had alluded to, even though it made no sense. But something in his face had given him away to his visitor.

'Help yourself.'

The rector slid one deftly from the proffered pack but refused the lighter. Instead he rolled the firmness of the little white tube in the tips of his fingers. He might still not smoke it. Not yet.

'Michael, shall we start with a prayer?' Then, since it was more a statement than a question, he bowed his head and began. 'Lord God, may everything we do begin with You and continue under Your guidance with Your help and blessing. Give us strength and wisdom for difficult times, and forgiveness for our failings. Amen.'

'Amen,' Michael Radcliffe echoed dutifully.

'Where to start then, Michael, practical things or perhaps something personal? You know you can speak freely here. If you prefer, we'll step across to the church, we can use the side chapel. We wouldn't be disturbed.'

'About Mary? Talk about Mary?'

'Yes, about Mary, about anything.'

'Yes, Mary,' the new widower replied, but did not expand on the statement, neither did the rector encourage him further. Instead the two men sat in the sticky heat of the rectory drawing room, blue smoke curling up and out into the garden, perspiration seeping beneath jacket and cassock alike. Michael Radcliffe seemed to be studying the carpet, while Philip Fox-Lomax pondered the honeyed oak beams of the ceiling, the unlit cigarette still twizzled in his fingers. Where the thoughts of the two men took them was impossible to tell from their closed faces. They may have considered the centuries of silences or urgent conversations that had filled that room or even the thousand years that priests and followers had attended to matters of the soul in the church beyond the garden wall. They may have reflected on more recent events, those that touched them both in their different ways. They may even have considered events yet to come and the parts they might play in shaping them. Whatever occupied them did so for nearly three cigarettes until at length the rector grew restless and enquired again. 'Mary?'

'They've found the girl you know. I heard they found her.'

'So they say.'

'It'll stir it all up again.'

'Yes, I expect so.'

Silence fell on them once more, broken only by the quickfire click and snap of the silver lighter. The rector asked for a third time, 'About Mary?'

'Dead. You knew? Yes, of course you do.'

'Do you want to make some arrangements? Fix a date and so on?' The rector did not want his visitor drifting off into a reverie again.

'Date?'

'Michael, you will need to make the arrangements for Mary's funeral. I assume there's no reason for delay, no formalities left?'

'No, not as far as I remember.' He paused, pre-occupied by unspoken thoughts. Then, sharing one glimpse of that private world added, 'Funny how people can look so good when they're dead. Ever thought that, Philip?'

The silver lighter flipped and flamed in the rector's hand.

6

'Are they saying things that aren't being broadcast, things they don't want us to know?'

'I don't know, probably.' Diana Samarasinghe was a little irritated by her brother's persistent questions almost as much as his reluctance to answer her own. 'Anyway, what are you talking about, the Duncan girl or your Melanie Staples?'

'About Melanie. And she's not mine.'

'Amma says you were friends, and you went to the police and made a statement about her. I didn't know that before. What did you tell them?'

'You weren't here, you were in Lanka, at opa Wikram's.'

As with most talented and beautiful women, Diana Samarasinghe enjoyed a degree of success in getting her own way with men. So long as she didn't overreach herself, didn't challenge their status or go for the big prizes too quickly, it was amazing how compliant the male sex could be. She'd learnt to smile or gently cajole, to look demure or flash her eyes, all according to the demands of the situation. Fathers may sometimes be persuaded by similar tactics, but, as most talented and beautiful women also know well, their charms usually fail to move their brothers. Brothers drive the hardest bargains, particularly younger brothers with their own talents and attractions and who have spent much of their youthful lives in shadows cast by their sister's glittering achievements.

Despite the habit of seeing a sister for exactly who they are and what they are, sibling love and loyalty can still leave a brother vulnerable to persuasion. The slightest suggestion of unwelcome attention from a would-be suitor, or perhaps a perceived disloyalty from a friend, ideas such as these once planted in a brother's head can sometimes be turned to advantage where flattery or a direct appeal has failed. For Diana Samarasinghe a change of subject always seemed like a good way to try a new tactic.

'Anyway, when are you moving to London, when do you start in your chambers?'

'They aren't my chambers, they aren't anyone's chambers, they're just chambers. I start at the beginning of September.'

'Are you going to let me come and see your flat?'

'Maybe, when it's ready and I'm settled in. If you stop being so annoying.'

'I don't mean to be, but there's so much pressure in the office, cutting back on this, cutting back on that. It looks like they're trying to get rid of someone. Someone said maybe it would be me, people might think I should be contributing more than I do.'

'I thought you were the shining star! I thought you would soon be reading the ten o'clock news to the nation.'

'Oh as a journalist there's no real problem at all, they like most of my pieces but,' and here the subtle sister paused slightly be sure the hook was properly baited, 'you know what it's like.'

'No, what do you mean? Because you're a girl?'

'Maybe a little, but,' again the little hesitation, 'remember we have to be better to be equal.'

Diana repeated the old phrase, the suggestion of prejudice, the unspoken bar to advancement, the secret priorities for redundancy, even though she had never encountered the slightest hint of it in the BBC. From time to time people tentatively asked about discrimination, curious to see through brown eyes for themselves, anxious to demonstrate their own liberal attitudes, but never had her skin worked against her. On the contrary, she'd found it usually worked in her favour where men were concerned, although admittedly less so with women.

'Is that what you find, is that what it's like?'

The indignation in her brother's voice was all Diana needed to hear, in good time he would tell her anything she wished to know about his interviews with the police, statements he might make, snippets he might overhear.

'You'll see soon enough,' she told him in her most worldly and superior way.

He was reminded how he'd felt that subtle shift among those he knew in the village, nothing specific, but he'd sensed a change. A look here, a harsher note there, not from friends, they were none of them friends, but from people he'd grown up amongst, people he'd known for half his life. Was it only this week, only these last few days, or had it been here since he'd come down from Cambridge? Not that he'd really spent that much time in the village, now that he thought about it. He'd been here in his home, but not seen many people. He didn't go to the pub or have friends he went into town with. Even Jack, the one person he might once have called a real friend, the one person he would have spent time with, was away climbing mountains halfway round the world.

For all it was his home, for all he'd grown up in Whyncombe St. Giles, for all he knew faces and names, the warmth of familiarity had leaked away. In its place he'd found a coolness reserved for the outsider, the incomer. He wanted it to be the flood, the distress, the missing girl; he wanted it to be nothing to do with him, nothing to do with unfamiliar names or brown skin; he wanted it to be the weeks and months he wasn't here, the new faces at the school, the families grown and flown.

It was different in Colombo, where the memories were of a different childhood, a different life in a different world. It was a world he'd been plucked from before his tenth birthday, a world whose sights and sounds and smells he'd found unchanged when he'd twice returned to sample them. How much of what he thought he remembered was true memory, how much was adopted from his parents' or his sister's memories, he couldn't tell. He thought he knew the cool perfume drifting through the evening shade of his grandparents' garden; he might recall the dust that coated his grandfather's black Mercedes no matter how often the gardener's boy washed it; he could cringe at the scolding he received for writing his name in that dust. Or it might be that he had heard these things from his parents on those rare occasions they spoke with any fondness or nostalgia for that world.

Like the child of any family, of any creed or caste in any land, he wanted to be able to set sail for a new life in a new world himself, yet always find his home as it was in his childhood. How much easier it was for his grandfather's scented garden or the raucous teeming city of his early years to remain exactly as his false and selective memory described. They were frozen, archived memories, photo-album memories, to be dusted down and opened now and again, then put away for a few more years. Whyncombe St. Giles was still where he called home, along with his sister and his precious Amma, it was his base, his ever-present, reliable foundation. And whatever he might do, wherever he might go, that was how he expected it to remain.

'Thomas,' his mother called from upstairs, 'that police girl is back again.'

From the same vantage point that she and her son had stood in wonder at the deluge two days previously, Upeksha Samarasinghe watched as two figures emerged from a car parked beyond the barrier closing Upper Orchard while urgent repairs were made to a gas main. They could be estate agents she thought, valuing a property, or insurance assessors come to check damage, if it were not for the girl. As the pair ambled along the road towards number eight she recognised the jet black hair and rounded figure. Quite distinctive, even if she was a little too blatant, a fraction too obvious, for a mother's discerning taste. And she had a man with her this time, probably a more senior rank despite the casual air with his jacket slung over his shoulder. She supposed they were still looking for the missing girl, and wondered at their apparent lack of urgency. Then as she watched them turn in to her gate, she wondered what more they might want from her family.

'No, we're here on a quite different matter,' Lavi Pitesteanu explained. 'An older enquiry, something I'm sure you'll remember. You've probably heard something about it already.'

The chief inspector had elected to watch and listen, as was his preference. He'd told his constable what line to take, not that there was any great science or subtlety to it. He hoped to learn something about how she handled herself too, see what advantage she might gain from having previously interviewed the man. He'd detected a fleeting shift of expression, a hint of a smile, when he'd said who they'd visit next, and he was curious to see the reason for that.

Diana Samarasinghe was also watching and listening, but trying very hard to become invisible lest she should be asked to leave the room, although she couldn't imagine why she should be. She could have put her mind at rest on the matter if she'd understood the policeman's intentions more fully. He wanted to interview the whole family, understand their attitude to Melanie Staples' disappearance and now to her discovery. The file about the Samarasinghes was thicker and more interesting than might have been expected, not least because it contained a couple of notes from two senior officers not otherwise connected to the case. That Miss Samarasinghe should turn out to be singularly attractive was simply an added bonus. If she had tried to leave the room the detective would have found a way to prevent it.

To complete the circle of watchers and listeners Upeksha Samarasinghe took up her customary place in her customary seat.

77

Despite being the smallest person in the room she contrived to dominate the group. The respect and love of her children was far deeper than any of the trivial differences they had with her. They might tease her about her habits, complain of her old-fashioned attitudes, they might even bend the truth from time to time if it might spare her some anxiety about them, but she remained the pivotal centre of their lives. This respect was apparent to the visitors and combined with her diminutive stature gave added weight to her every gesture and expression. Lavi Pitesteanu had spoken to Thomas, but it was his mother who replied.

'You're here about Melanie Staples, then. So it's true what they say then, you've found her at last.'

'Yes, it seems so.'

'What do you think we can add after all these years?'

'We don't know, Mrs Samarasinghe, we don't know if you can add anything. But you might. That's what we've come to talk about.' The constable was conscious of how often her own name was mangled by English tongues and had practised the Sri Lankan name several times in preparation for this encounter, rolling the unfamiliar syllables silently across her tongue. She had managed it perfectly, without the slightest hesitation. It was a small detail, but one noted by all present.

She turned to Thomas, only to catch him looking intently at her, his joyous smile implying a compliment yet somehow inappropriate to the seriousness of the occasion. Caught between returning the smile and her duties she struggled for a moment to compose herself.

'Do you remember the day, remember anything about it?'

'The truth is I'm not sure. But I imagine you still have all the statements, all the details and notes that from the time.'

'Oh, yes we have all those, in fact we have your statement right here,' she withdrew a buff folder from the briefcase at her side, 'but it is the statement of an eleven-year old boy, and as I'm sure you know, probably not your own words, and signed by your mother. Can you tell us what you do remember?'

'What I remember is mixed with things that have been said, things people have suggested, like pictures in a book I don't know if they are real memories or adopted ones. I would not make a good witness.'

'It's not a witness we need right now,' Donald Smallborne cut in, 'nor even a new statement, just your own words on what you think you remember.'

'Very well.'

Diana Samarasinghe could scarcely contain herself at the prospect of this retelling, of being let in to the very heart of the story. Had her brother not already closed his eyes and sunk back into his chair he might have caught a trace of this eagerness in her face.

'It was the last day of school, we came out early, there was a fuss about it being the last day ever at the school for our class and because it was the end of term, there were more parents than usual in the playground. There were even visitors' cars parked in the playground, there was no special area fenced off like there is now. Outside there were cars parked all the way along the road. It was warm, not like it is now, and cloudy. We were supposed to have a picnic tea in the evening but it had been raining and someone said it was cancelled.'

As he paused to consider the detail it seemed for a moment that the spell he'd cast on the little group might be broken, but they sat rapt and motionless waiting for him to continue.

'I don't know who said that, or whether it was cancelled, or whether I heard that afterwards. Melanie and I went down the path by the school, down into the combe, they'd not long planted the new trees and made the pond, it was all different to how it is now. We used to cut down that way to get home sometimes. When we were down there it started raining very hard, and we sheltered under the trees, just about where the bird hide is now. It just kept raining and raining. The pond filled up and then it all started flooding. I climbed up in a tree for a bit, Melanie was alright, she had her boots and raincoat, but I didn't and was getting soaked. I wanted to go home but she said she'd lost her key and couldn't get in her house, so I said she could come home with me, but she didn't want to. We arranged to meet later, up the track on Whyn Hill.'

As he told his story, the first telling in all the years since he'd sat with his mother in the police station, the smile had gone from his face and much of the life along with it. Once again he seemed to be privately weighing some detail in the sequence of events but when he spoke again it was to reveal a different kind of memory.

'We used to like going up there.'

Donald Smallborne cast a wary glance towards his constable, lest she should again be tempted to some indiscreet intervention, but she remained silent.

'I went home after an hour or so, the rain eased a little and I ran all the way up the hill, all the way home. I was completely soaked through.' At this the slightest twitch of his mouth suggested another stray recollection, 'Amma was not pleased with me,' across the room his mother nodded a small agreement, 'but later she let me out again. I went back down into the combe but it was too muddy to walk through, so I came back up and then round by the road to the track and up the hill. I went up to the fence and waited there, but she never came. Then I went back down. I saw her father on the track, he asked me if I'd seen her. Then I came home again.'

Of those listening to this commentary one was pleased and three were, in varying degrees, disappointed. Upeksha Samarasinghe was proud of her son's memory and the succinct manner in which he had recounted exactly the events of the day as she knew them to be. Thomas felt the warmth of her pride when he opened his eyes to see how his feat of memory had been received. His sister was hugely disappointed with the tale, having expected a great deal more from her brother than she could have found for herself from any contemporary account of Melanie's disappearance. She wondered what Thomas could have edited out, perhaps unconsciously, perhaps not. She knew almost nothing of the girl's disappearance, but she did know her brother.

Constable Pitesteanu had hoped he would shed more light on those distant events than he had, and would've liked him to have talked for a little longer since to her ear his voice had a certain melody. Her senior officer would also have liked a greater insight, he'd hoped to get much closer to the events of the day by hearing directly from a key witness. But although he'd heard nothing new of the girl's disappearance, he had learnt one thing - Thomas Samarasinghe had a remarkable memory, if not for the actual events then at least for the contents of the statement in the buff folder, since apart from a couple of personal asides, he had just managed to repeat them almost word for word.

He wondered if the clever, articulate, personable young man had perhaps recently re-read that statement, a copy of which would certainly have been given to his mother. He wondered also if the account had been entirely concocted by Mrs Samarasinghe, a bland

and innocent version of another, more incriminating sequence of events. And if not the mother, perhaps the classified father, beyond reproach according to the little note in the file and, for the present at least, beyond his reach. Had Melanie returned with Thomas to the Samarasinghe house after all? No one had ever been found who saw the boy run home with or without Melanie Staples and apart from Thomas' story the last sighting of the girl by a reliable adult was by Mary Radcliffe near the school playground. Had some awful accident occurred, some childish game that went terribly wrong? Had they covered it up in the panic of the moment and now repeated the lie years later. He was not the first to harbour such suspicions, even though the basis for doubt was flimsy in the extreme. It was possible that the girl's bones might yet provide something more than her identity, but he was not optimistic.

'When you were hiding under the trees – '

'We weren't hiding, we were sheltering from the rain,' Thomas corrected him.

'All right, when you were sheltering, when you used to go up Whyn Hill into the woods, what did you and Melanie Staples do? What did you talk about?'

No one had ever asked Thomas this before, and while it was true he had omitted some small, and to his mind irrelevant, details from the account he had consistently given, he wasn't at all sure that he wanted to reveal any of those childish things he and Melanie used to do and dream about. And besides, she was his friend and he still felt the bonds of that friendship and the loyalties that went with them.

'On that day?'

'On that day, on any day.'

'I told her about school in Colombo, about living in a city so different from this village, about my grandparents' house.'

'And Melanie, what did she talk about?'

This was more dangerous ground, this might touch upon those intimacies he still kept to himself. But there was plenty of scope to still speak the truth.

'Well, you may not believe this, but sometimes we talked about maths,' he said self-consciously. The admission genuinely discomforted him, he'd seen easily how it might not have been believed by an adult when he was a boy and how years later it might not be believed by a policeman. As if to endorse such a far-fetched claim he added rather weakly, 'Melanie was good at maths.'

Donald Smallborne looked slightly sceptical, but simply nodded, it could be true and it hardly mattered. Upeksha Samarasinghe nodded too, but could not resist adding her own observation, 'So were you, Thomas,' which briefly brought the smile back to her son's face.

'What else? What did you do, what else occupied you?' The detective was not to be deflected by a mother's pride.

'We played games, we told stories,' and sensing that the policeman needed something more concrete to be satisfied, 'Sometimes we watched what was going on. It was different then, there was a spot up on the hill where you could see right across Germans up to St. Giles and nearly round to the quarry.'

'And when you watched what was going on, did you see anything interesting?'

'We used to make up stories about what we saw, we'd pretend the postman was a spy, things like that.' The truth of the revelation, innocent as it was, caught him unawares as he remembered too the times he and Melanie had shared rolling on the ground in hysterics at their own nonsense. He grimaced as if in pain as the vivid flash of memory caught him by surprise.

'Something else?'

'No,' he said softly, his eyes cast down, 'just that we used to laugh a lot. We were just children laughing.'

'Was it just you two, laughing and talking about maths and watching from the hill? Or was there anyone else who went with you?'

'No, not up on the hill, that was just Melanie and me.'

'Was it a special spot, just one place you'd go?'

'Usually.'

'Could you take us there now? Would you still know it?'

'It's gone.'

'Was it marked in any way, you liked maths you say, did you mark a tree with a number, say?'

Thomas smiled a crooked smile. 'A number? What number?'

'Eight.'

The realisation that the policeman knew their place, had seen their sign, took the smile from his face. 'You've found our tree,' he said dully. 'It was not eight. Much more than that. It was infinity. We marked our place with infinity. It was our sign.'

'Ah,' said the policeman and paused a moment to let the significance sink in. He was certainly not about to divulge the intimate connection between the sycamore and Melanie's sad remains.

'Did anyone ever see you up there? Or anywhere else?' he continued.

'Now and again we'd see people walking.'

'And did they see you?'

Thomas had to think a little before answering. 'I suppose so, I don't remember anyone in particular, but yes, people must have seen us sometimes. We weren't hiding.' He could have added 'all the time' but didn't, it would only complicate things, the policeman would want to know what or who they were hiding from, what they were doing while they were hiding.

But the policeman had already noticed this second denial and the idea of the two children spying on the good folk of the twin villages had formed in his mind. Who could guess what they might have seen, what secrets they'd witnessed?

★

In the Duncan household things moved from bad to worse. Laura's mother, Kathy, had taken to her bed, overcome by tears, anxiety and a recurrence of her chronic sciatica. Laura had succumbed to fatigue and was sprawled senseless on the sofa while her brothers continued to make noise and nuisance of themselves. Colin Deeley had called partly to catch up with who'd been flooded out and who hadn't, and partly to see what new mischief the Duncans had been up to that would warrant so much attention from the local constabulary. After Laura's brother Aaron had given him a garbled account of Eysha going missing, heavily interspersed with cursing the police, the school and a few other blameless parties, Colin found Eysha's grandfather, Alex, in the back kitchen, wreathed in smoke with a bottle of Teachers and a packet of king-size. For a few minutes he gave him the sympathy and support that could only come from a friend and fellow grandfather who had, uniquely, suffered similar agonies.

Alex Duncan was never a man to say much and for the most part he simply stared into the bottom of his glass, grunting the occasional 'aye' or shaking his head as appropriate to what was being said. Then it dawned on him that his friend knew nothing of the discovery of what everyone believed were his own granddaughter Melanie's remains.

'Colin, wait a minute,' he stopped his friend in mid flow, 'You'll not have heard, right?'

'Heard what?'

'Oh God man! Its worse than you think! You're saying about your Melanie, but has no one told you? It seems they've found her. Well, you know, not official, it's just what they're saying.'

For a split second Colin Deeley thought his granddaughter had been found alive, wandering lost and unaware of who she was. The question of how his friend Alex would have known such a thing was starting to form itself when the other meaning, the dead Melanie, the found-her-body meaning, hit him like a brick. It was the truth he'd always known, and now they'd found her. He thought next of his own dear daughter Susie, Melanie's mother, and how someone would need to tell her and how he didn't even know where she was except she was on holiday in Cuba and not back for another week at least.

'Oh my God, Colin, I'm so sorry. I knew, I just knew nobody had said.' The host poured a little whiskey, previously refused, into a glass for his visitor.

'No, nobody said. They're not sure you say, not official yet?' Colin said, looking up pleadingly, clutching for the slenderest of straws. 'What about her father, what about Peter, someone been there?'

'Police there yesterday and today. There's one on the door, same as us.'

Colin Deeley considered the amber liquid in his glass and swirled it slowly round before taking a mouthful. The subtle blend which he might usually relish tasted like bleach.

'Was it where them other girls was found, up north near Preston was it? Somewhere like that?'

Alex Duncan felt the weight of knowledge heavier than ever and sighed a deep and heartfelt sigh. 'No old friend, not up north, closer to home than that. Not fifty yards away right by the school. You'll have . . .' he was going to add that his friend would have passed the spot that morning but left the words unsaid.

The heat in the cramped little room, combined with the deeply ingrained smell of chip fat and nicotine only added to the nightmare. Trickles of sweat ran down the faces of the two men as they looked at each other, almost as strangers might see for the first time the lines in their faces, the sunken eyes and grey stubble of a few days' growth.

'By the school,' he whispered to himself, and then again a little louder, 'By the school. All that time they were looking in the wrong place,' Colin Deeley's voice rose as his grief and anger found a target. 'So bloody convinced they were, so sure she was the third of them girls that got taken, that was all they went on about. What vans there were in the village, what deliveries there were, vans with dogs, men with dogs, and they never thought to look right under their bleedin' noses. Not even when they found those other poor mites and our Melanie wasn't with 'em. Bloody shameful.'

'Aye,' Alex Duncan resumed the monosyllabic responses and turned his attention back to the contents of his glass.

Colin Deeley's pent up grief, the gnawing, relentless absence of the last eleven years found form in a seething anger, fuelled by the whiskey and a minute later by a second glass. He pulled another cigarette from his pack, lit it, drew deeply and cursed Chris Rogers for not having his usual max-strength variety.

'Here.' Alex Duncan slid his own pack across the table.

'It's a shock to know, after all this time, you know what I mean?'

'Aye, I see it would be.'

'Bad times, Alex, bad times,' and then with a more perceptive insight he added, 'Maybe it'll serve your Eysha better, maybe they won't be making the same mistake again, maybe they'll find her soon enough.' The thought was genuine although his voice carried little conviction.

'Maybe.'

'I saw the helicopter, the dogs and all the uniforms. Doing a proper search this time are they?'

Alex Duncan gave a derisory snort.

'What's that?'

'Try this one then. Seem to think her father's got her and we're all in it to make money.'

★

Most of the population of the twin villages who were not pre-occupied with the cleaning and repair of their homes tuned in to the early evening news to catch the latest on the search for Eysha and the official word on Melanie's remains. The search still featured, but had slipped to third place behind the deaths of two elderly motorists overcome by heat in a traffic jam and the violent eviction of a group of travellers from an unauthorised site. Even then Eysha's story was tagged onto a congratulatory report on the emergency services' clean-up operation after the deluge and closed with a strong suggestion that the missing girl was more likely to be a victim of the flood than of foul play. There was no mention at all of Melanie Staples.

As Eysha's story slipped down the list, so did the number of sightings. She was already old news and it would take something dramatic or salacious to promote her story, or perhaps one of those infamous public appeals where the audience rates the likelihood of the distraught father being the culprit. Except of course, for Eysha there was no father to make such an appeal. Neither was there the more common 'mother's partner', so often the perfect fit for the role of child-abusing adult.

'You'd have thought there'd have been something more on the local news,' Margaret Westerleigh said.

'There's plenty going on down the hill.'

Her husband was not usually in the house at such an early hour, but he'd dithered over which of his many tasks he would start after a day of paperwork and phone calls. A huge lethargy had overtaken him, his energy drained by a lack of sleep and the endless fall of the bloated ewe. And all the while the sliding, flopping, saturated fleece was only a substitute for worse. In the end he'd done nothing but a quick round of the water troughs on the quad bike. Yesterday's pools of water had baked to a thick smooth crust, already cracking. The dark scar that ran from behind the barns down through the wood to The Chequers and the school grew lighter as the sun sucked the moisture from the earth, bleaching the soil and the fresh turned stones.

He'd stopped by the smashed fence above the wood to look out across the villages and the activity within that familiar Cotswold fold. In every road and lane there was some action or movement of people or vehicles, many with blue or orange flashing lights. Where the lights were not visible, the circling reflections of their beams twinkled from windows and cars as if there were a summer fair under way instead of the aftermath of appalling events, both natural and unnatural.

The gash in the wood allowed more of the scene to be taken in, from the back of The Chequers, past the school and right down to the combe where a spectral mist persisted, lingering in the trees and obscuring the detail like a soft-focus lens. On the far side of that pleasant dell were the cottages on the road out to the quarry and above them, up on the gentle slope of the hill, the new houses, built when he was a teenager. They'd ripped out the trees just as they'd come into blossom - those old orchards would never again provide fruit for the Lisle Estate or the villages. Neither would they provide a soft and gentle courting ground for young couples in search of privacy for their lovemaking. It wouldn't have been the first village girl who'd fallen pregnant after a summer evening spent in the long grass under those sweet branches. Those old orchards had provided many a euphemism to enrich the local language, 'blossoming', 'fruiting', 'scrumping' and the like being used according to the season and accompanied by a wink and a nudge. His had been just about the last generation to enjoy the varied bounties of those fruit trees.

Margaret was occupied with her own concerns. She didn't want to add to the catalogue of woes, but she needed to find a way to tell him about Mary Radcliffe. She'd hoped he might have heard from another source, but he hadn't left the farm all day. In normal times someone from the village would've been sure to call and tell them such a thing, but most people were pre-occupied with their own dramas. If she hadn't stopped at the rectory to check the rota for church flowers she might not have known herself.

'John,' she said after letting him sit for a little longer staring into space. 'John, there's no end to the bad news, not yet anyway.'

He stirred from his reverie enough to twist round in his chair and look at her.

'John, it's Mary, Mary Radcliffe, she died in the flood.'

In the instant before memory came, he imagined Mary Radcliffe caught in the tidal wave that flowed down the hillside from High Whyn and saw her sliding backwards down the side of the big bucket, her dress stuck to her swollen fleecy body. Then a vision of the blue car nose down in the brown sea, the recollection of Michael Radcliffe misplacing his Rover and his own reluctance to become involved in someone else's crisis all came rushing back to him in quick succession. And since then, to his shame, he had not given the Radcliffes another thought.

'Oh,' he said, more as a drawn out groan than as a meaningful word. 'It was her then, it was Michael's car.' His voice was flat, lifeless.

'You saw her? You saw her in the car?' Margaret was astonished, indignant. So carefully she'd prepared herself to tell him and here he was saying he knew already. 'Why didn't you tell me?'

'No, I didn't know, I saw the car, thought no more of it, then Michael's car was missing, and then what with everything else, I just forgot about it.' When he said it like this it seemed so lame, so pathetic to have forgotten that someone they both knew well, had known for years, might have been drowned not a mile from where they sat.

Despite her sympathy, her capacity for care and understanding, to forget such a thing seemed unbelievable to his wife. She'd made every allowance for all he'd suffered in the last days and much more before that, yet to have not mentioned anything about her friend Mary Radcliffe was unforgivable, at least for the time being.

★

Publicly, the search for Eysha Duncan continued with as much endeavour as ever. There were still conspicuously large numbers of officers in and around Germans and Whyncombe St. Giles, together with a few volunteers who'd spent the day walking the heath and the hedgerows. The dog handlers and underwater team had their vehicles parked in places certain to be noticed by the local inhabitants, a small advertisement of the unstinting effort. Officers had been told that they were not to stand in the streets talking together and if they were taking a break they must hide themselves away in the village hall or the back of a van, regardless of the heat and discomfort. Dogs and their handlers were exempted from this instruction.

Privately, and in no way that might later attract criticism, some expensive resources were quietly stood down. The police helicopter, so apparent since yesterday, no longer fluttered endlessly to and fro across the landscape, and the little pocket of airspace that had been closed to all other aircraft was quietly re-opened. This allowed the news helicopters to fly in and offer some continuity of background noise and activity that might mask the police withdrawal. The dog team had been reduced to two and a solitary diver remained working near the study centre.

Twenty-four hours of intensive searching had revealed not a single trace of the girl, neither had the widespread enquiries produced a worthwhile line of investigation. All of which led to a growing belief amongst the investigators that the child had been the victim of the deluge and had been swept away, to be found perhaps miles away in the days or weeks to come. Some thought otherwise, some thought there was a conspiracy amongst the Duncans, others that the discovery of Melanie Staples should be a warning to them all and that such a coincidence of events was an omen. In one respect the various strands were united: none thought Eysha Duncan was still alive.

Among those still going about their business as if there was a purpose to it were the solitary diver and his two supporters from the underwater unit. In the Centenary Wood where their work had been concentrated, the water level was slowly dropping, but it remained chest-high in places and as brown and polluted as ever, offering no possibility of anything but a fingertip search. It had been said that since the water was draining away and would probably be gone in a few days the searchers might as well wait until then to discover anything there was to be discovered.

The unit also had an inflatable which they'd paddled backwards and forwards through the trees as far as the shallow lake covering the farmland beyond. They'd looked around the bird hide, which was little more than a large wooden hut on a raised platform, and peered into the dim interior. Instead of windows it had viewing slits which opened and closed by shutters. Inside a bench ran along the wall by the slits so that a bird watcher could sit and rest their elbows on a wooden shelf, all the better to steady their cameras and binoculars. Between there and the neglected noticeboard on the back wall was a rough table and two more benches. It had once been better kept but was now more often used as a drinking and smoking club by the disaffected youth of Germans than by birdwatchers.

Within the building a collection of litter bobbed on the surface as a warning of heavier items lying unseen on the floor a foot or so beneath. Cigarette butts lapped together with chocolate wrappers, the odd beer can and a solitary condom. As a final act of a long and unrewarding day the frogman suggested he do a more thorough search than could be done from the dinghy. He needed no extra equipment for the task, but once inside he would have welcomed a mask, such was the stench. Even with a couple of the viewing slits left open the building had gently simmered its contents in the stinking heat. To judge by the smell the hut had also been used as a toilet. When mixed with the rubbish and rotting scraps of food the result was an impossibly foul atmosphere.

The policeman gagged as he opened the door and caught the first taste of the stink within. Cautiously he moved across to the closed slits and forced the swollen shutters outwards to give a little more light and air. Then with a powerful lamp set on the table he surveyed the scene. He was surprised to see an open pack of crisps, its contents spilled out and stuck like scabs to the table top alongside an almost untouched pack of king-size. Both items forgotten in haste perhaps as the waters rose, or deposited there by a receding tide - the high water mark looked as if it was about the same level. Either way, they were of little use to anyone now, saturated in their disintegrating packaging, but they did serve to remind him it was more than an hour since he'd had a snack or a smoke. Next he carefully inspected the surface of the water to see if anything of conceivable interest might be floating there. In the furthest corner a half-submerged shape or a texture, he was not sure which, caught his attention. Wary of his footing he made his way round the table to what looked like a bundle of rags and newspaper suspended just below the surface. Stooping down he reached out a hand to inspect it more closely, only to cry out in horror as the body rolled over to reveal the open jaws of a drowned badger.

'Alright in there, George?' called a voice from outside.

'Just slipped on something, nothing to get excited about,' he lied. He'd seen far worse in his time with the force, and his colleagues would have a good laugh at his expense if they ever found out, but all day he'd been half expecting to haul the dead weight of a drowned child from the water. The last thing he expected were bared fangs behind the black lips of a badger. 'I'll be done in a few minutes, I'll have a trawl, pass me up that net.'

The trawl produced a few bottles, paper fragments, a sock and a woollen glove both of which he put in a bag, more for completeness sake than in expectation they would be relevant. Finally, from behind the door, almost overlooked in his desire to breathe fresh air again, a more curious item found its way into the net. It was a clear plastic tub, in itself unremarkable and common enough, but this little tub was still sealed and when George carefully inspected it under the lamp it appeared to contain a decomposing picnic of cheese and tomato sandwiches and a chocolate bar.

7

At The Glebe House, Michael Radcliffe was composing himself in readiness to receive another visit from the police who'd requested an interview 'at his earliest convenience.' The phrase stuck in his mind as being old-fashioned and he wondered absent-mindedly if they reserved such ways of speaking for those of pensionable age. The girl on the phone had started by asking for Mary, which had unnerved him, and he'd stumbled over an answer. Extraordinary that the police would not know she was dead, they'd been the ones to tell him. Then the girl had been so apologetic, so polite yet so insistent he'd agreed on nine o'clock in the morning. He was still dazed from the loss of his wife and his car, still confused over whether he'd done all he needed to do regarding the flooded cellar and the funeral arrangements. He would have to think about the insurances for all three, but that required a level of concentration quite beyond him for the moment. And besides, in recent years Mary had looked after all those affairs.

In common with many who've suffered loss or trauma he felt a complete detachment from reality. In a strangely dislocated way he felt sure there was something else missing, something other than Mary or the car, something he'd forgotten to do, or something he'd simply forgotten, which when finally recalled would relieve him of a gnawing anxiety. There'd been times like this before, when he seemed to be watching himself going through the motions of life without having a solid grasp of events. At such times his wife had come into her element, taking charge of everything that needed to be taken charge of, slotting it all in seamlessly alongside her charities and church duties, her village hall responsibilities, the parish council, editing the little news sheet, and lately providing regular updates for the village website.

The girl on the phone hadn't been specific about the purpose of her visit, and when he'd asked what it was about, she'd been vague. It would most likely be about the car, and if not the car then about the girl, the one they'd found after all these years. Not that he'd have anything to tell them about her, not after all this time, but they'd be asking all the old questions again. Briefly, he tried to

91

remember her but couldn't place her at all. But thinking of her reminded him of the school and for a moment he wondered dimly if there was some problem at the school, a break-in perhaps, something out of order that they needed a key-holder to go there. As deputy chair of the governors he held a key and a certain responsibility, although usually only when instructed by the rector.

A car swished on the gravel drive. He pulled on his jacket and glanced at the kitchen clock – nine precisely. The heat of the day was already uncomfortable, the house airless and stale, an all pervading smell of damp wafting up from the cellar. In the kitchen sink a few days worth of dishes sat unwashed, the congealed scrapings of food already sprouting a furry coat. He opened the kitchen door to the garden to let out some of the used smoke and smells of fried breakfast. Then he felt for his cigarettes and lighter, reassured by their presence in his jacket pocket. As the doorbell sounded he stubbed out a cigarette and switched on the kettle ready for coffee. They would sit in the garden and have coffee and talk of whatever it was they were calling about.

'Mr Radcliffe, let me say how sorry we are about asking for your wife,' said Donald Smallborne the moment he'd introduced himself, 'the constable here had not been properly informed, it was not entirely her fault. On behalf of the force I hope you'll accept our apologies.'

Constable Pitesteanu sat beside her chief inspector trying to appear contrite and apologetic, not quite sure how it was that she was even partly to blame for the error.

'Yes, yes, well, these things happen,' Michael Radcliffe blustered. He wanted to know what they had come about, not hear more apologies over a trivial mistake.

'No, but they shouldn't happen Mr Radcliffe, we should be more on the ball than that. I can only apologise, I'm not sure what more I can do.'

'Well, thank you, now . . .'

'And the constable is very sorry too. Aren't you constable? I don't think she'll make the same mistake again, eh constable?'

'Yes, Mr Radcliffe, I'm very sorry.'

Like the interviews with Thomas Samarasinghe and Peter Staples and the stroll along the track with John Westerleigh, the detective liked to prepare a few words or comments which might unsettle the person concerned, might put them off guard just a little. It was Donald Smallborne's only attempt at subtlety and even then it was hardly an original ploy, yet in each instance he had discovered some snippet he might not otherwise have known. It appeared to be working again in the garden of The Glebe House: Michael Radcliffe was agitated. His statement from the original inquiry had been extremely brief, much the same as all the other governors had given about being at the school for the end of term meeting, then dispersing to their various homes. None admitted to having seen Melanie Staples at all, even though most had arrived before the children left. Now the detective sat silent, apparently in rapt appreciation of the pleasant aspect presented by the garden.

Michael Radcliffe could wait no longer. 'Inspector, you had something on your mind?'

'Hmm? Oh, I was just wondering if you were the gardener or Mrs Radcliffe. It's a lot of garden, and it doesn't look this good without a lot of hard work. I'm glad I don't have to dig all these beds over.'

'No, I don't, my wife does all the gardening.'

'It was really your wife we had been keen to talk to, a tragedy she can't help us now. But maybe you can tell us about it anyway.'

'About the car, the accident?'

'Oh no, didn't the constable mention it?' He shot Lavi Pitesteanu an exaggerated look of disapproval, 'It's about Melanie Staples.'

'Melanie Staples?' He knew he should know the name, did know the name, yet in the instant he was asked, he didn't recognise it.

'Yes.'

'Oh.'

'You remember the girl then, Mr Radcliffe?'

'No, not really, it's been a good few years.'

'And what about the day, do you remember anything about the day?'

'No, nothing at all.'

'Not the meeting at the school, the rain maybe, or the search for the girl?'

'The rain, yes it rained the whole afternoon, it rained a lot. We were inside, as far as I recall it was the usual end of term meeting. Apart from that there was nothing.'

'According to her statement your wife was the last known person to have seen the girl. Do you remember that?'

'Yes, she told me that.'

'Why was she at the school, was she a governor too?'

'No, but she was the secretary, she took the minutes, she was the clerk, if you like.'

'The minutes, would they still be available, those minutes she took?'

'I've no idea, but I suppose so.'

'So she saw the girl after this meeting you were all at. As she was leaving?'

'I suppose so.'

'But you didn't see her. Why was that?'

'We must have left at different times. I really don't remember.'

'Who left first, you or Mrs Radcliffe?'

The pace of the questions had increased along with Michael Radcliffe's discomfort. Neither were they all the old questions he'd half expected to hear again. He couldn't remember the detail he was being asked for yet it seemed he was expected to have answers. He reached into his pocket for the silver lighter and let his fingers run over its smooth round edges before taking it out along with his cigarettes. As he carefully selected one and took time to light it, only the flame betrayed the hint of unsteadiness in his hand. He inhaled deeply, drawing down that most satisfying first lungful of smoke. He took another moment to wipe the beads of sweat from his brow and upper lip. Having recovered his composure, he returned to the conversation, 'Sorry, what were you saying?'

The detective had again switched his attention to the garden, nodding almost imperceptibly as if in approval of the blousy lushness confined within neat borders and carefully trimmed paths.

'A very fine garden, Mr Radcliffe, it'll take some attention to keep it looking this good. And a lot of water, I expect.'

'Er, yes, my wife . . . ' he trailed off into silence, unsure of what he was meant to be talking about or why.

★

Four o'clock on a Saturday afternoon was the appointed time at which Dr B W C Samarasinghe made himself available for calls from his wife and, occasionally, his children. On only two Saturdays since he'd been in California had he been the one to make the call. Sometimes the calls were extremely short, especially if he had an excursion planned or intended to spend the day in his office. He usually said very little which partly accounted for the brevity, but increasingly his wife found less and less to say to him. He was completely disinterested in the daily happenings in Oxfordshire and only marginally less so with any opinion she had of wider events.

So when she sat at her computer to call him that Saturday afternoon, she was not expecting a lengthy conversation, neither was she expecting the little ding-ding announcing an incoming call from him. His round, bespectacled face flicked in the video box and she could see that he was not happy.

'Did you speak to the police?' he said without any greeting.

'Good morning Clarence,' his wife answered deliberately by way of rebuke. 'Yes, we all did. Why do you ask?'

'Because I am told that they made enquiries about me in connection with that girl, Thomas' friend who disappeared.'

'She has re-appeared, Clarence. They came here and asked questions again. And not just about the first girl but also about the second girl.'

'What second girl? Why didn't you tell me?'

'You are never interested in these things, you were displeased when I called in the week if you remember.'

'I do not like being disturbed without good cause. This missing girl is a different matter.'

'It is difficult for us to tell what is important and what is not important, so now we do not call for anything. That way we are more often right than wrong.'

Behind their mother, and carefully positioned out of view of the webcam, the sniping parents' children were stifling their laughter as they listened to this unhappy exchange.

'Is Thomas there now? If so then let me speak with him.'

Thomas slipped in beside his mother and contrived a slightly more serious expression.

'Hello Tatta, how are you?'

'Hello Thomas, I'm very well, thank you. What is happening about this girl? Are they bothering you?'

'No, not at all. They are just asking about all the old things.'

'Well, don't let them bother you. It was all a long time ago, she was clever enough I'm sure but she would've led you into trouble. Is her father still living down in those cottages?'

'Yes, Tatta, he's still there,' the smile had slipped from Thomas' face as he listened to his father speaking of Melanie and her family in his most dismissive of ways.

'He was a good man but his wife was less so I think,' continued the pronouncement from California.

'Tatta, what did you mean about leading me into trouble?'

'Do you want me to spell it out, Thomas? The little problem with the chocolate bars? Perhaps you have forgotten and probably just as well if you have. Her father came to me about it after she told him. He and I went together to the shopkeeper and it was all sorted out.'

Thomas' cheeks burned as he listened in horror to this revelation from the past come back to haunt him, now of all times. 'Oh, yes thank you Tatta, I didn't realise what you meant.' Then by way of distracting attention from further details of this childish misdemeanour he added, 'What are you doing today, will it be work or a visit to friends? And before you go I must ask you something about the lease on the new flat.'

'Yes, of course.' B W C Samarasinghe was no different to any other father when it came to being asked for advice - it was always a little flattering and the older the child who asked, the more flattering it was. 'What was it about the lease?'

'I'll get the papers, talk to Diana, she's here and wants to talk to you too,' he said to cement the change of topic, and also to irritate his sister.

Until that moment when his father spoke of the chocolate bars Thomas had thought it was his secret and his alone with Melanie gone. It had been one of their secrets and he could never have imagined that she would tell anyone else. But she'd told her father and he'd told Thomas' father and then the shopkeeper too. Even thinking about it now made him cringe, and that his father had known about it all these years and never said anything to him, probably his mother too. It was all too awful. Then a worse horror came to his mind. The shopkeeper might have told anybody or everybody: he might never be able to show his face around the villages again.

It was part of the excitement of being with Melanie, she dreamed dreams and said things that were fantastic and impossible for a young boy wide-eyed from his privileged life in Colombo. It was wrong to steal chocolate bars from the village stores, he knew that and so did Melanie. But it was also thrilling and daring and the chocolate tasted all the sweeter for being illicit chocolate, stolen chocolate. They'd worked out a simple method to take a bar without being seen and they'd never been caught. They'd even been careful enough to make their raids on different days when different people were in and out of the shop and they never took the same brand twice in a row. It was a great game, no more of a crime than taking cherries from the garden of The Glebe House where the branches hung close to the wall and they could reach handfuls from sitting astride it, each helping the other up. And when there were people in the garden they had to be like mice and sit concealed in the leaves and let the stones slip from their lips instead of spitting them out to see whose could go furthest.

And then suddenly he understood why she'd said they couldn't take chocolate any more. In case they were caught she'd said, but it wasn't that, it was because her father knew, his father knew and the shopkeeper knew.

There'd been other secrets too, Melanie's secrets that she shared with Thomas and he'd felt lucky to be allowed to know them. Secrets like stealing cigarettes from her mother and sometimes from one of the teachers in school and smoking them up on the hill or way down in the combe, out of sight of prying eyes. He hadn't much liked the smoking, but he liked the excitement, he liked the adventure and discovery of the world she showed him. Secrets like knowing exactly the right place to sit in the old yew tree by the church and hear what was said as people came and went. Secrets like where to sit like statues behind the curtain by the organ and hear the things that grown-ups spoke about when they thought no-one was listening and how they swore and used all the bad words they told children never to use. Secrets like how to stuff your mouth with a handkerchief to stop yourself from laughing when some of those same people came to school to tell them to be good.

All these years his father had known about the thieving, so what else might he know about, what else had he learned from Peter Staples, what else had Melanie told her father? He could hardly ask either of them now, he would be too ashamed to speak about it to his own father and could never look Melanie's in the eye again. He shuddered to think how many times he'd seen Peter Staples in all these years, smiled at him, talked with him, or simply waved in passing and all along he'd known about the chocolate bars, known how they'd worked together as a team to steal them and enjoy them. What must he have thought? Who else would he have told? In his torment a glimmer of light – soon he would be gone from here, gone to a new life in London and with poor Melanie finally found the whole chapter would be closed for ever.

★

'It would be better if you were here, that's all, Acantha.'

'Better? How better? It's not me they want to come and talk to, it's the vicar they want to see.'

'Well, if you want to be precise, it's the chair of school governors they're after.'

'Oh no, and there's you with your best black dress on too. Even less reason for me to spoil my evening with my friends. And just to play wifey so that you look something closer to normal than you are. Give me one good reason, vicar, just one.'

The rector could have given a dozen good reasons for his wife to stay at home that evening, but they would have started with concepts such as duty and loyalty which experience had told him were alien to her nature. But there was an element of truth to her barbs on this occasion, he did prefer to maintain the appearance of husband and wife normality, no matter how thin the veneer.

He wavered, struggling for a reason she might not dismiss with scorn. Her face was set and the glint of battle was in her eye, perhaps the glint of a battle already won, to judge by her smirk. 'Very well, I've asked and you've other things to do,' he conceded.

Which was hugely disappointing for Acantha Fox-Lomax as she was only just warming to the challenge. Her wretched husband grew less and less willing to contest anything, and besides she had no arrangements for the evening and at seven it was getting late to make any.

'All right. As you've asked so nicely, as you haven't mentioned any of those sick-making hypocritical moralities you're so fond of, I'll cancel my arrangements and play hostess to the constabulary.' To ensure that he understood on whose terms she was staying, she added a little whimsically, 'It might be quite amusing.'

'Please don't interfere, Acantha. Please.'

The two officers looked as uncomfortable as they felt when the rector's wife opened the door to them. They'd interviewed a dozen or so people during the day, made almost no progress with the inquiry, had hardly eaten, were dehydrated and sticky with sweat. After a bright start, Chief Inspector Smallborne was losing interest in the case which, as he'd feared, offered many tentative and

98

downright unlikely lines of enquiry, but little prospect of success. He'd found no encouragement from his temporary aide, constable Pitesteanu – he'd decided that 'temporary' was the correct way to describe her despite the attractions of her figure – and he was running late for a promised restaurant date with his wife and family.

'You two look exhausted, come in and have a cold drink,' she said, in the most welcoming, most hospitable, most wifely way she could manage.

'Thank you,' Lavi Pitesteanu dabbed a little moisture from her face with the last of her tissues, 'a cold drink would be great, thank you. But just water will be fine.'

'Yes, thank you Mrs Fox, same for me too,' echoed the inspector, so unfamiliar and awkward with double barrelled names that he invariably made them singular.

'It's Fox-Lomax, I don't mind one way or the other,' she added in a hushed tone of confidentiality, 'but the vicar can be very particular. And he usually likes the title too, it's Dr Fox-Lomax.'

She showed them to where Michael Radcliffe and the rector had shared their silences and where the smell of tobacco lingered, then knocked ostentatiously on the rector's study door and announced, 'Vicar dear, the police are here to see you, I'm getting drinks, would you like one too?' He gave her a look of pure exasperation in passing before going into the drawing room.

Acantha Fox-Lomax paused by the door on the way to the kitchen to be sure to catch the exchange of pleasantries between the rector and his guests. Sure enough, she had her moment of pleasure as they stumbled over names and titles. In the kitchen she prepared ice-cold beers for the inspector and his dark-eyed beauty of an assistant. For her husband she considered warming a glass before serving but she was keen to join the little group and a little reluctantly gave him a cold one too.

'So, it's confirmed then, it's her, it's Melanie Staples,' he was saying as she slid the beers in front of the visitors. In the corner of her eye she might have seen the girl open her mouth to protest and she might have seen her chief inspector's hand momentarily raised to stop her. Her smile was that of the genial hostess as she put her finger to her lips in a silent 'shh'. Now they could drink and be damned or not drink and sit and watch the condensation drip down the glasses like the perspiration leaking from their brows.

Her own chilled glass contained nothing stronger than refreshing elderflower cordial.

'We think so, yes.'

'So how can I help you tonight? I suppose you'll want to go over the statement I made back then? Not that I can add anything to it, nothing at all.'

'No, we've heard the same story from everyone, vicar. We've spoken to everyone we can who was at the school that afternoon and a few more besides. All you governors say pretty much the same thing and nobody's had anything to add.'

'Right,' the rector said slowly, 'so what can I do for you?' He'd expected questions about the day the girl went missing, the who and the where and the when, but these were apparently accepted without further question.

'Well, a couple of things,' suggested Donald Smallborne, his tongue flicking his lips and catching another droplet of sweat. 'First, I wonder if it's common for so many of you to be on the school board for so many years. Your neighbours the Radcliffes, Sir Bernard, Mr Deeley, Mr Staples, oh and the farmer . . .'

'Mr Westerleigh,' supplied his constable.

'Yes, Mr Westerleigh. And yourself of course, you've been there along with the rest of them for a long time.'

The Reverend Philip Fox-Lomax was mightily relieved by this new line of questioning, simple technical stuff about the governors that required simple answers.

'It's a small community and there are usually few volunteers, each of us is proposed by a different section of community, mainly the church of course, but the parish council too, the county council and so on. But you mentioned Sir Bernard Stoner, have you spoken to him?'

'No, not directly, he's abroad we understand.'

'Ah, yes. Strictly speaking, not a governor, it's an honorary position.'

The detective took the beer bottle from the table in front of him and held the cool glass against his forehead. At this cue, his constable cupped hers in her hands while Acantha Fox-Lomax watched across the ice bobbing in her cordial.

'I see. And you vicar, you're always the chairman are you?'

The rector stiffened a little at the implied criticism, 'It's an elected position, not one everyone would choose,' he replied defensively.

'I'd like to look at the minutes of the meeting you had that day. Do you have them?'

'I'm not sure, it's possible, but I don't know of what value they might be.' Having been put on the defensive, Philip Fox-Lomax remained there. He'd been chair of governors for the sixteen years that he'd been priest of the parish, following an unbroken line of priests since the school, then St. Germaine's, had first been created by the church in 1841. He knew to within an inch or so exactly where he could lay his hand on the file in question since all his school papers were labelled and filed on a particular shelf in his study. Barring some clerical accident the minutes of the meeting could be accessed immediately. Although his wife did not share the precision of his knowledge, she was almost sure that she could find the file in a matter of minutes and eyed her husband doubtfully.

'No, you're quite right vicar, I don't know of what value they could be either. But I'd like to look.'

'I would have to give that some thought. There are confidential matters discussed by governors, certain things are never made public.'

Asking to see the minutes was a spur of the moment idea, born out of a frustrating, exhausting and fruitless three days, during which he'd repeatedly heard that nobody could remember anything and if they could it was exactly as they had stated at the time. It seemed only when he'd ventured onto peripheral subjects had he glimpsed the shadows of something more substantial. More than once he'd also been made aware that insofar as school matters were concerned only the chair of governors could answer questions. So now that he was sat with the great man, he thought he might question the basis of this cosy little club, see if he could stir up anything by apparently irrelevant enquiries. There might be nothing in the minutes of any value to him, the evasion might simply be the vicar being protective and keen to demonstrate his petty authority. Or there might be something there.

'What kind of confidential things?'

Philip Fox-Lomax immediately regretted having given this sweaty dull policeman a reason to press the point. The last thing he wanted was to have a conflict over such minor matters as a parent's financial status or the social services report on another.

'The current year's minutes are available for inspection at any time, that's the law, but the governors reserve the right to make confidential any discussions on . . .' he hesitated, still unsure what trivial example he could give to deflect the enquiries. His hand was at his chest, his fingertips touching his crucifix and immediately the answer came to him. 'Look, there are sometimes children whose parents wish to opt them out of Christian activities, the governors discuss such things on the basis of strict confidentiality. Which is best for the child, the parents and the school.' He settled back into his chair and took his first sip of the welcoming chill of the drink, which only served to remind him of how profusely he was sweating.

'Oh, I see, that kind of thing,' the policeman replied with an air of finally understanding the point.

While he considered whether to pursue the matter he absent-mindedly brought his cold bottle to his lips and tipped it to drink. The cold beer fizzed on contact with the warmth of his mouth and he swallowed gratefully without a second thought. Mid tip, he looked across at the rector's wife who was offering him the widest of encouraging smiles. His constable looked on dejectedly, straight-faced and pale; it was one thing for a detective chief inspector to take a beer on a hot day, quite another to join him without specific invitation, which was not forthcoming. The temptation to bring her bottle to her mouth was almost unbearable, and in the oppressive atmosphere of the rectory drawing room her mind wandered to the end of the day's duty, to sitting by the river in Oxford and letting cold beer trickle down her throat. Surely these simple pleasures could not be denied her much longer. But Donald Smallborne seemed determined to have something to show for his sweating efforts.

'I think I'd like to see them, for that year, the year Melanie Staples went missing,' then after a moment's additional consideration, 'and for the year after. And the confidential stuff, that too.'

The rector sagged at this setback and offered wearily, 'Yes of course, it may take a while.' As a final defiant gesture in a losing skirmish he added with as much authority as he could muster, 'I'll need to check on anything confidential, in case it's still relevant to people today. Many of the children still live in the village you know, grown up now of course, as do their parents and grandparents. But rest assured if it could be relevant I'll let you know.'

'Very good of you, sir.'

★

When Lavi Pitesteanu walked under the Saxon arch of the south door into the parish church of St. Giles it was the first time she'd entered a church since being a self-conscious teenage bridesmaid to a cousin, ten years previously. Now, much against her will, she'd been pressed into working on her only scheduled rest day before the following weekend, and not only working but attending the Sunday morning service in the blighted village. What had eventually persuaded her was the suggestion that she could carry the Melanie Staples case while the chief inspector was on holiday. She'd have to report daily to someone more senior, but she could continue to collect information and, subject to certain limits, follow up anything worthwhile. Implicit in this idea was that the inquiry would peter out for lack of any new information or evidence, despite the full forensic report on Melanie's remains having not yet been received. There was also the question of resources, which had been stretched considerably by the need to support two inquiries and to do so in a conspicuous manner. The initial mistakes had cost the force dear, both in the probability of success and in overtime payments, a fact well understood by the chief constable, who would also be attending the service as a token of support to the community. Most Sundays found him offering tokens of support to one community or another.

The detective had been delegated to collect the papers promised by the rector and it had been strongly suggested she should also make herself visible around the villages, lest anyone should think that Sunday was a day of rest in the inquiry. While she went to church her chief inspector intended to spend his rest day repairing the damage done by his failure to reach the restaurant the previous evening.

Given the events of the previous days it was no surprise that the service was better attended than it might have been, boosted not only by the chief constable's party, but also the presence of the local TV crew covering his visit. She could have made herself known to him, there in the front row by the pulpit, she could probably have sat with his followers, but that would have made her visit as ceremonial as his. From her seat near the back of the church she watched as the great, the good and the ordinary came with their various motives to worship. The number of nudges, whispered asides and turned heads told her most had noted her presence. Some did so because they recognised her, others because they did not. It was a curious position she found herself in, knowing the names of many, having sat in some of their houses only yesterday, yet hardly on nodding terms with any and they having all forgotten her name, if not her face.

The church had one great blessing to offer all who entered on that morning – it was cool. Notwithstanding the heat of the day, the ancient stones soaked it all up and left the inside virtually unchanged, just as they had done for a thousand years or more. Indeed those who'd arrived hot and sticky in skimpy cotton tops found themselves grow chill in the unaccustomed air. Margaret Westerleigh was fussing about, apparently with some duty or responsibility for the electric fans that had been set out along the side aisle, while her husband sat head bowed, apparently in prayer, beside Colin Deeley and his neighbour Mrs Webster. Upright and alone, the new widower Michael Radcliffe sat in the third row back, one hand in his jacket pocket, untroubled by the cool draft of air.

Slightly to the constable's surprise Mrs Samarasinghe and her son were also present, another little lesson in not making assumptions based on names and skin tone. They too sat alone in a row and she couldn't help noticing that when the son looked round at her the smile she half-expected was absent. Perhaps he thought it would be improper, but she felt a hint of disappointment. Not only was the smile absent but all vitality had gone from his face.

Just as interesting as those who were present were those who were not. Unless he'd slipped in unnoticed, Melanie Staples' father was elsewhere. For no particular reason she'd thought he was a pillar of community and therefore certain to be at the service. Perhaps he was not ready to be consoled for his loss, not ready to resume his normal place in village society. The vicar's wife was another absentee, otherwise every one of those she'd seen in the course of the inquiry were at the service. As she thought about Acantha Fox-Lomax, she wondered if the beer had been a calculated trick or a kind thought. It was presented as a kindness yet the effect had been cruel, and something about the woman unsettled her. She'd been all eyes and expressions, yet had hardly uttered a word beyond a greeting and a goodbye. He'd seemed tetchy, prickly over his title – was it rector or vicar, she couldn't remember even now – and unnecessarily formal over being chair of governors, as if he were governor of some far-flung province of the old empire. Pompous was the word, she decided, as the man in question mounted the steps to the pulpit.

The service was dry and singularly uninspiring, Fox-Lomax making only a passing and obscure reference to caring for children and spending more time on the natural disasters and their effects. The two subjects came closest when he referred to an Old Testament verse about floods not drowning love, but it might also have been a reference to Mary Radcliffe. When he made the call to Communion she remained seated, awkwardly unfamiliar with the ways of the church. Apart from a handful of children, Thomas Samarasinghe was the only other dissenter, although the unmistakeably diminutive figure of his mother made her way forward to receive the sacrament.

As the congregation left the cool shadows of St. Giles to endure once again the glaring furnace of the day, the Reverend Philip Fox-Lomax bade them his customary goodbye, standing by the door and exchanging a word or two with each parishioner as they passed, more with visitors, especially important ones. Lavi Pitesteanu hung back to be last in line, competing with John and Margaret Westerleigh for that place until she recalled that the farmer was also a governor and there was no need for the niceties of a private conversation with the rector.

'Do you have the papers here or shall I come to the house?' she asked.

Despite his promise to provide them, the rector had not expected to do so until Monday at the earliest, and had certainly not been prepared for the raven-haired detective to appear in his congregation that morning. He'd half guessed her purpose and found her presence distracting throughout the service, an unwelcome intrusion of the temporal world into the spiritual. He could not get out of his head the idea that she had no right to be there, the more so when her failure to take Holy Communion made her official purpose all the more obvious.

'Oh no,' he said dismissively, 'not here, and I've had no opportunity to copy them yet.'

'Don't worry vicar, I'll get them from the house and have them copied in the office in no time.'

'We do have a visitor at the rectory this morning,' he motioned towards the chief constable who was talking earnestly and shaking hands with anyone who offered theirs.

'Perhaps he'll get them copied and pass them on, shall I ask . . .' the constable was simply being mischievous and would never have dreamed of doing such a thing, but it had the desired effect.

'No, no, come across now,' the rector replied with ill-disguised irritation, then turning to the bemused farmer and his wife, 'John look after our guests for a few minutes will you.'

★

Of all the families in the twin villages, the Duncans were almost certainly the one most in need of prayers, for their loss remained the unknown loss, their anxiety swinging wildly between hope and grief, pausing occasionally at anger on the way. But, perhaps unsurprisingly, they had not been represented at St. Giles that Sunday morning, none spoke for them nor prayed for them by name although doubtless there were some good souls who had included the lost Eysha in fervent pleas to their god.

A little before one o'clock a policewoman called with a request that Laura might go to the incident centre. A display had been arranged in the village hall and she was asked if she might look to see if there was anything she recognised. Arranged on trestle tables was the carefully collected debris from hedge-rows and paths, bus shelters and bins from all round the villages and the neighbouring lanes. All had been painstakingly labelled and laid out, not just for Laura Duncan to attempt to identify, but after her for anyone who could be persuaded to come and look. Also on parade was the chief constable, pulled hastily from the first mouthful of Sunday lunch with Lady Stoner, who'd returned to Lisle House to oversee plans to restore the grounds to their former glory and to mourn the loss of several irreplaceable treasures from the still waterlogged cellars.

Along with Laura went her mother and brother Liam, her friend Vicki Gardner and Vicki's daughter Molly. Kathy Duncan and her daughter both looked exactly as they had a right to look: pale and waxy, their reddened eyes sunk in purple circles, hair straggling and stuck to their necks, sweat darkening their T-shirts. Liam Duncan appeared a little less distressed, a little less unkempt, as did Vicki Gardner who'd managed a smear or two of make-up for the occasion.

In the incident centre they were met by an icy blast from a malfunctioning air conditioning unit and a sergeant who briefed them on the purpose of the inspection. They were told it was imperative that none of the items on display should be touched, they should all take their time as if it were an identity parade. If an item was worthy of attention then they should ask for it to be held up or turned to be seen from a different point of view. From there it was only a few baking steps across to the village hall where an ill-prepared chief constable shook their hands and offered hope and assurances while a local news photographer took pictures. In his haste he'd left his cap at Lisle House and was pre-occupied by this error of dress.

There were perhaps sixty items in all ranging from a pink wellington boot and a solitary white sock to disposable lighters and several single gloves. Some were contained in clear plastic bags, others lay on squares of paper denoting their place of discovery. Amongst the collection were two or three items the police were quietly hoping might be recognised, if not by Laura then by someone else.

They had their answer rather more quickly than they'd imagined. While the adults dutifully examined the first two tables and paused to examine a cigarette lighter more closely, Molly had roamed further, rushing back to her mother shouting, 'It's Eysha's lunch box! Mum look! It's Eysha's!' and holding the trophy in one pudgy little hand, the plastic evidence bag in the other.

8

It is said that three o'clock in the morning is the very worst of times to be awake and worrying. Every difficulty is magnified by the loneliness of the hour, fatigue turns every concern into an insoluble crisis. Add in the stifling, sultry heat and the stink of a receding flood, then have it happen two nights running and you have the perfect recipe for distress. In the small hours of Monday morning Thomas Samarasinghe woke from a restless sleep littered with dreams of nameless terrors, culminating in the horror of being buried alive. He was bathed in sweat, his sheets wrapping and trapping his body like clingfilm, so he could scarcely tell waking from sleeping. Desperately he fought with the bedclothes until by chance he freed an arm, then hurled himself from the mattress and escaped the half-bed half-grave confining him.

He snapped on the light and sat wet and shivering trying to shake the images from his head. Eventually the tremors passed and he made the bed afresh with clean dry linen. It soothed his body but not his mind. All that had passed between himself and Melanie Staples, and all that had passed since, swirled in confusion. He couldn't bear the thought of his father knowing of his crimes. No matter that he must have forgiven Thomas, simply his knowing was the worst possible thing. As this burden weighed on him, so it compounded with each additional person who would certainly know every detail – the whole of the twin villages, everyone at the school, his whole family both here and – the shocking realisation that his precious opa Wikram probably knew he was a thief was like a fist in his stomach. The shame was almost too much to bear.

How could he have been so wrong about Melanie, how could he have trusted her with everything as she'd trusted him? But she was at the root of this misery, she hadn't trusted him with everything, had she? She hadn't told him her father knew, and if her father then probably her mother too, and goodness knows who else. What could possibly have happened to make her confess these things? And if she hadn't told him all her secrets there might be other secrets, different secrets, she hadn't shared with him. The pleasure and relief of the clean sheets began to wane as his body oozed sweat. In vain he tried to lie quite still and let the fan by his bed blow a gentle breeze across him but no position offered any comfort for more than a few seconds. The sheets grew damp and twisted, the fan too noisy, the light too bright.

Yet when he returned to the dark silence of the humid night his fears only multiplied. His father had thought Melanie might be a bad influence on him, yet who was to say what the girl's father had thought. He probably held the same poor opinion of Thomas, that it was he who was the bad influence on his clever and beautiful daughter. He could hear Peter Staples saying to his father how she'd never been in any trouble until she fell in with Thomas and what was he going to do about it. And what he did about it was go and 'sort it out with the shopkeeper'. The shopkeeper! Sour-faced, ill-tempered, never-a-good-word-for-anyone Chris Rogers who'd glared at him with such hostility the day of the flood. Did he know, did he remember, did he hold a grudge all this time, did he resent every moment that Thomas was in his shop, did he watch him carefully, check his every purchase? Did he cheat him with short-change, a few pennies at a time to get back what he was owed for the chocolate bars? And what had his father meant by 'sorting it out', had he paid him off all those years ago, to add resentment to the shopkeeper's ingrained sense of injustice?

Thomas had not a single answer to any of his torments, other than those which begged more questions, and in doing so opened up worse possibilities. Simply quitting the place, starting a new life in a city far away was the best possible outcome he could hope for, and it was his great good fortune that he would be doing exactly that within weeks. But even as he reached for this salvation he saw the new life, saw his whole career stretching before him all blighted by the crimes of childhood. How could he now become a barrister of all things, a defender of the innocent, prosecutor of the guilty, above all an upholder of the law, when he himself was no more than a common thief? And somewhere in the shadows there'd always be a finger pointed, an accusing whisper waiting to be heard. Not once in all the years had he ever felt any guilt or remorse, in fact he had barely thought about it at all. Now with shame of discovery clouding every moment, he could think of nothing else.

As despondency threatened to overwhelm him he found one small ray of hope. His father had made little of the affair during their conversation, so little that he'd been easily distracted. If it hadn't been for the rain and the awful aftermath he might never have mentioned it and Thomas would have been none the wiser. Although it had meant more at the time, enough for the two fathers to smooth things over, his Tatta hadn't seen it as so terrible and wicked a thing as might have been imagined. Perhaps Melanie had been loyal to him after all, and despite whatever pressure had made her reveal the chocolate secrets, she'd given Thomas the junior role, the less blameworthy role, in the crime. As this idea took hold he found new faith in that old friendship and thanked her for such protection as she had given him, unworthy of it as he knew himself to be.

As the darkness retreated in the light of the new day, so the sweats and torments lessened. His punched and pummelled pillow finally produced a place to rest his head and his thrashing limbs lay still. Nothing had changed, nothing was resolved, there would be embarrassment and shame still to come, of that he was sure, but finding a little trust in friendship was a help. Perhaps, just perhaps, he might still find a way to wipe his own slate clean through confession or penance or both. But a new quandary presented itself: how best to repay his friend's loyalty – by keeping her secrets or revealing them?

★

The question of secrets and revelations was also uppermost some thirty or so miles from Whyncombe St. Giles, in the forensic laboratories at Culham. In a specially prepared room, kept locked and sealed, humidity and temperature carefully controlled, were the collected remains of Melanie Ann Staples. Here, in the silence before the working week began, she waited for the final indignities of examination. She had arrived in twelve white plastic boxes, each labelled and sealed and signed for, each brought to the special room, her own private suite, as luxurious in its way as anywhere she'd ever been in life. An adjoining area allowed one-way observation of the process without any chance of corrupting evidence, while the whole of her stay was monitored by video from the moment her first box was placed on the examination benches.

Four polished glass surfaces, each lit from every possible angle were arranged in the room, three occupied by different categories of finds, while the fourth remained empty. Melanie's re-assembled remains had pride of place on the main table, another displayed items of clothing, a third carried miscellaneous articles. Measuring

110

equipment of every kind lined the walls, ready for every conceivable analysis - no part of her need leave the room before the examination was complete. Then, when science and the coroner were satisfied she'd given up everything she could, she would be handed to her parents a final time; then, and only then, would they be able to give her the final goodbye so long delayed.

A little after nine o'clock an unseen hand increased the lighting level from the soft night-time glow, the permanent background minimum which allowed the cameras to function, to the artificial sunlight in which all examinations were made. A minute or two later white-robed and masked figures entered Melanie's suite. They checked lights on measuring machines, reset base points to zero, and tested the slim microphones hung from threads so slender it seemed they floated in the air above each table. By their movements the two figures were male and they were shortly joined by two similarly covered but distinctly female forms. All four gathered round Melanie and stood briefly motionless, as if in silent prayer. In their private, ritual world they might easily have been high priests and priestesses of the white-slippered cult who'd brought her sacrificial body to their temple.

For most of the morning they went about their gruesome business, swabbing this and examining that, weighing and testing, recording and photographing at what might seem to an outsider, to a non-believer, as a wastefully slow pace. But it was a steady pace, a painstaking pace, the prescribed pace, and it served their purpose well, since it came as close as possible to ensuring that nothing was overlooked or misinterpreted. From time to time they were watched through the mirror glass from the viewing room but whether they were aware of the watchers or not, it made no difference to their progress or their method. At regular intervals one or other of the figures spoke quietly of their findings, lifting their heads from their work to speak directly to the hovering microphones. A fanciful observer, or a religious one, might have imagined them intoning their creed.

There was little her bones and fragments of flesh and hair could say, beyond the nature and depth of the soil they had been buried in, the length of time she'd spent there, the species of tree that guarded her. But as important as the presence of some clue or revealing fact was the absence of any. Her body had not spent long in water, neither was any blow or cut apparent although she was still without her left leg between the knee and ankle as well as several smaller bones from her feet and hands. Her teeth matched her dentist's x-ray perfectly apart from the missing one, yet there was no certainty that it had been lost as a result of violence, nor if it had been detached from her skull pre- or post-mortem. Her remaining teeth showed what was well known to that dentist and to her parents, namely that she neglected them. They had been under sustained attack from a sugary diet for some time. Since the last record of her mouth had been made the very day she'd disappeared it could hardly have been more up to date. The hygienist who'd cleaned Melanie's teeth that morning had also noted the tell-tale signs of nicotine. Sufficient traces of tobacco tar remained to be visible under the microscope at Culham for those notes to be confirmed.

Modern fabrics wear very well in a shallow grave. The combination of synthetic and natural fibres endures far longer than textiles made from purely organic sources. Young Melanie wore almost nothing of purely natural material apart from a bracelet or wrist band, no more than a few twists of gold, crimson, green and orange cotton. This tiny fragment lay on the second table, alongside her red macintosh, one boot and all her school clothes. It was noted that her underwear was on her body at the time of her burial. Initial examination had shown no traces of DNA from a second person on her clothes or her body. It wasn't evidence, but if confirmed it would be an absence of evidence, an absence that might bring a small comfort to a parent, or even to an accused should it ever come to such a point. Although her left leg was mainly missing, the fact that both her feet and one boot had been recovered from the mound by the school gate, suggested that she and her boots may have been separated before burial, but that too was conjecture rather than definitive.

The third table held few articles and it was far from certain that they belonged in the same room as Melanie. The puzzle was to decide which belonged and which did not. Most had shared the mound by the school or been picked up somewhere along the route of the old track or up in the wood simply because they looked interesting. A few items were by definition connected to Melanie, taken from her raincoat pockets: two chocolate bar wrappers, a disposable cigarette lighter, a few coins amounting to thirty-seven pence and a key-ring with a single key on it. Among the remaining, apparently random selection, were the inevitable glove and a second lighter, together with the metal parts of a purse clip, a child's yellow sunglasses with one lens missing, a dog's broken collar without a tag, a penknife with a bone handle. Along with this trivia were the skeletal remains of what had at first been taken to be a fox, but had subsequently been identified as the bones of a dog, probably a retriever. Each item had been labelled and given an initial examination, which had revealed nothing beyond the obvious, and nothing further was learnt from them despite the attention they received. The key could probably be identified if it fitted the back door of the Staples' cottage, the glove might yield DNA of the owner as might some of the other items, but as evidence of anything they amounted to almost zero.

★

Molly Gardner's unfortunate identification of the lunch box, confirmed by Eysha's mother and grandmother, did little to influence the course of that inquiry. It was embarrassing for the chief constable to be present at such a moment, but that was the least of it. He'd been rapidly ushered to his waiting Jaguar and whisked back to Lisle House to be re-united with his cap and his Sunday lunch. The investigation remained split in purpose, each faction taking encouragement from the discovery. The abductionists reasoned that she would not willingly have left her lunch and it was evidence that she had been at the bird-hide the day she disappeared. To the flood-victim party it was a sure sign that she had been skulking in the bird-hide when she should have been elsewhere and then been trapped by the rising water, only to get into difficulties when she tried to escape. Those supporting the conspiracy theory saw sinister meaning behind the way the lunch box had been removed from its evidence bag in the presence of Eysha's mother, uncle and grandmother.

In fact little Molly's actions made no difference, it was Eysha's for sure, but it held no significance other than where it had been discovered. Regardless of which scenario might be closest to the facts, it did suggest that the girl really had been seen by Molly on the track down to the study centre and that she'd gone down that track nearly as far as the car park, then forked right to the bird-hide. This assumed that she'd left the lunch box there herself and in truth it was difficult to imagine any other reason for it being there.

All of which may have only moved her along a few hundred meters and ten or fifteen minutes, but it was progress of a sort.

Whatever had happened to her then still begged the question of why she was there, and there were several suggestions on that subject. Two of the theories shared one important idea: both the conspiracy and abduction groups agreed that she met someone there, although whether by chance or design was open to question. The accidental-drowners saw no reason or opportunity for her to have met anybody, she'd simply been skipping school for a few hours, something she was known to have done quite frequently.

Eysha's family hadn't recognised anything else from the village hall display, although Liam had been tempted to lay claim to a gold chain which was very similar to one he'd lost a month or two previously. Of the fifty or so other villagers who'd volunteered to inspect the collection since the Duncans, only one identified anything and that was an eighty year-old lady who was delighted to be re-united with a black leather glove. Exhibiting the results of such a huge effort served two purposes: a public demonstration of the commitment to the inquiry and the chance of something meaningful being identified. The exercise had netted a solitary item of any real interest and even that gave no new impetus to the search.

As important as anything the police were doing was the fact that the water level in the combe – as in the surrounding countryside – was at last dropping significantly as the flow from the hills slowed from torrents to trickles. Each of the different strands of the inquiry shared the view that as a result Eysha would be found quite soon. This was as much a hope as a calculation, for without some new information all lines of enquiry would soon be exhausted and inevitably personnel and resources would be wound down even further. As it was, the search phase had come to an end by Monday afternoon. If new information came to light or the receding waters revealed some new fact a fresh search could be mounted quickly enough.

*

At High Whyn Farm John Westerleigh should have been in better spirits than he was. His insurance company had instructed him to go ahead as quickly as possible with rebuilding the slurry lagoon. They had even conceded that the lagoon could be replaced with one of a higher specification than the corner-cutting one swept away. There was concern too for potentially larger losses if the farm were to go out of business and they were also alert to the possible liability for the clean up of the road and repairs to The Chequers' car park. The twice weekly tanker service to remove the animal waste from temporary storage was already racking up expenses and there is nothing an insurance company likes less than an open ended liability. Their policy absolved them from paying out for many things including the familiar 'war, civil disturbance or acts of God' and they had briefly debated whether or not The Great Whyncombe St. Giles Deluge could be classified as the latter. Legal advice had been taken and come down in favour of the claimants of which there were several from the neighbourhood.

Such news should have given him reason to be cheerful but he'd remained in a dour mood, more introspective than ever. As distressing as the events had been, they seemed to have had a disproportionate effect and he became more morose by the day. His wife's sympathy had grown thin and she could not quite forgive him for saying nothing about Mary Radcliffe. Her conscience pricked her over this, since she felt it her duty to forgive him. Indeed, she felt it her duty to support his every thought and action, but she had been angry with him, so she consoled herself with the thought that she would one day forgive him, even if it were not today.

He'd done the bare minimum of jobs around the farm, almost as if he had lost all interest in it. When he was in the house he kept himself shut away in the office, only grudgingly emerging for meals for which he had no appetite. Monday evening was no different except that he was slumped in his chair in the parlour. Margaret's attempts to engage him in conversation all failed until she spoke about the encounter between the rector and the detective after the Sunday morning service.

'Philip said she was after the minutes from the governors' meeting.'

'From last week? I thought it didn't happen?'

'No, not last week,' she said a little tetchily, 'From years ago, from the time when . . . ' she hesitated over whether to use the girl's name, and wished she hadn't spoken at all.

'From when?' her husband said, as if he'd half guessed the answer.

'From all those years ago, from when Peter Staples' girl went missing.' It was as close as she dared go to saying it.

'Huh,' he snorted, 'and a fat lot of good it'll do them.' He sank further into the chair, deeper into himself, a distant expression across his face. Then as if he had forgotten something important, he returned to the present. 'Did he say why? What did they want?'

'Nothing, most likely. You know what they were like when they were round here, all sorts of odd questions. Philip wasn't at all pleased, he told me they wanted some other stuff too.'

'What kind of stuff? What would he have about her?'

'Seems there might have been some private notes, you know, "governors' eyes only", that kind of thing. You've probably still got them yourself.'

'No. Not that far back.'

The denial was easy to believe and accept, after all they were talking about a few notes taken at a meeting over a decade ago, notes that would have no relevance to anything current and had probably never been looked at since the day they were made. But later she wondered how he was so certain and how it was that amongst the collected paperwork of more than twenty years these irrelevant pages had been selected, almost uniquely, for disposal.

The old farmhouse was rarely silent, too much going on in and around it for that. In the heat and humidity of the summer it had done nothing but creak and groan. Last week's deluge had added a new set of sounds to its repertoire but as the farmer and his wife sat in the parlour all was silence save for the scratching of a chimney cowl gently turning in the evening airs. Each day it expanded as the sun rose and contracted as it set; at each change metal caught metal by just a millimetre. Scrit-scrat. One scrit-scrat for every turn. Scrit-scrat, turn, scrit-scrat, turn. John Westerleigh slipped away again to wherever it was he went when he left his body sitting in the house.

Margaret Westerleigh looked at her husband's unseeing eyes and the unfamiliar set of his mouth, slack and down-turned as if in disgust. In the space of a few days he'd aged horribly, his ruddy health replaced by sallow skin drawn across gaunt features. A thought crossed her mind and she gave it voice before she had time to stop herself.

'John, do you know something about Melanie Staples?'

She saw the muscles in his cheek twitch as his jaw tightened and he turned his head a fraction to look her square on.

'I know some things, some things not everybody knows. Like you do probably, if you gave it some thought.'

'I don't think I do, what would I know about her?'

'Well, for a start you know the same as I do she used to come up here sometimes, her and her friend.'

'Yes, I'd forgotten, but what's that got to do with anything?'

'Nothing, but you and I know it and probably no one else does.'

'I didn't mean that, you know I meant something else, something important.'

'That might be important, who knows. I know she was a little thief and a liar and had a nasty way with her.'

'That's a terrible thing to say about the poor girl!' Margaret was taken aback that her husband could say such a thing. 'What did she ever do to make you say that? Poor Peter would be heartbroken if he heard you say such things.'

'Peter Staples didn't hear me and never will. But he knew well enough she was no angel. And she was taking that Thomas the same way by all accounts. Or they were both as bad as each other.'

'Thomas has always been such a lovely boy. Well, a man now of course, don't tell me he's all those terrible things too,' she complained.

'I don't know what he is, I've never known what he is. I do know he's always around. All these years there's been something not quite right about him, always anxious to please and so on, but that wasn't it. Then only today I saw him twice in the village, looking as miserable as sin and stood outside the shop, then again by The Chequers and I thought that's it, that's exactly why, for all that politeness, all his cleverness, all his good looks and good fortune, that's why he's so unsettling: he always seems to be everywhere you look. If you see him in the shop, he pops up in the churchyard five minutes later, or if you go to the school he's there. Go to the quarry and you'll meet him in the lane. And every time you do it's that big smile and a wave and a hello Mr Westerleigh. Even if he's waved the same not five minutes before.'

'You're being horribly unkind, he's lovely, and his family are too.'

'Maybe. But you asked me if I knew something about the girl, I'll bet your lovely Thomas knows a thing or two, he and she were thick as thieves.'

'You've always spoken so well of him, everyone has, what's made you this way now?'

'Maybe it was seeing the inside of her skull, maybe that's what's made me this way now.' It was the first time he'd expressed any feeling at all about his grim discovery, and he expressed it with unexpected anger and bitterness. When the flurry of words ended, the animation left John Westerleigh's face and his eyes resumed their distant focus, leaving his wife as mystified and rejected as ever.

The last of the sun's heat leaked from the metal as the evening thermals gained strength. Scrit-scrat, turn, scrit, turn, turn, turn.

★

'Have you gone crazy?'

Upeksha Samarasinghe could scarcely believe what her son was saying. He'd moped around the house all morning then volunteered to get the few things she needed from the village store only to come back an hour later with none of them, apologising lamely that he'd forgotten what he went out for. Then after their meal he'd become agitated waiting for his sister to leave for her late night shift at the BBC. Finally when she'd gone he'd sat long-faced and unspeaking until his mother had told him he could tell her what was going on or he could leave her in peace to watch her favourite soap. Then he'd just blurted it all out, about Melanie, about chocolate and the shock that his father knew and maybe half the village and his family too and did she know and how sorry he was to bring such shame on the family and how he was going to go and apologise to Mr Rogers and pay him back for every bar and talk to Melanie's father. It was at this point that his mother had held up her hand to interrupt the flow.

'You are not thinking at all, this is all nonsense,' she said firmly and deliberately. 'Of course I knew about the chocolate, her father came to see us, he was full of apologies. Then your father and he went and spoke to the shopkeeper. It is all over, finished, there is nothing left to say about it. It was years ago. You were children and children do such things.'

He had spent a second day in agonies until he could bear the torture no longer and risked more humiliation by confessing his sins. Now his mother's words brought a little relief, she had not been shocked by the revelation, more angered by his proposed remedies.

'Oh but Amma, why didn't you tell me you knew, why didn't Tatta say anything?'

'Her father said he'd make sure it stopped, which I suppose he did. Your father was going to say something to you, but we waited a little and the time came and went. Then it was gone and no point

118

talking about it. And really there is not much point talking about it now, and certainly not bringing it all up again with the shopkeeper or anyone else. And give a little thought to Mr Staples, do you think he'd be wanting to be reminded of all that just now?'

After all the anguish, all the guilt, it felt quite wrong that he should not have some penalty, some punishment. At the very least he should be saying how sorry he was for doing such things, yet here was his Amma, his wise and trusted Amma, telling him to forget it.

'Tatta said it was sorted out, what did he do, how did he sort it out?'

'I don't know, he and Mr Staples and maybe someone else, I'm not sure, they all spoke and it was done. It was better, we didn't want any fuss. You must remember this was a new home then, we had been here less than a year, it was best for everyone.'

'Did they pay him, did they pay him for the chocolate?'

Upeksha Samarasinghe looked at her beautiful, clever, son. Fresh from Cambridge and his First Class degree, soon to be living fashionably in London, diligent and thoughtful of his mother and father. One day he would marry well and give her beautiful grandchildren. A son any mother would be pleased to call hers. But with so little idea of how the world worked it seemed incredible that he should have got so far without falling.

'Yes, of course they paid him.'

'How much?'

'They paid him whatever was necessary, I don't know how much, I don't even know if it was money or something else, but it was all arranged, it was all agreed and arranged so that everyone was perfectly happy. No fuss, and that was the main thing for us, no fuss. And that is how it should be now. Your father will be very unhappy if there is any fuss now after all this time. You should think very carefully about even mentioning it to your father again, and anybody else too, I should say.'

Thomas already had much to be grateful to his father for, apart from the love and respect that was his right, and to cause him some new anxiety over the chocolate was something he would avoid at all costs. But he desperately wanted to know who else knew of his crimes, and if not who then an idea of how many, how far, how wide his shame had been known.

'Amma, did Diana know about the chocolate and Melanie and Tatta sorting it out?'

'No. It had nothing to do with her.' His mother paused, uncertain as to whether she should say more to Thomas, then judged it was better he should know. 'Diana is a clever girl, she does not miss things. She spoke to me after your Tatta called and asked what he'd meant by what he said. She may say something to you about it.'

'Did you tell her?'

'No!' she said in exasperation, 'Haven't I just been telling you it's all better left in the past?'

'But in the village, who else knew?' Thomas pressed on, having come so far he might as well find as many answers as possible, get the agony over once and for all.

'I don't know who else. Not many I think, that was something agreed, that it shouldn't be spoken of again, the matter was ended. It was best for everyone. Now, is that everything? Because I do not want to speak of it again, neither do I want it spoken of again in this house.'

'And is that how it has been, never spoken of again until Saturday?' Thomas couldn't quite believe that such an arrangement could be made and that the bargain, however well struck, could be kept.

'Yes, as far as I know, yes.'

He knew he would comply with his mother's wishes and by default those of his father too, but the carefully made agreement that resolved the matter years ago had not included Thomas in the vow of silence. He could see that a public penance or repayment of a few pounds for chocolate long forgotten, was out of the question. Much too much 'fuss', of which his father would have none, but he might yet make some personal, private, apology. Did Melanie make an apology, he wondered? For a moment he tried to remember exactly what she'd said to him when she called a halt to their raids. They'd been sitting in one of their trees up in the wood, the leaves just out enough to hide them if they were quiet, and she'd said they had to stop in case they were caught. He was almost certain she'd said that, 'in case they were caught', but it might not have been those words, it was a lifetime ago, he and the world were altogether different. But the sense was surely right, even though they may have already been caught. So was that what she couldn't risk, that they be caught again? Was it part of the secret agreement that one offence was allowed to pass without fuss but a second would have a harsher outcome?

He turned to his mother again, and was on the point of asking just that, but she was watching her programme. In her glance towards him, she looked once, then dipped her head to see him over her glasses and in that look he caught her meaning. The subject was closed, now and forever.

★

Monday evening found Peter Staples still in the dust and dirt of Maiden Quarry, where he'd been all day and most of the weekend putting the finishing touches to the gargoyle for St. Giles. It was finally ready to replace its corroded predecessor high on the tower at the base of the steeple. It need have taken far less time than he'd spent on it, but he'd worked deliberately slowly, expanding the work into the infinity of time he had available. He had other jobs that demanded his attention but did not get it: a local builder had twice left messages about progress on materials to build a gateway for a new house nearing completion; an Oxford college needed a quotation to repair a medieval arch; the diocese had called about repairs to the rectory stonework. He hadn't spent all that time on the gargoyle out of any obsessive attention to detail, or perfection of finish, rather it was a job already under way, a continuation of life before The Great Deluge and something he could just sit and do. He did more sitting than doing, but the illusion of work and busyness satisfied his immediate needs.

The quarry, the workshop and all his tools were as permanent a feature of his life as the stone he worked. While he was there, even when he was simply planning a job or choosing stone, but mostly when he was shaping the rock, he felt at one with the very fabric of the universe. The hard bright stone laid down those tens of millions of years ago stretched time back to its very beginning and forward beyond his short life to the end of eternity. He understood himself well enough to see the quarry was also his refuge, and although it welcomed him, it was an inhospitable place for visitors. Neither did he make any attempt to have it otherwise. Even in his little office there was no seat for a visitor and hardly a space to stand. The answering machine offered no pleasantries or gratitude to a would-be customer, it simply stated Maiden Quarry and the caller should leave a message. On rare occasions he would answer himself, but more often he would check messages each morning, returning the call only when essential. On Monday morning he hadn't called anyone.

Had it not been for the need to give a cheek swab to refresh his DNA sample on Saturday, he might well have spent the whole weekend at his workbench. A routine procedure at the appointed time had become complicated by the absence of the appropriate staff in the village and he'd obligingly agreed to go to the police station in Oxford. Needless to say, at St. Aldates his appearance was quite unexpected and he'd had to wait for an hour before the two-minute process could be done. He'd somehow expected the procedure to be different from the one in the days after his girl had gone, enhanced perhaps by an advance in technology. But the masked technician made no attempt at conversation while taking the cells from his mouth. To some it might have appeared insensitive but to Peter Staples it was a blessing, he was never one for small talk at the best of times. The journey to the city at least provided an opportunity to collect a few groceries from the safe anonymity of a supermarket rather than the stale familiarity of Chris Rogers' shop in the village. If he'd been sufficiently interested in looking it could have provided a variation in diet too.

All day as he'd attended to the intricate detail of the carving, shaping it almost grain by grain to slow the process, then lifting his goggles to check again, he'd been pushing back the thought of the painstaking examination to which his daughter was being subjected. Grain by grain, strand by strand, fibre by fibre, her remains were being listed and categorised, tested and reported. In some nonsensical way he'd linked his work to that of the examiners, only when he'd finished, only when he'd taken the greatest possible care of the grotesque goat's head, could their terrible work also be completed. Bizarrely to his way of thinking, there'd been a suggestion that if he wished to attend the process at Culham, it might be arranged, although that had been accompanied by heavy hints it was probably not a good idea. Whichever way he'd looked at it he couldn't see the need, not through love nor duty. As to what her mother might want, well that was her lookout, she hadn't been in touch and he'd not contacted her. For all he knew she'd been there watching Melanie all day long.

For twenty more minutes he sat, his fingers idly stroking the smoothness of the curves in his handiwork, when noises beyond the silent workshop brought him back to the present. He listened again and his sharp senses knew the source at once: a cyclist, one with a saddle that squeaked very slightly as the right foot pressed down on the peddle. Knowing the source identified the rider, it was Melanie's grandfather, Colin Deeley.

He stepped out of the building to find to his surprise that the light had all but gone. In the gloom his ex-father-in-law's white shirt appeared to be moving eerily headless and limbless across the quarry towards him.

'I thought I'd find you here, Peter,' said the shirt when it was still a distance away.

'Colin. Time you got that bike fixed.'

'Yeah, well maybe it is,' he said, dismounting and leaning the old machine against the workshop. 'Time you were home, too, unless you're planning to sleep up here tonight. You had any food lately?'

'Chicken sandwich at lunchtime.'

Then a silence fell between the two men and they turned away from each other and looked to the heavens where a handful of stars winked through the heat haze. As the darkness deepened and their eyes grew accustomed to seeing, so the sequinned sky began to reveal itself.

'There's nothing to be said,' Peter Staples said at length, there being only one subject in both their minds.

'No, not that hasn't been said already,' said the grandfather.

'Spoken to Suzie?' He hardly ever used his ex-wife's name but he said it with as much grace as he could manage.

'No, she's away, on holiday, but I found out where, left a message for her.'

More stars appeared before Colin Deeley added, 'It wasn't her fault, Peter, it wasn't then and it isn't now.'

'Maybe not, maybe not. But you can't help thinking what if, can you?'

'You're not the only one, we all do that. And the older we are the further back it goes, you'll see one day. You'd both be better for speaking about it.'

'Maybe, maybe not.'

'Well, you would, and that's a fact. And here's another fact. If you start hiding up here again, keeping yourself away from people it'll do no good to anybody, especially you.'

9

It was late Tuesday morning before the minutes of the governors' meetings received any attention from those investigating the death of Melanie Staples. The real point of obtaining them had been to inconvenience the rector and send a few ripples through the cosy little world surrounding him. The investigators had nothing of the slightest substance on which to base any particular line of enquiry, so looking at the girl's school from a slightly different point of view seemed as good as anything else. A few ruffled feathers might prompt someone to say something they would regret, but it was little more than fishing.

Melanie's re-appearance had proved the main thrust of the original inquiry had been misguided, but little else. The forensic examination had revealed nothing that wasn't known or couldn't have been inferred from the circumstances of her re-appearance. The report was heavy on corroboration of everything already known about the girl in life - her health, her teeth, her clothes – but light on anything which might give any clues to her death. There were still a few test results to come, but they were unlikely to do more than confirm she had not been poisoned. The primary cause of her death and the circumstances of her burial remained highly suspicious but unknown. There wasn't even any evidence that the poor girl might have been deliberately killed.

Donald Smallborne had two priorities for the last day of work before his trip to South Africa. First was his expense claims. He'd failed to complete June's by the deadline and with his holiday starting tomorrow he certainly wasn't going to miss July's. Second, by a narrow margin, was handing over all his cases in as complete a manner as possible, either sideways or temporarily downwards in the chain of command. Another inspector would nominally take charge of the Staples case, but the only actions would be delegated to Constable Pitesteanu who would report daily to a sergeant. Handing over the papers and briefing the pair in the suffocating little office at the back of the mobile incident centre, he made it plain to both he didn't expect any progress and was candid about the chances of establishing the truth.

'We've upset a few people, we've stirred things round a little and poked our noses where they obviously aren't welcome, but the fact is that's all we've done. There's not a scrap of difference between what people recall now, and what they saw or thought they saw eleven years ago. And the sum of that is nothing at all, nothing of any interest. But somewhere, probably no more than a mile from where we're sitting, there's someone who buried her or knows who did and knows how and why she died and why it was kept quiet. And you'll notice I haven't used the 'm' word at all, accident or manslaughter are still as likely as anything else.

'The last presumably reliable witness to see the girl died herself last week so there's no testing her memory. And the second last was aged eleven at the time and was probably coached by his parents on what to say and what not to say. He's remembered everything he said and that's a bit odd, but not odd enough to see what can be made of it. There are bound to be people in the village who know more than they're telling, but whether what they know has anything to do with how she died is another matter. That boy is one of them, but his father is apparently untouchable and some of that has rubbed off on the son. He and his parents might have been pressed a bit harder than they were first time round if they hadn't all been sprinkled with magic dust from someone on high. That young man is a bit too good to be true, if you ask me.'

He looked at the constable in what he meant to be a meaningful way, a way intended to convey something like 'you looked as if you might fancy him but you'd better be careful if you think he might be a good catch because you might get your fingers burned, and remember you're in CID while he's a witness in a suspicious death.' But to Lavi Pitesteanu such subtlety of meaning was completely lost, instead she took it as an invitation to contribute to the assessment.

'Could there be a connection between Melanie Staples and the Eysha Duncan case, sir?'

'Yes, there could, of course there could. But what would you call a connection? Same village, yes, same school, yes, but that's no more than saying the same village. Circumstances similar but not the same, not by a long way. And for now at least, the Duncan girl's a missing person, although it's a pound to a penny the poor kid's drowned somewhere, while this is a suspicious death. What else?'

'Well, strictly speaking it's not the same,' added the sergeant, keen to contribute and not wishing to be upstaged by a female one rank and many years his junior, 'They're quite particular about being different villages, so in fact the Germans girl went missing in Whyncombe St. Giles, while the Whyncombe . . .'

'Thank you, sergeant, for that correction,' the chief inspector interrupted him, more than a little irritated, 'So, one less thing in common.'

'One less, but does it promote the school to being a common element?' ventured Lavi Pitesteanu.

'Probably, and all that goes with a school, teachers, parents, governors, dinner ladies and lollipop ladies too, for all I know. Which all take us back to saying same village.' He glared at the sergeant, daring him to suggest another pedantic correction, but he wisely chose to remain silent.

'There's nothing happened for eleven years then finding her might've been the break, but it wasn't and anyway, it doesn't look as if anyone's getting ready to flee the country,' he concluded, then with a little joke he'd been saving for just such a moment added, 'apart from me of course,' an attempt at humour which drew dutifully appreciative smiles from his meagre audience.

Once he'd gone, back to clear his desk in Oxford, the constable braved the rising heat of the day to walk purposefully around the village, obeying the order to not only be seen but to be seen in action. Anything was better than being in the oven of the incident centre, so she paused in the church for twenty minutes or so, her new-found cool spot. She saw nobody there or in the churchyard, but tucked round a corner not far from the gate she noticed a fresh dug grave, carefully marked off with yellow tape. Curiosity led her to take a closer look, although there was nothing to see but planks covering the hole and mats of artificial grass over the spoil. It was a well tended area yet with apparently no burials in recent years. There was hardly room to squeeze in an extra body and she wondered what might qualify someone to be interred there.

A closer look at the inscriptions gave her the answer, for there layeth the once great and good of the neighbourhood: Lisles, Lomaxes, Beaumonts, Radcliffes and their wives. Old power, the detective thought, how often it ran in families, little groups loosely aligned and intermarrying to protect their influence. It was the same the world over, she reflected, as she enjoyed the shade of the ancient yew, casting its benevolent shadow wide across the churchyard. With a little further thought she wondered if it was not just old power that was vested in these names but new power too. A little more discreet in its execution perhaps, less blatantly corrupt, but still wielding its influence, insidious tendrils still seeking to shape the lives of lesser folk.

When she returned from the church the carefully copied notes of the governors' deliberations were waiting for her. They'd been passed from hand to hand until they'd ended up in a new filing tray freshly marked with her misspelled name. Attached to the file was a note from the sergeant suggesting she check them to see if they were relevant. Her haste to obtain them on Sunday, the extra effort to be sure they were on her chief inspector's desk for Monday morning had been a waste, for the envelope was still sealed, his name in her distinctive backward sloping handwriting crossed through and hers written beneath it.

She'd skimmed through most of them as she'd copied them on Sunday when the rector had grudgingly handed them over and knew for the most part they would be a dry and uninteresting read. Even those intimately connected with a special subject find committee minutes excruciating. Those of the St. Germaine and St. Giles Church of England Primary School governors would have bored the two saints themselves. There were eight sets in all covering the four meetings for each of the two years, no more than twenty sheets in all. Each meeting was recorded in a formulaic way, the start being the clerical business of who was present, who'd sent apologies and rather pointedly who was absent without apology. For some reason it made Lavi Pitesteanu smile to see the name Colin Deeley invariably appearing in that section. He clearly lived up to his reputation as being something of a village character.

More clerical niceties opened and closed the record of each meeting, leaving the discussions sandwiched in between. And they made an extremely thin filling, little more than 'it was agreed that' and 'such and such was discussed'. Even the election of the chair and deputy each September was noted with no more than 'chairman and deputy re-elected.' No dissenting points of view were recorded, no record of who had contributed what, no discussion of budget priorities in allocating the slender resources at the governors' disposal. The subject of money was mentioned once each year with the line 'budget (see attached) approved after discussion'. It seemed to Lavi Pitesteanu that the governors should have taken no more than a few minutes to complete their business, since according to the record so little attention was given to each topic. And yet, apart from July's, each meeting started at seven o'clock and closed at precisely half past eight. The consistent time matched the length of the printed minutes, each just a page and a half, give or take a line or two.

From the eight meetings she learnt little more than who attended and who did not. Statements had been taken from all those present the day that Melanie Staples was last seen alive, and all except two had been re-interviewed in the last few days. Mary Radcliffe had gone to meet her maker and Frank Wheeler, the previous head, having retired now spent half the year completely incommunicado on a Greek island painting and sketching.

A more casual observer might easily have missed the references to confidential matters, for they were hidden where all secrets are best kept - in plain view. The last but one item in each set was the innocent note 'confidential items noted elsewhere: none': in each set that is except two where the entry read 'confidential items noted elsewhere: one'. Whether it was intentional misfiling or a little additional burying, the two extra sheets were the last pages of the bundle and appeared at first sight to be part of the budget annexes. They were filed in reverse order so the first she came to simply gave the date and stated 'SR65 travel costs from GBF after discussion.' The meeting in question was in the Spring following Melanie's disappearance. The second was for the previous year, also from the Spring meeting and was equally obtuse: 'Miss Stephens: payment from GBF after discussion, SR54 review by MG.'

There was no doubt the notes were deliberately obscure, but in itself that was hardly suspicious; they were, after all, intended to be confidential. But these notes were written in a naïve code, obscuring their meaning to all but those who understood the references. It seemed absurd that someone should go to such trouble over the trivial happenings in a country primary school. They appeared to be not so much a secret society as children playing at spies, yet these were supposedly responsible adults administering the education of the next generation. Some connection with the idea of spies or secret societies, a connection she could not quite identify, took the constable's thoughts to Thomas Samarasinghe.

The truth was she found it difficult to not think about him for more than an hour or so at a time. Apart from the apparent regularity with which he cropped up in relation to her work, he had all the attributes to make him re-appear in any healthy young female's thoughts. His good looks, sharp brain and obviously excellent prospects were augmented by a winning smile and a smooth athleticism of movement. But above all these, or perhaps as a combination of them, he had something very physical about him, almost animal; yet as an animal is unaware of the power it possesses, so was he. She found herself staring out from the cramped corner of the desk into the wilting green and pale blue of another blistering day in Whyncombe St. Giles, perspiration trickling down her neck, her thoughts straying to quite different ideas of investigation than were altogether appropriate.

The air conditioning unit, on maximum continuously for nearly five days, had stopped abruptly soon after ten and there was no prospect of repair or replacement. Lavi Pitesteanu needed to find some new reason to escape the building and inevitably the cool relief offered by the church came to mind, even though she'd already wasted enough time there. She could go back on the pretext of looking for the vicar or whatever he called himself and have him explain the schoolboy code in the governors' minutes. And once she'd cooled off if she didn't find him in the church, she might go to his house and make further enquiries there.

★

It is practically common knowledge that a standard part of any investigation into a missing child is the discrete monitoring of the immediate family's communications. At times this may be extended to checking on movements or embrace the wider family and friends. It usually requires few resources as for the most part it's no more than recording of phone calls or the interception of texts and emails. It's a process which can be maintained at minimal expense over a period of months or even years if necessary. It's dry stuff and rarely uncovers anything pertinent to the immediate inquiry although it has been known to throw interesting light on other matters.

For a couple of days the activities of Liam Duncan, the older of Laura's brothers, had attracted growing interest from those watching the family's communications. By Tuesday afternoon they had the prospect of a most appealing new line of enquiry, not one with much potential for locating poor Eysha, but one which might certainly enable them to settle a few scores with the Duncans.

Liam had a cousin who had a friend who knew a news reporter on the Oxford Times. Between Liam and the cousin they'd hatched a plan to sell an 'inside story' of Laura, Eysha and Eysha's father to the local press, and through them to a national newspaper with far deeper pockets and fewer scruples. They weren't stupid enough to be naming names, but they intended to provide enough detail, and paint a sufficiently lurid picture to ensure a handsome payout. At the same time they hoped to take a hefty swipe at the police efforts to find Eysha. It didn't occur to either of them they would at worst be confirming police suspicions of family complicity in Eysha's disappearance and at best be guilty of deception.

The scheme was doomed from the beginning. Not only did the two cousins overlook the possibility of their communications being less than secure, but crucially they misjudged the nature of the press and the worth of the story. Not once did they question whether their exposé would be believed or whether their contacts were reliable and discreet. And it never crossed their minds that if the scam were revealed and Liam were arrested, that in itself would be story enough for the media. Indeed, it would be a great improvement on some tired old gossip about who slept with who. A few minutes' serious thought would have told them 'Callous Uncle Exploits Missing Niece' would make a far better headline than one purporting to reveal his sister's sex life nearly twelve years previously.

But there were bigger gains to be made than simply selling a few more papers. The newspaper, having recently been disgraced for hacking into phones and interfering in other criminal cases, had spotted an opportunity to gain not only a headline but also some badly needed credit by taking the story to the police. Some cynics later proposed they did this only after a senior officer had told the paper's owner of the monitored conversations, and suggested that disclosure would help restore reputations. In return for this co-operation, the newspaper would also be given a front row seat for Liam's arrest.

The whole affair would do the police no harm either, since any lingering discontent with the manner and progress of the inquiry could more easily be rebutted or better still, refocused on the Duncans: little wonder that they had not found the girl while they were undermined and distracted by having to deal with her delinquent relatives.

At the house in Germans that Tuesday evening none of these plots and conspiracies had yet impinged upon the wretched state of the remaining occupants. Liam had gone off to his date with destiny in Malmaison, one of Oxford's swankier hotels which is, quite fittingly for the occasion, an innovative conversion from a former prison. His brother Aaron had stormed out of the house, roundly abusing his father for some mild rebuke he'd received for burning the carpet with a fallen cigarette. The carpet was already stained and scorched from years of abuse but it had been the potential for starting a fire that had caused the disagreement between father and son.

Kathy Duncan, driven to distraction by the oppressive heat, her worsening back pain and her idle husband, was in no mood to listen to the row between him and Aaron. No sooner had their son left than she turned on Alex and let him have both barrels of her anger and frustration. In itself this was not uncommon, but the gnawing ache of losing her Eysha, the Duncan's only grandchild, gave her tongue fresh venom. There was no ill that had befallen the family that wasn't her husband's sole responsibility, either through his actions or his lack of them. For his part, Alex Duncan had little doubt his wife had contributed largely to the anti-social behaviour of their wayward offspring since not only had she carelessly conceived them, but she'd failed in every respect to give them the care and attention which was their due. So far as he was concerned, it was pure luck that the social hadn't removed all of them years ago, or ill-luck in the case of *her* two sons. This was too much for Kathy who despite her sore back and her tears landed a fast right hook in the shallow hollow between nose and cheek, a little below her husband's left eye.

Alex Duncan may have been many of the things his wife accused him of being and probably more besides, but he was not a man to put his fist in a woman's face. Instead he covered his head and ducked away from the continuing onslaught, dripping blood from his nose across the kitchen floor. His wife pursued him, shouting obscenities at him, emphasising each point with an additional blow, battering him about his lowered head and shoulders until she ran out of steam.

The first strike was the bloodiest, despite the noise and force of her swinging arms they did little actual bodily harm. She stepped back, breathing heavily, her fists still clenched even though her

131

fury was all but spent, unsure of either her own or her husband's next move. A splash of his blood had stained her pink T-shirt and was merging darkly with the spreading patches of sweat. He lifted his head to check if another attack was coming. His left eye had already closed in a fat purple puff ball, blood and mucus ran from his nose and dripped down his neck to his shirt. At his feet the floor was splattered dark red, trodden over and turned to skid marks all round the corner where he'd stood.

Attracted by the volume and ferocity of the conflict, their daughter Laura stood in the doorway surveying the wreckage. Smashed glass, the dregs from a mug of tea, a torn and scattered packet of biscuits, had all joined her father's blood and her mother's sweat and been trodden into the grimy floor. For an instant as the three looked at one another, mother and father became the children, she the parent. A moment of stillness in an ocean of tumult, a moment which lasted longer than most, expanding to fill the whole of time before abruptly collapsing back on itself.

'You two got nothing fuckin' better to do?'

Her mother made as if to speak, her loosened fingers clenching into fists again. Laura's arms stayed folded across her chest but she stiffened a little, just enough body movement to say she would stand her ground. For once she held the upper hand, both physically and morally. She seemed to grow a fraction taller, as if she had acquired the dignity her parents had lost.

The tableau might have stayed frozen that way had her father not turned to the sink and splashed cold water onto his swollen face. Her mother set her jaw and lowered her eyes, brushing past Laura to the hallway, whispering something which might have been an apology on her way past. The girl herself took a deep breath and turned too, returning to the sofa and her cigarettes where once she might have sworn and stooped to clear the mess. A short time later she heard the sound of her father cleaning up and cursing as he did so and knew he'd suffered no lasting damage. A little after that her mother came down the stairs and put her head round the door.

'I'm going to your Auntie Wendy's. Call me,' she said, waving her phone, only to return a moment later. 'Love you,' and with that she was gone out the front door.

Laura drew another cigarette from the pack open on the table. It was damp before she touched it, wet from her fingers by the time she lit it. Even before her parents had descended from verbal abuse to physical attack it had been a truly terrible day. No one had called, no one had knocked, hardly a word had been spoken in the sweltering house. Even the police, despite earlier promises, had made no contact, and no ransom note - a fanciful notion she'd entertained when she'd woken that morning - had dropped through the letterbox. Her Eysha wasn't mentioned on the television, nor the radio so far as she knew. Nothing had happened at all, until her mother had blacked her father's eye.

Since the moment her girl had been missed, Laura Duncan had swung from anger to sorrow, from hope to grief. She'd cursed her for bunking off school, wept when Molly had run up with the plastic box and the rotting cheese sandwich her gran had made for her. She'd believed it when they'd said how she'd be found soon enough, safe at a friend's when all the commotion about the rain and the flooding had died down. She'd been bewildered but happy, yes unashamedly happy, when it turned out it was the Staples girl they'd found, not her Eysha. But now the pendulum of pain had come to rest at grief and sorrow. Today she knew beyond all possibility that Eysha was gone for ever. She just couldn't bear to hope she'd be safe and well, to hope her spiky, cheeky, disobedient, gorgeous girl would slip in by the back door with some stupid story about why she was late and how it wasn't her fault she'd lost her lunch box 'cos someone had nicked it. It was so much better to think she was gone for all time, to know she would never come back, than to dream of something different.

★

When Michael Radcliffe reached into his jacket for his lighter it was almost ten, the light still lingering in the western sky, edging northward before true darkness wrapped the land in its blanket. Warm and firm, smoothly rounded corners met his seeking fingers. Beside it, nestled in the pocket, was his packet of king-size. For a second or two he tested whether he could leave them there a little longer. Then he remembered that it hardly mattered, he was completely alone in his garden, apart from the friendly company of a glass of scotch. There was no one to frown or tut-tut if he had another cigarette or if he had another ten.

He'd stopped wondering where Mary was, whether she would be back soon or why she'd taken his car. He knew exactly where she was, where his car was and why neither would be returning.

133

The clouds of recent days had lifted and clarity had returned to his memory, despite one or two blanks. And after all, who didn't have the odd blank? What he recalled, he recalled accurately, and the gaps were really quite small. He knew not only the last few days, but the last months and years too. He could go further back, way back into his childhood or he could be in his twenties again, the prime of his life although it never felt like it at the time.

And now that he was alone again, he could do as he pleased, when he pleased. He took out his cigarettes and lighter and weighed them a little in his hand, anticipating the small pleasure to come. Something was not quite right, the weight was wrong. The pack was down to the last two, an emergency in the making. Instantly the anticipated pleasures evaporated, the friendly scotch was forgotten, anxiety overtook him, his body now craving the drug more than ever. Nothing increases demand so much as lack of supply. His desk drawer was empty, he was sure it was empty, he'd checked earlier, made a note to restock. He sprung up from his comfy seat by the French window and in a second he was by his desk, the top drawer pulled wide again, rummaging through the collected minor debris of the last thirty years. There were no cigarettes, not even a stale one to go with the assorted books of matches that made a little gazetteer of a certain period in his life.

His watch showed three minutes past ten, three minutes since Chris Rogers had closed his shop not more than a hundred yards from The Glebe House, three minutes since the petrol station up on the main road had turned out the lights. Two cigarettes to last him until when, until seven when the service station opened, until seven-thirty for the shop? The hours between three minutes past ten and early morning seemed to stretch into infinity. Who could he call on at this time of day? The rector would still be up but probably have none to give him. There were others who would have a few spare, but who, who could he call on?

After a few moments' thought he found there was not a single soul whose doorbell he could ring and ask for a cigarette.

He could drive further, to the motorway perhaps or Oxford or Banbury, somewhere open twenty-four hours. He could drive further if he'd put fuel in Mary's car, but he hadn't, so it would stay where she'd left it. Almost casually he thought how it was probably no longer Mary's car, it was probably his car. How long would it keep its pristine cleanliness, its new-car smell despite being more than two years old? How long before the never opened ash-tray would receive its first grey sprinkling, its first stubbed butt? Stubbed butts! He had more than enough of those, he could be rescued by today's dog-ends. He rarely smoked down to the filter tip, put all together there was probably another smoke or even two to be recovered from the sand box on the patio.

He sat again and leaned over to pull each of the filter ends from the dust to see what might qualify for a second lighting. As he did so, some peculiarity in his posture, some oddity of the stretch over the arm of the chair caused an unfamiliar pressure against his left breast. He put his hand to the top pocket, never used so far as he'd been aware, and felt a squashed cardboard packet. Amazingly and quite delightfully, when he withdrew it he saw at once it was a ten-pack of cigarettes, a little crumpled and flattened and only three left in it, but a little miracle, a wonderful gift. Fleetingly he glanced towards the hidden bulk of St. Giles, as if he might catch sight of the departing angel who'd answered his prayer, but there was none to be glimpsed. Someone else's jacket then? As much chance of that as an angel in the parish church, and yet these cigarettes could not possibly be his, not his brand and 'lite' as well, so someone had given them to him. Who would give him cigarettes, and in tens, who bought tens? Perhaps he'd picked them up, found them where they'd been carelessly dropped. He simply couldn't remember ever having seen them before. They were damp too, but then what wasn't damp, in that house or the whole village? Examining the pack more closely he saw smudged felt-tip writing. It could have been 'mine' or 'mums' or even just a squiggle.

No matter about any of that, they were exactly what was needed. Now, with a total of five available, he could happily enjoy one immediately without the awful knowledge of the next one being the last one. The time between flipping the lighter and the shop opening suddenly shrank from far longer than two cigarettes to less than five. He sank back into the comfort of his chair and brushed the collection of dog-ends back into the sand box, wondering why he'd pulled them out. The silver lighter flipped and flamed, deeply he inhaled the unfamiliar smoke of the new brand, exhaling it steadily into the clammy night air. Tomorrow he would buy fresh supplies and attend his wife's funeral.

★

In the sticky heat of the night there was no respite from earthly cares, or heavenly ones come to that. Prayer would not lower the temperature, nor lessen the humidity. It might, at best, improve Philip Fox-Lomax's ability to cope with both, in much the same way as he relied on it to cope with his wife. He would've been the first to admit his prayers were not always answered, although he would never have blamed his God for this, rather the selfish nature of the prayer, or the weakness of the supplicant.

Through the still air the metallic scrape of chair on stone carried to him and he guessed that his neighbour was still in his garden. Knowing that, and knowing he'd be sitting drinking and smoking, the rector fancied he could catch a hint of tobacco in the air, and perhaps a few molecules of whiskey had been liberated from the glass and found their way through his bedroom window. Both compounded his inability to sleep, both served only to conjure unwanted images in his mind.

The two houses were hardly close, such houses were never close, but they were nearest neighbours, not counting those at eternal rest in the graveyard. The plot which the Radcliffes occupied had once been part of the church lands, like the rectory itself, but it had been given away a couple of hundred years ago to a local worthy as a reward for some service or silence. It had changed hands many times in the intervening period, but almost always through death and inheritance, which was how the present occupants had come to be resident. Over the centuries the church had reason to be grateful to its neighbours for gifts and deeds both large and small. As a result, successive generations had regarded the church, and by church they meant the ministers of the church from the bishop downwards, as being permanently indebted to them. The Radcliffes were no different to those who'd gone before them, St. Giles was their church, not just by membership, but through tradition and habit, by ownership. The rector was their priest and servant, as he was to all his parishioners, but some, like the Radcliffes, put more emphasis on the latter than the former, which was a different thing altogether.

He'd performed his various duties regarding both Mary and Michael over the years, some more difficult than others but he'd never wavered, never flinched from taking what he saw as the path of righteousness. Soon he would be performing the latest of those duties, conducting the burial service for Mary, a duty to her certainly, but also to Michael. For many, perhaps most of his parishioners, that would be the last demand they could place on him, to give them a decent burial. But for a few, including the

Radcliffes, his duties went beyond the grave for he was required to include them in his private prayers and, on certain days, his public prayers also. Duty and conviction also forbade him from breaking certain confidences given in life but which endured beyond the grave.

No matter how arduous they might be, those duties and convictions were not normally the things that kept him awake at night. If anything, they were the things which offered him the deep and peaceful slumber of those who are certain of their faith. The crumbling fabric of the church and more recently the rectory itself, those things kept him awake; his wife and all her mischief - the word evil always wanted to insert itself in this context but he resolutely refused to use it, even silently - those things also kept him awake; the wretched heat, the suffocating humidity, they kept him awake at night, along with many others.

And in a peculiar way the absence of pyjamas also kept him awake on these terrible nights. For Philip Fox-Lomax, and probably the majority of his countrymen, nakedness, even semi-nakedness, in a bedroom was inextricably linked to sex. In the bathroom it was about washing, privately and avoiding sight of oneself in a mirror, but in a bedroom there was simply no other reason to be without clothes of some kind. That was another of his wife's unfortunate habits, to sleep with far too little on. He was almost certain at that very moment she would be lying on her bed, sheets tossed aside and not a stitch of clothing covering her body. She had probably worn nothing in bed for months, perhaps years. She simply had no modesty. And here was he, struggling to stay dry enough and cool enough to sleep yet supremely uncomfortable wearing nothing but his boxer shorts, the same shorts Acantha once derided as hiding little but ideal since they had so little to hide. She had a wicked way with her, yet even as he thought such a thing he felt guilty for condemning her so. Even if he was more charitable, there was no denying her tongue was as sharp and quick as a flick knife.

As was so often the case, all his distresses, from the heat and leaking roofs right through to the lack of pyjamas, they all distilled into the torture his wife applied each day. No matter what he said or did, no matter what penance he'd performed, she simply had no forgiveness in her.

10

It rained again. It started in a small way, just a few spots streaking the windows, a few drops darkening the earth, a few rippling circles on garden ponds and ornamental lakes. As if to mark the passing of a week, the skies over Germans and Whyncombe St. Giles darkened again. One minute it was blue and blazing, the countryside grimly braced for another day in the oven; the next, a grey veil, thickening, darkening by the second, formed over the land. Residents from each side of the combe, from the highest to the lowest, young and old alike looked to the clouds with apprehension.

The roofers on the parish church stopped roofing, the bin collectors stopped their collecting, the insurance assessors stopped counting; all turned their faces to the heavens and wondered. The customers in Chris Rogers' shop ceased their chattering, the children paddling in the muddy bottom of the combe hushed each other as the drops splatted on the leaves of Centenary Wood, the librarian closed the skylight she'd forgotten a week ago; all held their breaths and hoped. One or two sent silent prayers, but none smiled, none spoke, not a sound was heard across the twin villages but the pit and pat of raindrops.

Up at High Whyn the farmer was in the barn with the vet checking the condition of a sick ewe. They looked at each other for a moment, uncertain as to what the noise could be, more like a sudden wind through trees than anything else, then as recognition dawned, they quickly abandoned the sheep and stood in the entrance to watch the scattering of drops caught like jewels in the last glimmers of the clouded sun. They were mesmerised, Pacific islanders watching their first snowflakes, not that there was any joy or amusement on their faces. John Westerleigh wondered what new horrors would unfold from such gentle beginnings, what further curse might be inflicted on his life.

The other side of the combe, way up where the farmer once courted a village girl who was said by his friends to be out of his league, three members of the Samarasinghe family looked out of

138

the bedroom window of the youngest. Their faces were expressionless, eyes darting here and there straining to catch where the rain was falling on each roof, each driveway and path they could see from their vantage point. Across the road their neighbour's house remained as the flash flood had left it, a brown tide mark still evident, the garage door sagging and crumpled by the weight of the roof it supported after part of a wall had crumbled and collapsed. The owners remained on holiday in the Seychelles, unaware - and presumably blissfully so.

In Maiden Quarry, Peter Staples worked on, oblivious to the change in the atmosphere. He'd resolved to catch up on all the calls and orders he'd let drift and he'd been cutting and shaping stone since seven. Even when the compressor paused from driving his tools, his earplugs prevented him hearing the little drum-roll of droplets on his tin roof. The tunnel vision of his goggles blinded him to the splashes of dust kicked up on the quarry floor.

In the larger of the two cottages at Six Lanes, Colin Deeley saw the streaks on his windows and thought not of the pleasures he'd enjoyed with Margery Webster when last it had rained, but rather the consequences of that deluge. Knowing his little Melanie's fate, knowing she would soon be finally put to rest once and for all, these were not the consolations he'd once expected them to be. Ignorance had been far better than the resurrection of pain and the extinction of faint hope. There'd be more tears to come on Saturday when her mother returned, more explaining to be done as the story was retold. There'd be more anger like his anger, more recriminations over misguided searches and wasted time, more indignation and accusations over old mistakes. It could rain till doomsday so far as he was concerned.

Acantha Fox-Lomax paused in dressing for her date with an exercise machine at the gym. It was not so much the sound of rain for there was no more than a whisper, neither was it the hiding of the sun for the grey veil had thickened almost imperceptibly. Instead it was the absence of sound, the lack of shadow that made her look from the bedroom window. Her husband was in the middle of his short commute from home to office by way of the door between rectory garden and churchyard. He was always striding, he never walked anywhere, he always strode with his black cassock flapping in his wake. It was one of those tiny irritations which over the years had grown out of all proportion to become one of his defining and unbearable characteristics. Wherever he went he always walked in that dramatic way as if trying to show purpose and direction when there was no purpose at all, no business or urgency to attend to. That, and to make his cassock flutter about his ankles, a reminder to one and all that he wore his badges of office both on and off duty. She so despised him, so loathed his cant, so hated herself for once having thought she might love him, yet remained in their deadly embrace long after she knew better. A few drops of rain held nothing more for the rector's wife than the potential to add to damage already done and thereby distress her husband still further.

From the kitchen window of The Chequers, Alan Miller looked out at all the work needed to restore the garden and car park. It wasn't that it was so great a task, nor too expensive, but it was beyond his own abilities for now and maybe the whole summer. The crutches and the plaster-cast made it impossible to do more than hobble about and serve a few pints. He would need help to even get the pub open again, never mind fix all that needed fixing. But if he didn't open the doors in the next day or so there would be no business left. The broken tables, fallen walls, they were all insured and replaceable, but he had nothing to cover loss of business. As it was, the disaster tourists had already left, warned off by police and a few angry residents and disappointed in the scale of the damage, the absence of corpses. As if to remind him of the cause of his troubles, the sky had clouded and the rain had started the moment the ambulance had deposited him at his front door. There wasn't much damage, he'd known roughly what to expect by reports from the loyal Colin Deeley, but getting it all organised, recruiting some full-time help, maybe even replacing his kitchen maid-of-all-trades Kathy Duncan, it was all a little daunting. The broken bone, the immobility, the forced reliance on others had all taken their toll on his confidence. Quite suddenly he'd seen a far older man in the mirror than the one who'd cheerfully run The Chequers just seven days ago.

As the rain briefly quickened, the solitary occupant of The Glebe House looked up from his long-cold bacon and sausage at the streaks slanting across his kitchen window. He glanced at his watch and wondered if it was a passing shower or set for the day. It didn't seem right to have a funeral in bright sunshine, a grey sheet of slanting drizzle would be so much more appropriate to the event. He had a few hours to ready himself, get his face set right, get the words in the right order to say 'how kind of you' or 'thank you for coming'. The first task of the day had gone smoothly enough, he'd slipped into the shop a few seconds after Chris Rogers had flipped his little sign from closed to open. The usual king-size, Michael Radcliffe's constant companion for twenty years, were out of stock, but luckily the angel's gift of last night made choosing an alternative all the easier. As a token of gratitude to the makers of those three little miracles, he bought a hundred more, and was delighted to note they cost him a good deal less than usual.

The few little drops of rain falling on the main street in Germans brought the same reactions as elsewhere in the twin villages, the same apart from the Duncans' troubled house where they went completely unnoticed. Neither Aaron nor Liam had returned from the previous night's adventures. Aaron was still sulking in his girlfriend's bed ten doors along the street, while Liam enjoyed what he confidently expected to be the first fruits of his journalistic coup by staying in Malmaison, all expenses paid. Laura's mother had not returned from her sister's and had no intention of doing so. Which left Laura and her father still clinging to the wreckage. Alex Duncan was on his hands and knees washing the kitchen floor, hardly his usual position but he'd complied willingly enough with his daughter's prompting. Laura tidied the front room, emptied ash-trays and vacuumed with a surprising energy. Neither father nor daughter heard or saw the rain.

As if to tease the watchers and the worriers, the shower momentarily intensified before ceasing completely, leaving nothing more than damp steamy roads and streaky windscreens. In a few minutes the grey veil was drawn back and briefly the air smelled sweet and fresh, a reminder of different times for all who breathed it. Visitors and residents alike turned back to the business of their days and allowed themselves a smile or two before the damp evaporated, dust again kicked up with each car that passed and a familiar stink returned to Whyncombe St. Giles and Germans.

★

'Hello,' said a friendly voice.

'Oh, hello,' Lavi Pitesteanu replied, surprised to hear a greeting from anyone in the twin villages, and pleased it was Thomas Samarasinghe, although the last place she'd expected to meet him was the dentist's waiting room, such was the healthy pinkness of his gums, the whiteness of his teeth.

The instinctive pleasure of contact was quickly replaced with a shared awkwardness. For Thomas she reminded him of his criminal secrets, a burden he'd carried so lightly for so long but which had weighed so heavy since Saturday. And who did not feel guilty of some offence, real or imagined, in the presence of a policeman? For the constable, she remembered she was on duty, and more, she was making enquiries which might involve him. Worse still, those enquiries might even implicate him in some obscure way she couldn't yet imagine.

'Check up? Or something worse?' she said, in the way that acquaintances might when they have no interest in either the answers or a deeper conversation.

'Wisdom teeth,' he said, looking anywhere but directly at her, 'An X-ray last week, a plan of action today.' The awkwardness continued into a silence until he remembered his manners and returned the enquiry, 'And you?'

'Business.'

'Oh, I see.'

The silence fell round them again before the muffled but unmistakable whine of a high speed dental drill reached them. Each felt the need to look at the other, engage in some exchange more meaningful than a waiting-room platitude, yet each had their reasons not to. Eyes lowered they searched desperately for a subject until inspiration struck them both at the same moment.

'Did you . . .?' and after an exchange of awkward smiles, 'No, after you,' he said.

'Thank you, did you say you had an X-ray last week?'

'Yes, why?'

'I didn't remember you mentioning it. Did you see anyone else here, waiting like we are now?'

He thought about this, wondering what significance it might have, trying to remember who or what he might have seen that morning.

'I don't know. It was the day it rained and I can't remember much before the rain started. I think I was first here at eight o'clock. There was a delay for some reason, I was seen about ten past. It only takes a few minutes to have it taken. Then I went home and had some breakfast. A little later the rain started. I don't know what else to say.'

'Was anyone else here?'

'I don't remember. Wait, yes I think so. When I left I think there was someone else in here, sitting in here. There was something, a movement, a voice, I don't know, I just went out past the door.'

They both looked up as one of the staff, anonymous behind the frosted glass of the door, moved down the little corridor between the reception desk and the treatment rooms.

'Like that, except it was me going down the corridor. Maybe the door was open a crack, maybe there was someone else here, maybe I'm imagining it, I don't really know,' he concluded, then added quickly, 'but why don't you ask them, surely they will know who had appointments and so on?'

'As I said, business.'

Which is where she should have left it, but she felt the same urge to keep the conversation going, to keep him engaged, as she had done that first day in his house. It had been the missing Eysha Duncan that took her there whereas now she had Melanie Staples in mind. Seeing him here once again linked the two girls, linked them through him and perhaps also through the dentist.

'Do you remember way back, the day Melanie disappeared, did you come to the dentist that day, Thomas?' She'd not meant to use his name like that, and quite involuntarily her voice had acquired the slightly patronising tone of an adult encouraging a child. She had an eleven year-old girl in her head along with the girl's eleven year-old friend and the images confused her speech. Hugely embarrassed and blushing fiercely she quickly apologised, 'I'm so sorry, I didn't mean to say that, it came out all wrong, Mr Samarasinghe, I don't know what I was thinking of.'

He was highly amused by her discomfort. A smile briefly lit up his face, banishing the hangdog expression he'd worn all day. 'It is nothing! Call me Thomas, of course,' but to be sure the trade was fair he added, 'and I will have to call you something in return, something other than Constable Pitesteanu.'

The precise pronunciation of her name, a rare enough event especially from one who'd heard it no more than twice, surprised her. For a moment she wondered, hoped a little, he might have practised it as she had done with his. Immediately she saw it was a foolish notion, he wouldn't have done any such thing, he simply had an excellent memory and a quick mind to match it. Now she was caught between the personal and the professional and it was all her own fault. Could she risk a hint of something more by reference to off-duty names or should she simply reinforce the apology and leave it at that? Rescue from her dilemma came in the form of the dental nurse, who at that moment called Thomas to his appointment.

'Mr Samasingee,' she said, 'please come through.'

The near-miss with the sound of his name was not lost on either the constable or the witness.

★

The reflection looking back from his bedroom mirror did not altogether displease Michael Radcliffe. Despite a grey pallor to his skin, he looked well enough. He had a certain roundness of face that went with generous helpings and was exaggerated by an evenly receded hair line, but the overall impression was not too bad for a man in his sixty-seventh year. And yet there was something slightly troubling about his appearance. It wasn't his shirt or tie, both carefully chosen for the day, and it wasn't that he'd forgotten to shave or had toothpaste on his chin. The troubling thing to Michael Radcliffe was that the man in the mirror looked slightly, well, he would hardly have believed it possible, but the only word he could find was unfamiliar. It was certainly him, no doubt about it, he wasn't going mad or anything like that, he hadn't forgotten what a mirror was. No, it was more that he hadn't remembered how he looked and, on what might turn out to be a difficult day, that was an odd way to think of yourself.

He was also slightly troubled by exactly what else to wear. He had only to walk a few yards to the church, and then walk back again when it was over, but it didn't feel quite right to go in his jacket, and he could hardly go in his shirt-sleeves. He had plenty of suits, a whole wardrobe of suits, all pressed and covered and neatly lined up like a tailor's rail, but Mary had usually directed which one was appropriate for a particular occasion. Quite possibly there was a suit whose only purpose was to be worn at funerals, if only he could be bothered to look through them all and see which one it was. He was almost sure that the suit she'd previously selected

144

was one with false pockets in the jacket, something which annoyed him intensely and which gave him nowhere to put his smokes. And thinking of them made him want one.

The new brand's garish red and yellow packet was subtly inferior to the stylish perpetual gold of the old favourites. It had sharper corner's, opened less smoothly, and he'd already found it less resistant to being squashed in his pocket. They were an altogether cheaper product, but these minor irritations could be addressed if he started using his old cigarette case again, and as a bonus it would fit slimly into the pocket of a suit jacket. It had been years since he'd last used it, but he knew exactly where to lay his hand on it. In last night's desperate search for cigarettes he'd seen it at the back of his desk drawer. It was another old friend that matched his lighter and for the moment he couldn't think why it had fallen out of favour. It only took ten cigarettes so perhaps it was because it needed such frequent topping up, but for special occasions it was ideal. He could remember having it when he and Mary would go out to dine or to the theatre, and as he took it from the drawer its silver smoothness was at once reassuring.

He chose the first dark suit he came across and was mildly surprised how easily he got into it. For a few years he'd been outgrowing his clothes and now here he was fitting easily into something from at least two years back. When he tested the slimline cigarette case it too slipped easily into its place in the jacket pocket. He inspected himself again. Perhaps that was why the image he saw was only half remembered, perhaps he cut a slimmer figure. Mary had always been there to advise on the shirt, the tie, the shoes, so he'd had little use for a mirror apart from shaving. Shoes. Yes, they would need improving. He would probably need his best black ones and they'd need a shine.

When he was satisfied with his clothes and the fresh polish there was still an hour before the service. He remembered he needed to fill the cigarette case, and while he was about it he would fill the silver lighter too. He patted his pocket, reacquainting himself with their shapes under the fabric. Then he slipped his hand in, fingertips exploring the soft warmth of the metal, the roundness of the corners. Everything felt exactly right, it would be so much better than the sharp edged card of the new brand. As he tried to open the case, instead of flipping up as he expected, the lid stuck. He pressed the little silver button again and eased it open with a fingernail. To his surprise it was not empty. The dried remains of four once-wet cigarettes were embedded in the congealed stickiness of two old-fashioned boiled sweets. No wonder he'd stopped using the case, but he couldn't imagine why he would have left it in such a state. The thought crossed his mind that despite its apparent familiarity it might not be his case at all, but one he'd found, or maybe it was very similar to one he'd once owned. He examined it closely to see if there were initials engraved on it but found none. From the smudged marks he could see the cigarettes were his previous golden favourites. Whatever the answer might be, it was not something he felt like sorting out now, he would clean it out another time.

As he was putting the case back, letting his fingers linger on it just a little, the doorbell rang. He started at the interruption, quickly shutting the drawer as if he'd been caught with his hand in the till. Through the glass of the inner door he saw it was the Westerleighs come to call. He looked at them a little quizzically before opening it, they were unexpected callers and he couldn't guess their motive.

'Hello, Michael. How are you getting along?' Margaret Westerleigh asked, as gently as she knew how.

'Er, fine, fine,' he replied, not exactly sure what she was talking about.

'Are you alright? You look a bit wobbly, you'd better get back inside and have a sit down. Did you have some breakfast?'

'Eh? Yes, had a bite or two. Didn't feel up to much.'

John Westerleigh had more than once found himself cast as Michael Radcliffe's friend and supporter, mainly through the closeness of their wives. The two men had little in common beyond their church, the school and their standing in the community. Their paths crossed frequently but without adding depth to their friendship. So far as their wives were concerned the closeness was all on Margaret's side with precious little being returned from Mary Radcliffe. Mary didn't do closeness like Margaret did, Mary did efficiency, Mary did businesslike, Mary did functional. Where Margaret did a little hug and a peck on the cheek as a greeting, Mary did a stiffened back, a turned cheek and pursed but unkissing lips. But in fairness to that recently deceased lady, she did all those things well and, had she been able, she would probably have acknowledged Margaret as the nearest thing she had to a friend.

The two guided an unprotesting Michael Radcliffe back into the house and eased him into an armchair, exchanging looks between themselves and wondering if he was like this already, how would he get through the funeral. But with a few moments to recover his senses and light a cigarette, the widower rallied.

'That's better, a little unsteady just then. Good of you to call round, I think we're all set for the off.'

'Good, I'm sure it's not been easy,' Margaret said encouragingly.

Easy? Once he'd got his bearings it had been easy enough, so easy he couldn't think what all the fuss was about. He had only to be, he had no need to do or to think, that was all being done by other people. The day had been arranged with little input from him, all he'd had to do was nod and sign his name. Between the rector, the undertaker and Margaret Westerleigh, everything had been taken care of.

'No, it's been fine, just fine.'

'I'll bring the food in, Michael, I'll leave it covered but get it set out ready,' she said.

'Yes, get it all done now. But I hope you haven't done too much, I don't expect many will come back.'

'Can I open a few windows?'

The house was no longer how Mary would have wished it to be, nor how her friend wished it to be on her behalf. In the space of a week the perfect neatness, the unsullied freshness, the spotless cleanliness had all been lost under a layer of ash and casual neglect. From the disaster area of the kitchen a widening circle of discarded crockery and newspaper was spreading through the house, as mould spreads outwards from the initial point of infection. To add insult to the defacement of Mary Radcliffe's pristine home, ashtrays overflowed beside sticky abandoned glasses. The farmer's wife set to work clearing and cleaning as best she could. Whenever the opportunity presented itself she opened cupboards to put things back in their place, opened drawers to check where best to put the silver cutlery. And although this was entirely practical and essential in the process of restoring a little of Mary Radcliffe's pride, it also provided an excuse to peer into the private spaces of The Glebe House. In part it was that special curiosity about another's home, more pronounced between females than their spouses, but it was also a chance to know her friend better, to be that much closer, to lay extra claim to a special friendship. In exploring the closed nooks and crannies of the house she might be able to share a secret or two that would make her Mary's true confidante. In life Mary Radcliffe would never have allowed such an intrusion; in death she had no say in the matter. When curiosity was sufficiently satisfied and tidiness sufficiently restored, Margaret Westerleigh returned to her husband and Michael Radcliffe in the garden.

'It'll do for now, Michael,' she said, preparing the way for a future browse through cabinets and wardrobes. Mid-way through the cleaning and tidying she'd realised that she could have free run of the house any time she liked, she had only to offer her help to cook a meal or wash some clothes and she would be admitted freely. She could help with the sorting out and disposal of all Mary's clothes, her books, her jewellery, her make-up. And in providing that small service she might even be offered some recompense, be invited to take a little trinket as a keepsake of her special friend.

★

'I thought you would be going, I thought we'd all be going.'

'Why should we go? We hardly knew her, we hardly know Mr Radcliffe,' Upeksha Samarasinghe complained to her son.

'I think everybody else will be going.'

'We are not everybody else.'

A sudden vision of his father dressed in a dark suit with black tie and white shirt came to Thomas. He couldn't think of any occasion from which he might have dragged such an image but it prompted him to say something quite out of character.

'I think father would want us to go,' he said stiffly.

A false authority had crept into his voice, along with a formality his mother had never heard from him before. She looked at him a little puzzled, wondering what might make him speak in such a way. As a wise parent she chose not to confront his assertion, but to adapt it to her own position.

'I think your father, your Tatta,' she said, gently reminding him of his more usual and informal reference, 'might go to Mrs Radcliffe's funeral, and we might accompany him. It would be quite right for him to go, as a man of standing he would feel it his duty, and it might be expected of him.' She paused to let the idea take root, lead her son to his own conclusion. 'But that would be for him to choose.'

'Then perhaps I should go to represent him.'

148

'Perhaps you should, but that is also for him to decide who represents him. I do not think it is something you should do without asking him and I doubt he would be pleased with a phone call so early in his day.'

Thomas scowled and chose a different point of argument. 'What did you mean when you said we are not everybody else?'

His mother looked away from him, back to her magazine before answering peevishly, 'I meant that we do not do things simply because other people do them.'

'You meant more than that,' he said flatly, a detached statement of fact rather than a rebuke.

Again her son surprised her with the coolness of his tone, a tone not unlike the one her husband sometimes used and which both Thomas and Diana had been known to mimic in good humour when they thought he couldn't hear them. Now she heard it again but without the humour. A tiny gap had appeared between her and her son, like a cold draught in a cosy room. She took her eye from the page to study him. In the last few days the smile had come less readily to his face, there was a dullness to his eyes and almost an indifference in his responses.

'I did mean a little more than that,' she said. 'but it's true, we do not do things just because everyone else is doing them, and you should remember that.'

'Yes, Amma, I'm sorry,' the hard edge left his voice as a son's affection re-appeared.

'Yes, Thomas. But neither are we like everyone else. We are not always as welcome as you might think. We have done well here, there's never been any real trouble, we have found our place here and that place is a fine place, a happy place. But we are not from here, we will never be from here, we will always be from Lanka. Or worse.'

'And does Tatta feel like that? He always seems to belong here.'

'Your Tatta is different. In a way he does belong here, his heart has always been here, but he has never really done much living here, if you understand. He has always had his work which takes him away. When he is here he plays a full part, he does everything necessary but then he is off again. It is not quite the same. It is like you going away to school, going away to university. Now you will be going to London and another life there. When you are here you do everything, it is your home, but it is not the same. You haven't really lived here for very long. And Tatta has always known when to step back and say nothing, he has the sense to know when and where he's wanted or not wanted. That's a very valuable thing to know in a new country. Which is something else you would do well to remember.'

Thomas was a little taken aback by this blunt assessment of their life in Whyncombe St. Giles and would have protested had the truth of it not been immediately apparent. His own vague feelings of insecurity were at once crystallized by his mother's astute comment.

'Is that why you don't want to go to Mrs Radcliffe's funeral?'

'It is not want to go or not want to go. It is a village thing, they are all village people, and if not this village then the next one. We are from away. It is not an event for us. People would look and say to themselves "what are they doing here?" They will not see us in the street tomorrow and say "why weren't they there?" And before you say anything, Thomas, yes, Clarence might well go if he were not in California.'

'So you think I'd . . . '

'I think you must make your own decision. You will be away again soon, then it will not matter what people think or say. You will be finding your place in another country.'

He began to protest that London was hardly another country before he grasped the meaning of his mother's words and smiled at his own naïvety. A few minutes previously he'd expected to go to a funeral, expected to be part of the mourning congregation as a matter of duty. Now it might be his duty to stay away, to step back and say nothing even though his father might do the opposite. He'd been ready to take his father's place, walk and talk with other men of standing in the community, now his own place might be elsewhere.

'When you said there had never been any trouble, was there something while I was away, I don't remember anything, perhaps I was too young.'

Upeksha Samarasinghe knew exactly what she'd said and hoped her beautiful and clever son, the soon-to-be lawyer, might not have picked up on it. But since it was becoming a day for truths, she would answer him truthfully, even though doing so would take them back to the unmentionable subject of Melanie Staples.

'We were still settling in, Diana had a very difficult time for a while at her school, although you seemed to fit in right away. Your Tatta was very happy you were getting on so well. Then there was

the business we spoke about, the problem with Melanie Staples.'
She paused to see if he would contradict her veto on further
discussion of stealing chocolate, but he simply nodded. 'Then she
disappeared and nobody knew anything or saw anything. Except
you.' She looked him in the eye, testing his reaction, but saw
nothing but dullness beneath the drooping lids.

'I can remember how worried you were about it all.'

'I was worried, I didn't know how these things would be dealt
with here, what the police might do. Of course, Clarence was not
concerned, he spoke with some people through work and the
police left us alone after that.'

'Is that all? Is that the trouble you spoke of?'

'No, it cast a shadow over everything, over the whole family.
People would look away, step across the road rather than speak to
me. The police thought we'd done something, I think they let that
idea go round the village. You were away at your new school, so
was your sister and your Tatta spent most of his time in
Cheltenham. That was another reason people were suspicious,
your father's work, they didn't know what he did.'

'I still don't, although I can guess at some of it.'

'Most of the time I was here on my own. It was not comfortable.
Then a year or so later something changed or it was long enough
that people forgot their suspicions and one by one people came
round to speaking again. The rector started it. It was his Christian
duty, but I'm grateful to him.'

Some thought, some idea, some fleeting image momentarily
connected the rector and Melanie Staples. It joined all the other
thoughts about her which had been jumbled in Thomas' mind
since the brief interview with his father. For the briefest moment
he could smell the fruit, feel the gritty stone scratch his legs as they
crawled along the wall between the rectory and The Glebe House,
giggling and shushing each other as they went.

'Do you remember anything now about all that, about the girl,
about what happened, what you saw?'

His mother was asking him about a different time but the two
momentarily fused. 'We didn't see anything, we were hiding in the
trees.'

'In the trees? When was that? You have never said anything
about hiding in the trees before.'

'No, not then, I was just remembering something about
Melanie. You know what happened, you know what I saw, it is

151

what I have always said, I left her in the combe and ran home in the rain. I don't really remember any of it, but I know it is what we said, we went over it. I can remember the police station and the green paint and the little glass blocks that made up the window in the room we sat in, but I can't actually remember seeing Melanie at all. But I know I must have done.

'There have been a few things I've thought about recently, things about Melanie, things we did together. I hadn't really forgotten them, just hadn't thought about them for a long time. I keep thinking about how much we laughed. Sometimes we laughed so much it hurt.'

'But nothing about the day?'

'No, should I? Are there things I should remember, things you know about, things I saw?' His voice rose as he spoke, anxious to know and anxious not to know. He stopped himself from going further, from pressing his mother with another question that popped horribly into his head, the question of whether he had forgotten not only what he had seen but what he had done. He had barely come to terms with the awful knowledge that their thieving was an open secret, the prospect of uncovering additional crimes was almost too much to contemplate.

'If you don't know, don't remember, then none of it is important. It is like your Tatta said, it was all a long time ago.'

'Amma, Amma, what is it, what happened? Tell me please, tell me even if it is awful, terrible.' His voice was pleading, child-like, all trace of the earlier aloofness gone. Then he blurted out his darkest fear, the nightmare question only a mother might hear, 'Did I do something, something to Melanie? Was there an accident? How could I forget such things?'

'No, no, Thomas, you did nothing, what could you have done?' Upeksha Samarasinghe was shocked her son should even think such a thing was possible. 'Of course you did nothing, I would have known, I would have seen it in your face if you had lied about anything. No, it was as you said, you ran home in the rain, you were dripping wet, you left her and came running home.'

'Then what is it I don't remember, did I see something, see someone?'

'Yes, you saw many people, you saw cars, you saw dogs, you heard this and that and many things and all of it is all forgotten. And not just by you, but by everyone else also. There is no reason to remember the trivial little things of a day. But you have always seen things and remembered things more than most people see and it was true that day. When we asked you later what and who you had seen and where and when you reeled off a whole list of people, some you knew and some you didn't, children and grown-ups. It seemed you saw half the village that day.'

A huge sense of relief swelled up from his stomach, filling his whole body, swamping all other thought and feeling at his mother's words. He hadn't forgotten anything of importance at all, he hadn't done anything, or left anything undone, he hadn't hurt or harmed his friend. Above all he had no new crime to repent. Then a niggling idea wormed its way into his thoughts.

'So what are we talking about?' Then before his mother could speak he had the answer himself, 'Why didn't we tell the police all these things, why didn't my great list of people and dogs and cars get passed on to them? Or did it? Was there something I told you, something I thought nothing of that you thought important, important enough to . . . to what?' The pleading child had disappeared again, pushed aside by the man suddenly freed from the burden of guilt.

'Have I not already said to you, have you heard nothing I've told you?' his mother responded. 'Did you hear me say what a valuable thing it is in a foreign country to know when to speak and when to step back and say nothing? We showed you how to do that, to step back and say nothing of who you'd seen where and when. Now it has all been lost in time and time has shown that it made no difference to anything. And do not ask me what was forgotten because like you, I have forgotten too, I forgot it the moment you said it.'

He fell silent, digesting this new revelation about not only himself but his parents. So much for truth, so much for honesty. Fleetingly he saw himself aged eleven again, felt the rain hammering down as he ran up the track, out on to the lane and turned for home into Lisle Gate beside the dental surgery.

'Amma, did I go to the dentist that day?' he said abruptly.

His mother frowned and shook her head. 'That day? I don't know, perhaps. Why do you ask?'

★

Considering it was the holiday season and the distance that the close family - if cousins, nieces and nephews can be called close - would have to travel in suffocating heat, it was what most people thought of as a good turnout. Mary Radcliffe had been by several years the youngest of a family of five and her two surviving sisters were confined to nursing homes where it was thought unwise for them to leave the safety of air conditioning. Two nieces, two nephews and two distant cousins represented her family while from the Radcliffes there was only her husband and her brother-in-law Andrew.

After the service, this little band, augmented by the Westerleighs, gathered round the open grave, while the undertaker's men held the coffin poised on purple straps ready to lower it into the ground. Standing a little further back and tiered by its own notions of importance were the rest of the congregation. Furthest away were those who'd no particular reason to be there but didn't want to miss anything. They hovered near the gate in the deepest shade of the yew, ready for a fast exit and to be first at the trough for food and drink in The Glebe House, a building into which they'd never previously been invited.

Nearer to the burial party stood the various volunteers, charity workers and acquaintances who'd had the privilege at one time or another to be under Mary Radcliffe's command in one of her guises as secretary or chairperson of village, district and county affairs. A select few of this group had previously been admitted to the inner sanctum and were looking forward to taking tea in the company of at least one Sir, a Lady and their member of parliament.

Closer still were the representatives of the various councils and commissions who perceived they owed Mary Radcliffe a debt of attendance at her funeral. Some wore their chains of office, some their uniforms or insignia which caused them great discomfort in the blistering sun. Since they were so close to the actual committal it was inappropriate for hats or caps to be worn and several balding pates quickly began to burn. A move to the shade involved stepping down a tier in the social order, something that for some was difficult to contemplate even if the alternative was being boiled alive. A few had taken the precaution of bringing their golfing umbrellas and stood slightly smugly in their exclusive shade. The front rank of this group contained the great and the good from both village and county and included such luminaries as the chief constable and Lady Stoner.

Peter Staples and his ex-father-in-law Colin Deeley, along with Acantha Fox-Lomax formed an uncomfortable buffer between the titled ranks to their rear and the untitled clustered round the grave. The rector's wife saw little contradiction between the fact that she hardly ever spoke to her neighbour and yet was attending her funeral. Apart from anything else it gave her a chance to people-watch, one of her more innocent pleasures. Melanie's father and grandfather were both grimly conscious of another funeral still to come, one that would need a far smaller coffin. Standing in a group of one, yet attempting to appear inconspicuous, was Lavi Pitesteanu, who'd felt she should be present to underline her commitment, yet had regretted every moment of being there, despite the cool respite afforded by forty minutes in the church.

Philip Fox-Lomax reached the point at which the coffin might be lowered and signalled to the pallbearers to begin the final descent. ' . . . we therefore commit her body to the ground, earth to earth, ashes to ashes, dust to dust, trusting in the mercy of Almighty God, to whom we shall all give an account.' As he spoke the final phrase his eye fell first on Michael Radcliffe and then, since she was standing in the same line of sight, his wife. If he had not remembered where he was and what he was doing he might have allowed himself a small smile at the appropriateness of the words. The purple straps slid through gloved hands and the polished oak disappeared from view until it rested in the cold clay.

Throughout the proceedings, during which various tributes had been paid to the deceased, Michael Radcliffe had but two things on his mind. One was the number of minutes that must pass before his next cigarette. The other was what exact state of decay his wife's body had reached. It had been a recurring fascination in the week since she'd been pulled waterlogged and lifeless from his car and he'd seen her beatific corpse in the mortuary. He'd mused on the details of temperature and humidity and what extra precautions might be taken by the funeral directors in such hot weather. As he stood by the grave waiting for the last act, he had a fear that her body would start to smell under the sun's unwavering blast. To see it descend, to know that it was going into the cool darkness was a great relief to him. The pre-occupation with flesh and decay acted as a distraction from the details of the occasion so that to a casual observer he had an air of detached serenity quite unjustified by the workings of his mind. To those who looked more closely he cut a forlorn figure, a shrinking man in a baggy suit, incessantly twiddling the lighter in his jacket pocket.

11

'You've heard about Liam?'

Vicki Gardner burst through the back door of the Duncan house a little after eight o'clock, desperate to be the bearer of the news of Liam's arrest, desperate that just for once she might know something her friend didn't know. She didn't hold out much hope, but she was in luck. Laura Duncan looked up from the bowl of cornflakes she'd been dolefully prodding. Breakfast of any kind was not a regular feature of her life, but she'd risen and dressed early and on impulse poured herself the cereal. Some sixth sense may have warned her that she would need a breakfast to help see her through the day. As unusual as the cornflakes were the blank screens on each of the five televisions in the house. In normal times the kitchen and sitting room were treated to all the digital world had to offer twenty-four hours of every day, the sound often muted, the channel often changed, but the off button rarely pressed. The whole family might be asleep in their beds - or someone else's - but the flickering screens never slept. Until last night, when Laura had turned off everything in the house, even her phone, and sat still and silent long after her father had gone to bed.

'What's he been up to now?'

'He was on the telly, arrested in some hotel in Oxford, there was cameras there and everything, they said it was . . .' she paused, uncertain how to complete her story. She'd been so full of the news, so keen to be the one to tell, she'd not thought for a moment what she was going to say to her friend.

'That's all we bleedin' need.' She pushed the bowl away and reached for her cigarettes. 'If he's been doing herbs again Mum'll go mental. When was this then?'

Vicki took the opportunity of lighting her own cigarette to delay further comment, exaggerating the need to have it lit perfectly and drawing deeply before venturing, 'This morning, I'm pretty sure it was this morning, about seven I think.'

'They'll be round here soon then, turning the place upside down.'

As the bearer of bad news, Vicki was conscious that she'd not yet told the worst part and was keen that any anger was directed where it most belonged. 'Bastards,' she said with feeling.

'Yeah.'

'See, the thing is, Lor,' she eyed her friend carefully, 'the thing is I don't know if it was maybe something else this time, might not be leaf or that.'

Laura Duncan had known her friend too long to mistake the slightly plaintive, wheedling tone that frequently preceded some little request or confession, but today she'd let her squirm a little longer, see how long it took her. 'Yeah, whatever,' she said with complete disinterest.

'No, see, the thing is, Lor,' Vicki tried again and found a little inspiration, 'they never said it was, you know, smokes and stuff. It might've been, but they do that stuff everyday don't they, and it's not on TV, is it?'

No, thought Laura, it's not. Her friend had a point. Cameras, TV news, Oxford hotel, they all added up to more than a few packets of a class B drug. She rounded on Vicki, took a step towards her so the girl flinched in anticipation of the blow to come. 'What's he done? Come on you stupid cow, tell me. What's he done?'

Cowering, eyes lowered in submission, Vicki could only manage a single word. 'Eysha,' she whispered, then a little louder in case she'd not been heard, 'Eysha, it was something about Eysha.'

No blow came. Laura was stopped in her tracks, stunned there could be a connection between her lost daughter and her brother's arrest. Unless Vicki Gardner had got it all wrong, which was quite possible. 'Are you pissing about? 'Cos if you are, Vicki Gardner, I will kill you,' she said, slowly and deliberately so there would be no doubt she meant it.

'No, no, honest, Lor, honest, they said something about Eysha, "helping with enquiries into the disappearance of his niece Eysha Duncan" they said, honest they did,' she wailed, her mouth puckering and tears starting in her eyes. 'There was someone else they took too, a cousin I think, I forget who.'

Without speaking Laura turned and flicked on the TV, skipping through channels until she found News-24 which was showing pictures of a train crash in China. Then she turned on her phone to check for any messages. 'Watch this and call me,' she directed Vicki, pointing at the Chinese carnage. On the big plasma screen in the lounge she tuned to Sky, which had the same pictures of the smashed train and littered bodies. Then she called up the stairs to her father.

When Sky had shown enough mangled Chinese corpses - 'no British casualties' - it turned to things closer to home with a poor quality picture of Liam Duncan behind the caption 'UNCLE OF MISSING GIRL ARRESTED'. Laura didn't recognise the picture, which had the look of a still from a mobile phone sequence. Then the report cut to a voice over some footage from the road by Oxford Castle, by the old prison, saying how two men had been arrested, both related to the missing girl, and both in connection with investigations into her disappearance.

'Dad, come down here,' Laura yelled again.

Vicki Gardner was standing half in and half out of the room, uncertain whether she should still be in fear of her life or had been forgiven. On the screen two figures, both handcuffed to uniformed police, were hustled out of the glass doors of the hotel into waiting vehicles. In the background a battery of cameras could be seen, along with a posse of extra police. To fill out the whole report the thirty seconds of footage was repeated three times in quick succession, culminating in a still from last Sunday showing Liam shaking hands with the chief constable in the village hall. A big operation, performed in clear view, planned and timed to catch the morning news, orchestrated with the press and TV in mind. No accusations were made, the men were assisting with enquiries, but the implications were hardly concealed: the two were heavily involved in Eysha's disappearance, had possibly abducted her for their own perverted reasons and were trying to obtain money for information as to where she might be found. There followed an interview with a prominent Oxford academic about how it was frequently not strangers who presented a danger to children, but members of their own families.

Laura tapped another button and the news item was replayed. As Liam emerged from Malmaison she slowed it to single frames until she came to one that showed his face clearly, full of anger and looking straight at the camera lens. She played the little snatch a couple more times, straining to hear what he was saying, reading his lips. All he seemed to be saying was 'No'.

Alex Duncan, dishevelled in string vest and baggy boxer shorts, pushed his way past the hovering Vicki Gardner. Father and daughter looked at each other for a moment then he took her wordlessly in his arms. It might have been months or years since he'd done so, in recent times all such hugs and kisses had been reserved for his granddaughter, now in Eysha's absence Laura resumed her place from childhood.

'I saw it upstairs. He'll not have done anything, not the stuff their talking about.'

'No, I know.'

'But they'll have fitted him up for it, have him trussed up like a turkey.'

★

As mid-day approached, Alan Miller looked forward anxiously to the prospect of re-opening The Chequers. Very little was how it should be but almost everything was just about good enough. He would be able to provide those two summer essentials of an English pub, ice-cold lager and tepid beer. A half-a-dozen tables with umbrellas to shelter from the sun had been arranged at the front of the pub, so places to sit and smoke were also available. Food would be restricted to packaged snacks since the kitchen was out of action, not through malfunction but lack of staff. There'd been no word from Kathy Duncan and once he'd been told of the latest turmoil in that household he'd abandoned hope of seeing her. Finding a replacement would not be easy, although someone had mentioned one of the Gardners as a likely candidate.

Colin Deeley had been a great support, working many hours the previous day and late into the evening to get the place ready. His neighbour from up on the hill, John Westerleigh, had come down about five with his tractor and levelled the track round to the back of the pub, then he'd cleared half the car park of rubble in a fraction of the time it would have taken with a shovel and wheelbarrow. Not that Alan could use either, handicapped as he was by his plaster cast.

As the appointed time approached the landlord propped himself up behind the bar with all the most likely drinks set up within reach. His friend Colin, who also happened to be his best customer, had happily volunteered to fetch and carry as required. As a first job, he took out the chalkboard and set it up on the edge of the grass by the road. He wrote 'WE'RE OPEN AGAIN!' in big white letters and stood back to admire his handiwork. Across the road the school was deserted. Down the lane towards his cottage nothing stirred. Along towards the houses of Germans and beyond to Whyncombe St. Giles he could see no movement. Over the little valley towards the row of cottages where Peter Staples lived and above that the new houses of Lisle Orchard, he couldn't see another soul. The whole scene was completely still, as if worn down by its sorrows and finally exhausted by the relentless sun. A film of dust covered everything. Plants not washed away in the deluge, drooped in the heat.

He couldn't resist turning to look up at Whyncombe Wood and the scar that cut through it. The gash so dark and raw a few days previously, had baked dry and pale, all moisture scorched from the new surface, all colour sucked from the stone. His Melanie had been somewhere up there all these years, looking down on all that happened in the pub, in her school, across this little fold in the land and far beyond. She would have seen him come and go a good few times, seen her friends grow and leave for college or brighter lights or greener grass while she stayed cold and still. She'd have seen her Mum leave the cottage, seen her Dad walk his lonely path and bury himself in the quarry. Then she'd been washed right down to almost where he stood and he'd gone right past the spot and hadn't a clue what was going on, he'd never thought it could be his Melanie's bones they were sifting soil for. On Saturday Suzie would be back to hear it all, live it all again, know this and that and everything there was to know, everything he couldn't tell her, everything he couldn't talk about on a bad line to Havana.

No bird sang, no breeze rustled the trees, even the various renovations to the flooded homes were silent. The whole country might have been abandoned for all he knew. In the few minutes since writing the sign every living thing might have been wiped from the face of the earth. He was reminded of an old black-and-white film he'd recently yawned through, something called *On The Beach,* an apocalyptic vision of deserted countryside after a nuclear war. Those who weren't killed saw the end coming and took their own lives. Perhaps he'd fallen asleep watching it and he'd wake soon to the old world, the world of a laughing grandchild, of cucumber sandwiches and Sunday cricket between the showers in a green and pleasant land.

A single distant sound penetrated his depressing reverie, the muffled buzz from the cooling unit in the little beer cellar beneath The Chequers. It reminded him there was still a life to be lived, and how thirsty his work and the end of the world had made him.

★

The decision to withdraw the mobile incident centre from Whyncombe St. Giles was greeted with unashamed joy by those officers who remained in attendance. The office was good for only one thing - to demonstrate a police presence. It was poorly equipped even after a week of operation, still with only a single working internet connection installed, and had been positioned at the worst possible place for radio communications. But what made it truly unworkable was the lack of insulation. When deployed in winter months it required constant and expensive heating while in a normal summer air conditioning was certainly desirable. But this was no normal summer and air conditioning was essential. Since the broken unit had yet to be repaired, it was simply too hot to stay inside once it was past ten o'clock.

It was two in the afternoon when Lavi Pitesteanu received the happy news. Her sergeant, who had escaped to the comparative luxury of the station in St. Aldates, called to confirm the rumour and to say she would be working from a desk in Banbury as from tomorrow. With the exception of one consideration, the change of location came as a relief. Being adopted by the chief inspector as a new favourite had been an opportunity she'd happily seized, but with his absence and little expectation of progress, the Staples enquiry was fast becoming a cul-de-sac. If she was not careful she would find herself as the only one assigned to the case, with little to do and retained purely as window dressing in an out-of-favour backwater. Back in Banbury, better still if it were Oxford, she could find ways to get involved in other cases, look for other sponsors and patrons.

The one negative aspect of leaving Whyncombe St. Giles could be summed up in two words: Thomas Samarasinghe. She remained caught in the eternal dilemma between duty and desire, and where a clearer sense of one or other might have resolved the problem, she couldn't satisfactorily define either. She would simply wait and see which pulled the hardest, she still had one more excuse to speak with him and that might decide the matter. She might arrange to see him tomorrow, depending on what progress, if any, she made with her two outstanding queries. The coded items of the governor's minutes remained a mystery, something she hoped to resolve with the rector shortly, and the dentist might have some information for her by the end of the day.

161

Aside from those, and the formality of a new statement from Melanie's mother when she returned, the detective could see nothing for her to do at the new desk in Banbury.

Rumour had reached her of the Eysha Duncan enquiry also being wound down under cover of some trouble with the girl's uncle. There was simply no sign of her, she'd vanished as surely as Melanie Staples had vanished, yet beyond that sad similarity and the location, there was nothing to link the two cases. And a gap of eleven years hardly suggested a serial killer. In fact nobody was suggesting a killer of any kind, certainly not for Eysha, who officially remained as missing during a once-in-a-thousand-year rainstorm. Melanie may have been killed, but might have suffered some accident, admittedly in unusual circumstances. Certainly a crime was committed, even such a burial was a crime, and when a young girl disappears there are few who don't think immediately of abuse in one form or another.

Dropping in to the church had become a daily, sometimes twice daily event. Along with the chance of seeing the rector it provided a few minutes of blessed cool air. It also had the advantage of appearing as if she was doing her job as directed and a chance to order her thoughts. Now she really did want to see the rector she hesitated at the gate by the yew. Another quiet sit in the holy shade or straight to business at the rectory?

The shade won, and she entered the churchyard close to where she'd watched Mary Radcliffe lowered to her final rest. It had been an uncomfortable mistake, but at least those present, in particular her chief constable, knew she was still on the job. The grave was marked by a mound of earth and a half-dozen wreaths. She paused to see which had been selected for the honour. Predictably, Michael Radcliffe's tribute remained in place, along with those from the rector and his wife and other neighbours and friends like the Westerleighs. Of those sent by mayors and their councils, by knights and their ladies, none remained. In their stead was a little posy with a note attached saying how all other floral tributes had been placed in the church where visitors were welcome to view them.

While she was bending down to read the cards, the gate squeaked opened again, followed by urgent footsteps along the path under the yew.

'She's here every day, everywhere I look there she is, even at the funeral yesterday. Most people probably didn't know who she was, but it was embarrassing. I've no idea what she expects to gain from hanging around.' The rector sounded weary and frustrated, but his voice was distinctive, despite being little more than a loud whisper. He was evidently using a mobile phone for the next voice was also his, 'No, not yet.' Then he seemed to respond to some assurance he'd received. 'Tomorrow?' but the rest was lost as his purposeful steps took him away from his accidental eavesdropper.

Her crouching position was threatening to cramp her calves but the constable sunk even lower. Unless the rector turned and looked directly at her he'd have no reason to see her. She was sure the complaint must have been about her, but to whom? She disliked the man, Donald Smallborne had been right about him, and it gave her satisfaction to know she'd upset him by sitting in his church a few times and attending a funeral. The pompous fool, did he think he was above being asked simple questions about his precious school committee? She heard him open and close the side door of the church and slowly and painfully raised herself from the crouch until she was sure she wouldn't be seen.

There was good reason to follow him into the church, ask him the meaning of the cryptic initials in the governors' papers, but she drew back from doing so. A little more thought before the interview might be repaid with some fresh insight. She might even wait until tomorrow when it seemed he expected to be rid of her irritating presence. An alternative course presented itself: knowing well that he was in the church, she could call at the rectory and double the annoyance. As she turned back towards the gate she met Margaret Westerleigh coming in. They exchanged smiles by way of recognition and it seemed to the constable that her presence would shortly be reported to Fox-Lomax. So much the better. Now there was no need to call at the rectory, she could save that for another day.

★

By evening the whole world knew that Liam Duncan had tried to sell his story to a newspaper. Exactly what story was not quite clear but it probably involved the abduction of his niece by a cousin or some other accomplice. And since the whereabouts of the girl remained a mystery, the world was told hope for finding her alive was fading with every hour that passed. Although the world was told these things there remained some who did not altogether believe what they were told. The Duncan household certainly kept their miserable faith in Liam, but they might have been surprised to learn of another family, in the last house on the right of Upper Orchard, who were also sceptical of the version of events being promoted by the evening news.

Upeksha Samarasinghe summed up the feelings of herself and her two children with a simple question: 'Is he clever enough to do all that?' Hardly a ringing endorsement, but it was a pertinent question and accurate observation.

'Yes, allegedly,' replied her morose son, who'd spent much of the day trying to bring forward the move into his new apartment in Southwark.

'Well, I doubt it,' said his mother shaking her head and missing the finer point of language.

'Thomas, you're being horrible,' scolded his sister Diana, ever willing to be the little mummy.

'No, I am not. I'm being precise, which is quite another thing.'

'Well, you're being horribly precise.'

'Stop please,' their mother requested, 'I am too tired for this silly talk today. You both think you are so clever.'

The three fell back to silent viewing, sharing the fascination of seeing places they knew, faces they recognised, but each with their own particular reasons for watching. Diana added a professional broadcaster's perspective, her mother found the possibility of such sins utterly compulsive, while Thomas felt somehow responsible for all the ills of the parish. His own perceived shortcomings, compounded by discovering those of his parents, had brought him to a new low. Such was the depressive effect that he wallowed in reports of fresh offences and new crimes, taking some aspect of them all upon his own shoulders, finding equality with abductors and abusers. The news faded into the all too predictable weather forecast.

'Not a word about your Melanie,' Diana commented dismissively, hoping either the tone or words might draw out her brother.

'I've said before, she's not my Melanie, she never was. If she was ever anybody's, she was her father's and her mother's.'

'Too precise. You know what I mean.'

Their mother sent them both warning looks over the top of her glasses.

'Yes, I know what you mean. Perhaps she was my Melanie, I don't really know any more. She was my friend, or I thought she was. Now I can't even be sure of that. I don't remember what I should remember, and what I do remember may not be true at all, it may only be what I learned to remember.' He was half talking to his sister, half to himself. His mother heard well enough but chose to be deaf.

'Do you think you knew something? Something about how she died?'

'I may have done, but now I don't know whether I did or not.'

'You remembered how much you used to laugh, the fun you had, you said that when you were telling them last week.'

'That's different, I know that was true, like I know other things were true, I remember plenty of things like that, just not the little details of that day. Amma knew things I never knew, and she has forgotten them too, haven't you Amma? But you've chosen to forget them.' It was no accusation, simply a dejected statement.

Neither his sister nor his Amma had ever heard him sound so miserable, so totally desolate. His mother, knowing something of what had brought him to this point of despair, still thought it a great over-reaction to long-forgotten events. She had only to look around at her fine home and fine children, had only to consider the prosperous and successful eleven years they had spent in Whyncombe St. Giles to know the course she and B W C Samarasinghe had chosen was the right course.

'We did what was best for everyone,' she said, abruptly rising to leave them. 'You were children, you knew nothing of what was best. I will not listen to all this nonsense again.'

'What's the great secret, Amma?' Diana called after her mother. 'Thomas, what happened? Come on, this isn't fair talking like this when you both know a secret and I don't.' An appeal to fairness sometimes bent Thomas to her will.

'The great secret is . . . ' theatrically he spread his arms wide as if opening a magician's cloak, 'Ta da! There is no great secret! Or if there is, we have all forgotten it!'

'You're talking nonsense.'

'The truth? Amma and Tatta decided that I should stick to the plain and simple facts about the day Melanie disappeared, that I should leave out all the little details of who and when and where, leave out the trivia of the day, the trivia I was so clever at remembering. And having told them all those details, they have also forgotten them. So nobody knows if there was anything important to tell. There is no secret.'

'Doesn't sound like a big deal to me.'

From the bottom of the stairs where she had paused on her journey to bed, Upeksha Samarasinghe allowed herself a small smile and a nod of the head. Of her two children, both her favourite in their different ways, Diana momentarily took pride of place. She at least understood immediately how things were decided for the best.

'There is a piece missing and I may have had that piece and I lost it,' Thomas said, and in saying everything slipped into focus. That was it, plain and simple, all in one sentence. Reduced to this level it became manageable, something he might in time come to live with. Now if he could only do the same with the other childhood crimes they too might become manageable, forever regretted, but ultimately accepted.

'Is that it, is that what's made you so miserable? No wonder Amma is unhappy with you.' She paused a moment as another thought came to her, a recollection of something more recent than eleven years. 'Is it what Tatta said on Saturday, something about chocolate and your Melanie?'

The idea of confession to atone for his sins had already come to Thomas in the sweaty, restless small hours of the night, now the same idea recurred. He had considered the girl detective, she might listen and advise, or even Chris Rogers, the man whose chocolate he'd systematically stolen, he might forgive, even after all this time. But what greater penance could he perform than to confess to his sister. She would certainly make him pay in one way or another, punish him with reminders for years to come, punish him more severely than he had the courage to punish himself.

'Yes, in a way,' he began.

Diana said nothing, waited with delicious anticipation while he summoned the last ounce of courage needed to tell her about the plans, the thrills, the sweet tastes of chocolate and of successful thieving. And when he'd told her those secrets, he told her how they came to stop their thievery and how terrible it had been to discover after all these years that his Tatta and Amma knew all about it, as did half the village.

'Is that all? You took a few chocolate bars and someone told Tatta?' Diana was utterly scornful of his confession, his soul-searching anguish. 'You're lucky nothing more was made of it, especially as we're incomers, and brown incomers too, but it's not exactly crime of the century, is it?'

'You think it is nothing? The embarrassment, the shame, you think it is nothing?' he cried, foiled in his search for punishment and forgiveness, meeting only with derision.

'You're upset that Tatta and Amma knew, knew their golden boy Thomas was just like everyone else and would steal a chocolate bar.'

'What do you mean, everyone else?'

'Oh, do grow up, little brother. You are so clever, so quick, so observant, but you know nothing, see nothing. In all your time at school, didn't you ever know anyone else steal things? From shops or friends?'

Thomas was shocked at his sister's suggestion, dumbly he shook his head.

'Well, you must have lived in a bubble.'

She drew closer to him, lowered her voice a little and told him lurid tales of crime and immorality rife amongst her school friends, tales which would have instantly lost her mother's favour had she stayed at the foot of the stairs.

'And did you do these things too?' he asked, wide eyed.

'Do you think I would tell you if I had?' she laughed, then, more seriously she said, 'It is nothing, forget it, you were ten, a child doing childish things.'

'Amma said the same as you. Well, not the same, but she said to forget it all. Now I don't know what to do.'

'Perhaps you'd better go with Amma to confession one day.'

'Confession? Where?'

'Where? In the church of course, where do people usually go for confession? Go and confess your sins to our creepy vicar.'

'I didn't know about that. Amma goes to confession, here, at the church here?'

'Yes, here. Maybe she doesn't any more but she told me about it once. There's a special time or service or something.'

Thomas had stopped listening, all he could see was the green curtain with the gold embroidery by the organ in St. Giles, all he could feel was the hard stone in his back while he and Melanie went purple trying to hold their breaths to stop laughing. Confessions. They'd listened to confessions.

★

It was a little before midnight at High Whyn Farm. John and Margaret Westerleigh had been in bed more than an hour and neither were sleeping, although they were pretending to do so. Both lay still and breathed softly with the gentle rhythms of sleep, and both guessed the other lay awake. A single sheet covered them, although even that was too much under the black roof of the old house, where the heat was trapped all day with no relief until an hour before the sun rose again. But a single sheet preserved the modesty they'd never been able to overcome in their many years of marriage. A single sheet was insurance against a nightdress that rode up too high on a restless night, or the revealing fly of pyjama trousers. Though they both lay in their own trickles of sweat and their own pools of guilt and anxiety, neither dared move lest the silent spell be broken.

Despite sharing a bed, it seemed to them both it was no more than a place to lay their heads, a place to sleep if they were lucky. The whole house was a place to live and function as best they could, no longer a home they'd made and cared for. Wider than that, the farm had become a place of grinding toil and little else, no longer a rewarding return for honest labour. Into this misery the sun had poured its unwavering heat day after day with the single exception of the day of rain, the day of new disasters and old horrors. It was a cruel irony that the Great Deluge had brought them physically closer than they had been for months, maybe years, as they'd clung near drowned to each other while the lagoon and half the hillside had cascaded through the woods.

John Westerleigh was angry. The focus of this anger changed day by day, hour by hour. It often rested on his wife, but was as likely to fall on a sick animal. He would be angry with the animal for being sick, just as he would be angry with his wife for being his wife. He was angry with the heat, the unalterable, endless heat that magnified every task, every disagreeable action, until it needed ten times the energy. He was angry with himself for being so easily prevailed upon by the school, the church, his neighbours - yet he never failed them, never complained or refused. He was angry with Melanie Staples for being dead, for waiting all these years to be found and then to be found by him. He was angry with the sheep that slid into the bucket in that fat heavy way and splayed its legs as it hit the bottom.

He was angry with himself that he hadn't said more about the girl when he'd had the chance, hadn't told what little he knew, even if it had nothing to do with her lying in a shallow grave for a decade or more. When they'd asked for anything at all about her,

168

he could have said how she came to the farm sometimes, how he told her more than once not to smoke in the barn. He could have said how she looked at him, half smirking, and it seemed as if she knew something he didn't. He could have said how she stole sweets and cigarettes but got away with it, how she spoke so badly of her mother. He was angry that he'd thought it better to say nothing in case it was irrelevant, or he was wrong, or it upset the balance of the way things were. He was angry with her when she was alive and he'd thought it better to keep that anger to himself. He was angry now that he'd probably do the same again.

He'd thought about Laura Duncan's girl all through the day, ever since he'd pulled on clean overalls and found the still damp but legible list of pupils on the expedition to the study centre. Not recognising it for what it was, he'd carefully unfolded the paper out of curiosity before realisation struck. He'd have preferred ignorance, but it was too late by the time his eye had been drawn to Eysha Duncan's blurred but unmistakable name, third on the list. He'd prayed there was nothing he could say about her, nothing he knew of her stealing or smoking, cheating or lying. It was his only prayer to be answered. He truly knew nothing at all about Eysha which could be of any possible interest to anybody.

Margaret Westerleigh had her own anger to deal with. Unlike her husband she was not angry with her life and everything in it. She was angry with him. She'd become increasingly confused, isolated, rejected and many other negative things for a while, but anger had been confined to the usual annoyances of life, a flash here or there and quickly followed by remorse. All her life Margaret had been encouraged to believe she was a worthless sinner. First by zealous and strict parents and then by a zealous and strict priest. Even now, the ever-willing Philip Fox-Lomax, for all he emphasised her many positive attributes, held steadfast to the concept of sin. Some sins amounted to less than others and could more easily be forgiven, but they were still sins. Margaret's new-found anger had been born the moment she discovered her husband hadn't told her Mary Radcliffe was dead. All her other angers had coalesced round that hard seed and fed on each other, even though she knew such anger was sinful. It was as if that event, that omission, had been a critical turning point, trivial in itself when seen in the great sweep of life, it nonetheless marked the moment when she set a new course. She was less generous, less forgiving, and wilfully so. A meanness of spirit was creeping in to take the place of openness and humility, trust usurped by cynicism.

To this sleepless brew of resentment and anxiety the afternoon had added fresh turmoil to her life. The Margaret of ten days ago would have declined the offer to rummage through her friend's belongings, been a little offended by the very idea that she might take any pleasure in doing so, even though there would have been some guilty truth in it. The Margaret lying silently sweating at half past midnight was confused and a little angry with her dead friend, puzzled that Mary could have presented one face to the world - and what a face, a face that chaired a thousand committees - while keeping another face hidden in the private places of The Glebe House. Margaret felt cheated of her friendship when only yesterday she'd thought she might get closer to Mary, might become her extra special friend even after death, now she realised how distant she would always be. On the scale of criminality the discovery had been nothing much beyond petty larceny, but finding Mary's collection of shoes had been both shocking and disgusting.

At first Margaret had simply been a little surprised that Mary would have so many pairs, and of so many different styles, all boxed up yet nearly all well used. But as she opened box after box it dawned on her that they were different sizes and not pairs at all but single shoes. Almost all were simply the left foot of the pair. Only when she recognised one of her own long-lost shoes, a moccasin whose right-foot partner she had stubbornly refused to dispose of, did the real meaning of the collection slowly dawn on her. Mary collected other people's shoes. Almost all were women's or children's shoes, and to judge by the styles some dated back decades. Amongst the sandals, slippers, high heels, boots and trainers Margaret also recognised some that wouldn't have been out of place in her grandmother's house. Mary had been collecting for years. A shoe here, another there, perhaps one from every house she'd visited. And who would ever think of a single shoe being stolen by anyone, certainly not by Mary Radcliffe. No, just as Margaret herself had done, the victims would assume they'd lost the shoe, thrown it out by accident or tucked it in a cupboard and couldn't find it. Robbery would simply not have been considered.

She was at a complete loss as to what to do with the shoes or the knowledge. Michael Radcliffe had been glad of her offer to start sorting his wife's clothes and given her free run of the bedroom.

The shoe collection had been right there, all neatly stacked in the walk-in wardrobe. He'd said to take what she wanted, do whatever she thought best with whatever she didn't want, a charity shop, a jumble sale, anything to have them gone. In the end she'd done nothing but roughly box them all up again after sitting surrounded by tissue paper and left foot shoes opening just one more box in fascinated horror.

She'd left her own moccasin there too, uncertain whether after the years that had passed she wanted it back, whether she'd ever be able to wear it again without the discomforting thought of Mary Radcliffe stealing it. And having stolen it, what else might the woman have done with it? Margaret Westerleigh's imagination strayed to places it had never been before.

12

It had been a long time since Peter Staples had been up in the scrubby growth bordering the edge of the quarry. He had no reason to go there, up between the fence and the crumbling edge that dropped fifty feet, in places sheer, in others over tumbled rocks, to the dusty floor where he spent most of his time. He'd taken a grim satisfaction from watching the policeman struggle through the brambles looking for the poor Duncan girl a week ago, now it was his turn to curse the undergrowth. At least he'd thought to bring his machete to hack his way through to the fence. Most likely kids playing, he'd thought, broken a few planks and squeezed through to run dares on the edge of the rocky drop. His neighbour had seen something up there a day or two back and thought best to mention it. 'You wouldn't want some fool claiming against you for a broken neck,' she'd said and she was right, he wouldn't.

He almost missed the break in the fence, so carefully had the planks been replaced. A few branches had been roughly dragged across to hide the opening, but the brambles were less dense and the grass was trodden down where someone had been using the spot. A short tunnel had been worked through the undergrowth, leading right into a thicket. Crawling through he came to a little clearing, recently well used and with the litter to prove it. It was as private a spot as you could wish to have. He'd been right, youngsters playing, making a den, the thrill of secrecy, seeing and not being seen. Or older ones perhaps, with the urgent drive of youth, happy to suffer a few scratches in return for privacy and an hour or so of fondling intimacy. Much may seem to change, he thought, and much does, but some things remain as they have always been.

As he bent to collect the litter he saw the little plastic bags with their traces of grey-green dust, the hundreds of filter tips scattered and sunk in the grass, the empty packs of roll-up paper. The brown and flattened grass also hid ring-pulls and bottle-tops and as he looked closer, a few condoms too. He thought better of his litter collection. He'd come back later with a bag and pair of gloves for the party leftovers and a hammer and nails and a warning sign for the fence. There'd be no come-back on him then if someone decided to launch themselves into oblivion.

It was only nine but already the heat was up, although not perhaps with quite the same ferocity as recent days. He paused on his way back to stand on the very edge of the drop and look east into the sun. The air seemed a fraction clearer than of late and a breeze stirred his hair. The possibility of change in the air? He stood a little longer, remembering what a fine place it was to stand, just below the brow of the hill, looking out across the gently undulating land. As far as he could see it was brown. Little ribbons of green stretched across a brown quilt, at once beautiful and terrible, the beauty hiding untold misery and hardship brought to half the country by the unyielding sun.

It was a moment of peace, something he'd found little of. He caught himself thinking when times were better he'd come up again to sit and look, and marvelled that he could still think that there would be better times. The eternal optimism of good things just round the corner, eternal and yet so often unfounded. As if to demonstrate the point his attention was taken by the figure of the female detective stopping her car by the gate and sauntering in, unaware she was being observed. She'd seemed a good enough girl when she'd sat in his house and watched him weep and made him tea. Looking at her now, with her casual energy, her youthful swing, he saw how she might also be attractive in that way a black-haired woman is so differently attractive to the blond or brunette. And that thought also caught him unawares, another little triumph for optimism over reality.

He watched as she leaned her head into his workshop and called out his name. Receiving no answer she disappeared inside. She must have taken the opportunity to poke around when she found it empty, for it was several minutes before she emerged, peering round the quarry with a hand shielding her eyes from the sun. He couldn't help but notice what unsuitable shoes she was wearing.

'Need some help?' he called down. 'Wait there I'll be with you in a minute.'

'Mr Staples, I came round to see you because I wanted to tell you a couple of things personally, not a phone call.'

He nodded in appreciation, having a good idea what she had come to tell him.

'First, about Melanie,' she said it softly, as if she'd known his girl, seen her sparkling eyes, kissed her hair as she'd lain sleeping, as if she felt the loss herself. 'Where would you like her taken? I heard from the coroner this morning that all the . . . ' she hesitated a fraction too long and the spell she'd cast with her gentle talk was broken.

'All the tests?'

'Yes, thank you, all the tests are finished.'

He nodded again, the start of a tear pricking his eye. 'I'll have something sorted out. Do I tell you or call someone?'

She handed him her card and wrote another name and number on the back. He studied it intently, as if the writing were Chinese, worthy of detailed examination and interpretation.

'There's another thing too,' she ventured, 'not really official, just something I wanted you to know.'

He said nothing as he looked at her.

'The incident centre, the mobile police station behind the village hall, it's being taken away today.'

Still he said nothing.

'I didn't want you to think we'd stopped looking, or stopped asking.' She looked at him hoping for some sign of approval, some understanding of her intentions in telling him this small operational detail.

'What about the Duncan girl?' he said sharply. 'Too late for my Melanie, but what about her?' The old anger, the old bitterness threatened to surface once again.

She held his gaze and replied as best she could, even though she knew how inadequate any answer would seem. 'They haven't stopped looking or asking about her either.' She was going to add a reference to the business with Liam Duncan but decided against it. She hadn't been really convinced of any of it herself, so it probably hadn't convinced many others.

'And you and your boss, are you being taken away?'

'Only as far as Banbury. I'll be working from there. But please call me any time.'

He nodded again, although not with any thought that he would ever do so.

'There was one other thing you might help me with. I missed the vicar yesterday, I was going to ask him about some references in the notes from the governors' meetings. You're a governor aren't you, Mr Staples? Can you help me?'

'I can try.'

She'd carefully chosen the note from the year after Melanie had gone missing, according to the record it was Peter Staples' first year as a governor. She pulled out the paper and showed him the cryptic line 'SR65 travel cost from GBF after discussion.'

It took him only a moment to recognise the meaning. 'It's a shorthand so that any casual reader won't know who was being helped. I don't remember the detail, how long ago was it?'

'Ten years or so.'

'Well if it is the same as now then the SR65 is a reference to the pupil. That would mean number sixty-five on the school roll was getting some travel expenses paid. That usually means whenever there's a school trip to a museum or art gallery or something and the child, or rather the child's parents, can't afford the fee. The governors can then decide to pay the cost, some of it or all of it out of their own funds.'

'Is that GBF? I thought that was somebody's initials.'

'No, GBF is the Governors Benevolent Fund. It's a little pot of money set up for, well, let's just say discretionary payments. Things like paying for a pupil to use a musical instrument or a school trip they can't afford.'

'Anything else it might be used for?'

'Could be anything I suppose, like I say, it's discretionary, but you'd best ask the rector.'

'Thank you, I will.'

*

The really uncomfortable thing about the man in the mirror was not his sweaty grey face or the red-rimmed eyes sinking deeper into his skull as each day passed. No, for Michael Radcliffe the awkward fact, the unpalatable fact, was the man looked not so much like him, but exactly like his father. Of all the resolutions in his life, and there had been many, few of which had lasted more than a few months, there had been one which he'd made when he was barely ten years old: he would never, ever, be like his father in any respect. For well over fifty years he had by his own reckoning, kept the promise. But here, now, the one aspect over which he had no control, made a liar of him. He was his father. How could that have so suddenly happened without any warning, without a tell-tale sign? He gave a little shudder at the prospect, and was

175

horrified to recognise one of his father's mannerisms shuddering right back at him.

As if to test the pain threshold he stood a few moments staring into his father's eyes, defying him to resist the confrontation, defying him to speak or command obedience, defying the belittling phrase or dismissive sneer. Defying him to raise his hand, or worse. It was the smallest of victories, addressing memories but ignoring reality. His father had been dead for many years and not once in life had Michael, or so far as he was aware, his brother, resisted their father's power over them. Indeed, it was several years after they'd cremated him before they confessed even the slightest anger or resentment, and then they scrupulously spared each other any detail of pain or humiliation. Their closeness went only as far as acknowledging they shared a bottomless well of bitterness and neither could speak his name nor his parental title. Once they were past nine or ten their mother had withdrawn her protection and left them to fend as best they could with all the ills *that man* and abusive regimes at schools could heap upon them. For this they half forgave her and half despised her, for she could no more withstand him than she could resist the sweet release of alcohol.

In vain he studied the man in the mirror for some likeness to his mother. There was none to be found, not least because Michael Radcliffe could not really remember what his mother looked like. He had a few photos of course, pictures of a young woman, of a young mother, but none from the later years. She'd taken to locking herself away from the world for days at a time, where she'd eventually drunk and smoked herself to death. Only later, much later, long after she and *that man* were dead, did anyone suggest she might not have locked herself away, might not have deserted her boys for days at a time, but instead had been shut away by her husband with the promise of harm to herself and pain for her children if she dared complain.

The chain of thought and the memories so vividly and painfully brought to mind had two predictable results. He looked at his watch and wondered if he could reasonably pour himself a scotch at eleven in the morning. He could certainly light himself a cigarette, although he was finding his new brand not much to his liking. They had given him a slightly sore throat and made him cough more than usual, especially in the mornings. He might have to switch back to the old gold. And thinking of old gold brought him right back to the prospect of a glass of scotch. The Chequers would surely be open, and if he could buy a scotch in The Chequers then he could certainly pour one for himself in the comfort of his own house. His wife had been many things and he was grateful to her for most of them, but there was no denying the pleasure he found in being free to sit and smoke and take the odd glass of Scotland's finest whenever and wherever he chose.

The house was already unbearably hot, so after turning on the lawn sprinklers he sat in the garden, blissfully unconcerned by the ban on such flagrant waste of precious water. The lawn at The Glebe House was perhaps the only one which needed cutting in either of the twin villages, it was certainly the lushest. Sitting under the fruit trees in the shadow of the venerable old wall that separated him from the rectory, the dancing droplets of water playing before him, a glass in one hand and the first deep draw on a new cigarette in his lungs, Michael Radcliffe found a few moments of genuine peace after the ghosts of past anguish had so tormented him. It was a spot Mary had often chosen to sit with whoever came to call, discussing whatever the business of the day might have been. With all the comings and goings in the village of the last week, she would have been in her element, volunteers to be marshalled, committees to be formed, recovery plans to be hatched, bodies to be buried. By an unhappy irony the house would have been full of, well, full of many of the same people it was full of just a day or so ago.

Without her guiding hand there would be so many things to be organised he wasn't sure where he should start. That toady little woman, the ever helpful Margaret Westerleigh, might be useful, he'd given her a free hand to clear out all Mary's clothes, but she seemed to have done nothing yesterday so far as he could see. She probably just wanted to poke around to find what she could take for herself. As that uncharitable thought crossed his mind, Michael Radcliffe realised that he had no idea what Mary had in her drawers and cupboards, not even what papers or jewellery she kept. She almost certainly had some good pieces, family pieces most likely. He struggled to think of what she wore to the many functions she attended, to some of which he'd dutifully accompanied her. The undertaker had passed him her rings in that little plastic box, he knew about those, but nothing else. Perhaps it hadn't been such a good idea to give the farmer's wife free reign.

Mary's room seemed so much cooler than the rest of the house. It was quiet and still with an almost unnatural chill. So perfectly arranged was every ornament, every book, he hardly dared step beyond the doorway. The ground floor of The Glebe House was, until this week, regularly attended to by the cleaner - whose name Michael Radcliffe could not immediately recall - but the bedrooms were strictly off limits to all but their occupants. The unused rooms were closed up, all the furniture covered in dust sheets, 'mothballed' she'd called it, as if they were only preserved at all in case new owners might find a use for them. He hadn't been inside her room for years, but it was exactly as he'd last seen it. It was as if no one had moved there, slept there, dreamed there, in ten years or more. Cautiously he opened a wardrobe. It was filled with perfectly hung and neatly ordered clothes, not an empty hanger amongst them but neither was it too full. He opened a second and found the same perfect containment, the same perfect order. In her dressing room he found her shoes, astonishing how many pairs she had all arranged in their boxes, even if they were a little unevenly stacked with lids half on and tissue paper leaking out.

The drawers contained the predictable, if large, selection of all her scarves, sweaters, gloves, and underwear. He gave the intimate undies no more than an embarrassed and cursory glance despite his natural curiosity, perhaps because he feared she might still somehow discover his interest or worse, she might discover his presence in her room. He turned his mind quickly from such thoughts to something more likely to win her approval, the practical purpose of his visit, the removal of any valuables from temptation's way when Margaret Westerleigh next came to visit. In the back of his mind was a distant recollection of a black box, beautifully lacquered and inlaid with mother-of-pearl, probably valuable in its own right, regardless of its contents. He quickly found it in buried in a drawer, exactly as polished and tactile as he'd remembered. It was stuffed full with jewellery of all kinds, more than he'd realised she owned. He absently thought about insurance and having recently needed to locate those papers felt sure there were nowhere near as many items on the valuables list as he had laid out before him on the dressing-table. Perhaps they were cheap imitations, not worthy of special mention, although to his untrained eye they were certainly good imitations.

Amongst the diamonds - or diamanté - were silver and gold brooches, exquisite enamel pins and pendants, together with a few little bracelets she must surely have had since childhood, so slim was the wrist they would have fitted. A gold-coloured locket caught his attention, not for its beauty or value but the opposite: it was tiny and cheap in the shape of a full and rounded heart. He held it in his fingers, letting the little heart swing back and forth on the tiny chain. A piece seemed to be missing and the clasp was broken, no doubt a legacy of some pull or snatch from Mary's childhood. He began easing it open with his thumb nail, curious as to what picture or keepsake she might have kept in such a thing.

'Michael,' called her voice urgently at the door, 'I called, are you in here?'

In panic he closed his hand over the locket and pushed it deep into his jacket pocket, stood up and knocked over the chair he'd sat on. The door swung open and there was Margaret Westerleigh in a blue dress that might have been Mary's, and an expression to match.

'Insurance,' he muttered, 'checking through for insurance.' His voice had an improbable squeaky quality and he couldn't have looked more guilty if he'd been holding a knife dripping with the victim's blood.

'Are you all right, Michael? I called out, several times. I called out but you didn't answer. The house is all open, I said I would be here today, I've been held up, had to go and see the rector about something.'

'The rector. Yes. Yes. You said you were coming, yes.'

He moved as if to get past her out of the bedroom, then realised the jewellery was still scattered across the dressing table. To remove it now would be awkward, would reveal a lack of trust, but to leave it casually spread out might be too tempting. He looked at the jewels and back to Margaret. She read his mind perfectly.

'Are you finished with that?' she said. 'I'll put it all away if you like.' Then to cover all possibilities she added, 'There may be a couple of things there she might have borrowed.'

His fist closed more tightly round the cheap locket in his pocket, the same pocket that held the silver lighter and the cheap cigarettes. The urge to take one and light it was almost overwhelming but even he could not bring himself to do so in Mary's bedroom.

'Yes, thank you, Mary, excellent, if you would.'

He rushed out, half stumbling in his haste and anxiety. As he brushed by she caught the usual waft of stale tobacco, blended this morning with the pungent sweetness of Johnnie Walker, which partly explained his mistake with her name.

★

After a little delay the rector's wife answered the door, and appeared none too pleased to do so. 'Yes?' she said abruptly.

'Hello, I'm Detective Constable . . . ' she began, her warrant card ready in her hand.

'Yes, I know who you are, what do you want?'

'Is the, er, vicar available?'

The little stumble over her husband's title softened the hard line of Acantha Fox-Lomax's mouth. 'Sorry, he's still over at the office,' she tilted her head towards the church, 'with one of the faithful, but do come in, I'm sure he won't be very long.'

Lavi Pitesteanu hesitated, mindful of the cold beer torture she'd been subjected to previously, but unwilling to encroach on the privacy of priest and parishioner. Annoying the rector was one thing, but she wasn't going to overstep the mark. And who knew what might be learned from a chat with his wife. 'Well, if it's no trouble, I'll wait for a few minutes.'

She was ushered to the same seat as she'd sat in on her visit with the holidaying Donald Smallborne. The two women sat eyeing each other a little uncomfortably for a moment or two, the detective perched uncomfortably on the edge of the seat, Acantha Fox-Lomax in no mood for small talk or her usual games. Until a thought occurred to her.

'Coffee, tea?' then a little playfully added, 'Something cold?'

'Tea would be lovely.' Tea was surely safe ground.

Having brought the constable from the lounge to the kitchen while she boiled the kettle, the rector's wife took advantage of the informality to ask, 'It's nothing I can help you with, is it? Sometimes I seem to know more about things than Philip does.' She accompanied this with a knowing look that she hoped would suggest a feminine affinity between them. Lavi Pitesteanu thought she was making eyes at her again, but took the chance of a little heart to heart for her own purposes.

'Well, you might. There were a couple of things. One was about the governors' meetings, were you ever a school governor?' Acantha Fox-Lomax shook her head. 'A pity, there's a fund, a benevolent fund and I was keen to know what it was used for.'

180

'I've heard of it, I know that now and again the er, shall we say, better off in the parish are invited to donate.' She literally licked her lips at the prospect of some scandal or impropriety concerning the benevolent fund, adding as casually as she could, 'Nothing wrong is there, nothing missing from the kitty?'

'Oh no, nothing like that, just a question about something years ago.'

Disappointed and feeling a little outmanoeuvred, the master game-player tried again as she poured the tea. 'And the other thing?'

'Well, no harm in asking you as well, although you probably didn't know her very well, but it's about Melanie Staples, I wondered if Mr Fox-Lomax might remember her.'

Pure gold for Mrs Fox-Lomax who almost slavered in anticipation. 'Go on, ask away.'

'Do you remember having any contact with her, was she in church, did she come here perhaps?'

'Here? In this house? Has there been some suggestion she was here? We're talking about that unfortunate girl who went missing?'

'Yes.'

'I don't think she was ever here, not once. She might have been in the church, but you'll have to – '

'Have to ask the vicar about that. It seems to be the answer to every enquiry.'

'Yes, he does like to keep a finger in every pie,' she agreed. 'I wonder why you thought she might have been here, in the house. Has someone said something?'

'People have said very little, nobody can remember anything. So little in fact that she might never have existed. Which is no disrespect to Mr Staples, he has many memories, as does her mother I'm sure,' she added hastily, uncertain of what alliances might exist between the Staples and the Fox-Lomaxes.

'People will always talk, especially about vicars, won't they?'

'Yes, I suppose so.'

'Of course, it's usually about little boys and vicars isn't it? Not little girls,' she added with a little laugh and another of her meaningful looks, the meaning of which was lost on Lavi Pitesteanu, who wondered vaguely, and not for the first time, whether the vicar's wife was making a pass at her.

'Do people round here talk about the vicar and little boys?'

'Oh no,' Acantha Fox-Lomax cried out in theatrical horror, before adding the mischievous, 'not round here! Not that I've heard, anyway.'

'Somewhere else? Something else?'

Now the rector's wife had the conversation exactly where she'd wanted it to be, questions about her husband, asking whether he liked little boys, or little girls, asking if there had ever been any talk of such things, asking about rumours of misconduct. She dropped the smile and adopted a serious face, a face more appropriate to the moment, a face to show that she took these things seriously, not as flippantly as her previous comments might have suggested.

'No, not ever that I heard,' she said most emphatically. 'Not little boys or little girls, let's get that straight. But as you ask, yes there was something, years ago now, but that was more in the way of bigger girls, if you understand.'

'How much bigger?'

Acantha Fox-Lomax's hands were about to describe two large curves when she realised the question had nothing to do with size, but with age. 'Oh,' she said with a little girl's giggle, 'well over the age of consent, in fact nearer the upper limit than the lower.' Her mouth described her sense of disgust, as if she had accidentally bitten into a slug.

The constable found herself wondering how the conversation had reached this point, how she was hearing about the vicar and gossip about ladies of a certain age from a previous parish. Whether it was true or not was open to question, but his wife had seized the opportunity to tell her all about it. A double bluff to hide something worse? The vicar's wife did not appear to be the loyal type, no, she appeared to be more the silent stabbing-in-the-back type. True or not she had to agree on one point - it did sound unpleasant. Unsure of what to say, she said nothing, but gave what she hoped was a knowing look and a nod to seal their female secrets, and perhaps elicit one or two more.

'I'm sure you'll have a pretty good idea of what else people are saying, not about your husband, but about other things, about Melanie, maybe about Eysha Duncan. Are there whispers, rumours that someone like me, an outsider, would never hear?'

'We're all outsiders,' then, to confirm their new bond, she added, 'Tell me, have I got it right, it is Lavi isn't it? Is that how you say it?' and without waiting for an answer went straight on with, 'We're all outsiders, Lavi, unless you've been here a very long time, in which case you are promoted to incomer. Or unless you're from one of the county families, or the rector, or preferably both.' She smiled as if she was amused at her own play with words, but she was losing interest in the game which had brought her little apart from dripping a drop or two of acid about her husband. This detective seemed bright enough but she was turning out to be hard work.

'So once again it's a case of 'better ask the vicar', eh?'

'Yes, of course, but don't expect him to tell you, he'd never tell anybody anything he's heard in the church or here for that matter. But you must know that, confession is the great secret, even though some of what's confessed probably doesn't amount to much in this little dust bowl.' Again the conspiratorial nudge-nudge look, the raised eyebrows.

No, thought the detective, it probably doesn't amount to much: the odd infidelity, coveting the neighbour's oxen, worshipping a graven image, abducting a child or two. But it did make her think, reminded her that someone could do terrible things and still walk and talk and pray and laugh and live their lives as if nothing had happened. And that it applied equally to outsiders and insiders and everybody in between.

★

It had been a slow day at The Chequers. With Colin Deeley's help, Alan Miller had opened the bar at noon, but the pair had been the only occupants until two in the afternoon, when some hikers had stopped in to ask about the old sheep track and been shamed into buying orange juice and lemonade. They'd sat outside under an umbrella until Colin went out to have a smoke, at which they pointedly left, juices half drunk. When the door opened again at four the landlord looked up hopefully from his position propped up behind the bar.

'Alex, good to see you,' he said with as much enthusiasm as he could muster. Alex Duncan was an irregular, that is to say he would have spells of being a regular customer and spells when he wasn't seen for weeks at a time. His regular periods often terminated when he'd not exactly been thrown out, but certainly asked to leave, usually as a result of some argument with, or about, one or other of his sons. Alan Miller was pleased to see neither Liam nor Aaron were accompanying their father.

'Aye, right,' he replied, with little warmth or feeling. He'd come to the pub because after being cooped up for more than a week he

183

was desperate to get out and he'd nowhere else to go. Laura was in Oxford with her mother to see Liam, who still languished in a police cell. For several reasons Laura had thought it best if her father stayed away. Aaron had decided he was better off keeping his head down and remained at his girlfriend's house, which left Alex alone, hot and miserable. He took his lager to join his friend Colin at a table outside.

'Any news, Alex?'

'Nah. Nothing.'

The two fell silent again, drinking quickly then brooding over the last inch, each with their own troubles but well aware of the other's.

'Suzie's back tomorrow.'

'She knows it all now, does she?'

'Knows enough. But she'll want all the ins and outs when she gets here.'

'She and Peter still at each other's throats?'

'Maybe, we'll see. I saw him a couple of days ago, up the quarry again till all hours, but something's changed.'

'I suppose it would.'

'What's happening with Liam?'

'Charged with conspiracy and deception for now, should be out on bail, but they've got all kinds of other stuff they're lining him up for.' He lifted his eyes from his beer and met his friend's. 'And he's got nothing to do with Eysha, doesn't matter what they say, or what they wish he'd done, he's got nothing to do with it. It was their stupid idea in the first place and he's thought it was clever and he'd make some money and walked right into it. It's like they set the whole thing up.' The plight of his family, the injustice and sheer misfortune should have made him angry, should have had his voice rising, his fist banging the table, but he was exhausted by tragedy, bewildered by events beyond his worst nightmares.

'That's not good, not good at all,' Colin agreed. In the brief conversation with his daughter on the crackly line to Cuba he'd said nothing of Eysha, she'd no place in the conversation about their dear Melanie, but Eysha Duncan's disappearance was sure to be mentioned tomorrow, would need to be mentioned, and would provide yet more agony. And he was fairly sure he knew the answer to his next tentative question, 'And Eysha, what about your Eysha, has anybody seen anything, said anything?'

'About as much as was seen and said of your Melanie. If you ask me I'd say they've stopped looking, given her up.'

The two men shook their heads and stared a little longer into the empty glasses.

'Oh God, Alex, it's an awful thing, the waiting.'

'Aye. But here's a thing, our Laura's not waiting any more, says it's easier to think she's not coming back at all, better than hoping. That's bad enough eh, when it's better to think she's gone, than to hope?'

'Suzie said the same. I hoped, I think Peter hoped, and waited for his girl, but Suzie said she'd gone. You'll see about Eysha, but whatever happens I wouldn't wish eleven years on my worst enemy.'

★

It was an unusual request, certainly, but a straightforward one. Even so, the dentist's receptionist was uncertain how to handle it.

'Sorry, Mr Smarsinger, but we just don't have the appointment books that go back that far. The police were in here the other day, wanted the same thing and had the same answer.'

'You explained that, which is why I would like to see my records. They will have a note of every appointment I've ever had, won't they?'

Behind the counter were four filing cabinets of patient records, each containing row after row of little cream folders, vital statistics written on the outside, details of every visit, treatment and check-up on index cards inside. In the fourth cabinet, third drawer down, were the records of each of the four Samarasinghes who were registered with the practice. While he was talking another assistant was taking the tray of records used that afternoon and replacing them in their alphabetical positions. Over the receptionist's shoulder he could see the drawer open where Samarasinghe B was filed in front of the Samarasinghe D, T and U. With long enough arms he could pick out his record himself, yet still the receptionist was unwilling.

'They're confidential records, not meant for anyone but the dentist,' she protested weakly.

'Or the dental nurse.'

'Well, yes, the dental nurse too, they usually write them up.'

'And the hygienist.'

'Yes, them as well.'

185

'And you, when you make appointments, you write on the record, right there on the little folder they're kept in.'

The girl grew more uncomfortable and moved her hand to cover just such a record she had in front of her. 'Yes, well I don't see the record itself,' then knowing that he could sense the lie added, 'not usually, I don't see them usually.'

'Then we will compromise and to save much trouble to us both, please get my record and then read out the dates of my appointments since I was first registered. I am only interested in a few dates, it will take no time at all.' To give the girl an extra reason for this little task he gave her a beaming smile and added, 'It is most important and you will be doing me a great service by helping.'

'Well, if it's really important,' she said, anxious to find a way out of the corner she'd painted herself into, and swivelling her chair to find his record.

To avoid further embarrassment he spelled out his name as she flicked beyond S and into the Ts. A little red-faced she turned back with his record, a slim one, in her hand and began reading the dates and times while Thomas noted them down. At the third he stopped her. 'Excellent, that is the precise information needed. Now, if you look on the first card of the record, you'll see what I was here for on that third visit.' The receptionist looked doubtful. 'It will take just seconds.' Again the smile, less beaming but with a nod of approval.

'It was a regular check-up. There's some squiggled numbers, you'd need to ask the nurse about them.'

'Perfect, now one last thing and you can put it back in the file. Did I come for that appointment? Does it say if I was here or only that there was an appointment?'

'Oh yes, you came in for that, look.' She turned the card so that he could read it, her finger pointing to the little tick in the second column.

'Good, thank you. Now let's put it back, let's keep it confidential.'

Now he had the information, he was unsure what to do with it. It had no meaning for him, no significance. Even knowing that he had been to the dentist that day jogged no memory. It had merely satisfied his curiosity. He stood at the top of the steps leading down from the surgery entrance by the little space for a half-dozen staff and patients to park their cars, straining to recall whether it had been the same all those years ago. The road was a dead end, a little branch off Maiden Lane, no more than twenty yards away down the slope. Turn right and go past the track down to the Centenary Wood, a little further were the cottages, last one was Melanie's, then keep on going to the quarry and somewhere, eventually, the wider world beyond. Turn left and go past the bottom of Lisle Gate, the shop, the village hall, the rectory and St. Giles, then fork left up to the main road or right to Germans, the school and Six Lanes.

Everything stays the same, the same as it has been for hundreds of years, but everything changes. The roads are resurfaced and re-marked, new roofs and fresh paint on houses, wires and aerials sprout and grow, trees flourish and die and are cut down, there's a missing phone box outside the house that's no longer a pub. The monochrome of winter is coloured in by spring, the sun of summer turns green to brown, soft mists of autumn blur the sharp angles of August. And the people change too, laughing children into smirking teens, the old to their coffins while the newborn are wheeled out with pride, even those who would once have been hidden in shame, for what's right and what's wrong changes too. And fashion changes the hair and the shape as much as it hides what was shown and reveals what was not.

Not that Thomas saw the subtlety of change and continuation, he couldn't see the centuries flick by, he could barely understand how much and how little a decade had touched the scene. Looking around him, down the lane and across the combe through squinted eyes, he tried in vain to see what his eleven-year-old self had seen as he left the dentist, down these same few steps on the morning of that last day of term. Why did it matter, if it mattered at all? It did not come to him, none of it came back to him, why should it. As he opened his eyes he recognised a figure who might know an answer or two. The dark haired detective was standing at the end of the lane watching him.

Her presence decided him, just as his was deciding her. He would give her the answer to the question she'd asked while they'd sat in the waiting room, then he'd see what else might be said. She had the excuse of a chance meeting to fall into conversation, redeem her little faux pas over his name. And she too would then see what else might be said.

'I have the answer to your question,' he said as he skipped down the steps towards her.

She stood and waited as he approached, watched how his limbs moved so easily, how loosely he seemed to be joined together and felt her heart thump a little harder in her chest. Whatever happened she must not call him Thomas.

'Mr Samarasinghe, how are you?'

'Don't you want to know?'

'About the dentist? Your wisdom tooth?' Then remembering what she'd asked, remembering what her excuse to see him again would have been, added, 'Ah, the appointment, of course.'

'Yes, but before I tell you, you must tell me why it matters.'

'It probably doesn't, but,' she hesitated. They had turned and fallen into step with each other, as much as a tall and lean young man and a shorter more rounded young woman can, and had reached the top of the track leading down to the wood. 'Will you walk down with me?' she asked, 'It's either that or walk by Mr Staples' house and I'd rather not.'

'There's more shade down the track.'

He'd made his decision in the space of a few steps, he would talk to her about Melanie, about their games and other things, so long as it was private. His sister's warning about whether she could be trusted came back to him, be careful she'd said, don't forget she's police. He would try not to.

'Before you go on,' he said seriously, 'don't tell me anything you shouldn't. And if I tell you something, it is for you only, there are things which may mean nothing, private things, not secret but private.'

She looked at her watch. Twelve minutes past five. 'I'm off duty,' then smiling added, 'if that means anything.'

'Maybe. My name is Thomas.' He held out his hand and for a moment she was uncertain.

'Ah, yes, hello Thomas, I'm Lavi.' Her hand seemed tiny in the great cup of his.

'So why does the dentist matter?'

'It might not, you know Melanie went to the dentist that day? I wondered if she saw something, someone. And this is all private, yes?' her dark eyes looked earnestly up at him. 'You remember I met you when I was working on the other girl, on Eysha Duncan? She'd been to the dentist that morning. It may mean nothing, just an odd coincidence, no more.'

He drew his own conclusion immediately. 'I had appointments on both days, Melanie's day and then Eysha's. Another coincidence. Anybody else?'

'No records left. Not without going through all the medical cards to see who was there. And that needs a decision from on high, very sensitive area is medical records.'

'But,' he thought a moment longer, 'are you only interested in who might be common to both days?'

'Yes, maybe, I don't know.'

'Well they must have the appointments book from last week. See who was there, then find out if any of those people went the day Melanie . . .' The sentence trailed off as he thought less of the theory and more of his lost friend. They had reached the parking spaces at the bottom of the track. Ahead of them was the slope where he'd launched Jack's canoe, to the right the path to the bird hide and the trees where he'd said goodbye to her and arranged to meet her later. Thinking of her again here, close to where they'd been, brought her back more clearly, teeth a little too big for a face that had yet to grow, rain trickling down her cheeks mixing with smudges of dirt, water and mud everywhere.

'The rain is another thing,' he said rather absently, 'another common thing.'

'Yes, the rain. They say Eysha came down here, she was seen at the top and maybe half way down too, then nothing, gone.' She looked at him and his half-there, half-distant expression, dreaming of young days with his friend and she felt embarrassed to be intruding, as if they were talking of a former lover. She guessed in some ways they were, a first love perhaps for them both, even if they didn't recognise it at the time.

'Lavi, there are some things I want to talk about.' He put a hand on her shoulder as if to turn her more squarely to face him. 'Things I must trust you with, even though they are private and really just fragments.'

He hadn't asked a question but she answered it anyway. 'Yes, tell me anything you like, no one will ever know, unless you've done something I can't ignore.' She wanted to add, 'in which case don't tell me,' but resisted. Off duty only went so far.

He dived straight in before he had a chance to change his mind. 'Melanie stole things. I stole things, we stole them together, we stole chocolate bars from the shop, the shop here in the village.'

189

The confession came as a great relief to them both for their different reasons. But unlike his sister Diana, Lavi Pitesteanu didn't make the mistake of treating it lightly.

'Often?'

'Every week. For a while it was every week. We had a system.'

'Did you get caught?'

'Somehow. One day Melanie said we had to stop. I found out her father knew about it and,' he hesitated to say the worst part even now that he'd confessed to the crime, 'and my father, my mother, they also knew about it. They and Melanie's father made things right with the shopkeeper, with Mr Rogers. That was the end of it.'

'Did you steal anything else?'

'No.' He'd been staring at the path at their feet, now he looked up at her again, 'But this is hard to say, I think Melanie did, I know she did. She stole cigarettes from her mother and money too, and maybe from other people, I don't know for sure. I know there were some others who gave her cigarettes and money, 'easy' she called them, 'they're easy' she'd say and then she'd laugh and we'd both laugh. She never said exactly what it was about or if she did then it didn't mean enough to stick with me.'

'I didn't know that, nobody has said anything about her. She was the invisible child, except to her parents of course.'

'We were both invisible,' he said without thinking.

'How was that?'

'Remember what I said about how we were in the wood, playing spies, climbing trees? You were with your boss when you came to our house the second time.'

'Was it more than that?'

'Yes. And no. I don't remember enough to be sure, it was all just games we played, or I thought it was. Now I wonder what else it could have been. It was only a week ago I discovered my parents knew about the stealing, and other people knew too. It's made me wonder if other people knew other things too.'

The off-duty detective was beginning to regret the way the conversation was going, it all seemed far too much like being on duty. She'd imagined something lighter, reflective perhaps as suited the day and their reason for meeting, but still lighter and not devoted entirely to Melanie Staples. Despite the flashing smile and the quick wit, her companion was really a most serious-minded person. While he was still talking, her boss's sour comments about worst killers being best actors and how they couldn't resist showing off how clever they were, popped into her thoughts. It sent a shudder down her sticky wet spine. This man and his family had once been half suspected of some involvement in her death, until it was squashed by senior ranks. He'd been a thief and got away with it, along with the same girl, again thanks to his father's intervention. For an instant she went cold at the thought of how wrong she might be, dreaded the fall from the crumbling edge she found herself standing on. Right or wrong she knew she must hold her nerve.

'What's wrong?'

'Nothing, go on, you were saying about people knowing things, I'm not sure what you mean.'

'I was saying how we listened to people talking, we climbed walls, climbed into trees, people never think to look up do they? We would be in a tree and they would stand right underneath and talk about all sorts of things. Sometimes we thought we would die laughing. It was like stealing chocolate, it was the thrill of not getting caught. It was just a game to see what we dared ourselves to do.'

'What was the biggest dare?'

'That's probably worst of all. It's what made me sure about telling you.' She looked expectantly, waiting for him to get the words assembled in the order he wanted them. 'We hid in the church and listened to conversations in there. I don't think we knew what it was but now I think we listened to confessions.'

'What did you hear?'

'That's it, I don't really remember, it wasn't important what we heard, it was just that we did hear, that was the game, to not be found out. I have an impression of people talking about cheating and stealing, it seemed to us that everyone said how they cheated and stole things. But as to who said what I don't think I knew even then. One or two voices we'd recognise and that would make us laugh even more. Later we might see them in the street and we'd keep extra straight faces until they couldn't see us.'

'I suppose you've already had the idea that if somebody found out what you were up to they might be pretty angry, to say the least of it?'

'But how would they find out? We would have known.'

'Did you ever go alone, hide in the church on your own?'

'No, never. It wouldn't have been the same.'

'And Melanie?'
'No. I don't know. Why would she?'

13

Suzanne Mortimer, once Staples and originally Deeley, left the car behind The Chequers. She and Andrew Mortimer, her husband of eight years, had arrived in the small hours, jet-lagged from two days of travel and the shortened night of an Atlantic crossing. They'd done no more than fling their cases into their house, showered and driven on to her father's cottage at Six Lanes. There, father and daughter consoled each other and shared a hug and a few tears. Colin Deeley's were for his daughter as much as anything or anybody else. Suzanne's were tears of bitterness and anger as much as for sorrow and loss. Coffee to keep her and Andrew going, a quick exchange with Marjorie Webster from next door, then they were off up the lane to Germans, to see just where her daughter had been discovered, to know better how she came to be there. As they drove where her father had so recently cycled in all innocence of what was to follow, he described as best he could the sight of Lisle House as an island in a sea of mud, the cloying humidity and the smell of decay.

'Still stinks now,' she said as the car door slammed. Andrew Mortimer thought better of asking his wife to close it more gently. 'So show me what happened, Dad.'

For the next few minutes her father did exactly that, and since he had not actually seen anything but the aftermath, and like everyone else was still ignorant of the extent of the slurry lagoon catastrophe, he told the story second hand and in parts third and fourth hand. Lacking sufficient words to adequately describe the noise, the scale, the truly frightening nature of the deluge and all it had brought to the twin villages, he ended simply standing mute, shaking his head, still amazed at the story he'd just told.

'Where'd they find her?' Right after Melanie went missing her mother had suddenly been unable to say her name or her pet name, even to whisper them to herself. She'd never been able to speak either since.

The trio trudged from the car park to the school gate.

'Here. You can see the line of the top.' A brown high tide mark showed where the washed down earth and rubble and slurry had piled against the railings. A muddy stain covered the road and footpath marking the extent of Melanie's burial mound. Cooked in the sun and mixed with the tarmac, it was an indelible reminder.

'Couldn't get much closer, could she?'

'No.'

'And John Westerleigh was the one, he found her?'

'Thought she was . . . thought her mac was a fertilizer bag. Went to pick it off the pile, apparently.'

'You spoken to him?'

'No.'

Suzie nodded at this and fell silent. Despite a mouth with the accumulated taste of thirty-six hours of airline snacks, nicotine, tar and coffee, she drew out another of the duty-free king-size and passed the packet to her husband and her father. They shared a light from Andrew Mortimer's Zippo. It was almost ten, and the sun burned down on them through the humid air, while from the houses of Germans a hint of wet plaster and rotting wood drifted in the atmosphere.

'Poor sods in Germans got the worst did they?'

'Bad everywhere, Suzie. But there was worse than that in Germans.' He'd set himself to say something about the Duncans before they went any further and waited to find some reason to speak of them. His daughter turned to him, quizzical. 'You remember my friend Alex and his family?' She nodded, but her lips pursed in disapproval. 'Don't look like that, it's another bad business.'

So he told her and her husband the tale of another lost girl, lost in another rainstorm, lost from under the very noses of her mother and the teachers and all her school mates, lost without a trace and now lost without much in the way of looking going on either. It was almost as an afterthought, just to complete the whole sorry picture that he mentioned Kathy Duncan leaving Alex, and her son being arrested for some scam or involvement in Eysha's disappearance. It seemed to be the last straw for Suzie, who fought back more tears, dragging a white sleeve across her eyes and running nose. Andrew Mortimer moved to console her, with a comforting arm round her shoulder, a handkerchief ready in his hand, but she seemed not to notice him.

'That poor bloody girl and her mum. She was just a kid herself when she had her, I remember her pushing that baby out in the pram, pleased as anything she was. She let our Annie hold her, I remember that.' As if she had found not just her name but the girl herself she repeated it softly, 'Our Annie, our Annie. Bless her.'

They stood there a few minutes longer, but for all Suzanne Mortimer wanted to see everything, be told everything, there was little left to see and nothing much left to tell.

'Shall we walk into the village?' her father suggested.

'I don' t want to see anybody. Suppose Laura Duncan saw us, what could I say to her?'

'As you like Suzie. What about Peter?'

'What about him? Have you seen him, spoken to him?'

'Yes, I told him it was time you two spoke about it, about Melanie, time you spoke about it again. I told him you'd be coming over this morning. He might be at home.'

'Dad, you'd no right to do that. After the way he treated me you'd have thought . . .' the sentence went unfinished as she struggled again with old emotions, old bitterness and blame, old guilt and agonies. 'Anyway, he's probably buried himself up with the stones again.'

'He said he'd stay home this morning.'

'I'm, er, I'm not sure it's a good idea if I, I mean if we, go to the cottage,' Suzie's husband suggested, shifting uncomfortably from one foot to the other.

'Go back to the car then Andy, I told you not to come over. It's got nothing to do with you.'

'Oh, it's always had a lot to do with me, or so you've told me,' he said, turning on her. 'Wasn't she going to - oh leave it, today's not the day.' He moved away and stood apart from his wife and father-in-law, drew out a fresh cigarette and lit it without sharing the pack, his gaze following the gash through Whyncombe Wood to the hill above and the distant roofs of High Whyn Farm.

They left him there and walked on past the houses of Germans, not exactly going to see Melanie's father, but heading in that direction, the decision deferred. They'd just passed the Duncans' house, where they might have caught a shadow of movement behind the frosted glass of the front door, when Suzie said casually, 'Did she ever say who the father was? Get him to pay up, or what?'

'Laura? Well, not to me, and I don't think to anyone else. Alex has never said and I've never asked him.'

'We were just here, just past their gate,' she stopped and turned to look back down the road towards The Chequers, the school and the chimneys of Lisle House nestling in the combe, 'she and her dopey friend had the baby, Annie asked if she could hold her again and she let her.'

Colin Deeley said nothing, wondering where memories were taking her.

'Then she said something not quite what you'd think, she said, "Has she got a Daddy?" and I thought what a waste of time all those sex education classes were and the talks we'd had. Poor little Laura looked at me not knowing what to say and Annie looked at me all wide-eyed and innocent and I could see right away she knew well enough the baby had a Daddy. Then Laura took her back quickly and her friend said something about everyone's got a Daddy and they walked off back down the road.'

'I wonder if Laura remembers that.'

Their walk took them on through Germans, past St. Giles and the village hall, neither asking where they were going. To Suzanne Mortimer the place had a curious half-familiar half-strange feel to it. She'd lived there for years, raised children there, albeit neither of them reached their teens, but now she'd been away ten years and more. She had a different life, still attached by the pull of family, but her life was away. Very soon it would only be her father and memories that might bring her back and she found only resentment in that. She turned to him and caught his arm as he was about to go into the shop for his Saturday cigarettes.

'Dad, I don't want her buried here, not here in this place, I hate it. I don't want to have to come back to see her here. If she'd been taken up North like they said, it might've been different, but not now.'

'Peter might want it,' he said quietly, then as gently as he could, 'he wanted it before.' The reference to his grandson was as oblique as he could make it, there was enough pain in the day without adding to it.

'He can want it all he likes, but no, not here. Cremated and scattered. Tell him.'

'Not seeing him then?'

'No, not today. It's too hot, I'm too tired, we'll only shout. But you tell him please, and I will talk to him, tell him that too. I'll see about tomorrow, I might come over tomorrow.'

With that she turned and walked back the way she'd come, shouting back over her shoulder that she'd call him later and putting her fingers to her lips in the sign of a kiss.

★

'Isn't there a wedding later?'

'Cancelled. The groom's mother had a heart attack or a stroke or something. Acantha took the message, so I'm not quite sure of the exact details. But cancelled is all that really matters, so no bells to be rung this afternoon, John. I thought Margaret might have told you.'

Philip Fox-Lomax was not particularly unhappy about the wedding, cancellations at short notice were rare but this was understandable and it meant he had a day without any official duties. Nonetheless he was dressed in his usual black, standing on a step-ladder inspecting the latest set of repairs to the vestry roof when John Westerleigh had found him.

'No, she didn't mention it. She's got things on her mind at the moment, helping Michael sort out Mary's clothes and so forth. And then there was a visitor last night and that probably put it out of her mind. It was that I wanted to see you about.'

'Oh, who was it?'

'That woman detective, came up all of a rush about seven last night.'

'She's been hanging around here a lot all week, and at Mary's funeral, do you know what she's doing?'

'She was asking about the governors again. Same as last time. Said she kept missing you, maybe I could help.'

'Missing on purpose I think. She'll find me soon enough I expect.' The rector stopped checking the ceiling and looked down at his visitor. 'And did you? Help her?'

'Maybe, that's why I thought you ought to know.'

The Reverend Fox-Lomax descended the steps, folded the ladder and placed it precisely against the whitewashed wall beside the cupboard. For a few seconds he stood making minuscule adjustments to its final position.

'What did you tell her, John?'

'She seemed to know a lot already, but she asked about the notes again, about the private notes, she had them with her. She asked about one in particular. You'll know which one.'

'I can guess. Did you tell her to look in the roll to see who it was?'

'No! I knew straight away who it was! And what it was about.'

'What did you tell her?'

'I told her Melanie Staples was apparently stealing money, cigarettes, all sorts from other pupils and from a teacher and we'd discussed what should be done and agreed to pay the teacher compensation from the benevolent fund. Which is all perfectly true and I don't know why we didn't say so before. And anyway, that girl detective seemed to know about the thieving already.' he concluded with ill-concealed irritation.

In fact he'd told the girl detective a little more than that, but suddenly he didn't want to admit it to the rector. She'd asked about the cryptic *review by MG* and he'd told her MG was the sub-committee of governors, the Management Group, and how she'd have to look at the start of the year to see who was on it because he couldn't remember, but it would certainly have included the rector as the chairman.

'Then you remember even less than you think. It was better for everyone to keep it confidential, it served no purpose to make it public, which I think you agreed with at the time.'

'That was all very well back then, we all thought the poor kid had been abducted and goodness knows what else with those other girls and taken off to Manchester or wherever it was. All the stuff about her stealing didn't matter then, it had nothing to do with anything.'

'And, it is a bit overused I know, there was nothing to be gained by speaking ill of the,' he stumbled momentarily of the choice of word, 'of the child, and there isn't now. And at this particular time, her father could probably do without any talk of thieving, as could her mother, who I saw in the village earlier.'

'Yes, I know all that, but what if the way she was had something to do with what happened to her, what then?'

'You imagine she was killed, and buried up in your field for stealing a bar of chocolate and a few cigarettes? John, you're getting carried away here, what could it possibly have to do with what happened to her?'

'My field? Who says she was in my field? She was not on my land!'

'Well, as good as, by all accounts. And you're suddenly very sure of where she was buried. A lot of talk about things that happened too long ago for people to remember will do no good today, just as it would've done no good then.' Having put the farmer onto the back foot he wanted to keep him there, so added, 'Of course, John, we must all follow our consciences, I do, and I'm sure you do too.'

'I try to.'

'And it's not always easy, I know. Look at your good wife now and her problems with poor Michael. Where should her conscience lead her?'

'What are you talking about, problems with Michael?'

'It's your affair, John, but you two might gain much from talking to each other a little more. I suggested the same to Margaret and I hoped she would have said something. She came to see me yesterday, seeking advice on something, something very difficult for her. In its way not dissimilar from your difficulty over what should be said and not said about Peter Staples' poor child.'

'What's Margaret's problem with Michael? I know he's losing his memory half the time, I don't know what'll become of him.'

'Margaret came to me in confidence, John. I must respect that. I've said too much already. Ask her, I'm sure she'll be happy to tell you. These are difficult days for us all, shall we have a prayer together?'

Before he could answer they heard the heavy iron latch of the south door crank open and fall back, metal on metal, as it had done for hundreds of years, sending its brief echo round St. Giles.

'I wonder if this is your friend now.'

'My friend?' protested John Westerleigh, 'Who do you mean?'

The rector pulled the vestry door open a few inches, in time to see the figure of Lavi Pitesteanu ambling down the south aisle. 'Your friend the detective of course. And yes, it is she. I doubt she'll be here for a prayer.'

'I'll go then, I'll slip out this way,' he said, moving to the side door.

'Out of action, John, you won't avoid her like that.' He pulled the door wide and called out, 'Can I help you, constable? Or have you all you need with the cool and the peace of St. Giles?'

John Westerleigh muttered an acknowledgement as his path crossed the detective's.

'A few minutes of your time would be a great help,' she said, with a weariness born of many hours' research.

'Here? Is it church business?'

'Maybe. But school business first. Or maybe both, it is a church school, isn't it?'

'In a way, yes, in a way no. A technical detail.'

'The governors' Management Group, what does that do?'

'Anything it is delegated to do by the governors. It could be anything, that's the idea of it, once it's been delegated to do something, it does it.'

'Does it report back?'

'It might, it might say something was done or not done.'

'But it doesn't have to?'

'Not, as I say, if it is delegated to do something, no.' The rector knew very well where the conversation was leading, but was certainly not going to assist its progress. Lavi Pitesteanu was fairly sure he knew too, John Westerleigh's fleeting presence left little doubt about that.

'So can you tell me who was on the Management Group eleven years ago?'

He saw the danger sign easily enough, there was no point in an outright lie. 'I can make a good guess. I would say it was myself as chair of governors, the chair is always a member, almost certainly the vice-chair and sometimes one other. It depends. It changes year by year, sometimes term by term.'

'But that year?'

'As I say,' he began.

'You don't actually seem to be saying very much. You were on the group and the vice-chair? That would have been Mr Radcliffe?' She had done a great deal of homework since last she'd seen him, she didn't need the answers to the questions, she needed to know if they would be answered truthfully.

'Probably.'

'So what did you and Mr Radcliffe do, what did you delegate to yourselves, when it came to reviewing Melanie Staples' reported thefts from other pupils and teachers?'

'From memory, I'd say we spoke to the parties concerned.'

'Parties?'

'The thief and the victims.'

'Might the police have been a better option?'

'This is a small community, things are done in the best way for everyone. What could possibly be gained from involving the police? Completely out of proportion,' he pronounced dismissively.

'And what was the result?'

'As far as I know, the best possible result, there was an end to the thefts.'

'What did you say to her?'

'I don't remember exactly.'

He didn't remember exactly for the very good reason that he had never spoken to the girl about thieving or anything else of substance. Not as a priest, not as a governor nor as a member of the Management Group. It was something his deputy had taken on. Tucked into the top right-hand drawer of the vestry desk was a packet of cigarettes. Alongside the packet was a little book of fold-out matches, a souvenir of Stratford-On-Avon from a time when matches were considered suitable advertising. Both cigarettes and matches had been there, untouched, for several years. Their presence had been both a comfort for emergencies and a daily accolade for good behaviour. If he turned a little, his right hand could reach the drawer handle, a little tug and it would slide open. Deft fingers would have a cigarette in his lips and a match struck in thirty seconds at most. The urge was almost irresistible.

The detective half saw, half sensed his discomfort. She was about to speak when she remembered the sun-seeking Donald Smallborne and how he might have conducted the interview at such a point. She said nothing for nearly as long as it would have taken to light a cigarette. Then she changed tack.

'Simply amazing, isn't it, the way they built these places? I'm always so surprised by how cool it is in here. And wonderful acoustics, you can hear every word, even the whispers.'

'Yes, wonderful.' He swallowed hard. The rector was not accustomed to telling lies, not downright lies. He'd tried to not lie about Melanie Staples, but he'd bent the truth so far it had broken.

'Have you changed much in the church since you've been here?'

'No, hardly anything, what do you mean?'

'I don't know really, I suppose there are things that get worn out?'

Far safer ground was beckoning, ground that had no connection to the discreet actions of governors, no connection to a missing girl, ground he felt secure to stand upon and offer a discourse if necessary. 'Oh yes, show me something that is not worn out, it's a never-ending headache. Church finances are very stretched, it's hardly possible to keep the buildings themselves in good repair, never mind replace things that wear out. Shall I show you around?'

The answer he got was not what he expected.

'Can you show me where you hear confessions?'

'Confessions?'

'Yes. Confessions. Here in the vestry? Kneeling at the altar? Sitting in a pew? In your house? Where?'

'I don't understand what you mean, what's this to do with anything?' Having glimpsed safe ground he found it disappearing in the mist, and resorted to his more familiar bluster.

'Maybe to do with nothing, but a simple question,' she persisted.

'It might be anywhere. It can be anywhere. It doesn't have to be here in St. Giles.'

'And if it is in St. Giles, then where?'

'Most people feel more comfortable in the body of the church than in here. The vestry is more for business.'

'Unusual isn't it, hearing confessions like you do?'

The rector wondered who else she'd been talking to apart from the Westerleighs. Or maybe the farmer had told her more than he'd admitted, maybe told her more about all kinds of things. As long as she kept to the general he would go along with her, give her the lecture she seemed to be wanting.

'Only by degree. It would be a rare priest who'd not heard a private confession.'

'Most people think it's a Catholic thing, but it's not is it? Anyone can confess, yes?'

'There is an old adage in the Anglican Church which goes along the lines of *All May, None Must, Some Should.* I've always thought it summed it up quite well,' he said, managing to find a convivial tone.

'And whatever anyone tells you, whatever they confess, you can forgive them, absolve them, is that the phrase you use?'

'Oh no, that's not how it is at all. Confession of sin is about repenting sin, not so much of the forgiving, although people see it that way. And as for me, I am not really here, I listen, I'm an ear, a receiver. I hear the sinner repent, not the sins they repent of. Hearing confession, it's quite a different thing to offering forgiveness.'

'What's the worst thing anyone's ever confessed?'

'I can see where this is going. You have no right to ask and I certainly have no right to tell, even if I could remember, which thankfully I don't. They would be heavy burdens to carry,' he said, in a manner suggesting he was sharing a personal insight she was privileged to hear.

'No, vicar, I don't think you know where this is going at all. Unless you know already, unless someone has confessed and truly repented of listening to other people's confessions in secret. Here in this church.' Such colour as was left drained from the rector's face as she spoke. 'While you've had half the population pouring out their worst sins, someone other than you was listening. But maybe someone already told you that.' With no attempt to disguise her contempt she added, 'Not that you would remember of course.'

The rector's instinctive reaction was shock and disbelief, but before he could protest the error of her assertion two memories came unexpectedly back to him with great force. One concerned someone who had fallen out of the church and moved away many years previously and who'd once come accusing him of breaking the seal of the confessional. She had been adamant that she'd confessed to nobody but her God and her priest. The second was no more than a snatch of conversation, one parishioner saying to another, 'She knew about it! Can you believe that? She knew!'

*

'The dentist? She wanted to know about the dentist?' Diana Samarasinghe could hardly believe what she was being told. Having seen him and his 'detective friend', as she put it, walking up from the combe the previous night, she'd been very anxious to know what had passed between them. Work, sleep and their mother's presence had delayed the questioning until nearly two on Saturday afternoon. Now the best he could come up with was the coincidence of dental appointments.

'No, not the dentist, but about appointments, who had appointments on the day Melanie disappeared, who might have also had appointments last week, the day it rained, the day Eysha Duncan disappeared. Melanie had an appointment and so did Eysha. And I was there both days too.'

'Which makes you a suspect? You and the dentist and the nurse and probably the hygienist and the receptionist and the assistant?' Her tone was one of utter scorn.

Thomas was taken aback by this instant analysis. Why had he not considered that? Why had Lavi Pitesteanu not said the same thing? From being in some mysterious way important the coincidence of the dentist looked suddenly silly and irrelevant. But his sister had not finished the demolition.

'And what about those who go with them? What about Amma going with you, because I'm sure she did. And Melanie's mother or

203

father, and who went with Eysha Duncan? And it's not just children is it? Who gave so-and-so a lift? Who went with his wife because she was nervous? Who took their neighbour?'

'Yes, all right, thank you, I get it it,' he interrupted, before she found reason for half the population to be there.

She couldn't resist a final kick. 'And the dental supplies rep?'

He was annoyed that he hadn't seen the flaw in the idea himself. For all he was quick of mind, his sister had always been at least his equal. 'It was just a starting point, there might still be something in it,' he said by way of justification.

'Sounds more like an excuse for a walk in the woods.'

'Yes, maybe that too. Although she doesn't really need an excuse does she?'

'Not her, little brother, you. An excuse for you. What else did you talk about?'

'About when we were children, what we did, where we went.'

'You didn't tell her about the chocolate did you?' She saw the look on his face. 'Oh you did, you did! What did she say? I see she didn't arrest you.'

'She wasn't very interested, we talked about all kinds of things. She was off duty.' And as soon as he'd said that he wished he hadn't.

'Off duty!' his sister screeched, 'Dear Thomas, you are so wonderfully trusting. They're *never* off duty, didn't I warn you to be careful? So what did you get out of this happy little off duty walk in the woods? What little gems did she let slip? Or were you too distracted to notice?'

'After we'd walked for a while she said there was something she needed to do and she was going to put herself back on duty to go and do it. That was about it, nothing much to it.'

'Not for you, sadly, or for me, but I'm sure she got all she wanted.'

★

'No, thank you, there's nothing I want,' she assured Michael Radcliffe.

After her conversation with the rector, it had taken Margaret Westerleigh another long and sleepless night to decide what should be done about Mary Radcliffe's shoe collection. Philip Fox-Lomax had been less helpful than usual with his advice that she should follow her conscience, particularly as she was not at all sure what her conscience was saying. Even when she'd told him as much as she could without revealing the repugnant details, he'd been quite ambivalent and found no scripture or lesson to guide her more directly. He'd been very matter-of-fact in his reaction too, as if revelations of bizarre criminality amongst respected members of the community were all in a day's work. Perhaps they were.

When she'd woken, sweating and exhausted, as her husband had risen at six, she'd made her decision. The less-than-grieving widower of The Glebe House had given her free reign to do whatever she wished with his wife's clothes, and she would solve her dilemmas by destroying them all. It was not too difficult to decide on the shoes, they were so odious to her that destruction had always been their fate, regardless of any thoughts of finding their owners. No, they would all be burnt, not sent to recycling or the land-fill, but burnt. She would make sure of that. For good measure she would also contribute the right foot moccasin she'd kept in the hope of finding its partner. It had occurred to her at two o'clock in the morning that when Mary Radcliffe had taken the left foot moccasin she might quite easily have picked up the pair and indulged whatever fetish she had before leaving the right and stealing the left. At that moment she knew she would be unable to touch either shoe again. A little later as she'd lain thrashing in her sheet it had come to her that if she felt that way then every other victim of her former friend's crime would feel the same. They must all be destroyed. She would remove everything in plastic bags and bring them back to High Whyn and burn them where no one would see or ask any questions.

Later still, as light was filling the room and the lowest temperature of the day had already passed, she opened her eyes to the stark thought of further discoveries. She'd not had the stomach to look deeper once she'd collected the jewellery Michael Radcliffe had scattered across the bed and the dresser. As for the bed, she couldn't even bring herself to think about it. But what if those rows of dresses, drawers full of tops and jumpers, carefully ordered blouses and skirts, what if they too had been snatched from the bedrooms and - oh God forbid! - the washing baskets of half the county? She wrestled with this, toying with the idea of sending only those clothes she knew to be Mary's to charity and burning all the others. The sheer waste of it all appalled her, especially when she knew from the most casual of looks that so many coveted labels were present. The charity shops would be more than happy with them, but what if one were seen by its original owner? No, they must all be burnt too, although it would take a long time. There was no hurry, the priority was the shoes.

'Well, if you're sure,' Michael Radcliffe was mildly surprised that she wanted nothing, but hardly interested or concerned. 'It's very good of you to help out like this. Much appreciated. There seem to be a lot of bags, can you manage them all?'

'This is not the half of it, Michael,' she said as they surveyed the front hall of The Glebe House where she'd stacked a dozen black bags full of shoes. 'Didn't you know Mary had so many clothes and shoes?' A small part of her wanted to ask the question outright, did he know about his wife's peculiar hobby, but she was scared of the answer or the further questions that might result.

'Never really counted. I know she liked picking up second hand things sometimes, things that caught her eye. Never a big spender so far as I know, but it's all a bit of a closed book to me. Jewellery too, I think. Did you have a look yesterday? She had lots of good pieces of course, family pieces, hers and mine, it all came her way over the years. But she liked to find little things as well. Charity shops I suppose, she used to help run one or two. Charities I mean,' he laughed, 'not so much the shops.'

No, thought Margaret, not so much the shops, not Mary's kind of thing at all. She'd arrange for Margaret or any of the other lesser folk to take a turn helping out here or there, making jams or cakes, serving teas at the fête, reporting for duty at this hour, signing off at that, but Mary wasn't one for pouring the lemonade herself. Mary was more one for stealing shoes. The shoes would not, could not, leave Margaret's mind until they'd been incinerated, purged by fire from the face of the earth. Even though she'd worn gloves to bag them, she felt dirty, almost infected by the task. The stuffy heat of the room hadn't helped, but she'd found both windows to be locked shut.

'Quite a mix of things, I saw that when I was putting them away yesterday. Some little chains and pendants I can't imagine her ever wearing. Inexpensive little things, more like a child's, maybe from when she was very young.' Again, other questions hovered behind the words, again she was wary of asking them.

Before he could answer, Michael Radcliffe was struck by a fit of coughing, so much so that he gasped for air and clutched the door-frame to support himself. Margaret brought him a glass of water and urged him to sit. After a few minutes he recovered well enough to offer her a smile and hoarse thanks.

'Changed my brand, haven't quite got used to the new one yet,' he spluttered, reaching across to the packet beside his chair. He vaguely waved them at Margaret, to which she held up a latexed hand.

'You don't look good today Michael, it's no use saying you do.' In fact, when she looked more closely he looked terrible. Thinner by the day and skin the colour of the ash leaking from the tray across the arm of the chair.

'It's the heat, it's getting me down.' He coughed again as the first intake of smoke grated on his raw throat.

'That's all I can do for you today, Michael. See you in church tomorrow.'

For reasons she couldn't be quite sure of, she was cross with Michael Radcliffe. She was cross that he sat there smoking and drinking, coughing and sweating, but apparently doing little else while she'd laboured with such a secretly awful task, even though she'd volunteered and never asked for any help. She was cross that he knew nothing of Mary's strange collection and had a nagging feeling that if he had known he would have said it was none of his business. She was cross with herself too, cross it was she who would now be instrumental in preserving Mary's reputation, cross she was somehow tainted by association and was protecting herself as much as Mary or even the useless Michael.

★

Alex Duncan had just watched the end of the early evening news during which he'd had the misfortune to see a report from outside Oxford Crown Court. From this he'd learned of his oldest son's remand into custody. It was stated he'd been denied bail because he had somehow contrived to offer a threat to a key witness, namely the local reporter who was the friend of a friend. Sadly, Alex was drawn to the conclusion that it was quite plausible, Liam could be that stupid, he would almost certainly have offered to kill the man if he could lay his hands on him. Liam was full of such idle threats. The notable missing element with nearly all of them was the person being threatened. Liam offered all sorts of violence and retribution to people who'd crossed him in some way, but never in person, never face to face. When he was feeling really brave he might say loudly how somebody the other side of the bar had better watch out, but that was as close at it usually got. Now he'd probably told a cell-mate or a friendly custody officer how he was going to sort out the reporter who'd stitched him up. Such an outburst would have been duly noted and passed up the chain to the court, who rightly took such matters seriously and promptly denied Liam Duncan the release on bail he might otherwise have obtained.

Alex had his head in his hands when he heard the front door slam shut. It certainly wouldn't be his wife Kathy, unless she'd had a change of heart and returned to the marital home. He guessed correctly that it was Laura, back in ill temper from the court hearing he'd just seen reported.

'Liam is a complete bleedin' idiot!' she announced at full volume, her father nodding in mute agreement. 'I ain't bothering about him again. That's it, he's on his own. Twat.'

'Was your mum there?'

'Yes, she was there. If she'd been close enough she'd have smacked him one right there in the court, she was that mad at him. You'd think he could keep his big mouth shut just for once wouldn't you?'

'Aye, you might.'

After a few minutes of his daughter circling the kitchen and cursing both her brothers, when he sensed the worst of the storm had passed, Alex said, 'Get yourself a cuppa and sit down, Laura. Liam's only half our troubles.'

'What's happened now? There's nothing left is there, Dad?' All the sound and fury left her and her shoulders slumped. Head bowed, soundless tears trickled down her face. Her father put an arm round her and held her close.

'Oh, nothing new, pet. Something old. But before I say anything, hear me out, don't get mad till you hear me out.'

She eased herself away from him, her nose running and her lips twisted with weeping. She nodded to him.

'Hear me out, right? Colin was round earlier. Suzy's back, Melanie's mum, used to be Suzy Staples, now she's Suzy something else. Colin says she was asking after you, would've come in if she'd known what to say. She said something about Eysha, about when she was a baby. She said Melanie held Eysha a couple of times, you let her hold her.'

'Yeah, maybe, I dunno now. Why? What's this got to do with anything?'

'Suzy thinks there was a time when Melanie said something about Eysha's father,' he held up a hand as mention of the forbidden subject hardened Laura's face. 'No, I'm not asking, nobody's asking, but listen. Does anybody know who Eysha's father is? Anybody but you and, I suppose, him?'

'Maybe,' Laura sniffed, 'but what's it got to do with anything?' Her senses had switched to full alert. What were Colin Deeley and Suzie Staples doing wondering about Eysha's dad? This was and always had been her greatest secret, shared in part only once and regrettably with her greatest friend. She'd been pressured one way and another about Eysha's father by her family and social workers and benefit officials and more lately, the police. She'd held out against them all, sometimes giving them whatever silly idea had come into her head, but more often refusing anything.

'I don't know what it might mean. Have you ever told anybody, anybody at all?'

'I might've. Once.'

Alex Duncan may not have won many parent-of-the-year awards, but he knew his children well enough. When Laura might've done something he could be sure she had, but didn't want to lie and didn't want to tell.

Despairingly he said, 'Not Vicki, don't say Vicki Gardner.'

'Could've been. But not exactly.'

He sighed deeply. 'So anybody might know, she could've told anybody.'

'No, she wouldn't 'cos she knows what would happen to her if she did. And if she did, then I'd know about it. Anyway, it was just after I found out, I was all upset, you know how it was, happy one minute down the next. Me and Vicki were really close then, she wanted a baby too. If I hadn't fallen for Eysha she might never have had Molly.'

'Aye, I know how it was.' His arm went round his daughter again.

'Dad, I never really said this before, the thing is I didn't want Eysha's father to know, didn't want him knowing and being here and seeing me again. Or Eysha. It was bad enough without having him as well. It was all a kind of accident.'

'But you told Vicki who it is?'

'No, not exactly. But I told her how it was we came to,' in a rare moment of embarrassment she blushed at the memory and stumbled over the words, 'you know, how we came to do it.'

'Say no more, pet, it's your business. But you never said anything to Melanie Staples? You did let her hold Eysha sometimes?'

'Yeah, her mum was nice and she was a cute little kid, she liked babies, I let her hold her, but there's no way I would've told her anything.' She waited a moment for her father to say more but he was silent. 'Are you going to tell me what all this is about? Is it about Eysha or about that little Melanie?'

'I've no idea. Colin has it in his head there's a connection, something with Eysha and his Melanie, I know he's trying to help, trying to help us, but so far as I can see there's nothing more than you'd expect from living near each other.'

'Living near each other?' More tears filled her eyes and overflowed unchecked. 'Yeah, Dad. And dying near each other if you ask me.'

★

He'd been there for her, if she'd wanted to come and see him. But she hadn't. Instead she'd sent her father with a message. Not that he'd put it like that, not that he'd been sent, nor that he carried a message, but to Peter Staples that was what it amounted to. And what a message. Cremated and scattered. She wanted their Melanie cremated and scattered. It had shocked him when he'd told him in his reasonable way that he thought it best if his granddaughter was cremated. 'We've had no grave to tend all these years and she hasn't meant anything less than the day she went, so what's the point in digging one now.' That's what he'd said, 'what's the point in digging one now.' The point was, they'd had nothing to put in a grave, not while there was a chance, not while there was a hope left. But he hadn't said anything, hadn't argued or protested, whatever he thought, he knew he'd agree to it, just like he had before.

That had been half way through the day, when he'd come knocking on the back door, him instead of the ex Mrs Staples, the jet-lagged Suzanne, the long-gone mother of his two long-gone children. It had been at that moment, seeing Colin Deeley standing at the open door, one arm leaning against the frame, he caught a glimpse of his son Anthony. That's just how he would have stood there. He'd carried himself the same way as his grandfather did, no doubt he'd have grown to be like him and like his mother too. Although he was never that far from his thoughts, never forgotten, Peter Staples was slightly surprised to realise that for ten days or more he'd not crossed his mind once. Now with his sister's funeral to dispute and his mother honouring them with a visit to the neighbourhood, Anthony had returned.

His boy had neither grave nor marker, only an entry in the *in memoriam* book kept in the hushed little flower room at the crematorium. Each day a page was turned so that on the anniversary of a death the entry would be there for anyone to see, if they could be bothered with anyone other than their own fathers or mothers or sons or daughters. He never went, he'd never liked the idea, but he was, after all, a stonemason. He imagined whole pages being turned in the book, unseen by anyone who once cared, no more than a curiosity to those who delivered flowers. Now that was to be Melanie's final entry too, a line in a book, invisible for all but a few hours once a year.

By the time the light was starting to fade he'd become more accustomed to the idea. Melanie's grandfather was right in his own way, there was nothing to be gained from a grave, it made no difference to memory, nor to love or to loss. Anthony's sudden decline from noisy boyish health to hospital mortuary in the space of a few weeks had given them a little time to understand and prepare themselves, but the loss was no less keenly felt. The memories remained, a little faded it was true, and they would have been none the sharper for a plot and a stone by the yew in St. Giles churchyard. But it nagged away at him that she might want a cremation just because he'd want a burial. She'd have known, without needing to ask, what he'd prefer. And it also nagged away at him, as it had done for eleven years, that they might have all been saved from this day, she might have grown and had a family of her own by now, or be at college, or in Australia on a gap year, she might have done anything, been anything, if her mother had not chosen to be out with a friend that soggy afternoon.

He stood at the bedroom window, looking out across the little valley until the heat began to leak away and there was no light left. A sickly yellow moon, distorted and lopsided just past the full, hovered low over the horizon. In the cupboard beside him, a few inches from where his hand rested, were Melanie's last few things. Soon he'd sort them out, give all but a couple to her mother, if she wanted them. He'd keep Princess for sure, maybe something else too, but he wanted to get it done before the funeral, he didn't want to come home to that.

14

'I'm not sure I want to go this morning.'

John Westerleigh eyed his wife slightly suspiciously. He'd said nothing of his conversation with the rector, asked no questions about her problems with Michael Radcliffe. Neither had he taken the advice to talk more with his wife, preferring to wait and see if she would tell him herself. Since the rector had suggested a problem with Michael Radcliffe along with a hint of some parallel with Melanie Staples' little sins, he dimly imagined the widower might have made some improper advance to Margaret. But she showed no sign of talking about The Glebe House or anything else until her unexpected announcement about not going to church.

It followed a tendency he'd noticed during the week, a harder edge had crept into her words and there were fewer of them. She'd stopped making regular attempts to engage him in conversation, her usual running commentary on the meal she'd prepared, the water rationing, events in the church, how healthy, or not, he was looking, all these topics had dried up, as if all the strands of her life had finally begun to wilt in the heat. Maybe that was just it, the heat was sucking not just the land dry, but also the lives of those who walked on it. Energy was being conserved, unnecessary speech or actions were suspended until further notice.

'Oh?' he said by way of mild curiosity.

'I'm not in the right mood to be in church this morning.'

He looked at her, surprised. She'd never said such a thing before, not about church or anything to do with her faith. In normal times she would have been going to church whether she was in the right mood or not, it would be her duty to go, her bad mood something to be repented, not given in to. He wondered vaguely if the business with Michael Radcliffe had some connection to her mood, and again the idea of some improper suggestion occurred to him. Or perhaps it had been the visit from the detective on Friday evening, she hadn't said anything about that either, but her displeasure at being excluded from the interview had been apparent.

'Not like you.'

'No, I'm not feeling much like me at the moment.'

'Well, if you want to talk about it,' he ventured, which was as close as he was ever likely to get to heeding the rector's advice about his marriage.

She stopped tidying away the breakfast things and looked at him. 'Talk about it? Talk about what? When did you last talk to me about anything?' She shook her head in disbelief. 'I've got things to do this morning.' Then, thinking she'd best mention having a fire, 'I've a lot of Mary's things to get rid of, some to be burned. I'm going to make a start before it's unbearable. Behind the barn, it'll be in the shade this morning, all right?'

'Make sure you've got a bucket of water handy.'

So, he thought, it was all about Mary, this mood of hers. Clearly he'd not been forgiven for forgetting the sight of the Radcliffe's blue car in the mud. 'I think I'll still go down, shall I send your apologies?'

'Who to? God?' which was so unlike her, so hard and sharp, he wondered if he'd heard her right, wondered if there weren't more to her mood after all.

'No, of course not, I mean to the rector, I think he relies on you, on us both, that's all.'

'He'll have to manage without me today.'

'And Michael?' he suggested, without quite asking what had upset her in The Glebe House.

'He'll have to manage without me too.'

★

Almost as high on the hill as High Whyn Farm, but on the opposite side of the valley, Sunday morning was following a more familiar course in the houses of Upper Orchard. Some remained curtained and asleep, a couple of others had cars being discretely washed, supposedly from buckets but the eagle-eyed would have seen a hose coyly snaking to one garden tap. Two doors further along, the Seychelles sun-seekers remained in their distant paradise, while their home continued to rot. In one, and only one, the occupants prepared themselves for worship in St. Giles.

Upeksha Samarasinghe remained troubled by the conversation she'd had the previous afternoon with her husband Clarence. She hadn't discussed it with either of her children, nor had she any intention of doing so until she'd decided how she felt about it herself. He'd suggested, perhaps more than suggested, his wife and even possibly his two children should join him in California for

213

the remainder of his secondment, or for much longer if he was, as he expected, invited to stay. Her reservations were numerous, especially on behalf of Diana and Thomas, whose preferences their father had largely ignored. It would, he had said, be better if they all got away from England for a while, away from the heat and away from everything that was happening. By everything she presumed he meant Melanie Staples, for the equally upsetting disappearance of Eysha Duncan had not seemed to touch him at all. He'd said it had all been arranged with both the university and with London, as he put it. The whole family would be welcome, he'd explained, the opportunities were unlimited in the Golden State, especially for such talents as Diana and Thomas.

He'd spoken enthusiastically of living in California, how different it was from England, and although he would always love England, California had so much more to offer, not just for him but for Upeksha and their children. He'd said too how they would all thrive in the fertile intellectual scene of the Greater Bay Area and come to love it as their new home. Of the many things to cross Upeksha's mind as he spoke, one of the last was that her husband had used almost exactly the same words as he had done years previously to persuade her of the many great advantages to be had by moving from Colombo to Whyncombe St. Giles.

She listened dutifully to all that he had to say and told him more than once that if it was his wish that she should join him then she would almost certainly do so, perhaps for a few months at first to see how they got along. But of her children she could say no more than that perhaps they might come for a visit soon, but that they had their careers to think about. To Clarence she always defended her children's choices, emphasised their successes, especially Diana, while she privately looked forward to the day when her daughter would make her a proud grandmother rather than a proud mother of a TV news reader.

As she prepared herself for worship in St. Giles that Sunday morning, another, somewhat unexpected, thought occurred to her: what would it be like to attend church in California? In many ways St. Giles was not so very different from her St. Michael and All Angels in Kollupitiya, and it had been one certain place in an uncertain world when they'd first come to the village. But what of California, what would her Sunday morning be like in the 'fertile intellectual scene' of Berkeley? She had only the sketchiest idea of the Anglican Church in America and what she saw in the sketch seemed alien and uninviting.

'Are you coming to church this morning?' she called out to neither child in particular.

To her surprise they both called back that they were. Thomas often accompanied his mother, more from habit and appearances' sake than for faith, but Diana was a rarer visitor. She too had motives other than worship, but that was hardly a novelty at a Sunday morning service in Whyncombe St. Giles. Something her brother had said suggested the detective might be in the village again this morning and Diana was curious to see her off-duty face. And just when the rest of the world had lost interest in Whyncombe St. Giles might be the very moment to learn something valuable about the place.

★

There was very little her husband could conceal from Acantha Fox-Lomax, especially when it came to his moods and pre-occupations. Their abrasive skirmishes gave her sport but increasingly lacked any real satisfaction. All too frequently she knew what he was thinking before he did and could judge his reactions almost perfectly, which was why he was such an easy target for her darts and barbs, why he fell so neatly into her snares and traps. So it came as a surprise to her when she spied him unawares, standing at the French windows gazing at the baked brown lawn with an unlit cigarette twirling back and forth in his fingers. She hadn't even spoken to him and here he was not much more than an hour before the Sunday morning service, distracted and distraught over what she wasn't sure. She slipped silently back from the room to collect a box of matches from the kitchen before walking round to meet him in the garden.

'Good morning,' she said brightly, ignoring his agitated expression and the cigarette.

'Good morning, Acantha.' he replied with little enthusiasm.

'Worried about this morning's message to the faithful, vicar?' which she knew would be the very last thing to ever bother him. The one thing he could do nervelessly, albeit tediously, was preach.

'No.'

She tried a different tack, a more personal prod straight to a soft spot. 'Oh, Philip, you haven't been a naughty boy again, have you? Not been caught with your fingers where they shouldn't be?'

Not a flicker. Oh praise be! she thought, at last there was a game to be played.

'Well, that's a relief, don't want any more pensioners getting all of a fluster do we?' She came close to him, making sure he'd smell her hair, her fragrance from the shower. 'Aren't you going to light up now, vicar?' she suggested in pouting tones, pausing before lifting the matches to his eye line. He stepped aside to show where an earlier butt-end, scraped out by his shoe, lay on the stone beside him. Looking up again she saw he held a cheap disposable lighter in the palm of his hand.

'Thank you, but I have a light. Something I picked up earlier.' he said without malice or sarcasm.

'Eeew, sounds very nasty.'

He flipped the lighter over in his hand. 'Left in the church. Along with two cigarettes. Imagine that, leaving your lighter in the church. Sitting there on the end of the second row, not dropped, not thrown, but carefully placed. Why would anyone do such a thing, eh Acantha?'

She'd quite misunderstood, he wasn't playing at all, he was his same joyless self as always. If she worked a little longer she could probably raise his temper, an unkind reference to the doting Margaret Westerleigh, or his manly closeness to Michael Radcliffe were usually reliable standbys. Then a fresh idea came to her, inspired by local events and the boring little police girl. 'Well, one person who wouldn't have left it for you would be that poor little girl, eh Philip?' she asked, mimicking his tone.

He turned on her, his expression apparently unchanged, but betrayed by the muscle twitching in his cheek and a tell-tale swallow. 'That's a terrible thing to say, Acantha. Even you should be ashamed of yourself for that,' he said sharply, his lips pinching into colourless lines as he spoke.

'Oh, but vicar, that rather depends on which poor little girl you have in mind, doesn't it? I was thinking of that poor little police girl who came round for such a nice chat the other day. Which little girl were you thinking of? Which one do you know most about?'

'You know nothing, nothing at all, you and your cleverness,' he sneered, while a little glint of saliva leaked from the corner of his mouth. Perfect, thought Acantha, although her face did not betray a hint of the triumph she enjoyed, a perfect way to prepare him for the office. She might even go along herself just to encourage him.

★

There were more bedrooms in The Glebe House than its
solitary occupant had remembered. He'd risen earlier than of late
with the single purpose of finding something he'd mislaid years
ago. He'd never really looked that thoroughly for it, rather he'd just
been aware he'd lost track of it, and thought one day he would
make the definitive search. That day had arrived and he began with
the bedrooms. For a start there were two at the top of the attic
stairs. If he'd have been asked how many there were while he was
still at the bottom of the stairs he would've said only one. But there
were two. Although it was not even ten in the morning, the
accumulated heat under the lead roof at the top of the house was
overwhelming. He just had time and energy enough to open each
of the two doors at the top of the stairs and glimpse two good-
sized but sparsely furnished rooms, before he grew so dizzy he
could barely get down again.

On the next floor down he went a little unsteadily to each door.
As before, there appeared to be an additional room. There were
four aside from his own which made a total of five plus the two in
the attic. Whatever else he might be forgetting, he was still fairly
sure that five plus two made seven. Not only were there two extra
rooms, but three bedrooms were mysteriously mothballed under
dustsheets, this in a house frequently full of people. He chose not
to disturb them and slowly descended to the ground floor where
he sat on the bottom steps, shaky, breathless and disoriented. He
was quite unable to account for the number and state of the
bedrooms in the house, which was a very peculiar thing to discover
on a Sunday morning. It was as if he was in someone else's house,
a house which had similar familiar possessions, many of the same
pictures on the walls, the same elegant furniture in the entrance
and as comfortable a sitting room as his own house, and yet was
not his, was not where he lived.

He sat there worrying for a minute or maybe ten, half scared to
turn his head and look up the stairs for fear of what other
strangeness he might see. A sudden chill passed over him and
roused his senses. He got to his feet, patted his jacket pocket to
confirm the presence of his essentials, and was momentarily
thankful for the drop in temperature. At the kitchen door it
appeared he'd been mistaken, for the outside air was as hot as ever,
relieved only slightly by the gentle sprinkle from the garden hose.

As he pulled out a cigarette, he paused over the garish packaging that had replaced the old gold. Why couldn't they leave things as they were, why did things always have to be changed, and so rarely for the better? He sat to light it, taking the first draw full and deep and felt the rasp in his throat. As he suppressed the coughing reflex, breathing out as only a smoker knows how, he reached for a drink and found the evaporated remains of one of the previous night's whiskeys. As he brought the neutered residue to his lips he saw a black beetle scrabbling inside the glass. It was one of their best glasses, one of a set of four antique crystal tumblers Mary's father had used, and his father before him. In disgust Michael Radcliffe threw it from his hand.

John Westerleigh turned the corner of the house at the precise moment the glass took flight. He'd come in by the unlocked side entrance, his attention immediately drawn to the illegal sprinkler. The cut crystal described a gentle curve through the dancing droplets, creating such an improbable sight that it was not clear what was solid and what was liquid as it sparkled on its brief journey. Equally improbably it bounced unharmed on the lush green turf.

'What's up Michael?'

'Eh?'

To John Westerleigh, calling for no other reason than he thought he ought, the glass hurler looked almost too feeble to have done such a thing. He appeared to have diminished overnight and to be withdrawing into his collar and tie as a tortoise might shrink into its shell.

'You'll have to turn this water off, Michael.'

'Yes, it's fine now, we'll leave it for today.'

The farmer wondered if he was being mistaken for the gardener, come to call and doff his cap at the big house. 'No, not for today, off off. It's not allowed, the rest of us have got no water.' He realised how easily he'd slipped into speaking loudly, as if Michael Radcliffe had not only shrunk but become deaf or foreign or both. 'Never mind, I'll do it. Are you coming to church this morning?'

'Church? Yes, why not. Have you got, um, Mary with you?'

'Mary? You mean Margaret?'

'Yes, yes, Margaret, that's it.'

The confusion of the recently deceased wife with his own, still living, spouse reminded him he had yet to discover what trouble she'd had here at The Glebe House, what trouble had required Philip Fox-Lomax's advice.

'No, not today, Michael. Haven't you seen enough of her lately?'

★

They'd hardly recognised each other, face to face on the front step at the Duncan house in Germans. Suzie Mortimer knew who she was calling on, but for a moment thought Laura was her mother, Kathy. Laura's first thought had been of another reporter or maybe police, especially when she'd been addressed by name in the way they do, 'Laura Duncan?', except if it's police they usually follow it up with 'Laura Jane Duncan?'

In other lives they'd have had no reason to meet or speak unless their fathers' friendship had brought them together. They certainly wouldn't have been calling on each other, exchanging private moments, walking arm in arm through the twin villages. But in this life they shared one miserable experience above any other that could unite them, they shared the loss of their daughters and the agonies that followed. It wasn't difficult for Laura to take up Suzie's offer of a walk, a chance to talk if she wanted to or not if she didn't, a reason to be out of the house. Laura picked up a big golf umbrella to give them shade as they walked through the stifling heat. Within a couple of minutes of answering the door, the two mothers were strolling towards the school and the path that wound its way down the side of the combe to the Centenary Wood, the lake and the study centre.

'I got stuck in the house for weeks, I couldn't go out in case she came back, which was silly really, she wasn't coming back, but it was how it felt.'

'Yeah. Do you know about Liam? That's my brother, my stupid brother. I've been out to see him, couldn't help it, but I know what you mean. It's not just staying in, it's just not being able to do anything, I can't even watch telly more than five minutes.'

'But the phone doesn't ring does it?'

'Not for Eysha, no, not for her. Not for anyone, there's no calls, no texts, it's like nobody can speak to us.'

'Scared. They don't know what to say,' said Suzie Mortimer, remembering her own isolation, made worse by the estrangement from her husband and abstinence from her then lover, Andrew Mortimer. Not that either of them had known what to say. Friends had evaporated, just as Laura was describing. 'What about that girl you were always with, Vicki wasn't it? Is she still around, are you still friends?'

Laura's alarm bells started ringing again at the mention of Vicki's name, perhaps this was all it was about, this friendly walk was nothing more than some quiz about Melanie and Eysha and Eysha's father. She stopped abruptly on the path, pulled on Suzie Mortimer's arm and said crossly, 'Is this about Melanie and Eysha when she was a baby? Is this got something to do with Eysha's dad?'

'No, it's got nothing to do with anything. Except you and me, and talk or not, 'cos I never had anybody, and I don't suppose you have.'

Laura loosened her grip and turned to walk again. 'I've got Mum and Dad. When they're not killing each other.' Hearing herself say the word she started to apologise, 'I didn't mean kill –'

'No, it's just a word. We none of us mean kill.'

They'd reached the bottom of the slope where the path forked. They chose to walk in the direction of the little lake and the study centre. Both women knew only too well where they were walking, what ghosts they might disturb.

'Have you been down here since?' Laura asked, a catch in her voice betraying her own unease.

'On the day I did, we were frantic and her friend showed me where they'd been. Otherwise no, not since. That was another reason to come down here. It's taken too long to be brave enough, I thought maybe it'd be easier together.'

'Sorry, I don't really know much about Melanie and her . . . '

'It's alright, I don't know much about your Eysha, except she's gone and nobody's found her. But Dad says she was down here, like my Annie was, then next thing she was gone. Have they said what they think has happened, the police, have they said anything?'

'They asked a lot about all sorts,' Laura paused, Eysha's father again hovered unwelcome on the edge of the conversation, 'asked about her father, they thought he might've snatched her, about us making money out of it all. But nothing else. They've got Liam, which keeps 'em happy, and as for my little girl, they don't say it outright, but they think she's drowned in the floods. Oh and they found her sandwiches floating over by the bird house and that seemed to confirm it for 'em.' That was it, she realised, in a few words she'd said all there was to say about her lovely daughter's disappearance, she was there one minute and the next there was just a box of sandwiches.

'I don't know the bird house, where is it?'

Laura led the way, telling Suzie where the water had been lapping, how the class had been cut off then rescued on the tractor and how her girl hadn't been with them. She desperately needed a smoke, but was conscious of having only one left until she could get some more from the shop. As they approached the building in the woods the unmistakeable smell of tobacco hung in the humid air, with evidence of recent occupation scattered all around. Laura could bear it no longer and reached for her cigarette.

'Do you? I've only got one,' she said lamely.

'Yes, duty frees. Have one. Have the packet, I've got another one. Is this the place? It's changed but I'm sure it's where Annie's friend brought me. If she'd been here, your girl, what would she have been doing here?'

'Truth? Just between us?' Melanie's mother nodded. 'Same as us, most likely, having a ciggy and bunking off.'

'Nothing changes. Annie did it too, I expect you did it. Looks like there's plenty of others who like this little hide-away,' she said pointing to the beer cans and cigarette ends under the tyre tracks.

'There's all sorts goes on down here, always has been so they say. The joke was when they put the bird thing up was how a roof on the place was long overdue.'

As they turned away, their arms linked naturally as a mother and daughter might do. A casual observer would have taken them for just that, and thought what a good thing it was for a parent and child to walk together like that, enjoy the shade of the trees together, little knowing that these two mothers would never know such small pleasures.

By the time they'd climbed sticky and breathless up to Maiden Lane by Suzie Mortimer's old house and old life, the two were talking freely of their daughters, good and bad. They had nothing to lie about or cover up or pretend was better than it was, they had no cause to make their girls cleverer or prettier or more loveable than they were. They just talked about them. And in the talking they found so much that seemed alike, their little ways, the sideways looks, and both so quick of mind but only fleet of foot when a fast exit called for it. They both thought how they might have been cousins at least. All the talking let them smile about their children, smile without fear of censure when the expected face was sorrow and tears.

★

The congregation in St. Giles was smaller than usual, holidays and the heat having taken their toll, as to a lesser extent, had events in the Radcliffe household. The Reverend Philip Fox-Lomax surveyed his parishioners at their worship as *Let There Be Light* wound its desultory way to a close. They were a far from inspiring gathering and, if he was honest with himself, he'd given them a far from inspiring sermon. In these trying times of blistering heat and water shortages he'd thought it right to remind them of the virtues of patience and good humour. He felt well qualified to advise his flock on these subjects, in part because his own temper was so frequently tested by those around him.

One or two had shifted uncomfortably as he'd touched on saving water and sharing resources, although his neighbour from The Glebe House had continued smiling blithely up at him. More than a few had looked at the floor as he'd spoken of keeping tempers under control. Several had nodded, a little smugly he thought, when he reminded them of neighbourly duties and care of the vulnerable. Some gave him no reaction, like the Samarasinghe woman from Upper Orchard. She was certainly one of the most dutiful yet also one of the least forthcoming. Her daughter on the other hand gave little reaction because she paid so little attention. The revealing glow of the screen on her mobile phone may have been hidden from most but not from his vantage point in the pulpit. And they were all spread out, all with little buffer zones of empty places or empty rows separating them from their fellows. Nearly all, anyway. His neighbour Michael had the worrisome farmer in close attendance and Margery Webster inevitably had Colin Deeley in a similar position.

The persistent little constable was back again too, after her unwelcome enquiries of yesterday. She'd left him to guess at when the sacrilege of eavesdropping on confession had happened and for how long, but he knew without asking it was all tied up with the Staples girl. The whole affair had slept through the years with nobody any the worse off through ignorance, and some might say better off, then chance takes a hand and one thing leads to another and all manner of unhappiness unfolds.

He offered the final prayers and the blessing from in front of the altar then moved towards the door, ready to exchange a few words with each worshipper, as was the custom. The congregation filed out, subdued and apparently unwilling to leave the sanctuary of the church. The brilliance of the light outside brought each of them squinting from the shade into the glare. The better planners, or fashion conscious, had hats and sunglasses at the ready.

Suzie Mortimer and Laura Duncan had stopped under the yew by the gate, Suzie to join up with her father Colin, Laura to stay in the company of the older woman a little longer. They'd smoked all round their walk, yet here at the church gate they stood a little awkwardly, their cigarettes half hidden by their sides.

'Did your Annie,' Laura had adopted Suzie's pet name for Melanie quite naturally, 'did she nick her ciggies off you? Eysha does, she thinks I don't know, but I do.' With all the talk of her daughter she'd quite forgotten to speak of her in the past as she'd started to do.

'Yeah, and a few other people too. Nothing to be proud of, but I think she nicked some and cadged some too. I'd ask her where she got the money from and she'd say so-and-so had given her one. It got her in trouble a few times, at school and with Peter, he hated it.' She looked at the ash at the end of her cigarette, the blue wisp of smoke curling up from it. 'Still does,' she said.

As the door opened and the worshippers spilled out, blinded, into the sun and heat, the first to emerge were Suzie's father with Margery on his arm, which brought a nod and a knowing look from his daughter. The two stopped and turned to talk with John Westerleigh who was hovering around Michael Radcliffe. A little gaggle of people followed, before the Samarasinghes and Peter Staples, lingering to speak earnestly with the rector and a couple of Laura's near neighbours, the only members of the congregation who lived in that corner of the parish.

One moment it was all heat and slow movement, a summer buzz of insects and after-prayer conversation, the next it was shouts and saving lunges as Michael Radcliffe tripped with his hands caught in his jacket pockets, feeling for his smokes. John Westerleigh deflected some of the fall but his friend still went sprawling across the path, ending on his back between two ancient tombstones. One hand remained trapped in the pocket, the other was bent under him, released by the fabric tearing as he fell.

After the shouts and dives a moment's hush as all eyes turned to the half hidden figure struggling to raise himself from between the graves. Then the quick-witted darted forward to offer assistance and eager hands reached out to haul the faller gingerly to his feet. Thomas Samarasinghe was too far back to help directly, so he contented himself with picking up Michael Radcliffe's wallet, cigarettes and lighter which had dropped from the torn pocket. As he bent to reach the silver lighter the glint of a coin also caught his eye. Retrieving it he found it was not the brassy gold of a pound, it was not a coin at all, but a locket with a broken chain. He held it out in his hand, almost certain of what he held, but doubting such a thing could be true. A thousand possibilities screamed for attention while the impossible calmly lay across his palm, glinting its cheap shine into his eye. He would not believe such a thing, not until he was quite certain.

'Have you got Mr Radcliffe's things?' said a voice at his elbow. He snapped his hand closed over the locket and mutely gave up the wallet, the cigarettes and the precious silver lighter.

'Was there some money?' the voice enquired suspiciously.

He shook his head. 'No,' he said thickly. Turning, he watched as the valuables were re-united with their owner and the little knot of people began to dissolve and drift apart. He desperately wanted to be able to stop the scene just as it was, to hold all the actors on their marks until he could remember, or work out, what the next lines were. Unless he did something right there and then, he might never be able to do it, the world would never ever be aligned in just this way again. His mother's words about his father *to know when and where he's wanted or not wanted* suddenly made better sense to him, there was indeed a time to speak and a time to be silent. In a moment he knew this to be both.

Looking round for his mother and Diana he saw them talking to Lavi Pitesteanu. His sister saw his look and made a face for him to come over. Beyond them, still by the church door was Peter Staples saying goodbye to the rector. At the gate, Michael Radcliffe was being escorted slowly away to his house, enveloped in a cloud of blue smoke. He could see Colin Deeley there too, and by association he thought he recognised Suzie Staples, with Laura Duncan close beside. Eysha's mother had no part to play in the scene, but her presence somehow endorsed his plan.

'Diana!' he called to his sister. Grudgingly she came over to him, his urgency intriguing her. 'Listen and please, please do exactly what I say. Take this.' He took her hand and dropped the locket into it. 'Show no one and say nothing to anyone until I come back. Keep everyone here. Amma, her,' he pointed at the constable, 'Mr Staples, and all of them,' he turned to the group chatting under the yew.

'Thomas Samarasinghe, have you gone crazy?' she hissed.

'Maybe I have. And maybe you will have your special report for your news desk. Maybe this locket is Melanie Staples' locket. Keep them all here, I will be five minutes, ten perhaps - at most.' He clasped her closed hand in his so the metal bit into her palm, 'Do this,' he urged her.

Once he was briskly past the village shop without a backward look he broke into a jog. Within a few steps he was soaked in sweat, the sun nearing its high point seared him from above while the treeless tarmac of Lisle Gate roasted him from beneath. He increased his pace, fearful that his sister wouldn't keep the group corralled for long. Once before, just once, he could remember running up these roads to his house in Upper Orchard drenched, not as now, but with rain. It was the day he'd run from the bottom of the comb leaving Melanie standing in the downpour, saying how she'd be alright. As he'd run with all the carelessness of youth, the cheap brassy locket had bounced up and down on the thinnest of chains at the neck of his white polo shirt. He could feel it now, feel it as he rushed into the house, into his room. He could feel it as he tipped out the drawer to find the box, feel it as he scrabbled to open it. Then it was there, back in his hand after so long in the dark. There was no doubt, the half he held was his half, the half he'd entrusted to Diana was Melanie's.

At the thought of his sister he was on his way again, pausing at the door when he thought he caught a hint of burning in the air. A lunchtime barbecue under way perhaps, or another field-fire eating its way across the parched ground. Across the valley, over towards Whyncombe Wood he thought he could just detect a dark layer in the atmosphere, streaked against the blue and green, but the heat played tricks with the light and he could not be sure. He looked back at the scattered contents of the box and turned back to grab something else and slip it over his wrist. Then he was off again, loping along to the end of the road, past the sullen Labrador, swinging right and helter-skelter down to the lane, all in no time at all. He was at once excited, euphoric even, free and light enough to fly if he wished, yet with the nervousness of an impending exam.

Almost to his surprise, he could see all the players remained on stage, awaiting his direction in the shade by the gate. As he ran towards them, he could see that his mother was least happy to be kept waiting. She wouldn't say so in front of strangers, but he knew from the hard line of her jaw what she was thinking. Diana was in conversation with Laura Duncan when his arrival hushed them all.

'Thank you so much,' he said, 'thank you for waiting. Now, I am back, I don't know where to begin.' He looked at Peter Staples and Suzie Mortimer separated as they were by Suzie's father, all three looking expectantly at him, and he saw them all again in the cottage along Maiden Lane, where he'd sometimes gone for tea or just called round before he and Melanie had slipped away to their games and hideouts. 'Hello Mrs Staples,' he began.

'Mortimer, it's Mortimer now. Call me Suzie, Thomas. What's this about?' If her face had changed since his childhood, her voice had not. With this reassurance he began again.

'Something I had to tell someone, I had to tell you all, because it's about Melanie. And at just the exact moment I had to tell you, you were all here together. Serendipity, we could say. She was my great friend. We did many things together, not all of them good things.' He looked at his mother and saw her warning look. 'Some of them were probably very bad, but we laughed so much together, we were children. I know we did maths together, which sounds incredible now, that we should have shared such a thing. We made promises to each other, the kind that children make and when we made them we believed they were for ever. Do you remember our friendship bracelets, Amma?' His mother nodded. She had made them, twists of cotton thread, yellow, green, saffron and maroon. He held his up to show his audience. 'Here is mine, I found it this morning.

'There was something else like these bracelets, too. I haven't worn mine or seen it for many years, until this morning.' He saw Suzie Mortimer's hand go to her lips as she took in a sharp breath. 'This morning I thought I'd seen a ghost. I saw Melanie's locket. I knew it was hers, but just in case I was somehow wrong, I ran home to find mine.' He turned to Suzie Mortimer who was hanging on to her father and trembling slightly. 'I think you bought this for Melanie to give to me didn't you?' She nodded. 'Here is its partner, the one I found here this morning.' Diana held it out for all to see and passed it to her brother. Carefully he opened the back of each, knowing precisely what to expect. 'Look, see, here is our sign, we drew them.' In each locket was a scrap of paper with the symbol for infinity drawn in blue ink. Then he closed them and held them in his fingers. 'They are made for each other, they go together like this,' and he slipped the one into the other to make a whole heart.

★

He could smell it long before he got there, and he got there as quickly as he could. An acrid burnt-flesh stench that stuck to your clothes. He'd just got Michael Radcliffe a cup of tea and settled him in a garden chair when he'd caught the first hint of it. An alien smell seeping through the air with nothing to carry it but the thermals rising from the oven baked land, a cross between singed hair and the burnt paint of new-car exhaust pipe. Then in a flash he remembered who was having a fire and where they were having it. He dashed from The Glebe House and got back to the farm faster than he thought possible. Through Germans the horrible odour was strong, then down by Lisle House and Six Lanes it was foul. He kept looking up from the road to the tree tops on the hill, half expecting to see flames leaping above them, flames consuming the barns, the house, everything that was High Whyn Farm.

As he turned into the gate, it was almost a surprise to see all the buildings intact and no fire tender hosing down the yard. Behind the end barn he found his wife, exactly where she said she'd be, tending a quite modest sized fire in the middle of a large circle of burnt grass.

'What the hell have you been burning?' he said, angry that she should burn anything, and quite forgetting that he'd approved it.

She hooked something from the remains of the fire with the fork she was holding and held it under his nose while it smoked and melted. 'Shoes, mainly.'

'Shoes?' He looked closer at the smouldering debris. 'Shoes?'

'The plastic burns, but leather doesn't, so I gave them a helping hand with all sorts of old junk. I've had quite a clear out.'

'Shoes? The stink is halfway across the county.'

'The stink was already halfway across the county.'

'The rector said there was some trouble with Michael, is that was this is about?'

He would know, sooner or later, and she had no reason to hide it from him apart from disgust and her own misplaced sense of shame. So she told him what she'd found and how she'd come to find it. She told him of the racks and drawers of clothes that had still to be checked and her fears of what might yet be found amongst them. And when he questioned whether she'd taken the right course in burning the shoes, burning the evidence he said, and might it have been better to tell the authorities, by which he meant the police, she could have brought up his own silence about Melanie Staples and how it had taken eleven years to tell the little bits he knew, so who was he to talk about a few burnt shoes. But she didn't say any such thing, she said yes and no and maybe while tending the diminishing fire until the last traces of the shoes were reduced to ash. And when all but the metal clips and stiffeners and buckles were gone she raked those last fragments together into a bag for recycling and considered it a difficult job well done.

15

Two whole degrees cooler than yesterday should have been a cause for minor celebration, but by eleven o'clock Lavi Pitesteanu was already too tired and hot to care as she parked outside the church. She'd barely slept for days and had spent far too long in this corner of the county. What might have once been an interesting challenge in a picturesque setting had become a sweating, unrewarding, labour. Finding Melanie's locket was progress of a sort, although the emotional impact could turn out to be more significant than anything practical. Having listened patiently at the church gate to all shades of opinion over what she should do about the discovery, she'd gone to the Samarasinghes' and taken a fresh statement. Formally. Mr Samarasinghe. Miss Samarasinghe. No Thomas and certainly no Lavi - how she regretted those off-duty moments of informality.

She had both halves of the locket carefully labelled and listed, although she knew full well that they were of no value in themselves. Handled by everyone, they were really for illustration purposes only. One thing about them had struck her, which was that they were equally worn, and neither was tarnished in any way. Neither looked as if it had been in the earth and both had probably been kept in a drawer for years. Her question was whether or not it was the same drawer. If so, then who else's but Mr Samarasinghe junior's? The sickening possibility that he was again showing off his criminal cleverness once more lurked in the pit of her stomach.

Her superiors had been of little encouragement, telling her to get on with it if she wished, make sure it was all logged, they were there to help but that she should weigh up the chances of success before she spent much longer on it. There were, they said, other matters she might be more profitably employed on and gave her some files to be considering. Being plucked from bicycle thefts in Oxford to help Donald Smallborne in a potential murder, glorious though it might have been, could be reversed in seconds. And probably would be when he returned.

If she were going to take the Staples case to the bitter end then there were two obvious places to continue: the unbearable vicar in whose churchyard the locket had been found or his oddly distracted neighbour, who'd been the last person seen to drop something in that place. The two halves of the self-appointed Management Group. It occurred to her that they not only appeared to be playing at spies with their silly secret codes but at gangsters too with the name for their gang.

She was sick of the pompous vicar, so she opted for the erratic Michael Radcliffe. But not before a few minutes of contemplation in the cool embrace of St. Giles.

★

'Me?' Acantha Fox-Lomax complained, 'I'm hardly qualified to be nurse-maid, you should get the Good Samaritan to go, she spends enough time there.'

Her husband had suggested she come with him to The Glebe House to check on their neighbour after his fall of the previous day. In some instinctive way he thought a female presence, even if it was in the unmatronly form of his wife, might be appropriate. He didn't mention to her that he'd already called Margaret Westerleigh without success.

He had a second reason to pay a visit, well outside the Christian charity he'd preached about the previous day. He feared events were leading inexorably towards unwelcome discoveries and fresh accusations, all beyond his control, perhaps beyond his influence and accelerated by the Samarasinghe boy's theatrical party trick with the lockets. The days since the Great Deluge had served to remind him how delicate was the balance of knowledge and ignorance in maintaining the smooth order of village affairs. The weakest link appeared to be Michael Radcliffe who seemed to be declining by the hour.

'I'll go round myself then, but if he needs something I'll call.'

'If he needs something call one of your caring flock or better still call social services. I'm going to the club for a swim.' A door banged shut and few moments later he heard the car swish out on the gravel.

At the mirror by the front door the rector checked his appearance, not through personal vanity, but as a priest he had a duty to be neatly dressed, clean-shaven and with his sandy hair tidy. Neatness seemed impossible when in a permanent pool of sweat and the heat flattered no one, but he would have to do. At his gate he stopped and noted the car parked across the entrance to the churchyard. He recognised it as belonging to the annoying police girl. If she was hiding in the cool of St. Giles on the pretext of looking for him again, then good luck to her.

The driveway at The Glebe House stood empty behind closed gates but the side entrance through to the garden was inevitably open. He found Michael Radcliffe just where he might have expected, sitting comfortably on the terrace, a cigarette in hand, an amber coloured drink in a small glass beside him. Less expected was that he was in his shirt sleeves.

'Still using the sprinklers, Michael? They're dishing out big fines, you know.'

'Keeps it a bit cooler, a bit fresher I find.'

'No doubt it does.'

'Mary's been back. Been upstairs getting things sorted out.'

'Mary?' for a moment the rector feared he'd forgotten his wife was dead. 'Ah, do you mean Margaret? Is she here now?'

'Margaret, yes, that's it. Yesterday. Or Saturday.'

'No broken bones after your fall? But sore I expect?'

'Yes, blasted steps, slipped right down on top of her, fearful yelp she let out.'

'Yesterday? A dog? When did you get a dog?'

'A dog? No, we haven't had dogs for ages, after that business with the sheep. No, no, this was weeks ago. I'm fine.'

'And yesterday? Coming out of church? You fell over, you tore your jacket.'

'Yes, my poor jacket is in Mary's good care. She's taken it to sew it back together. Pocket's all torn.'

Habit took his hand to his side to find the silver lighter and the cigarettes. A moment of anxiety, and then relief as he found them on the table beside him. He took a sip of scotch, then a fresh ice cube from the flask and plopped it into the glass, swirling the chill of the ice and the fire of the whisky into a blur, then letting them sit and slow to a stop. A fresh cigarette was pulled from the pack and the silver lighter, after a couple of tender strokes from his fingers, flipped and flamed.

'Well, I'm glad you're not hurt, you seemed pretty shaken up.'

'Eh? No, fine, just a tumble.'

The Reverend Philip Fox-Lomax eyed his neighbour uncertainly, suspicious of his exact mental state, and feeling the rising need of his own nicotine hit. He lowered his voice a little and tested the memory a little further. 'Michael, did you lose anything yesterday? When you fell?'

The sparkling droplets of the sprinkler rose and fell twice while he considered the question.

'Lost my wallet I think, and my lighter,' he reached out to touch it again.

'Nothing else? Somebody found a necklace, a little heart locket.'

'Locket!' he exclaimed, 'She had one, a little broken heart thing. I don't know why she picked up that cheap stuff. Mary came in just as I was looking at it.'

'Mary? Do you mean Mary? Or Margaret?'

He looked at the rector, clearly unsure of who had disturbed him. 'Margaret, yes, that's it.'

'Michael, they say it belonged to the girl, they say it was Melanie Staples' locket.'

'It might have been, I suppose, I don't know where she got it from. Staples? Peter Staples' girl? Oh, that girl, yes,' he lowered his voice a little and leaned forward in his chair, spilling ash down his shirt, 'nasty little mouth on her that one. Quite shocking, little thief like that and she comes out with all sorts of filth and lies. Shouldn't really have said anything to Mary. Should've kept mum. But, there it was and it couldn't be taken back. Anyway, we've said all this before, it was just one of those things in the end, eh?'

'In a way, yes, Michael, and we all must do what we believe is right, for the good of everyone.'

'I think we have, all along, it's been right for everyone. Made the best of a bad job, as my dear mother used to say. Do you want a drink or something? If you want a scotch I can sort that out right here.'

'A bit early for me.' Which was quite true, it was very early for the rector to even think of a drink, but the offer was extremely tempting. 'I'll settle for a smoke.'

'Help yourself, here, I don't much like these new ones, see what you think.'

'Michael, they'll be coming to see you again, coming to ask about the necklace, about whether you had it, how you had it, how Mary had it. Not all the old questions with all the old answers. New questions, like the governors meetings, the, er, conversation you had with the girl,' and he chose his words very carefully in adding, 'and anything Mary might have said. They'll be asking all that now, you know that?'

'Does it really matter any more, Philip? It was a long time ago, all that. We all did our penance, eh?' He spoke as one who was surveying the whole catalogue of history since the Domesday record was made and saw no more than a minor footnote.

The tension of the moment would have caused a nervous perspiration on the coldest of days, but in the midsummer heat Philip Fox-Lomax felt every stitch of clothing glued to his body. Even the palms of his hands grew greasy, and the white of his cigarette grew dark from sweat seeping from lips and fingers. He still had a precarious balance to maintain, one between public knowledge and private knowledge. In a life already full to bursting with contradictions, he could only see more crowding in. Every additional snippet and detail he learned only amplified his dilemma. For years the subject of 'the Staples girl' had never been touched upon by name, the arbitrary judgement of good over evil had been accepted and the peace of the parish had been more or less preserved. Silence also sustained the rightful and natural order of things, ensuring the continuity of centuries would persist. Now, in speaking as they had done the spell had already been broken, regardless of what consequences flowed.

As they carried on their strange, disjointed conversation, the two men ignored the presence of another person in the house. Philip Fox-Lomax thought they were alone and Michael Radcliffe couldn't be sure whether it was his wife or Margaret Westerleigh, or even if it was today. But there was another person and it was the farmer's wife, and from an upstairs window she'd seen the rector arrive. And it was true, she had offered to mend the torn pocket. All this money, she'd thought, and more clothes than they knew what to do with, and him wearing that old jacket day after day in the hottest summer since goodness knows when. How had she been foolish enough to offer to sew that foul smelling old thing when he probably had a cupboard full of jackets?

To begin her task she'd shaken out the collected litter and tobacco dust from the pockets onto a newspaper. Left dangling as she did so, caught in the tear, were a few tiny links from a fragile gold chain. A child's chain she'd thought, like some of those she'd seen in this house previously. She'd picked them out and discarded them in the paper with the rest. And then, when she got right down to it, the ripped pocket was more or less beyond repair. Not only the pocket but the lining was worn and torn in so many places she put it aside and began the unwelcome task of bagging up Mary's clothes. She'd entered the bedroom with deep misgivings, armed with plastic bags, gloves and a disinfectant aerosol, although quite how this would protect her she was not sure.

In the stuffy closed-up heat of the room it was all she could do to fill two bags before she needed a breath, and then two more before she needed another and a drink of water to go with it. Despite all her troubles and misgivings Margaret Westerleigh remained a considerate soul and thought to also offer the two men a cool drink. The open French windows of the drawing room gave out onto the terrace where they sat. She'd drawn the heavy curtains earlier to keep some of the heat and dazzling light out of the house. As she stepped into the room some word or gesture from the terrace made her stop. The two men sat outside in the brilliance of the sunlight as if on a stage, oblivious to the presence of an audience in the darkened playhouse.

Michael Radcliffe was talking about Mary, how she collected odd things and for a moment Margaret was horrified to think that he knew about her disgusting shoe thefts. Then she realised he was speaking of jewellery, how his wife liked little cheap things and how foolish she'd been to keep that thing from the Staples girl, and the rector was smoking and looking very uncomfortable with a serious face. *The Staples girl!* Her mouth grew dry at the sheer casualness of the reference. She edged a pace closer.

'I was never sure if you knew or not, or how much,' the rector was saying.

'We don't talk about it, but Mary took care of things.' He leaned towards the priest and lowered his voice, 'I don't see I had much choice really in the end, the girl had made up some filthy stuff, had me giving her money for cigarettes and all sorts. You didn't know that, did you?'

It seemed to Margaret Westerleigh that the rector looked ill, looked as a man might look on the point of death, his cheeks and lips quite bloodless. Beads of sweat covered his face and as he closed his eyes he might have been a corpse dragged fresh from the river. Margaret herself was faint from the heat and the words she was hearing. In staring at the bright-lit stage, all around her had become black and she was unsure if she stood or sat or floated. Beneath her feet the plush carpet grew plusher, a quicksand threatening to envelope her.

'Then that stuff about Mary, just nasty, nasty lies, like the rest. That deserved a good smack if anything did.'

The rector swallowed hard and brought the cigarette to his lips. The smoke lingered round his mouth and nostrils as he drew in a shallow breath. He fought back the knowledge of what were lies and what were not, knowledge that was private knowledge, forgotten and never heard knowledge, confessed knowledge. 'Michael, you need say no more,' he said in little more than a whisper.

Margaret saw his lips move and saw the smoke speak his words and wanted to cry out no, he did need to say more, although in truth she was fearful of what she might hear. The thought of prayer crossed her mind, but was driven out by the sun momentarily catching the crucifix sweatily stuck to the priest's black frock. A week ago, maybe less, she might have taken it as an answer to the unspoken prayer.

'That was the last straw really, but a girl like that? Something had to be done, I know you've said as much yourself.'

'I've not said that, I don't think, not like that.'

'Well there you are, what's done, is done. No bringing the kid back, not now. God knows where she is. Washed away most likely.' He contemplated his empty glass. 'Have a drink now?'

'Washed away? What do you mean, washed away?' She's been found.'

Then a hideous thought entered Philip Fox-Lomax's mind and lodged itself there like a deep and jagged splinter. It took a moment or two to frame a simple question.

'Are you talking about Melanie Staples?' he asked hoarsely.

Michael Radcliffe looked puzzled and considered the question. 'Yes, I think so. Who are you talking about?'

A nearby hammering, metal on metal, made Margaret turn her head and in doing so some reflection in her glasses caught the rector's eye. 'Michael, you should say no more,' he said earnestly while looking directly at her. 'Margaret will be down in a moment.'

'Margaret? Well, I'm sure she knows a thing or two about Mary as well, she'd know what lies the girl's been saying. I don't know where she's got the ideas from, terrible stuff for a ten year-old. Tagged me for a cigarette, then do you know what she said?'

'Michael, you've said enough.' His gaze remained fixed on the twin pinpricks of light twinkling from the darkness of the drawing room. As he stared into the darkness the shape of Margaret's face began to reveal itself.

'Told me to eff off, if you please, called me a pervert and all sorts.'

The glimmers twinkled brighter as she rushed to the door, out into the light, hurling herself towards the back of Michael Radcliffe's head. The rector was not quick enough, struggling to rise and lunge between her blows and the widower's skull. In the fury of the attack she struck only a glancing blow with her hand and another with the aerosol can before being pushed back by the rector. She squared up to him, her hands by her sides, his raised in supplication.

'Stop, Margaret, stop! Stop!'

She raised the disinfectant and sprayed straight into his eyes, cursing his sight and wishing him blinded for his evil. As he turned away pawing at his face, she returned to the main object of her anger.

'Mary! What's going on? For goodness sake, woman!' Michael Radcliffe cried, trying to rise, but Margaret's hand rested on his frail shoulder and was enough to keep him in his seat.

'For goodness sake, Michael? You disgusting old man, you foul and disgusting old man. You call me Mary? Your precious Mary was no better than you. Little kid told lies about her, did she? No, she didn't. Not lies, Michael, she told the truth. She knew didn't she, she knew about the shoes, knew about the perverted thieving, knew other stuff too, I'll bet. It was true, you sick old man. Do you understand that? Let's clean you up a bit too, shall we?' She leaned down to be closer to her target, waving the spray just beyond his reach, covering him in the liquid. 'You killed a girl for the lies she told, and the lies weren't lies at all.'

Then she launched another strike with her hands, then another. Michael Radcliffe sat transfixed, not comprehending the storm of anger and violence that had suddenly burst about his head, hardly defending himself against the swinging blows that brought the hard edge of the can across the side of his head leaving torn red stripes across his scalp.

'You'd probably have killed her anyway, wouldn't you? Put her down like you did your dogs, remember that? Somewhere to shoot them where people wouldn't notice the blast. Came and did it behind the barn, remember?' Even as she spoke the words a terrible image burst in her brain. 'Oh no, oh God, no, is that where you killed her?'

Her face screwed into an animal snarl as a final downward strike imprinted the circular base of the can on his forehead. Stunned, he fell back. The whiskey glass slipped from his hand and broke on the stone.

'Margaret, please! He hasn't killed anyone!' Philip Fox-Lomax was on his knees shouting, begging her to stop, while the lawn sprinkler waved its sparkling jets across his face. But she had already stopped, the awfulness of the picture in her mind draining the energy from her. She stood trembling, dishevelled, her hair plastered to her face, aerosol still clutched in her latex fingers but with arms hanging limp by her sides.

'Look at him, he's ill, he hasn't killed anyone.'

She lifted her head as the stream waved its last as the sprinkling finally ceased. If not the disgusting Michael then please, please not her priest, let it not be him, how could it be him? Let it be someone else not him, let it be Mary. Yes, let it be Mary. She mouthed the name. The dripping, pleading rector of Whyncombe St. Giles made no reply.

★

Suzie Mortimer couldn't help but notice just how at home Margery Webster was in her father's house. It had never been Suzie's home, but nonetheless she might have supposed that Margery, being only a friend and neighbour, would have deferred to her while her father was elsewhere. With Margery occupying the kitchen it left Suzie and Peter Staples as uneasy company in the little sitting room. It was as near neutral territory as could be found and both had been there since early afternoon, being brought up to date with events by a well intentioned, but poorly briefed, liaison officer. Not only was it neutral ground, it was away from the centre of activity close to the church, where a posse of sweating reporters had collected unhappily over the last few hours.

'Your dad'll be on in a minute,' Margery said as the national news ended and the local service took over.

She was right, the news of Suzie and Peter's daughter was the leading item, reported live from under the yew at the gate to St. Giles. Not only reported live, but by a local reporter with a special interest and knowledge of the case, the BBC's very own Diana Samarasinghe.

'You're sure you want to watch this?' Peter Staples asked his former wife.

'Yes, get it over with. See what the rest of the world are going to be told.'

Diana Samarasinghe's serious face appeared, behind her the churchyard still bathed in sunlight. It had been, she said, a harrowing day for many people in Whyncombe St. Giles, triggered in part by events yesterday, events to which she had been a witness, and indeed in which she had played her own small part. As if matters couldn't be made any worse, she added in an unscheduled aside, the water supply to the villages had been cut since mid morning. The plug for her own journalistic acumen having been established the camera pulled back to reveal two figures flanking her, who she introduced as the senior officer in charge of the investigation plus the detective most involved in the day-to-day detail. It was true that the senior officer put forward for the interview was theoretically in charge, although he knew no more than Melanie's name, and had needed reminding of that. He made a few standard comments about solid police work, no case ever being closed, sympathy with the family and so on, which, in fairness, was exactly why he was there, before the BBC's very own turned to the more photogenic Constable Lavi Pitesteanu. Such was the coup of reporting live on an important story, Diana Samarasinghe had not objected to sharing a little of her time with the dark eyed detective.

' . . . no, at this stage we are not expecting any charges to be made against any of the people helping us piece this sad story together . . . must emphasise that none of those being interviewed are suspected of any direct involvement in the death of Melanie Staples . . .'

'No involvement. One way of putting it I suppose,' Suzie Mortimer said sourly. Her ex-husband said nothing.

' . . . four local residents are talking to us at the moment, there may be more tomorrow, it is hard to say . . . a fifth person has already returned to the village . . .'

'I don't know how he looked you in the eye all these years,' she went on.

' . . . no, all have volunteered their assistance . . .'

'Not sure that he did, now you mention it.' said her ex.

'I don't expect it's been that easy for him, not when you think of all the things people must tell him, it must be an awful burden,' Margery Webster suggested with the greatest sympathy. Melanie's parents remained stony faced.

238

'. . . yes, as we presently understand events, it seems likely that the person most closely involved in the victim's death is themselves now dead . . .'

'Been dead a lot sooner if I'd have known what she did.'

'. . . there is no evidence of that at present, we may never know the exact circumstances. The death may have been purely accidental . . .'

The three watchers in the cottage at Six Lanes each had their own thoughts about how likely it was that Melanie had died in that way. To say it was accidental somehow suggested she had fallen from a tree and cracked her head, or choked on a toffee. It suggested that it involved nobody but Melanie herself, and might even have been her own fault for being up the tree or eating too many toffees. Accidental said nothing of it being in the presence of an adult, said nothing of the child being smacked hard across the mouth before she died, hard enough to dislodge a tooth deemed healthy and sound only hours previously. Accidental said nothing of being thrown unconscious into a car boot and later buried in the woods, as a dog might have been. As a dog was.

'. . . any suggestion of the exact cause or circumstances of the death is pure speculation at this stage and may remain so, we must emphasise that . . .'

And speculation it remained in the cottage at Six Lanes.

By the time Diana Samarasinghe had thanked the police, linked back to the studio for thirty seconds of archive footage from the first investigation, then re-introduced herself and the report, another of those helping piece Melanie's story together had returned to Whyncombe St. Giles. Thomas Samarasinghe joined his mother in the newly air-conditioned splendour of their house at the end of Upper Orchard. Despite a country-wide shortage of units, priority supply to the young and the elderly, an unmarked van had delivered one of the scarce machines earlier in the day, and an unmarked engineer had installed it shortly afterwards. It hummed softly in the corner of the room, anonymously cooling the air and sucking water from it. The cooled water was collected in plastic bins, an additional benefit when the mains supply had been cut off since mid-morning.

'Did you say all you wanted to say, Thomas?' his mother asked earnestly, hoping he had, hoping that finally she and her son could put the whole business of Melanie Staples behind them for good.

'Yes, I think so, I think it is done now, Amma.'

'Diana is talking.'

'Yes, I see her, Amma.'

' . . . *Mr Colin Deeley, Melanie's grandfather, who has kindly agreed to speak on behalf of the family . . .* '

'He looks terrible, poor man,' said Upeksha Samarasinghe.

'Yes.'

' . . . *only good thing is to have some kind of answer, know something of how she came to be taken from us. People will say all sorts, but I want to say right here and now, she was a lovely girl was Melanie. She got into all kinds of scrapes, we know that, but she was a lovely girl, no more than a . . .* '

'He didn't say how much fun she was, how much she laughed,' he said, full of regret, as if it were he who'd missed the opportunity to speak of laughter.

'He didn't need to.' Mother and son exchanged looks of understanding about a subject which only a few days ago would have been quite impossible. The veto on speaking of Melanie had been lifted.

' . . . *opportunity to mention another family who've lost a young child. That's the Duncans, their Eysha has been missing ten days now, they need all our help and support. We've got our Melanie back in a way, but they've got nothing . . .* '

'That's good, I think people have forgotten already.'

'That such things happen,' said Upeksha shaking her head sadly, 'That such things should happen here.'

' . . . *think there could be any possible connection, any link between your own family's terrible loss and the disappearance of Eysha Duncan?* '

'I think they'll start looking at all that again, and soon,' said Thomas.

'Did they say that?' asked his mother.

' . . . *know, you'll have to ask them. Personally, yes, I do, but whether there is or not don't let that family wait eleven years to find out what's happened to . . .* '

'No, but I think they will. There are so many little things, even if the dentist isn't one of them. Even the rain. We stood upstairs last week and watched it, remember that Amma? And we both thought about Melanie then.'

'What other little things?'

'All sorts, I spoke to Mrs Mortimer, Melanie's mum, and Eysha's mum Laura yesterday after the lockets were put back together. They'd been walking round the old places where we used to go, and they'd thought there were little things too. Like,' he hesitated momentarily, a residue of shame still clinging to his memories, 'like cigarettes, like stealing cigarettes. And other things too.'

'Nothing to do with the Radcliffes?'

'Maybe, I don't know about it all, they're going to speak to the detective about it.'

'The pretty one who can't take her eyes off you?'

'Amma!'

'Well, it's true.'

The little back kitchen of the house in Germans where Alex Duncan and his daughter were watching intently had no such luxury as air conditioning. Each sat with as few clothes as possible to remain decent, enduring not only the heat and humidity, but the renewed attention of the press, a small party of whom were loitering at the front gate. For the sake of appearances a uniformed support officer - Eysha's disappearance no longer warranted a fully-fledged constable - had been detailed to loiter by the gate with them. The intention had been for the support officer to be on hand when the water tanker arrived to distribute emergency supplies, but as it had failed to do so, duties had been switched.

'Did he tell you he was going to say something about Eysha?' Laura asked her father.

'Aye, said he would if he could.'

'Nice of him.'

'Colin's alright.'

'So's Suzie, a bit hard, but alright.' After a little more thought she added, 'That Samasinger boy's ok too. A bit la-de-dah but he's alright.'

'I know him, used to be a big pal of Suzie's girl.'

' . . . someone who knows this community very well and has been intimately involved . . . '

'Knows nothing.'

'Maybe knows nothing you know, Laura, but knows a lot of other things, or so it seems. Maybe knows things even now he's not telling.'

241

' . . . *deeply shocked and saddened too, by these developments. The church has supported the Staples family through all this tragic affair . . .* '

'Support? Looked after their own more like,' Laura Duncan snorted in disgust.

Then Diana Samarasinghe surprised her audience and the rector of Whyncombe St. Giles by cutting across his platitudes to ask him directly if he had known all along some of the important details which were only just now being revealed to the police. She'd chosen her words carefully being neither too specific nor too vague. The rector's expression flickered briefly from serious but benevolent to hostile and malignant. Then he composed himself.

' . . . *the church is often called upon to share a burden, sometimes of knowledge, sometimes of ignorance . . .* '

'What kind of bleedin' crap is that?'

Her father grunted in agreement.

' . . . *support of the family and withholding information seem contradictory. How do you respond to that?*

'Good for you! Int that the Samasinger girl?'

' . . . *no contradiction. The church has certain duties . . .* '

'*Excuse me, but why do you keep referring to the church when really you are talking about yourself?*

'*This is not a personal matter, this is a church matter, a pastoral matter.*'

'*It's difficult to think of the death of this young girl in what appear to be highly suspicious circumstances as either a church matter or a pastoral matter. Do you have any final comment?*

'*No, thank you, enough has been said already.*'

All trace of benevolence had long since vanished from the rector's face.

Father and daughter were both left unexpectedly satisfied by the interview, even though neither had previously held any particular grudge against the rector. It was true that in their eyes and in the eyes of their neighbours, he represented the 'haves' of Whyncombe St. Giles rather than the 'have-nots' of Germans. A minute or so after it had finished and the news had switched focus to the water crisis, the thought occurred to them both that Philip Fox-Lomax might possibly have some knowledge of their lost child, might carry some secret about Eysha and her whereabouts. The

242

possibility hardened Alex's face in determination, softened Laura's to fresh tears.

'I'll not wait eleven years for him to tell me,' he said, and his words sounded more like a promise than a prediction.

In the rectory, Acantha Fox-Lomax watched her husband's first live television interview with a mixture of contempt and amazement. To her great surprise she found there was also a trace of sympathy for his predicament. Witnessing him being ambushed by that clever Samarasinghe girl on the doorstep of his own precious church should have had Acantha rolling on the floor with laughter. Instead she saw a man whose carefully nurtured control over all that moved in Whyncombe St. Giles had been eroded in no more than a couple of weeks, washed away in the Great Deluge and shrivelled in the baking heat. What was left appeared as an angry man, bitter at his impotence and shorn of his vital supporters.

Mary Radcliffe, in many ways his influential patron, had been taken abruptly and while her glorious memory had survived intact for a week or so, that was now forever blighted. That stain could never be removed from all that she had touched, not from her charities, her committees, her pet projects, not from her church, nor from her priest.

Of her husband Michael, the rector's compliant deputy on more than one of the village's governing bodies, his days of valuable service had ended as suddenly as his wife's. For the time being he lay lightly sedated and heavily bandaged in a private hospital room. For company he had a constable outside his door and a succession of visits from detectives and lawyers. His complicity in Melanie's death was at once apparent yet unprovable. Where his recollection of events was clear, the context or the timing made little sense, where the memory was clouded, the chronology appeared perfect. As often as not his answers bore little relation to the question posed, and yet retained a sense of true recollection.

The Westerleighs had distanced themselves from any suggestion of involvement or even knowledge and to do that required a distancing from the rector. They'd easily justified their actions and statements to those who enquired, although justifying some of them to themselves was less straightforward.

Even as Acantha waited for his urgent step on the gravel, her normal appetite for baiting and tormenting her husband was absent. Once he might have been sharp enough to enjoy the game, once he might have been that worthy opponent. Once he might have been many things, she thought, more with sadness for the diminished man than regret for her own wasted years. With great clarity she saw the gaming days were over, he would never amount to more than he was today, and that was little enough.

16

From an upstairs window at the front of the house in Upper Orchard Upeksha Samarasinghe looked out towards High Whyn Farm. The roofs of the barns drifted in and out of sight between the grey veils of drizzle drawn like drifting nets across the valley. Carried on a steady breeze, the fine droplets soaked the ground and the people who walked on it, washing away the dust and dirt, filling the gutters and gurgling in the drains. Across the road she watched as neighbours, tanned and smug from their holiday in paradise, decanted from their airport taxi and stood aghast at their crumbling home. They would be wondering how such gentle rain in so soft a land as this could possibly have wrought so much damage.

It had started yesterday, the day of Melanie Staples' funeral at the crematorium. There'd been a surge of humidity as the cloud gathered in the west while they assembled awkwardly at the doors of the little chapel, waiting for the hearse with the tiny white coffin. Her father had carried it in his outstretched arms. By the time they'd watched it slide beyond the velvet curtains, shaken hands or stiffly embraced with other mourners, the breeze was up, the temperature down, and the first thin shower was in the air.

Watching from her window in the silent house, Upeksha wondered if the rain in California would be like English rain or if it would have a character all of its own. In a week she might find out if by chance the cloudless blue of Berkeley's sky unexpectedly delivered any during her visit. She would travel with her daughter for a holiday and a taste of life in the Golden State, and yes, she had assured Clarence, she would consider living there.

At the back door of The Chequers, Colin Deeley stuffed the last of the rubbish into the bin ready to trundle it out to the roadside for collection. He wore a jacket of the type described as rain-resistant but which seemed least effective against the clouds of drizzle sweeping down across Whyncombe Wood. He wore no cap and was happy to stand and let the water trickle down his face and neck, dripping from his nose and chin. In the space of a day the land had turned from bleached to brown and even as he looked a hint of green could be seen dusted across the fields. In a week or less, life in the little valley would pick up the familiar rhythm, and the upheavals of recent times would fall back into memory.

Some things would not be restored. Amongst these would be a pint or two with friends and neighbours at the bar of The Chequers. A country pub has many pressures on its existence, a lack of customers being most significant, but a lack of beer is a terminal blow. With the critical levels of drinking water had come a shortage of beer and to those little pubs like The Chequers that sold so little, supplies had ceased altogether. Alan Miller had been left with no option but to close completely, and there would be no coming back from this final collapse of his business. It marked the end of four hundred years of recorded ale-house keeping in the twin villages, where once four pubs had flourished.

Across the road in the school, workmen had begun their repairs and the schedule of summer repainting. As one of the new key-holders Colin Deeley had let them in early, then the head had arrived, fresh from her holiday in Crete and keen to pick up the pieces she'd dropped so abruptly. He'd chatted with her for some time, told her about the changes that seemed likely, how new governors would be needed, how old ones had ended their terms. Lorraine Gregson had never considered him a real governor, despite his name appearing on the list, now she saw a different side to him and wondered why he'd played so little part before. She was keen to preserve what might turn out to be an important working relationship, so she resisted the urge to remind him that even in the playground during the holidays, smoking was prohibited on school premises.

The contractors on High Whyn Farm were busy moving earth. The rumble of their machines had gone on all day yesterday and wouldn't end until the new lagoon's site had been smoothed and levelled ready for the piling and pouring of concrete. John Westerleigh had taken the expensive advice provided by the insurance company and had chosen a new site behind the big barn. It would not slide down the hill unless there was an earthquake or a ten-thousand-year weather event cursed this corner of the county.

The noise of the earthmovers masked an unusual quiet in the farmhouse. Margaret Westerleigh, still shocked from her discoveries and miserable experiences at The Glebe House, had

246

gone away. Each year she declined the annual invitation from an old school friend to join a small group for a few days walking holiday. They'd done little more than exchange Christmas cards for more than twenty years, but they'd been close once. The invitation had sat unanswered for nearly a month, before she'd seized the opportunity for escape at the last minute. In three hours she'd packed and gone, to the surprise of both her husband and the school friend.

There was nothing broken beyond repair at High Whyn, if he worked as hard as he usually did, John Westerleigh knew the farm could recover from all the setbacks. It was a fine farm on good land, he'd managed it well and borrowed wisely when investment was called for. Even in these days when farming was out of fashion, it could be sold for a large enough sum to pay off his debts and leave them plenty to take elsewhere. Such thoughts would not have crossed his mind a month previously, but the farm and the valley it looked over had lost their permanence, as had his marriage, once such a fixed and secure point in his life.

Chris Rogers was not pleased, but then he was rarely pleased. Some contortion of his roof caused by the heat or the Great Deluge or probably both, had resulted in a small crevice being opened up which was ideal for fine drifting rain to creep into. Once there it accumulated at one spot in the ceiling until no more could be absorbed and the excess began dripping onto his cigarette cabinet.

As if this was not enough, he had also made a mistake in his stock taking which was something he was quite meticulous about. Either that, or a new generation of rats were at work in his shop. It was a small but noteworthy compensation to have a new customer for his rescued cigarettes.

'A packet of the old gold, please.'

The shopkeeper was not one to engage in unnecessary conversation but on this occasion he couldn't resist.

'I didn't know you smoked, Mrs Fox-Lomax, and I don't suppose you're just starting.'

'Oh no, they're not for me. The rector likes to have one now and again, I thought I'd keep a little supply in for him, now that . . .' she trailed off, uncertain how to refer to Michael Radcliffe's absence. 'Now that his usual source has dried up.'

'Not much else has dried up today.'

'No, quite,' said Acantha Fox-Lomax, unsure if this was an attempt at humour, her eye taken by the steady drip drip on the cabinet.

By the time she'd be back in the rectory, the old gold would be very welcome. The Reverend Philip Fox-Lomax was at that moment engaged in a long discussion with the diocesan office, one of several conversations that had ensued following his brief and dismal interview with Diana Samarasinghe.

A uniformed constable was no longer stationed at the door to Michael Radcliffe's hospital room, although the patient remained inside, and continued to breathe and occasionally eat and drink. It was generally believed that he'd given up all he could, but many details had been lost forever when St. Germaine's stone hand had split his wife's head open. There were hints and glimpses of a connection with Eysha Duncan's disappearance, but nothing of any substance. For the sake of the record he'd been charged with various offences connected with Melanie's death, but without any prospect of prosecution or conviction.

The battering he had taken at the hands of Margaret Westerleigh had been bloody and painful, but hadn't resulted in any serious injury, despite her free and open admission of intent to kill. However, the precautionary x-rays of his skull had revealed something more serious, something malignant and terminal insidiously distorting his brain. Without Margaret's intervention he might have continued undiagnosed for weeks longer, dulling the growing headaches, the aberrations of sight, the failure of movement, with nothing but whiskey and nicotine. These would have become increasingly ineffective as he'd declined miserably and painfully towards death. Instead he was able to receive a whole range of drugs designed to ease his symptoms and control the pain, drugs whose sole purpose was to make the going easier. When it came, his would be a dignified, if lonely, exit from this world. He would slip painlessly away, albeit unloved and unmourned.

There can be few worse events in a man's life than the funeral of his own child. Peter Staples had the awful misfortune to have suffered it twice. At least with his dear Melanie there was the small consolation of knowing her fate after so long without any knowledge at all. He and her mother had also found a way to speak to each other without recrimination and bitterness colouring every word. These were the two crumbs of comfort to be found. He would never come to terms with the circumstances of her death, never believe that accident or misadventure played any part in it. The Radcliffes, one or other or both, had killed her to protect their own perverted view of their privilege, their right to live without regard to others, according to no rules but their own. That they should have been sustained in their evil by lord and lady this, by sir that and the right honourable the other, and by the priest of the parish was as sickening as the act itself.

Back in his workshop at the quarry he'd sat for more than an hour contemplating the pieces of stone, the work yet to be done, the work completed. From time to time he got up and walked round the various pieces, noting the curves and angles, mainly with satisfaction, before sitting again. When he listened there was no sound but the gentle hiss of rain on the corrugated roof, the trickle of water as it found the gutter and dropped down the spout.

At the centre of his attention was one piece in particular. It was finished and paid for, it needed nothing more than to be delivered and installed. Alongside it stood the weathered, almost formless lump it was made to replace high on the roof of St. Giles. There was no doubt about it, the new gargoyle was a fine piece of work, even if he did say so himself. It would last as long as its predecessor, perhaps longer if the air of the next two hundred years were less corrupted than the last two hundred.

He had several ideas about what to do with it. His first thought had been for it to accidentally drop from the roof as it was being fixed in place. It would be a lucky shot if it came off, but with a little stage management it might be possible for it to smash the rector's skull at the moment it reached terminal velocity. A second, more private idea had been to use his skills to cut a message into the stone, a message that would last down the years, unseen by human eye, untouched by wind and rain until in some far distant future the building crumbled or another mason replaced it. Then, as it was hauled into a workshop very much like his own and the worn remains of his work were examined, it would be turned to take the measurements for the replacement. There the stone-cutter would see that Melanie Anne Staples, a child of eleven, had been murdered and her killers given succour by the rector of St. Giles.

Even as he entertained these thoughts, he knew them to be fanciful. In reality he would do nothing so dramatic, nothing so poetic or fitting. At most he might mount the two pieces, the old misshapen lump and the newly crafted figure, either side of the gate to the quarry, and if asked about them he would tell the story of how they came to be there. And all who knew the story would think of it every time they passed the quarry. They might also think of it as they passed St. Giles.

'What time's he getting back?' Laura Duncan asked her father when he'd finished talking on his phone.

'Your mother says she'll drop him off about three if they let him out.'

'If? What's he done now?'

'No, the solicitor says it should be fine. But you know, things happen.'

'Yeah, things happen,' she agreed.

'It'll not be easy, you know what he's like, and being caged up in the house won't suit him.'

'Will he be tagged?'

'Who knows,' Alex said, shrugging.

The prospect of having Liam back in the house was not entirely pleasurable to either his sister or his father. Since Kathy Duncan had left, the two had found a way to get along well enough, and rediscovered some of the closeness they'd once shared. In part it was adversity which had bound them together, but there was more to it than that. Without the relentless aggression of Aaron and Liam, without the smouldering friction between Alex and Kathy there'd been a chance for father and daughter to better understand each other, to find a little respect for the people they'd become.

At Melanie's funeral Laura and Suzie had held each other and given each other the comfort that only two such mothers could give. It was not said, but it was understood that they shared the mourning for Melanie, as much as they shared the heartache for Eysha. As the mothers became as sisters, so did their daughters. The spell of silence that had cloaked Melanie down the years was given no chance to take hold over Eysha. She would be spoken of, smiled about, unashamedly kissed goodnight on an empty pillow. Above all she would be found, her fate would be known, Laura would see to that and learn form Suzie the mistakes to avoid.

'What about Mum? Think she'll be back?'

Again Alex shrugged.

'Dad, I've been thinking I might get away. Nothing fixed. Just so's you know.'

'Aye. Not before time.'

There is a pleasure in driving a new car, especially a first new car, especially an expensive and powerful new car, a pleasure which is impossible to deny, even for the least car-conscious. The smell of such a car, the embracing opulence of white leather, the silent surge of power gently pressing in the small of the back, all this and more will bring a smile to the lips of the meanest of spirits.

Thomas Samarasinghe was far from mean, either of mind or pocket, and he wore a huge grin as the crimson BMW flowed along the lanes towards the main road and beyond, to Oxford and London. He'd owned the car for all of two days, an impulse buy quite unlike anything he'd done before. His mother and father had both thrown up their hands in horror at the extravagance, even though the expense had barely dented his savings. What did he need a car for at all, in London it would be a burden not an asset, his father had complained. It would be damaged, vandalised within days, he warned. His mother understood a young man's desires a little better than her husband, who'd forgotten his own. Even so, a smaller more sensible car would surely serve the purpose just as well, she suggested. And what use was a car with an open top in a country like this when the sun was only out for five minutes at a time?

Thomas had more than one reason to smile. Beside him sat the pleasing figure of Lavi Pitesteanu, also wreathed in smiles. Her presence was as impulsive as the car itself. Meeting again at the crematorium to bid their final farewells to Melanie, they'd embraced briefly, almost by mistake as all around were embracing each other. Come to London tomorrow he'd said suddenly, come and look at the new flat now it's finished. Yes, she'd said, just like that before the old concerns had a chance to surface. All the warnings she'd been given were irrelevant now, no conflict of interest remained. He'd been quietly thanked for his help by all concerned, most warmly and touchingly by Melanie's parents. No matter what protest they made, how often he was invited to call them Suzie or Peter, they would always remain Mr and Mrs Staples until he remembered it was now Mrs Mortimer.

Despite her youth and inexperience, Detective Constable Pitesteanu knew enough to take credit when it was offered, for there were bound to be times more deserving when none was given. Even so, she was embarrassed by the praise heaped upon her, not least because of the way in which it had all fallen into her lap. Chief Inspector Smallborne had unashamedly accepted the praise for his insight and coaching of the promising Pitesteanu, and it would be his name forever linked to solving the riddle of Melanie Ann Staples. All thought of dispensing with his protégée's services quickly disappeared in the warm glow of success, so instead the constable had been offered the prospect of a dazzling future as his long-term assistant. And now here she was enjoying possibly greater reward in the smiling company of Mr Samarasinghe as they sped through the driving rain in the lap of luxury.

For a while they sat in grinning silence, like children tasting illicit pleasures, each scarcely able to believe they could enjoy such luck after so much misery, witnessed and felt. As Thomas turned the events over in his mind a question occurred to him.

'I never did understand how you came to be at the Radcliffe's at just the right moment. Was it just a happy accident of timing?'

'Yes, it couldn't have been luckier.'

'How so?'

'Remember the conversation we had, our 'off-duty' conversation before it all came out?'

'Yes.'

'The same applies now, ok? Some things are not to be repeated. Ever,' she said with great emphasis, although the smile remained.

'Yes, of course.'

'I fell asleep. I would have been at Mr Radcliffe's house much sooner, it would all have been different, but I fell asleep in the church.'

When he'd stopped laughing, when they'd both stopped laughing, he thought how much it was like the laughter he'd shared with Melanie, innocent laughter over childish things, each of them oblivious of the evil lurking so close.

After another mile or two he turned to his passenger. 'Would you like some chocolate? Press the little button in front of you, it works like a fridge in there when the air con is on.'

She pressed and the flap dropped down to reveal two silky bars of chocolate, cool and hard to the touch, but with the promise of soft and melting on the tongue.

'I'm addicted,' he said, eyes on the road ahead, 'always have been.'

DJ Wiseman

A Habit Of Dying was DJ Wiseman's first published novel. In October 2012 he edited and contributed to *Positional Vertigo*, an innovative collection of short stories. He also writes online as InkOnDemand. Lifelong interests include maps, travel and photography. In 2009, in conjunction with a close friend, he produced *The Further Bank*, a memoir of photographic expeditions around the landscape of the upper Thames.

DJ Wiseman divides his time between the UK and Canada.

A Habit Of Dying is the compelling story of Lydia Silverstream and her attempts to reunite a family heirloom with its rightful owner. Amongst the box of old photo albums she discovers a sinister journal, both the key to one puzzle and an enigma in itself.

Lydia's enquiries take her from her home in Oxford to Cockermouth and the Lake District, to Cambridge, Essex and the Sussex coast. Along the way she meets Stephen, who becomes the sounding-board for her theories. As the original purpose of her quest is fulfilled, the potentially homicidal secrets of the journal emerge. Lydia's worst suspicions appear to be confirmed when she uncovers the circumstances of the journal writer's death.

Positional Vertigo is a collection of very different stories from writers spanning three continents – this anthology is moving, disturbing and daring in equal measures. Writing in very broad interpretations on the theme of health, the stories take us on a journey through many minds and many places. Expect a book that transports the reader from hospital beds and health food stores to the Nova Scotian countryside and damp English woodland via the bizarre and the commonplace – all delivered with an unusual and uncanny intensity.

For further information about these and other titles from Askance please visit askance-publishing.com